PRAISE FOR
MOTHERLANDS

"Andrulis deftly portrays not only two vastly different cultures, but also two vastly different human beings—a stern, demanding mother and a daughter seeking her own identity in post-World War I New York. The result is a work of fiction that evokes the sights and sounds of a long-gone era and the tensions between two clashing generations of transplanted Americans."

—**TIM O'BRIEN,** author of *The Things They Carried*

"*Motherlands* is a compelling and beautiful read. The carefully woven story floats the reader along through the journey of a young girl from an old homeland to America . . . the book reminds us yet again of the incredible capacity of newcomers to the United States to become one with this country and contribute in unexpected ways."

—**DENISE GILMAN,** Immigration Law Professor,
University of Texas at Austin School of Law

"*Motherlands* is a powerful and emotional page-turner. It's a classic migrant's journey, but one that is far from straightforward. The characters that Andrulis gives us are vividly drawn and linger in the memory, but the real hero of this book is education. *Motherlands* never preaches at us, but tells us human truths in a way that only the most powerful fiction can."

—**GEOFF WARD,** Professor of Literature,
University of Cambridge

"How delightful it is to read a story that is truly novel. *Motherlands* is such a tale. This book shows us how both love and prejudice defy all borders. It reminds us that no matter how far you've traveled and how much you've encountered, the most important discovery is in yourself."

—JAMES "BIGBOY" MEDLIN, former writer,
E! Entertainment Television, co-writer of
screenplay *Roadie*, author of *Slap Noir*

"*Motherlands* is an immersive historical novel . . . Irene is a thoughtful narrator whose language is poetic . . . observes generational trauma within mother-daughter relationships with acuity, and she fleshes out old-world Hungary with affection."

—*FOREWORD CLARION*

"Self-love overcomes trauma in this powerful mother-daughter saga."

—*PW'S BOOKLIFE*, Editor's Pick

"*Motherlands* by Dennis Andrulis is a powerful story of one young woman's emigration and assimilation from Hungary to the United States at the end of World War I. . . . More than just a tribute to the author's mother, this is an exceptional read and a fascinating adventure. I highly recommend it."

—*READERS' FAVORITE*

MOTHERLANDS

An Immigrant's Story of Love and Loss

DENNIS ANDRULIS

This is a work of fiction. Although most of the characters, organizations, and events portrayed in the novel are based on actual historical counterparts, the dialogue and thoughts of these characters are products of the author's imagination.

Published by River Grove Books
Austin, TX
www.rivergrovebooks.com

Distributed by River Grove Books

Design and composition by Juan Díaz Rodríguez
Cover design by Alan Dingman

Publisher's Cataloging-in-Publication data is available.
Print ISBN: 978-1-966629-02-3
eBook ISBN: 978-1-966629-03-0

First Edition

In memory of my mother

Dear mother of mine
Was I ever worth your time?

Never will I forget the past
But I will step out from the shadow you cast.

"The Shadow You Cast"
by Reece Lennox

PART I
Birth of an Affair

CHAPTER 1

My mother, Mary, was only nineteen when she told her mother she was leaving Hungary for America, having made her unhappiness with her peasant life plain to anyone who would listen. But, in those feudal days, leaving was only what men did when marching off to war or dreaming of fortunes to be made in far-off lands. A woman striking out on her own in 1910 was unheard of, especially in what she left behind: me, Irene, her infant daughter. Little could three generations of women have imagined how my mother's world and mine would come together again across continents and time and forever haunt our lives.

***

Eastern Hungary at the turn of the twentieth century was a flat land where small towns and farms dotted the countryside and fertile fields set the course for a family's destiny. Unpaved ribbons of roads stretched as far as the eye could see, parting groves of apple trees and amber grains before disappearing into the horizon. The Körös and Maros rivers flowed through this landscape, giving life to crops and those who tilled them. This was my mother's world, and it was to be my world. But we would only come to know it separated and apart.

My family was beholden to Master Kovacs, a Jew among the few in Catholic Hajdudorog. Kovacs owned the land not far from the town where my mother lived with her brothers, Sandor and Josef, and my grandmother, Ilushka.

My grandmother's stories told me it hadn't always been this way for her. In the early days of her marriage, my grandfather made a good life for them as the town's only blacksmith. The people of Hajdudorog knew Peter Szuromi as strong, stout, and muscular, with straight hair the color of rust, and a full, round face. But what impressed everyone who knew him was the strength of his sinewy hands, molded from years spent practicing his craft.

Grandmother was small in stature like my grandfather, but that's where the resemblance ended. Her jet-black hair and wiry body belied her strength; she carried within her a quiet intelligence rooted less in her limited schooling than in her keen observation of the world and her grounded sense of what to make of it.

Their parents had set a course for Peter and Ilushka's lives that seemed cast in stone. Grandfather earned a living like his father but did little else, expecting a well-kept house and dinner on the table. Grandmother knew little beyond a life of responsibility. As the oldest child, she'd helped her widowed mother raise her younger brother, Johann. When, at nineteen, she met my grandfather at church, she already knew what lay ahead. Their courtship and ceremony followed the traditions of the times. She knew early on that her marriage reflected necessity more than desire.

In those first years, when Grandfather was more sober than drunk, townsfolk sought him out for his skills. The family's stone house, with three bedrooms and a kitchen, plus a front porch with a two-seated swing, was more than most possessed. And every spring, when tulips of maroon, cream, and yellow came into full bloom, neighbors on their way through town would stop to admire the seasonal beauty that my grandmother had nurtured with her hands.

Grandmother showed no favorites among her children. But while Grandfather would roughhouse with Sandor and Josef, the youngest, wrestling with them or kicking an old soccer ball around in a nearby field, my mother's affection and attention charmed him into a tenderness he rarely showed Grandmother and the boys. She was Grandfather's chosen one, and my mother adored him.

A few times a week, my mother walked over to his blacksmith's shop to tell Grandfather about her day and keep him company until dinnertime. She delighted in his stories about who'd broken what and how and why he was the only one in town who could fix it. But pride in his work wasn't all that they shared. During these visits, Grandfather introduced her to favorite folk songs from his childhood, some of them patriotic, others simple melodies. His rich baritone led many townsfolk on their way to somewhere to stop and listen.

It was on one of those days that Grandfather realized what he had passed down to his daughter. As he regaled her again with one of his favorite folk songs, "At the Foot of the Csitár Mountains," she at first began to hum along, then repeated the refrain in perfect pitch:

But we could live by the foot of the mountain
We could clear us a yard in the back
Build a home by the foot of the mountain
We could stay there and never come back.

"Where did you learn to sing like that, my little one?" he asked.

"I don't know, Papa. I suppose it's from listening to you. The songs sound so beautiful. Sometimes when I walk home from school, I sing them to myself. And the songs at the cathedral too."

"Well, you sing like an angel. If you'd like, I'll teach you as many as I can remember."

Nothing could have pleased her more. "Oh, yes, Papa. Then I can sing them with you." She added wistfully, "Do you think you and I could ever do that?"

"Do what?" my grandfather asked.

"Build a house at the foot of that mountain where the two of us can go."

"My, my, what a sweet thought, Mary. But I don't think your mother and brothers would like that."

From then on, if Mary wasn't meeting with friends after school, she would go by her father's workshop. On entering, without fail, she'd ask, "What are we going to sing today, Papa?" and plant a kiss on his cheek.

"Well, there's an old tune from my childhood . . ." he might say, and after hearing the song only a few times, she'd have it memorized by heart.

One day Mary came by with a surprise of her own. "Papa, Father Zalmond wants me to sing at the cathedral on Sunday! I've been listening to the songs for what seems like forever, so when Father Zalmond came up to me after Mass and asked, I said yes. He seemed so surprised that I already knew most of the hymns."

Peter put down his awl and hugged his daughter. "That's wonderful! Now not just our family but everyone in Hajdudorog can hear your beautiful voice."

Mary hesitated before asking what was on her mind. "Papa, when you take us to the cathedral, will you come in and hear me sing?"

Her father's face softened with a smile that told all. "Of course I will."

After that, it seemed that whenever they were together, father and daughter would harmonize, with his powerful voice and the sweet lilt of my mother's soprano. Every so often, they would come home as the evening sun came to rest on the horizon and tell the family, "We practiced a new song together. Would you like to hear it?"

All would eagerly gather on the porch, taking their usual places: the boys in the swing and Grandmother carrying a chair from the kitchen. After their serenade, one or the other in that familial audience would exclaim, "No one in town can sing like you, Mary! Father Zalmond and all the parishioners are lucky to have you." Because her brothers and her mother couldn't hold a note, let alone a tune, they could only listen, admiring the musical talent of their family members. But what drew my grandfather and my mother closer only set her further apart from my grandmother.

Mother never shared such intimacies with my grandmother. The seemingly never-ending repetition of the routine and chores bored her. Every day, Grandmother rose at four to knead the dough and bake the morning's bread, fry sausages, and boil eggs. She'd pick the fruits of the season from the small garden and set them in the ceramic bowl decorated with the green, white, and red colors of the Hungarian flag. She placed a bottle of blackberry brandy on the table for my grandfather, as it was his morning ritual to take a small glass before leaving for the blacksmith's shop. Once the children were off to school, she walked to the Cathedral of the Presentation of Mary to help with flower arrangements and upkeep, where she also spent time with her neighbors before returning home well before my mother and the boys returned from school.

As my mother grew older, my grandmother asked her to help clean, wash clothes, and cook. While my mother obeyed, as she knew the penalty for disobedience would be painful, she didn't take kindly to her role. When she came home from school, she'd do as she was told, soaking shirts, overalls, and underwear in the claw-foot bathtub, then hanging them on the clothesline that stretched to the aged birch tree in the back yard. That task finished, she sat in the kitchen and peeled potatoes, cut vegetables, and watched over whatever was roasting in the oven or cooking on the stove.

She'd finish her work as ordered, but that didn't stop her from complaining. "Why can't Sandor help more? When I was thirteen, I was cooking, helping you clean up all the dirt the boys brought in, and picking tomatoes and potatoes out of the garden."

"You're the oldest, Mary. When Sandor is older, he'll help your father."

"When I'm older, I'll have servants to take care of me. I'll have a big house with a beautiful garden filled with roses."

"Where do you get such ideas?"

"Do you remember when I told you I had to stay late at school?"

"Yes. You said something about studying for a test."

"Well, yes, I did study. But there was something else. Elizabeth and Andor told me about a great house not far from town, and they wanted to see it for themselves. The person living there—I think they said his name was Kopeks or Kovacs—owns all the land as far as the eye can see. So, we went for a walk. We walked for almost an hour and started passing people picking corn and wheat, and then, suddenly, there it was, sitting on top of a hill. The house was the color of the wheat fields at sunset. Windows stretched from floor to ceiling. I saw a woman on the porch by herself looking over a garden filled with flowers. I'd never seen anything like that house, not even in schoolbooks.

"As we walked back, I told them I wanted to live there someday. They laughed at me, but it's true. I talked to Papa about it at his shop today. He loved my story and told me to keep on dreaming."

My grandmother had no patience for such silliness. "Try to be happy with who you are and where you are, or you'll be unhappy not just now but later. I don't mean you shouldn't try to make a good life, but understand that finery and beautiful gardens won't take the place of the love in this home."

"I knew you'd say that. You don't think I can do it! Well, don't be surprised if one day I do." With those words, she stormed out.

The encounter fed a growing tension between mother and daughter, but my grandmother was determined not to let anything upend the life she had nurtured for her family.

What forever upset that faith in her family started Sunday mornings. Before Mass, Grandfather hitched the horses to the wagon and took her and the children to the cathedral, but, except for one occasion to hear Mary sing, the steps were as far as he would go. Week after week, my grandmother and her children attended Mass while Peter met up with his old friends at one home or another and sipped homemade brandy and beer. He'd stay there, trading tales with the others of times and places, present and past. The liquor flowed as did the conversation, often well past the end of Mass.

When he arrived late at the steps of the cathedral, his atonement elicited Grandmother's reluctant patience, as my grandfather launched into his excuses. "Kalman was telling us about the time he took on the Prussian army in battle! He was so funny, as we all knew he was telling a tale as tall as he is short." Even as he spoke the words, behind his tone Grandmother sensed—what was it, resentment? Impatience? She wasn't sure, but whatever was eating at him left an air of unease hanging over them.

Early on, Grandmother was inclined to forgive these Sunday morning events, but soon they metastasized, spreading in severity and number over the weeks and months. Vodka became Grandfather's morning beverage of choice. When she brought lunch to his workplace, more often than not he wasn't there. She served dinner as always, but usually without him.

Excuses flowed like the alcohol that was consuming him. Sunday tales began to appear on other afternoons and evenings. "I had to go to Arthur's. The cows broke his gate." Or "Joska needed a new railing." Or "Imre needed new tools." Grandmother knew they were lies, as the smell of alcohol trailed her husband like a spirit unwelcome in her home.

Over the following months, his excuses gave way to bitter words. "Why don't you stop asking where I've been? It's none of your business," and, before long, "Just leave me alone!"

Grandmother's patience was also thinning, as she determined not to let her husband get away with his deceits. "Where do you go during the day? At night? Why are you always late for dinner? Why are you drunk most evenings when you come home? What's happening to you?"

The stories Grandmother told me never masked the darkness of those days. She and Grandfather could sustain a fog of concealment for only so long. Furtive acts of condescension and longer silences masked the tensions that lay beneath the surface. Peter's absences became an odd relief from the bitterness, disdain, and threat of brutality he carried with him.

Grandmother said that during those dark days she did her best to protect Josef, Sandor, and my mother, sending them to school and having dinner on the table without their father. When arguments with her husband came, she sent the children to the neighbors, who could hear her husband's drunken rants and knew what was to come.

My grandmother worried about the children. For the boys, what came from them mirrored who they were. Josef, the youngest, was fearful and didn't understand. Sandor's innocence and gentleness, his hallmarks, never changed. He puzzled over what was happening to Papa, but trust in his mother was his carapace.

"This will pass," she told them. "I'll make sure of it. Sometimes people like Papa lose their way. We can try to help them find their way back, but we can't let them do the same to you. When that happens, it's time to keep true to your way, no matter what it takes."

These words didn't comfort my mother and seemed to have the opposite effect on her. She had always taken her father's side and now lay fault with her mother.

"What did you do to Papa? You always picked on him for not going to church, for spending time with his friends, and for having a good time. You never thought about what he wanted, just like you don't think about what I want."

Grandmother stared at her daughter, wanting her understanding but sensing futility. "I pray that someday you'll come to see, but I don't think anything I say today will make a difference."

The words left behind a silence that filled the room. But as much as she defended her father, my mother couldn't deny the dark reality that had taken its place in their home. That defense of Grandfather, I was to learn, masked her own sense of something vital between them slipping away. For all her bravado, the absence of those lilting intimacies they shared, the bond born of music and memory that she felt with no other in her family, left a hole in her heart. Like a passenger departing on a wagon propelled not by horses but by alcohol, he was leaving her behind. All my mother could do was bear witness steeped in sadness, as she felt helpless to change what was happening.

My grandfather eventually stopped making excuses, and his inebriation and rage filled the spaces in their lives. Conversation turned into confrontation, and the semblance of temperance into temerity. "Just shut up. I swear you're asking for it. If you don't stop, you'll regret it" were his responses to questions and to Grandmother's growing intolerance to what he'd become.

Alcohol became a living past for Grandmother. Drink had consumed her husband's father and his oldest brother. Children were abandoned, and marriages disintegrated. Good men faded into an infused haze, blurred in memory, indistinct but for the marks they left on those left behind. Not only did she feel helpless to stop Peter, but Grandmother also dreaded what she foresaw was to come.

And came it did. My grandmother had tolerated solitary hours at night before, as her husband returned and silently stumbled into bed, if he didn't pass out at the kitchen table first. However, she was not one to suffer fools, even if that fool was her husband. But even her worst premonition did not prepare her for what was to come.

It wasn't long after her latest quarrel with Mary that she became determined to confront Peter's escalating absence, hoping that some remnant of what had kept them together remained. And so, on yet another late evening, Grandmother put off retiring and waited for his return. With the children in bed, she busied herself, clearing dishes and getting ready for the next day. All was as it had been many times before, but this time the quiet of the room offered her no comfort. Her hands shook, and she felt as if the walls were closing in, the air suffocating. Stepping outside, she breathed deeply, feeling the tightness in her chest and throughout her body ease in the stillness of the cool night. But as she turned toward the kitchen door, the sound of her husband's carriage broke the silence. He pulled the horse up within inches of where she stood, seemingly unaware of her presence. Climbing down, he leaned against the carriage wheel to steady himself, gripping the wooden spokes as he did. My grandmother stood staring at what had become of her husband, strong and upright in his youth, now stooped and aged before his time. Keen to avoid drawing the attention of neighbors, she retreated to the kitchen.

Minutes later, my grandfather entered, weaving from side to side as he did. "So, you're still up," he slurred. "I'm going to bed." He moved to the stairs, tripping as he did, and reached for the banister just as he was about to fall again.

Grandmother followed, even more determined not to let yet another night of his alcoholic oblivion pass. Closing the bedroom door behind her, she walked over to his side of the bed and sat before him. "This can't continue, Peter. What in God's name will stop you? Can't you see where this is going?"

In that moment, his jaw, cheeks, and even his brow stiffened and became as fixed as a statue etched in porphyry. His first blow came with a force from somewhere unknown to her, pivoting her head and propelling her from the bed to the floor. "I told you to shut up," he said. "Now you're going to get what you deserve."

Not waiting for her to rise, Peter brought his right hand across his chest and struck her across her cheek. That second blow raised a welt above her right eye, but with it, she rose as well.

"Out!" she demanded. "Get out! I don't care where you go."

Her husband stood there, transfixed in confusion for the moment. "Me? Go?" he slurred.

Grandmother had moved to the other side, keeping her distance, never taking her eyes off him. As she steeled herself for whatever would come next, it was over. Peter reeled and slumped onto the bed. Having used up what was left of his drunken abuse, he passed out. She knew Peter would be there for the rest of the night.

***

The next morning, as Peter lay silent in their bed, Grandmother knew what she had to do. She told the children to climb aboard the wagon that Peter had left tied up the night before. Josef was the first one to speak. "Where are we going, Momma?"

"To your Uncle Johann's," came her reply.

Her younger brother, Johann, had moved to a farm on Master Kovacs's estate, the large property that my mother had once walked to with her school friends. The family visited when they could, and Johann was always happy to see them. They had enjoyed those visits, the boys playing hide-and-seek in and around the old, graying barn, my mother going for long walks along the dirt road, my grand-mother cooking her brother's favorite dinners. Although his modest home of straw and stone was small, my grandmother had felt safe there. As for the children, they cherished those visits. "Oh, good. Sandor and I have so much fun there chasing the chickens around that old barn."

"Well, you'll have plenty of time to do that."

The last remark seemed to rouse Mary from her sleepiness. "What do you mean we'll have plenty of time? How long are we staying? And where's Papa?"

My grandmother was not quite ready to tell her children the truth, as she knew the many questions that would follow. "Your father is going to stay in town for a while. As for us, we'll be at Uncle Johann's. I promised we'd help him with the tobacco and wheat." Her answer quieted their questions for the moment, until Mary noticed the welt above her mother's right eye.

"What happened to you? Did you fall?"

"Yes, I fell off the bed last night. It's only a bruise, and it doesn't hurt. It will go away in a few days."

Mary stared at her mother as if trying to see beyond the words she suspected didn't tell the whole story. For now she let it pass but reminded her mother, "School starts next week, and I don't want to miss class."

As the wagon approached Johann's house, Ilushka simply said, "We'll come to that when we need to."

Johann heard the horses as the wagon approached. Before they had come to a stop, all the children had jumped down and scampered off to the places they knew so well, just as Johann opened the front door. As he stepped out to greet his sister, his smile vanished.

"What's happened, Ilushka?" he asked, but Grandmother's face, swollen and bruised, answered his question. "I saw this coming."

She nodded. "I should have known he would end up like this. His eyes warned me. I saw his father in them. Peter's soul lost just like his."

Johann shook his head and with a sad grimace said, "Come. You can stay as long as you like."

"Thank you, Johann." She embraced him and kissed his cheek. No other words were spoken about that day, then and for the days to come.

CHAPTER 2

My grandmother said she made the transition from town to farm with determination driving her to break from the world of violence, deceit, and distrust her marriage had come to. Johann did his best to help, giving up his canopy bed for my grandmother, while my mother slept on a large, padded wooden bench, and Johann and the boys slept in the barn, making do with padding and straw.

Grandmother knew the old house well. Johann had yet to marry, so his home suffered from a lack of attention to detail evident in the hand-me-down dishes, dust, and random disorder of things. On that first morning, Grandmother went to work, knowing that Johann would happily adapt to a woman's touch. By the end of the first day, the chaos of his unkempt kitchen had become a place she could call her own, with clean dinnerware, spices, and preserves tucked away and vegetables where they belonged.

Grandmother's natural instincts eased her transition to the tasks of growing and harvesting tobacco, potatoes, and grains for Master

Kovacs. She, her brother, and the other peasants earned a quarter of the crop yield, and they added to those earnings by selling eggs and fowl from time to time. No longer able to visit with her friends at the cathedral, what little social life Grandmother enjoyed happened on Master Kovacs's estate. At tobacco harvest, my grandmother and her neighbors picked the leaves and brought them to the barn to hang and process. They sat around a long table and smoothed out the tobacco leaves one by one. The next day the piles of tobacco were taken to a tent, where the women hung the leaves. There they would stay until the men gathered them and brought the tobacco to town. Sunflower harvest followed a similar routine.

As she never learned to read or write, my grandmother was content listening to the stories of those who had lived on Kovacs's land for years. While the men pulled up chairs by the farm equipment and drank whiskey on those cool autumn days, the women got together for a glass of the sweet wine of Tokaj at the barn that sat not far from the lord of the manor's stately residence. The elderly Mrs. Karoly, who had lived on the land longer than anyone else, was always happy to get things started, spinning yarns about endurance in tough times, her gnarled fingers stabbing at the air, pointing to ghosts from the past. It was here that Grandmother learned about the deep snows from years ago, their drifts turning homes pitch dark by day, windows blanketed in a cover of white.

On another afternoon, Mrs. Karoly told of the drought that parched the land so that few chickens and pigs survived. Mrs. Czerny, a widow, who by her formidable girth seemed to have taken outsized comfort in the harvest over the years, spoke next. "One thing I'll say about Master Kovacs, he opened up the stored grain and corn to us. He said we could owe him, but it cost us much less than what it fetched at market."

Knowing little about him, Grandmother asked the women as they sipped their wine, "So, is this to say he's fair and kind?"

"I don't know about kindness, but he and that manager he hired, his name's Eisner, don't cheat us out of our share of the harvest," Mrs. Czerny said.

A few of the other old-timers nodded in agreement and then went back to gossiping about whose son eloped with the daughter of Mr. and Mrs. Karoly, who might have stolen a chicken from the Ballots, and how Jakob Esterhaszy broke his leg repairing his roof. My grandmother came to savor those times, especially as stories filled the hours. However, with three children to raise, cook for, and get to school, she had time for little else.

For Sandor and Josef, the farm became their playground. Adventures seemed to await them at every turn, among the trees that bordered the plot of land, in the river where the cold waters prickled their skin; even the waddling wild ducks became their playmates, racing after them around the barn and into the fields. However, early on, my grandmother knew that her daughter hadn't taken well to the move to Johann's home.

Squealing pigs and those incessantly cackling chickens replaced the relative serenity of their home in town. Instead of walking to school, Mary had to rise at five each morning to catch a ride with the neighbor, Charlie, who worked in Hajdudorog and drove his son to the school. She had little time to spend with friends at the end of the day, as she was bound by her neighbor's need to return shortly after work. My mother fell sullen and silent early on, showing little interest in her brothers' entreaties for their sister to join them or much of anything for that matter. Grandmother's pleas for her to help in the kitchen were met with nothing more than resignation to duty. Only the hymns she sang at Sunday service lifted her spirits, if only for that time.

My mother's resentment of Grandmother and her quotidian fate only grew over the next weeks and months. Her Sundays in choir were the highlight of her week, as compliments on her singing from parishioners fed her pride. And as much as she enjoyed school, it became only a brief refuge before work on the farm called. At seventeen, Mary had taken her place in the barn along with the others, where they stripped and dried the tobacco, siloed the corn, and stripped the sunflower seeds. For her, anything was better than the detested drudgery of planting and picking in the fields. My mother's determination persisted in her search for escape. The path she chose forever changed her life and became my destiny.

***

As Mother longed for a way out of a life she came to detest, she never let her own mother forget how much she hated where she was and who was responsible for it. Gradually, that hatred of land and lot, a constant din in my grandmother's day, became too much to bear.

On a cold, rain-swept Sunday after the family had returned from Mass, Grandmother sent the boys to fetch logs for the wood stove in the kitchen.

"Mary, after we dry off, go to the well. I'll make a big pot of tea. It'll help take the chill from that ride back from the cathedral." My mother stared at Grandmother for a moment. Then, without a word, she picked up the pail by the sink and left.

Josef and Sandor returned a few minutes later with armfuls of logs, and Grandmother said, "I'm making some tea for us."

"No thanks, Momma," replied Sandor. "We're going out to chase the chickens. They're so funny when it rains. We're already soaked, so we'll just change clothes when we get back."

"Suit yourselves. The tea will be here if you want a cup when you come back."

Just as they were leaving, Mary returned with the pail and placed it in the sink with a heavy thud that was impossible to ignore.

As she filled the teakettle, Grandmother turned to her daughter. "What's bothering you?"

My mother sat at the kitchen table, arms clenched across her chest. "You ask what's bothering me. Where to begin? Let's start with why we left Papa behind. Can you answer me that? Can you?"

She didn't give Grandmother time to answer. "And I think you said something about us being here for a time. Well, it's the last place I want to be! There's nothing for me here. Only dirt and work. No friends. When will this *time* be over?"

Grandmother had said little to her children, only that she and Papa needed to be apart for a while. "I know you love your father. We all miss him. But his drinking had got to him. Remember when you asked about my bruise when we were coming here, and I told you I'd fallen? It's true that I fell, but I never said how. Your father slapped me so hard that I fell from the bed. It hurts me to say this, but Papa is a drunk. I said he had to stop. That's when he hit me."

Instead of quelling her doubts, Grandmother's confession only added to them. "I know he drank," Mary said, "but I still don't understand why. I just know I miss him, miss the songs we'd sung, the times we were together." Then, after a moment's hesitation, she came to her pointed question. "What did you do that made him drink so much?"

Grandmother was startled by her daughter's question. "Mary, I don't think there's anything I could have done differently. Sad to say, but what happened to him I saw happen to the men in our families, time and again. Were they that unhappy with their lives that drinking was the only way he and the others could escape from what was eating them? That's the question I often ask myself."

"So there's really nothing else you could have done?" Mary said in a tone tinged with doubt. "Is that what you're saying? And the only way out was for us to leave and live in this place that's so far from where I want to be? Well, I'll never settle for here. Never!"

Grandmother had hoped her words would ease her daughter's unhappiness, but now her patience had run out. "I don't need to be reminded day in and day out about how you don't belong here at, as you call it, 'the end of the world.' You are your father's child: bitter, angry, forever unhappy. If you're so eager to change your life, then do so. Just leave us in peace, for God's sake!" Catching herself for a moment, Grandmother sighed. "Perhaps you should leave."

My mother's smile was pure disdain. "So that's what you want, is it? You've wanted me out of this house, and now you finally said it."

"No, Mary. I've never wanted this. Maybe it will teach you a lesson. But I know that whatever you learn won't happen here, and it won't come at a cost for your brothers and me."

My mother left the kitchen without saying another word. Grandmother seemed to sense that her daughter knew this day would come. Now that it had, she wished it were on her time and terms. *Where to go?* Mary had one school friend, Magdalene, who was just a year older, at eighteen, but already married to Karl, the coachman for Master Kovacs. Magdalene knew how desperate my mother was to leave home, and Mary planned to take advantage of their friendship.

The next morning, in freezing temperatures, carrying what she could in a small suitcase and bag, she walked the mile to Magdalene and Karl's home. She knew what she had to do. Greeted at the door, she worked herself into a burst of tears. "She threw me out. Can you believe it? My own mother," she lied.

Magdalene, I was to learn, wasn't surprised. "So you and your mother finally had it out, and now you've come here to see if we'll take you in. One time too many you talked back to her when she's trying to make the best for you and your brothers. You know, Mary, there's nothing in life as bitter as a mother's curse, and woe be unto her on whom it falls."

My mother ignored Magdalene's admonition. "I hate that woman. I have nowhere else to go. Can I stay with you until I come up with something? Help me get work. I'll do anything. Just don't make me beg her to take me back."

Magdalene's friendship with my mother and her family quelled her reluctance for a time. "You know our home's small, and I have a baby to care for. Karl's going to be worried about another mouth to feed, so you'll have to work. As for where to sleep, we only have the long bench in the kitchen that I can fix up. You can stay for a short time, but only a short time."

My mother stopped sniffling, took Magdalene's hand, and smiled. "You don't know what this means to me. Thank you. I promise to find another place as soon as I can."

Like Johann's home and all those nearby, Magdalene and Karl lived on a farm that wasn't their own. Mother always thought they were an odd-looking couple. Magdalene's tall, slender body and thick blonde hair seemed out of tune with Karl's calloused hands, wide girth, and hair that fell in thinning strands. Still, no one doubted their affection for each other.

Magdalene had spent much of her young life planting and picking for Master Kovacs. Now, with their newborn, fieldwork was out of the question. Karl helped as he could with the garden, chickens, and their one pig, but as coachman for Master Kovacs, his time was taken up with the horses and carriage year-round. He rose early, started his day by feeding and hitching the horses to the coach, and reported for whatever work was required, from running errands in town to taking the family on longer travel to visit friends at neighboring estates. He had worked for the lord for ten years, since he was seventeen, and had earned a trust that my mother would come to see as her way out.

Master Kovacs often spent the spring and summer on the estate but returned frequently to Budapest for business, sometimes without his family. During those times, he left oversight to Jacob Eisner, his appointed general manager. Eisner supervised the harvest, paid whatever taxes were owed, and accounted for monies spent and earned. In exchange, he lived in one of the largest and most well-appointed homes on the estate. No one knew much about him other than to say he was different: educated, from Budapest, and worldly. Karl made a point of saying he had the hands of someone who had never tilled a hectare. And, like the lord, being a Jew in a Catholic world, he lived in a cultural distance never to be forded beyond work and tasks.

My mother settled in as the weeks passed, helping Magdalene with her infant and doing chores around the house while avoiding work in the fields and the barn. When the subject of Master Kovacs did come up in conversation, my mother continually pressed Karl to see if he could help her get work as a maid. Finally, one day, as they sat for dinner, her wish came true.

"Do you remember me talking about Mr. Eisner?" Karl asked one evening. "He takes care of the estate for Kovacs."

"Yes," Mary said.

"Well, I don't have much to do with him, but today he came up to me at the stable just as I was about to leave. He said Olga, the woman who had kept house for him, had left for Debrecen with her boyfriend." Karl paused there. "They're looking for someone to take her place. He asked if I knew anyone."

What had been idle conversation now drew my mother's keen attention. "Doesn't he live in that big house next to the manor?" Leaning over the table, she tapped Karl's hand. "I bet that job pays more money, which means I can pay *you* more while I live here. I'll do whatever it takes."

Karl leaned back in his chair. "I thought you might be interested, so I told him a little about you—that you are a hard worker, you're young and able bodied. He asked if you could come by tomorrow morning, around eleven."

Magdalene told me stories about that first visit and so much more. As she recalled, the next day my mother dressed in a white blouse and long skirt, pretty in its patterns but also suitable for meeting a future employer. She thought about putting up her black curls and tucking them beneath a babushka, but it made her feel so plain, reminding her of the peasants she shunned. Standing before Magdalene's mirror, she admired the fit of her clothes, modest though they clearly framed the curves of her body.

The next morning Karl offered to take her, but my mother was so excited that she walked the two miles to what she hoped would be her new life. The narrow road took her through the fields of the estate, passing by the places where men, women, and children went about their routines day after day. The flat landscape gradually gave way to a gentle incline that led to an imposing two-story house set between two tall oak trees, grass, and a forbidding stone wall that separated the residence from the land around it. Beyond that structure, in the background, the lord of the manor's sprawling estate came into view. Approaching Eisner's house, my mother lifted the latch on the wooden gate, walked the short distance to the entryway, and knocked on the door.

A voice said, "Please come in. I'll be with you in a moment."

She pushed open the heavy oak door and stepped into the grand foyer. Jacob Eisner, tall, with clear skin and straight hair as black as night, greeted her. He was dressed in a ruffled shirt and trousers that, to my mother, spoke of his class and upbringing.

"Good morning. You're Miss Szuromi?"

She smiled and, for the moment, found herself speechless. There was something about this man. His eyes seemed to see into her, so much so that she couldn't look at him without blushing. A sense of warmth like none she had known before came over her. She felt small and insignificant as he stood before her, like a grain of sand in a great, elegant world.

"Karl told me only a little about you. You are looking for work as a maid?"

He paused to give my mother a chance to say something, but

when she didn't, he continued. "This house has an upstairs and downstairs to attend to. At the start, your tasks will take up much of your day, as no one has been here to take care of the house for a few weeks. As you get used to your job, you should have time to prepare lunch and dinner. I hope we can agree on the terms, as it would help me greatly with all that I have to do for Master Kovacs."

My mother listened, smiling politely, though her intimidation left her at a loss for words. "Yes, Mr. Eisner" was her only reply.

An awkward silence followed. There was something else to be said, and when Eisner spoke next, his voice softened, tinged with sadness. "There's one more thing, Miss Szuromi. My wife has been bedridden for some time. As of now, she needs considerable attention. She can be feverish and sometimes—to be straightforward—difficult and demanding. Katia will have a list of things for you to do in addition to your daily duties." He allowed a moment for my mother to take this new task in, but quickly added, "I will pay you well for your help, should you accept this offer."

My mother smiled. The salary, two krone each week, was more than generous, but it was the revelation about Katia that surprised her. Karl hadn't mentioned that Eisner was married, let alone that his wife was bedridden. Here was this man, no older than thirty, burdened with a wife so ill she could neither tend to his needs nor the needs of the house. She couldn't even tend to herself. Finally, my mother stirred from her silent state.

"Mr. Eisner, I'm happy to help as you wish, and I'll do my best to take care of Mrs. Eisner."

"Thank you, Miss Szuromi. It will mean a lot to me. And now let me introduce you to my wife."

With Mary trailing behind, they walked from the anteroom through the hall and stopped before a door on the first floor. "Mrs. Eisner will likely be up at this time, but I still suggest you speak in a quiet voice, as loud sounds unnerve her."

The door opened into a large room with a four-poster bed. Heavy drapes remained closed at midday. Oak night tables stood at each side of the bed. Elsewhere in the room were a writing desk with paper and pens, a fireplace, a two-seat couch, and two large-framed chairs, one of which was draped with a blanket and two small pillows, where my mother imagined Eisner slept from time to time.

The figure on the bed seemed small and out of place with the residence and the gentleman who met my mother at the door. Her cheeks were hollow, and her dark-brown hair lay in curled disarray. Her body was so barely outlined under a wrinkled white sheet as to seem a gossamer semblance of a woman. She reminded my mother of the ghost stories that her father used to tell on cold winter nights, frightening all the children to their core.

"Katia, this is Miss Mary Szuromi. She's agreed to the chores for the house and has said she will help you with whatever you need. Miss Szuromi, the housework and my wife's care will require you to be here every day except Sunday. On Saturday, pick vegetables from the garden for that evening and the following day."

"I understand, Mr. Eisner. Good morning, Mrs. Eisner."

Although she appeared frail and her high-pitched voice quavered, the woman spoke as one whose authority was not to be questioned. "As I'm sure my husband has told you, I'm not well. I do know this house needs much attending to. When you're here, you will see me first thing so that you know what I want you to do that day. There will be tasks that you must do for me immediately and others you can do later in the day."

"Yes, Mrs. Eisner." My mother listened intently, not wanting to forget or miss anything. However, as much as Jacob Eisner's words and worldliness captivated her, my mother felt a visceral discomfort with his wife. Still, she knew better than to show any reaction. Managing a slight smile, she asked, "When would you like me to begin?"

Mr. Eisner spoke first. "Tomorrow, if that's possible."

"You should be here no later than six," Mrs. Eisner added.

"Yes, madam."

"Katia, if that's all, I'll see Mary out," Mr. Eisner said without waiting for an answer. As they left the bedroom, Mary turned back for a moment. His wife's head lay on the pillow, but her eyes remained fixed on them.

As he closed the door, a smile came across Jacob's face. "Well, Mary, I hope my wife's wishes didn't discourage you. I think all will work out nicely once Katia is comfortable with you being here."

The warmth in his words eased her tension for a moment. "I'll do my best, Mr. Eisner. I promise."

"Yes, something tells me this will work out very well for all of us." By now, they had reached the front door. "We'll see you tomorrow morning, then."

"Yes. And thank you, Mr. Eisner."

Reticent to meet his gaze, she focused on a button on his vest. Then, stealing a glance, his piercing eyes touched a vein of attraction and something else, something deep within her. For that moment, she forgot all about his wife.

My mother couldn't wait to tell Magdalene about her good fortune once she returned to the cottage. Not only would she have income to quiet the concern about another mouth to feed, but she also no longer had to mix with the peasants, bend over in the fields, or sit in the barn listening to the tiresome talk of the other workers.

Magdalene saw her pride and arrogance reemerge along with infatuation with her new place of employment and, especially, with her employer.

"You know I'll be earning more than most," my mother told her. "I'll have enough for my room and food and extra to buy some nice clothes and do things I want to do. I can even save a little money."

"Karl will be glad to hear that. Staying with us will work for a while longer, but you'll still need to find another place. Karl and I want to have another baby, and this house will be too small for all of us."

That admonition did nothing to stifle my mother's elation. This was her moment, and she suffered no doubt about her decisions. Even before her first day at work, she began to chart her destiny. "In time, the Eisners will find they can't do without me."

"If you know what's good for you, be happy with what you have and the world you know," Magdalene told her.

"You sound just like my mother."

"You give her little credit, don't you? Your mother is wiser than you think." She said little more but feared that one day Mary's ambition and arrogance would be her downfall.

***

Mother arrived at the appointed time the next morning, greeted by Eisner. "Good morning, Mary. I hope you slept well. I'll show you around the house, and then you can attend to Mrs. Eisner. I know she's eager to see you."

Thrilled at being in his presence, Mother overcame her reticence in time to return his gaze. "Thank you, Mr. Eisner," she replied.

So began her routine. Each morning she'd listen to the recitation of tasks—attend to Madame, clean, dust, pick vegetables, and cook. The time spent with Jacob became her only consolation. He was always considerate, often asking about her day. She also found that while the distance between master and servant remained, his easy way around her eventually alleviated her awe and intimidation. A growing comfort in his company took their place.

Their conversations, at first, always concerned home and work. However, over time, curiosity led her to open other doors. "You work very hard, Mr. Eisner. You have so much to do for Master Kovacs with all the land he has, attending to the fields, helping keep up his estate, and overseeing the peasants and what they owe."

"Yes, it's a lot, but I manage. I often think about my family in

Budapest. But my wife and I have become accustomed to this land." Not waiting for her reply, he continued. "Can I tell you something? You know that Master Kovacs's family is Jewish, as am I. In Budapest, we had a community where we shared much in common. We went to synagogue together, celebrated births and bar mitzvahs, weddings, and holidays—not so different from your celebrations. I miss them—our friends, the people, and places."

Mother listened intently, eager to learn more about this man. Feeling emboldened, she asked what had been on her mind for some time. "How long has your wife been ill?"

Turning away from her, he gazed out the window in his study. "For some time now. Before she fell ill, Katia was a dedicated equestrian. If she had her way, she would be on horseback every day. I told her time and again not to take so many chances, but she wouldn't listen to me or anyone. Then one day, about six months ago when it had rained for days, a gully formed down by the abandoned barn not far from here. Katia and the horse didn't see it. The poor horse had to be put down, and Katia broke a bone in her leg that came through the skin. She hit her head as well. The doctor set the leg, but . . . " His voice trailed off. "He said that while she's out of immediate danger, her condition requires rest for her to recover."

Mother sat quietly, taking it all in, sensing that something more lay hidden behind his words.

***

As Mary's pride and confidence grew, so did her desire to show her mother the mistake she had made in underestimating her. One spring Sunday, as the snow and chill receded from the countryside, she waited to visit until she was sure her mother would be home from the cathedral. Six months had passed since her exile, since her mother set her out to find her way alone—and that she had.

My mother entered the house and walked into the familiar scene of Grandmother preparing lunch for Sandor and Josef.

"Mary, I'm surprised to see you," Grandmother said as she turned from the kitchen table. For a few awkward seconds, they stood before each other.

"Hello, Momma. I knew you'd be surprised that I came. How are my brothers? I wonder how much they've grown over these months. And you? You look the same."

Grandmother's eyes welled, but her memory of bitterness between them tempered a desire to embrace her only daughter. "Sandor and Josef will be here as soon as they finish their chores, so you can see for yourself." Turning to stir the pot on the stove, she continued. "Magdalene came by just the other day and told me all about you. It seems you've done well for yourself."

"Yes, I have. I'm very happy. I still live in their house, but I don't know for how much longer, as Magdalene's due to have another baby in November. My work at Mr. Eisner's home is going so well that I think they'll soon invite me to move in. I'm taking on more responsibilities and helping his wife. Both depend on me."

"I'm glad that you found a home for yourself. It seems your wish has come true."

"So it has, Momma. So it has."

"Will you stay for lunch? Your brothers haven't seen you in a long while."

"I can't, really. I must be on my way. I want to go to town while I can, before the sun sets. I just stopped by to let you know how well I'm doing. I know you probably thought I'd have a hard time."

"You're a clever girl. I don't doubt your ability to make people and circumstances bend to your wishes and will. What comes from your willfulness is what worries me."

CHAPTER 3

The next days and weeks passed uneventfully for my mother as she took on more responsibilities. She was disappointed that the Eisners made no offer of accommodations, but she never let on. My mother continued to do what was asked, tolerating demands from Mrs. Eisner, both small and significant, never showing displeasure, though she came to resent the woman's need for attention and the way she never let my mother forget the distances between education, wealth, and peasant poverty. It also didn't take long for her to realize that the more time she spent with Mrs. Eisner, the less chance she had to be with Mr. Eisner. He, unlike his wife, had become more relaxed in her company, easing the distance between master and servant. My mother responded in kind, making a point before she left in the early evenings to talk with him about their days and, more and more often, their lives. Before long, each time she prepared to leave, Eisner made a point of walking her to the door. He often brushed her hand or touched her shoulder before departing, leaving the sensation, the thrill of his touch, with her on her walk back to Magdalene's.

Mother came to accept these simple acts as gestures of gratitude. Then, on a typical Friday afternoon as she finished her chores, Eisner called her into his study.

"Master Kovacs has written to tell me that he and his family will return to Hajdudorog early this year, April instead of June, and that they'll need more help than usual with the children and their estate. He asked me whom I might suggest, and I recommended you. As he is anxious to fill the position, he approved. You'll have more responsibilities and living quarters. With my wife's health improving, she doesn't need care every day, though the house still needs attending. Perhaps you can find someone to take over your chores. I'd be most appreciative."

This unexpected news caught her by surprise. "How can I thank you, Mr. Eisner? I promise I'll make you proud. I have so much more to learn about your ways and those of Master Kovacs and his family, but I learn quickly. Being with Mrs. Eisner and you in this house, well, I've loved how beautiful it is as well as all the things in it. And now this. It just means so much to me."

With that, she rose to go. "I know Madame is waiting for me."

"My wife is napping, and she told me she doesn't want to be disturbed this afternoon."

"In that case, I'll prepare dinner for you and be on my way."

She entered the kitchen, lit the oven, and began to knead the dough left out to rise earlier in the day. Suddenly, sensing she wasn't alone, she looked up to see Eisner standing in the doorway, arms across his chest, watching her every move.

Mother smiled, flattered. The same desire she'd been feeling for months now welled within her. Finished with her preparation, she turned to the oven. But before she could take a step, Eisner was behind her, so close the feel of his breath on her neck sent chills of anticipation through her. At a loss, she could only go about her task, continuing to knead the dough and afraid to turn around. Seconds of uncertainty passed. Eisner's nearness left her lightheaded, and she leaned against the counter to keep her balance. Then, without a word, he laid his hands on her body. First her hips and thighs, and then slowly he began to caress her breasts.

Unsteady from his touch, she turned around. Their lips met with a kiss that took her breath away. "Mary, Mary," was all he said as she surrendered to him. In that moment no words came to her, so taken by this man whose way and world held such allure.

He pulled her to him, and they made their way from the kitchen, passing by Katia's closed door, and up the stairs to his bedroom. My mother never let go, fearful that if she did, all would disappear as if in a dream. As soon as they reached the top stair, she said, "Jacob, I love you. I have loved you from the first moment I saw you."

His reply came not in words but in his kiss that seemed to come from a place of unrequited longing.

Every touch, every movement of their bodies, even the rustle under the soft linen sheets became magnified. Every part of her was alive to the moment. Everything about him was new. Smooth skin untainted by years of servility, the softness of his hands, reminders of the distance in their lives, hair the texture of silk, and his scent— masculine and yet made lightly sweet by the faint fragrances of cologne and earth. His body spoke to her without words, moving in an inexorable rhythm. Her body responded in natural cadence, shuddering in utter surrender to their moment.

As they lay together, even that room she had come to know took on detail and color she'd never noticed before: the sliver of light not quite masked by the brocaded drapes, the corner lamp with its crystal petals, the filigreed bronze handles on the chest of drawers, the gash on the side of the rolltop desk. All and more came alive to her.

They lay together in silence after making love, but, as she was to tell Magdalene, her mind was racing with all she wanted to ask. *When will we be together again? When will you tell your wife that you're in love with me? Can we make love tomorrow and the next day and the next?* Just as she was about to break that silence, the grandfather clock at the foot of the stairs struck six. The chimes sounded an alarm, as it was the hour that Mrs. Eisner expected dinner, well past the time for my mother to have departed. She and Jacob heard the door to Madame Eisner's chamber creak open and a shuffling sound of slippers across the wooden floor by the kitchen. The high-pitched voice that followed made them both sit bolt upright in bed.

"Jacob? Jacob? Where are you?"

Startled, Eisner called down to her, "I'm upstairs changing for dinner. I'll be right down." Taking a deep breath, he called out to her once again. "Katia, why don't I bring dinner to you? I'll set that table next to your bed for the two of us. That way you'll be more comfortable."

"All right. Can you make me some tea when you bring dinner, that black tea I like?"

"Yes, of course." As if fearful of the silence, he added, "And if you feel up to it, perhaps we can go for a short walk afterward."

"Yes. That would be nice. I am feeling better. Come down. We can talk about it over dinner."

By now, the sense of panic on Eisner's face had receded. He rose from the bed and dressed quickly. Before he left, he looked over at my mother. "Give me a few minutes to prepare her dinner. Then you can leave. I'm sorry." With those words, he disappeared.

Magdalene's account of those moments was crystal clear. Soon, fantasies of the life-to-be were all that fit in my mother's world. She bided her time, looking for the opportunity to be alone with Eisner again, to feel him next to her and to ask him the questions that lingered. Now that Katia was up and about, being alone with him took on a hint of danger in being discovered that, to her surprise, excited her. Those few secret seductions, the hastily made straw bed in the abandoned barn, the high grasses beside the wheat field, only served to feed her passion and desire.

Gradually, awkwardness filled the days before she left, as Mrs. Eisner's health continued to improve. Whether by coincidence or suspicion, Mrs. Eisner began to take an interest in her. Her orders continued as always, but that's not all she had to say. Whereas for weeks Mrs. Eisner's condition had kept her confined to her bedroom, now she seemed to follow my mother around, as if studying her. Uncomfortable exchanges about home life, school, and friends became more frequent, until one sultry Friday afternoon in the kiln of August heat, Mrs. Eisner unexpectedly entered the kitchen. It was late in the day, and my mother was finishing up.

"Mary, I wanted to ask you something," she began, narrowing her eyes as if trying to penetrate my mother's thoughts. "You told me the other day that your friend Magdalene is married and has a child. Is she happy?"

"Yes, Mrs. Eisner. Very happy, I would say."

"Aren't most of the girls you know married at your age?"

My mother felt uneasy but kept her composure. "Many, Mrs. Eisner, but not everyone."

"What about you?"

"I haven't met anyone yet. Besides, now that I'll be working for Master Kovacs, I'll have my hands full with the house and children."

Mrs. Eisner went silent for a moment. When she continued, she spoke with a thinly veiled note of suspicion. "I noticed that Master Eisner has taken a new interest in gardening, especially when you're tending to it. I overheard him the other day talking to you. He seemed very interested in what you were doing."

Unsure where this interrogation was leading, Mary was about to reply when Eisner appeared. "Mary, I've been looking for my gold cufflinks but can't find them anywhere. Have you seen them?"

Realizing they weren't alone, he turned to his wife. "Katia, I didn't expect to see you here. I've misplaced my cufflinks and wondered if Mary had seen them when she was cleaning the bedroom."

"I was asking Mary about something too, but it's not important."

Nothing was quite the same after that day.

Whereas she'd always looked forward to Eisner greeting her at the door, reticence had now taken its place. He fell back on his erudition and politeness, engaging her only around tasks or the latest on her move to Master Kovacs's estate.

As she later confessed to Magdalene, my mother's self-assurance and arrogance turned to guesses and uncertainty, not over what had happened but how not to lose what she had possessed. Still, she felt certain that they would be together as lovers and, in time, as husband and wife.

***

My mother's eagerness to start work for Master Kovacs grew now that Mrs. Eisner was feeling better, and her recovery only sharpened her scrutiny of tasks and time. The more assertive Mrs. Eisner became, the more her husband retreated to his study and into his own world of work and books. Still, as my mother caught him watching her from across a room, in the garden, at the stove, she assured herself that, as he would miss her so, some distance between them would make him act.

Soon the day came when Master Kovacs's family called for her to work and live at their estate. Magdalene looked on while my mother packed her things. "I know we haven't talked much these past weeks, but there's something I want to tell you. You do know that Mr. Eisner has been very nice to me since I went to work for him."

"Yes, I know that. You've said so many times. Are you leaving Eisner on good terms?"

"Oh, yes! In fact, I'd say he's been more than nice. It happened a little over a week ago that he made love to me."

Magdalene stiffened in shock. "Oh, Mary, how could you? He's a married man!"

"He's in love with me, and in time he'll leave his wife," my mother said, rushing the words. "He hasn't told her yet, but when I move into Master Kovacs's house, he will. I'll be with him in that house. I'll go to parties in Budapest, where all the women dress in fancy evening gowns. We'll dine at fine restaurants with his friends and family. My mother will be disappointed that I did so well without her. Aren't you happy for me?"

"Do you really think that's your future? That he'll stay and work for Kovacs, and life will just continue except you'll be the center of his life? The two of you are so different. Where he comes from and who he is—that's not us. He's educated. You know how to read and write, but beyond that what do you have to offer?"

"I know he wants me, and it means I'll never have to live at home again."

"My God, how you despise your mother. You're so desperate to escape from your mother that it's taken you over. It's just not going to happen with you and Eisner."

"What makes you so sure?"

"When I say he's not 'us,' I mean there's one way you and he will never be alike. He's a Jew. They own the land and will always be separate from us. You've crossed a line that no one else in your family or our town has ever crossed."

"I don't care! I'll make him convert. Or I'll find a priest in Budapest who will marry us."

"I have nothing more to say to you," Magdalene said, shaking her head. "You have your fantasies, and I know there's no room in them for reality."

The conversation ended, and my mother finished packing. She washed and braided her hair, put on a white starched dress and her best shoes, and wrapped herself in her only silk kerchief, one resplendent with red roses. With that, she walked out the door into what she yearned to become her new life.

***

The next weeks were a blur as my mother took up residence in the modest servants' quarters on Master Kovacs's estate, caring for two children, ages seven and ten, and helping the other servants with chores and meals. Settling into this new life was easier than Mary had expected. All the while, she waited for Eisner to realize what she saw as his destiny: to be with her.

Then, as she dressed for work one day, my mother didn't feel well. Her breakfast didn't stay down, and the smell of cabbage cooking in the kitchen brought on waves of nausea. Making it through that day and the week ahead became a chore, while irritation replaced her patience with the children. My mother thought she had fallen ill. Something wasn't right. It was during this time that she paid a visit to Magdalene.

She found her friend in the kitchen, preparing lunch for her son, Antal. Surprised by the visit, Magdalene's greeting was more distracted than inviting. "I didn't expect to see you. Karl has been keeping me up on your work for Master Kovacs. He said you're busy but very happy at his estate and that things are going well for you."

"I told you when we last saw each other that I am where I belong. That hasn't changed. I enjoy the work, the children. As for where I live now, it's a dream come true, as it's taken me far away from the fields and that barn."

"Have you heard from Eisner?"

"A little. He's come by to see Master Kovacs a number of times. We haven't had any chances to be alone, but when he visits, I catch him following me around the room, that same way as before."

"And how are you feeling? You look tired and pale."

"You're right. I don't feel well. Days are a struggle to get through, and I've been sick to my stomach, though I don't have a fever. You know how I've loved to cook, but mealtimes? Well, they're not the same either. For some reason, it's been hard to keep food down. Mornings are the worst. But even later in the day, when I'm boiling the cabbage, I feel I'll be sick to my stomach."

Magdalene eyed her knowingly. "How long have you felt like this?"

"It started a few weeks ago."

"When did you and Eisner become lovers?"

"Seven weeks to the day."

My mother at first looked stunned, and then horrified. "It can't be! You're wrong. I just don't feel well. I'll be better in a few days."

"Actually, you'll probably feel much better in a few weeks, but that won't change what's happening to you. You might want to start thinking about your life differently. Put aside those fantastic dreams of yours, and think about what's growing inside you and how you'll care for your baby."

"I don't want to hear any more from you." With those words, my mother stormed out the door and started on the road back to the estate. However, the firm ground of her denial to Magdalene was now sown with further seeds of doubt about what Jacob would do. What if Magdalene were right? What would she do? As her friend had said, did Mary really believe that their child, if that's what this was, would make him leave his wife so they could be together? But even as Magdalene was not convinced of that happy ending, Mary told her it could work.

Distraction carried my mother along for another week or two as the nausea subsided. Time spent with the master's children in their home was put to good use, as she learned etiquette and the language of wealth, and came to covet the finery of and around the Kovacs family. Linens; silk; antique furniture; foods she had never dreamed existed, let alone eaten; and Jewish culture surrounded her.

Kovacs often invited Eisner and his wife to readings and dinner on Sabbath evenings. At first, Mary was satisfied to catch his gaze during those visits. However, doubts returned that she may lose the chance for the life she had imagined, and that was something she would not endure.

It was at this point that my mother accepted my existence, not as a gift to love but as a means to an end. She could no longer ignore my presence, as she felt the changes in her body, the tenderness, swelling, cravings, and a keen awareness of her sensuality.

She saw her chance one of those Sabbath evenings. Emma, the short, stout family cook, had her hands full as she prepared the carp and watched over the chicken soup and vegetables. Mother, who was in charge of the kindle cakes, turned to Emma just as she was about to open the door to the dining room. "I'm going to need someone to help get the flour canister down from the top shelf."

"Well, I certainly can't do it. If you're going to ask Master Kovacs or Mr. Eisner, make sure they're not in the middle of one of those Jewish prayers they're always chanting on these evenings. I never understand a word of it."

She listened at the door until hearing casual conversation. Entering the dining room, she spoke softly as if not to arouse attention. "I'm sorry to interrupt. May I ask for someone's help in reaching a canister of flour? It won't take but a moment."

All turned toward her, making my mother blush. Eisner was the first to rise. "I'll get it down for you."

"Thank you, Mr. Eisner," she said as he followed her into the kitchen. As Emma busied herself at the stove, my mother leaned into him as he reached for the canister and whispered, "I need to see you. There's something I have to tell you."

"All right," he whispered. "Meet me tomorrow morning, before seven, by Kovacs's barn." With that, he reached for the flour canister, handed it over, and returned to the service.

My mother hardly slept that night as the weight of two futures—one born of desperate hope, the other a bitter end—lay before her.

Parsing each encounter, each word Eisner uttered, her spirits rose and fell. The way he said her name, how he smiled at her, what she felt when they made love, and now the baby. She knew he'd want to be together. Then, that dream darkened as she saw a future where he'd never leave Katia, that she'd always be a peasant woman in his eyes, and a Catholic in a Jewish world he'd never abandon.

These irreconcilable fates stayed with her the next morning as she dressed quickly, promising Irina, Madame Kovacs's maidservant, that she would be back by the time the children had finished breakfast. My mother stepped out the front door and looked around and up. The dense fog of that night had yet to lift, concealing the world around her. Walking carefully along the road, seeing only the vague contours of farms and fields, she thought, *It seems Mother Nature is playing a cruel joke on me.* Like her life at that moment, she had lost her moorings, not knowing where she was or, for that matter, what would happen next.

When she arrived, Eisner was there, pacing back and forth in front of the splintered barn door. He greeted her with a wan smile and an all-too-brief kiss. "I have to meet Kovacs shortly. I'm sorry to be in a hurry, but this was the only time I could meet you. What's so important that it couldn't wait?"

"It *is* important, Jacob. I'm going to have a baby—our baby."

His face fell. "Are you sure? Can this really be? Are you certain?"

My mother took his hand and placed it under her blouse so that he could feel the slight but undeniable arc that was me.

A look of shock came over him. "Are you sure it's mine?"

She gasped, taken aback by his response, but then quickly composed herself. "There's never been anyone else. You must know that. I know you're busy, but now you know I don't have much time before everyone will know. I want to be with you. It's past time to stop hiding from others and ourselves."

It took Eisner a minute to regain his composure. "But I'm married. I may lose my job if Kovacs finds out. You won't be able to have a place with him and his family, so you must plan for that. Perhaps I can help. As for us, I don't know what to do."

"Don't make excuses! He can't do without you. He'll never let you go. As for your wife, I know you haven't been happy with her for a long time. I'm the one who makes you happy. I know it can all work out, but our lives are in your hands. You must do something about it, Jacob. Now you have more than the two of us to think about."

Eisner shook his head and walked away, repeating the words "I don't know" before leaving her beside the decrepit barn as he receded into the fog.

***

My mother knew there was little more she could do but wait for him to see things her way. As weeks passed, however, she could no longer hide the new life within her.

One afternoon, at the end of her workday, Master Kovacs called her into his study. She entered an office that radiated wealth in colors, tapestry, wood, and glass. A world of separation stood between them as he sat behind a rosewood desk, papers arranged in a small pile to his right, gilt-framed photos of his wife and children displayed in one corner. She took a seat before the overlord of all she knew and envied. His hairline, which was receding but without one strand out of place, and his well-trimmed black beard flecked with gray gave Master Kovacs a noble bearing. A voice of quiet command let her know his decisions weren't to be questioned.

"Mary, is there something you want to tell me?" He didn't wait for her response. "You're with child, aren't you?"

Although my mother knew this was coming, she found herself frozen and only able to nod.

"How far along are you?"

"Six months."

"You've set a very poor example for my daughters. They've already started to ask their mother about you. It's especially distressing, as they've grown to like you." He then grimaced, eyes shifting to his desktop. "This situation is impossible, I'm afraid. You should plan to leave immediately. Today is Wednesday. You need to be gone by the Sabbath."

A "But Master Kovacs" caught in her throat. She knew there was nothing to say that would change his mind. Instead, she straightened her back and nodded. "Thank you for allowing me to serve your family, Master Kovacs."

With that, she left the room.

In the fields, the sunflowers had begun to reveal their brown and golden beauty, and the tobacco ripened for the harvest. Even in her fecundity, my mother felt empty, bereft over the life she had briefly known and the future she wanted, seemingly out of reach.

Master Kovacs had left her with little time to pack her things and get out. My mother could no longer put off a dreaded decision.

CHAPTER 4

T he warm summer months were wonderful for Sandor and Josef. At sixteen and fourteen, their chores—feeding the animals and tending to the fields and small garden—took them from adventures among the trees and streams that crossed the lands only for a time. Tasks finished, they would lose themselves in that immersive world that surrounded them until suppertime.

Grandmother, too, was happy. Her brother's generosity had made life more than tolerable. The cathedral filled the void her husband had left, and she had come to a place of resolve and, in a way, peace when it came to the absence of her daughter. Mary's leaving seemed meant to be.

As she prepared lunch for the boys that day, there was a tap at the door. She wiped her hands on a dishtowel and went to answer it.

"Hello, Mother. I didn't want to surprise you, so I knocked first."

Since Mary had moved into Master Kovacs's mansion, my grandmother had continued to hear from Magdalene and Karl about how well her daughter was doing, but little else. Now the flesh and bones of reality stood before her.

"I know you're surprised to see me. I heard from Magdalene and Karl that you, Uncle Johann, and my brothers are in good health these days. I can see not much has changed since I left." She walked into the room, finishing her inspection of the kitchen and the small area with the bench in the nook where she had sometimes napped when she was younger.

"How have you been?" my grandmother asked, seeing her daughter's state but not wanting to say anything that would upset her. "How is working for Master Kovacs?"

"You can see how I am. As for Master Kovacs, he said I set a poor example for his girls and told me to leave. I didn't want to come back here, but I can't stay at the manor anymore, and Magdalene now has two children and no room for me. I'm here because I have nowhere to go."

Grandmother frowned as she held back tears. "Who is the father of the baby?"

"Jacob Eisner."

"Your employer? He's the estate manager who hired you."

"Yes. Please don't look sad. Jacob was—is—wonderful. He treated me very well when I worked for him." My mother stopped there. She didn't have to explain anymore, she was sure.

Grandmother's downcast expression didn't change. "Does he know you're pregnant?"

"Oh, yes, he knows. I told him I love him and want the three of us to be together. I know he loves me too."

"Have you talked about when you'll marry?"

My mother's next words seemed to catch in her throat. "There's one more thing I haven't told you. He's married."

"I don't understand. Is she leaving him? Or is she very ill?"

"No. She was ill, but now she has almost recovered. As for leaving him, I don't think she has any intention of doing that."

My grandmother averted her gaze, unable to look at her daughter. Still, maternal concern for her daughter and the new life growing within her took over. "What will you do?"

"I know he wants to leave his wife and be with me. If you had asked me a few weeks ago, I was certain he would. But now I don't know."

"Mary, you can't count on him. We can make room for you and the baby here. The boys moved into the house when you left, but we can make them comfortable again in the barn. I know this isn't what you wanted. I thought my life would be different too. But we've made a good life here." Then she added, "It would be for the best if you came home."

My mother's pride and resentment yielded to her mother's words. Speaking barely above a whisper, she acknowledged her fate. "Yes, I know that's what I need to do."

The revelation of Mary and Jacob's profane union remained only between them for a time. Johann and family friends knew Jacob Eisner only as the person who helped Master Kovacs, the man who made sure they did the required work. Conversations about him rarely went beyond fieldwork, crop yields, and getting paid. My mother and grandmother saw nothing good in changing that order of things. Even Johann seemed to know better than to ask questions of them, until the people of Hajdudorog made it so he could no longer turn away from what had come to pass.

***

As much as Eisner and work had dominated Mary's waking hours, she had never abandoned her love of singing at the cathedral. Sunday High Mass with its liturgy and choral refrains never failed to animate her and bestow peace of mind for a time. Before she left home, it seemed the only place free of tension, where mother and daughter could share a common space, uplifting both their spirits. In the days since, my mother found solace and support from ceremony and those who filled the pews.

The cathedral and its sacred days and secular events seemed to reach into the lives and homes of all in town. Sunday breakfasts, saintly feasts, holy days of obligation, and especially Christmas and Easter were times of rejoicing and renewal. Announcements of baptisms, weddings, and confirmations brought pride to the families of congregants.

However, one all-too-common tragedy seemed to bind all to the story of the town where the sacred songs fit as one with the people. The cathedral's graveyard silently told of the generations who had gone before and foreshadowed those to come. Dates on small stones marking those laid to rest told of many whose shortened lives marked the hardships of their time: families whose newborns never knew the light of day and darkness of night; young women for whom childbirth was their death sentence; those taken by pestilences passing over the town; and so many sons, fathers, brothers, and husbands lost to wars who left heartache as a companion to those who loved them.

My mother's singing voice was a source of comfort and consolation through these tragedies and losses. People would tell my grandmother after a service that her arias seemed like one with sacred consecration. With her quiet dignity, Grandmother let her daughter know time and again what it meant. "Mary, God gave you such a gift. I am so proud of what you have and what you've given to all of us."

None of this was lost on Mother. Everywhere she went, people expressed their gratitude. Over these days and years, my mother loved the attention, until it turned on her.

Family secrets didn't stay that way for long in this small community. Marital affairs, petty grievances, and social indiscretions were almost impossible to hide. It was unsettling for the entire family when rumors stirred about my mother's illicit liaison.

She offered little to them. Her devotion to the choir never wavered, even as she could no longer conceal her state, leaving parishioners and neighbors to solve the mystery. A secret admirer? A young man from town? Perhaps a soldier passing through? Nevertheless, in this insular community, rumors closer to the truth also spread, and with them came stories about my father. Where and how my family heard from the townspeople was the cause of their humiliation.

As my grandmother told the story to me, one Sunday morning as my family was leaving, one of the parishioners, Mrs. Matjas, approached them on the cathedral steps, just outside its arced wooden doors. "Good morning, Ilushka and Johann. How are you?" Not waiting for a reply, she continued. "Mary, it's good to see you too. I know you haven't said much, but I wanted to ask when you'll have your baby."

"In the next month; perhaps a bit longer," replied my mother icily.

"I understand you were working for Eisner and Kovacs, but no longer. I don't want to pry, but a few of us were just wondering who the father might be. Rumor has it that you and that Jew, Eisner, got to be very friendly when you were taking care of his wife and," she hesitated, "you were taking care of him."

The frozen silence from all told Mrs. Matjas everything. My mother turned away. My grandmother had kept from her brother the father's identity, but now that seal was broken.

Johann struggled to contain himself. "Mary, you've already shamed our family by your sin. Now this? You slept with a Jew and are having his child? This is a disgrace."

She turned to face him. "So, what of it, Johann? Yes, it's true. I didn't want to say anything to you because I knew just what you'd think. What do you want me to do—give it away? It's too late to do anything about it now."

"I wouldn't say that," Johann replied.

"What do you mean?"

"You have your responsibility to your baby now. And what I'll do is out of your hands."

***

A few weeks after that Sunday, my mother tried to take fate into her own hands. She knew that on Monday mornings Eisner bought provisions at the store in Hajdudorog, so she harnessed the horse to their cart and set out for town. "I need to pick up a few things for the baby," she told her mother to allay any suspicions.

She arrived before Eisner, stopped the cart precisely in front of the store, and sat gripping the harness so hard that her nails dug into her palms. A few townspeople went about their business on the dusty streets as the usual sun-drenched heat of the late summer day was already taking its toll. Their lives and that discomfort meant little to Mary, single-minded as she was to see Jacob.

Before long Eisner and Markov, his young assistant, pulled their carriage next to hers. Eisner glanced over absentmindedly at my mother as she waited for his greeting. It took a few seconds to say hello, startled as he was to see her there.

She knew what she wanted to say as she climbed down from the carriage but got no further than "Jacob" before Eisner motioned toward the store entrance to his assistant.

As soon as Markov left, she continued. "Jacob, why haven't you come to see me? Since I lost my job with Master Kovacs, I've had no way to see you. Besides, I assume that your wife is up and about more these days, so unless you've—"

"Unless I've told her about us. Is that what you are about to say?"

"Yes, isn't it time for that? Past time, actually." She rested a hand on her protruding middle.

Eisner hesitated for a moment as a man and a woman passed. Once they were out of range, Eisner spoke in a low voice. "Mary, I've thought a lot about us, believe me. I still want you. I often think about when we made love and our moments alone. But Katia needs me—and divorce is out of the question."

"So, what I thought we had was all a lie? Is that it?"

"No, no. Not at all. But now that you're going to have a baby, it makes things that much harder." He looked away just as Markov returned with meats, cheese, a box of candies, and a few other items.

"Is there anything else you need?" Markov asked, eyeing my mother's protruding stomach.

"No, Markov. That's all."

The assistant boarded Eisner's carriage.

Then, leaning in, Eisner said, "We can't talk here. I'll come by this afternoon. Katia knows I have to see about a fungus spreading in the cornfield. I'll meet you by the old, abandoned barn near you."

"Yes, the one where we've met," she started to say as Eisner and Markov pulled away in a cloud of dust.

***

That afternoon, knowing Grandmother would be furious if she knew about their rendezvous, my mother left the house without saying a word. Eisner was there when she arrived. He enclosed her in his arms before she could say a word. His kiss, languid and dizzying, left her lightheaded.

"It's been impossible to get away. It's not just Katia, but whether it's true or not, I feel the eyes of others on me."

"You must tell Katia for us and for what's to come in a few months."

With those words, he pulled away from her. "It's hard enough to see you now. Once the baby comes, it will be impossible. I don't know. I just don't know." Running his hands through his hair, Eisner hesitated before the next words came, unsure of what was to come from them. "Mary, now that Katia is better, I'll be returning to Budapest after the harvest and will come back here before the planting next spring. You and I have talked about Budapest and how much you would love to leave Hajdudorog and live there."

"Yes, Jacob. With you."

"I know that's what you wish. But should you agree, you must know I'll still be married to Katia."

She stepped back, away from him. "I don't understand. What are you trying to say?"

"I'm saying that it's our only chance. We can be lovers, away from here. I can take you to Budapest, where you can live comfortably. I can promise you that. But only you."

"Are you saying I can be your mistress but not your wife?" she asked. "And only if I give up the baby? That's your idea of how we can be together?"

"I don't know of any other way."

"You want to be with me, but you say you can't leave Katia," she said with exasperation. "You can find a way to take me to Budapest but only as your lover. I don't believe there isn't any other way, as you say." She stared at him, a solitary figure leaning against the rotting barn. "I don't want to see you unless you do find a way."

***

The late summer days gave way to fall, and the fertile fields offered their bounty. The green tobacco leaves, corn, and other crops ripened to the point that Master Kovacs required all his workers to harvest from dawn until dusk and into the night as the oil lamps allowed.

It was during these days that my father's world fell apart and the affair became a town scandal. As overseeing the harvest was his primary responsibility, he was a constant presence among the workers, supervising the delegation of tasks, making sure sufficient numbers were available for picking, and preparing produce and tobacco for market.

At first, he dismissed silences among the workers as he passed, thinking the drop in voices was nothing more than the usual private discussions. Then he noticed silences had given way to whispers and stares that conveyed, what was it? Anger? Menace? He wanted to dismiss them, but a sense of foreboding hung over his head like a scythe about to fell a sapling.

One evening, as he walked up the steps to the front door of his house, a missile sailed past and crashed through the stained glass. Katia burst through the front door as he approached.

"Did you see that? Someone threw a rock and broke our window!"

"Are you hurt? I didn't see who did it, but I heard footsteps close to me, close to the house."

"Why would someone do this to us? Have the workers been complaining about something? Did you do something? Is someone mad at you?"

"No, there's nothing I can think of. All they care about is their share of crops and money, and this has been a good year."

"Well, you need to find out. Kovacs won't be pleased. And I'm afraid."

"I'll ask around tomorrow."

My father went about his routine the next day, keeping track of which fields needed harvesting and directing workers to cut down the corn and tobacco and clear space in the barn. The peasants went about their work as usual, knowing their assignments all too well. All seemed normal that morning. Now an unknown fear gripped him as if a sulfurous presence circled about. His greetings went unanswered, and the silences from all once again left him bewildered.

Eisner struggled to understand yesterday's event and now this day's reaction. Suddenly it came to him: It had to be about Mary. At the end of morning work, just around lunchtime, he approached Johann and his friends.

"May I have a word with you, Johann?"

With his eyes riveted on Eisner, Johann accompanied my father behind the barn. As they turned the corner, Johann didn't wait for Eisner to speak.

"Do you know what you've done to us? To our family? Mary worked for you, took care of your wife. You come to our town from the city, and you think you can do as you please. You think you can sleep with our women? You are already rich from the land and live in that fancy house, and you take and take from us. And now you've taken Mary to your bed and have left her with child. You. A Jew. Don't you know you don't belong here? Now we have to live knowing that Jew blood will be in our family."

As he spoke, Johann's body clenched, fists tightened as he leaned in, so close that the spit he hurled dribbled down my father's face. Jacob drew back, anticipating the blows to come. And came they did, knocking him to the ground.

"I have one piece of advice for you," Johann snarled. "Leave this place and never come back. You've got a week, and if you're not gone by then, I'll kill you."

With that, Johann walked away.

My father rose unsteadily. Trembling and dizzy, he leaned against the barn. The life he had made was crushed. He had harbored the hope that my mother would come away to Budapest, where he could keep her, but that decision had been made for him, for Katia, and for my mother. He had to leave at once.

In the weeks that followed, Mother adjusted to life at home. She helped around the house as much as she could, preparing meals and seeing her brothers off to school, but the much-detested peasant work was out of the question, as she was now well into her eighth month. Grandmother did her best to comfort her daughter, but my mother shared little of what she was feeling beyond what had to be said to make it through the daily routines. She heard nothing about my father, a silence that kept her faint hope alive.

Then one morning my mother received a letter.

Dear Mary,

I am sorry I haven't written sooner. Katia and I have left Hajdudorog. As to why, I will only say that I couldn't stay any longer.

I still think of you, your kiss and caresses. I had so wished for us to be lovers. I offered you Budapest, but you would not come alone. And it remains impossible for me to leave my wife.

I wish you and our child well. I have moved back to the city but will send money for the child in the coming weeks. Should you ever change your mind, send a letter to that address.

Yours,

Jacob

Distraught and disbelieving, Mary read and reread his words. *Wish our child well? Impossible to leave my wife?* Perhaps it was my mother's despair in reading my father's words, or perhaps it's that I was the cause of such anguish, but on that same day I entered the world. I think my mother wanted me out of her body, wanted me to be separated from her.

I became a symbol and form of lost love, a lost life.

***

Maternal duties and attention didn't sit well with my mother in the following days and months. She remained in her own world, deferring responsibility and devotion to Grandmother. She took on whatever work earned money, even joining others in the fields and, at times, helping Karl feed and keep the horses, staying on well past dinner and into the night. She was driven, it seemed, by a desire to spend as little time as she could with me.

To my grandmother's relief, Magdalene came by to help with me as she was able, perhaps hoping that my mother might learn from her nurturing and loving way. Leaving her younger son, Frederick, with Karl from time to time, she was happy to bring Antal by and watch over the two of us. As I was to learn, these days kindled a bond of caring that transcended their difference in age. At one point, Grandmother recalled telling Magdalene, "Your visits are my gift. The way you are with Irene is what I hope Mary will soon become."

Her visits, however, made little impression on my mother, as once Magdalene departed, Mary did as well. She preferred to be alone, reading and writing letters to Jacob. Even with her responsibilities lightened, she spent these days shrouded in resentment. Motherhood, the farm, the town, the family—she yearned to be rid of it all. As for Grandmother, as her love and devotion to me deepened, so did my mother's discontent with her life.

Her resolution came about one morning at breakfast, a few days after my first birthday. My mother entered as I sat in an armchair, propped up on pillows at the kitchen table.

Grandmother said, "You went for a walk before breakfast?"

"Yes. I was up very early."

Then, keeping her distance, Mary began to speak about what Grandmother sensed was something she had been keeping from her but was now resigned to reveal.

"You know how I've been working so hard these past months? You know how I've been keeping to myself when I'm home? Well, it certainly isn't so I could live here for the rest of my life. I've been writing to Jacob. He's sent money, and I've saved some too. I have enough so now I can leave this place. I'm going to America. I've heard that it's the place of dreams, and I'll finally get to live mine."

My grandmother took a deep breath. "I know you hate your life here, but you have an infant to care for. It's not just about what you want. How will you manage?"

"Did you hear me? I said, '*I* am leaving for America.' Did I say anything about taking Irene? I'm not about to become you, never seeing the world, never being anything but a simple peasant woman, living and dying where I was born. No, I leave Irene to you. And the barn, the fields, this dirt and dust—you can have it all. She wasn't my idea in the first place. Oh, and Johann told me what he said to Jacob. He took away any hope I had of ever being with him. And what chance do you think I have of finding anyone in this town worthy of me?"

Those last words seemed to catch in her throat. With tears in her eyes, her voice softened. "All those Sundays at cathedral singing, how our neighbors and others would come up to me after. 'Mary, you sang so beautifully today.' 'Wasn't the choir so wonderful today, Mary?' Now I can't stand the way people look at me. I know the priest frowns on what I've done too and won't let me do what I love, so . . . " With a sigh, she leaned over to my chair and kissed my cheek. "I'm lost here."

My grandmother's eyes glistened as Mary spoke. Reaching out, she gently touched her daughter's arm. "You didn't say, but I felt it. I knew you hurt, and I wished I could take that pain away. You still can make a life here. People won't be so harsh and unforgiving once they see the love you have for Irene."

My mother stiffened. Resolution had returned to her tone. "Don't be naïve, Mother. It's too late for that. My life here is over. And you don't need to feel sorry for me."

It didn't take long for her to make arrangements. Within the week, on a clear spring day, she sat with Grandmother for the last time as I toyed with my porridge.

"I don't have much to say to you, Mother, as I haven't for a long time. I know you love Irene and that she's in good hands."

"Mary, I love Irene with all my heart and will watch over her," she said, gently brushing my black curls from my face. "I know you've made up your mind, but I still don't understand how you can leave her."

"I'll see what happens to my life. Who knows? Once I find work, I might send for her. Maybe I'll marry someone with enough money to bring her to America." Hesitating for a moment, she added one final self-reflection. "Maybe she can take care of me when I get older, just like I knew you wanted me to take care of you. Well, you have my brothers to do that. As for me, I say goodbye to them and to you."

With nothing more to say, my mother rose from the kitchen table, lifted her suitcase, leaned down and kissed me, and took leave from our lives. With that last kiss, as I was taking my first steps, my mother walked into her new life without me.

CHAPTER 5

My mother left little for me to remember her by. In my early years, with only a few clouded photos, she became indistinct, an abstraction, a black-and-white image. I committed to memory the stories I heard about her past, as they were all I had. What was said about her life in America was spoken in murmurs between Johann and my grandmother and only when a rare letter arrived. They both said little to me about the contents of those letters, but I would come to read my grandmother's silent expression well, as it belied the sadness she harbored within. As I grew older, my mother's absence left within me a yearning, a hole in my heart.

Grandmother did what she could to fill the emptiness. She became the center of my world and of my first and enduring memories of early days and years, from morning to night. The sweet, yeasty aroma of her bread baking when I awoke, her embrace when I came home from school, her kiss goodnight, her steady breathing as we slept in Johann's canopied bed all became a part of me. My reality and hers were one and the same, immersed as I was in what I saw, felt, and heard through my grandmother.

Home became our intimate world. Grandmother taught me early on to sew what I wore from clothes my mother left behind and fabric she purchased from the haberdashery in Hajdudorog. I was eager to help in the kitchen and quickly learned the simple magic of preparing evening and weekend meals for her brother and the boys. Although unable to read or write, she instinctively knew the value of both and would ask, or rather insist, that I bring home one of the few books the teacher allowed me to take from school, even if it meant rereading those already borrowed.

Her firm resolve and sense of what to do carried the day, even in my illness. One Saturday I awoke to feel as if my body had erupted with fever, chills, rash, a terrible earache, and sore throat as I had never felt before. Sending Sandor for the only doctor within miles, my grandmother learned that it was no ordinary condition. Scarlet fever had coursed through the town and descended on our home. The doctor counseled her to do what she could to control my fever spikes and soothe my aches and pains.

She sat by me as I tossed and turned for the next week, leaving my side only to feed the boys. She did as the doctor advised to reduce my fever. My grandmother, however, had her own ideas. She wrapped a cool towel around my neck at least once a day, giving me some relief. Then she did something that never ceased to puzzle me.

"It will help take away what's in your head and throat," she explained, and with that she picked me up by my shoulders and gently bounced me, as if trying to shake out whatever had taken me over. Too ill to protest, I let out a whimper until her treatment passed. Day after day, she performed this ritual until the pain eased. I had no sense of why, but old folkways, by her measure, had served their purpose.

***

As the farm was miles from my school, that distance left me with little chance to play with children from my class. Johann was always prompt in taking me to town and picking me up after school since fieldwork dictated his days. Magdalene's frequent visits were happy times. She'd bring Antal, a few years older than me, whenever she could. Among my earliest memories are the two of us on warm, bright spring days, playing in the grassy front yard with a rubber ball or wooden figures of a boy and girl that Karl had carved. Magdalene sat on the steps, smiling, watching, and sometimes joining in our revelry.

However, with few toys and playmates other than Antal, I was often left to create my own imaginary world. It was actually a visit from my grandfather's brother that led me there.

Uncle Janos lived near the city of Debrecen, about three hours from Hajdudorog. My grandmother didn't see much of her brother-in-law after separating from Peter, but she remembered him fondly. He had always been kind to us, generous, and good-humored. His full beard had turned grayish white, even though he was barely fifty. His well-rounded belly, I was to learn, came from a diet abundant in blood sausage, beer, and Tokaji wine. Uncle Janos's hearty, full-throated laugh brought to mind the image of St. Nicholas. Although I rarely saw him, his visits came with great anticipation and excitement, as I knew that just like Santa Claus, he would bring a present. So when he appeared at our door one day as August had ended, I ran to him. He picked me up as if I were a toothpick, his strong arms wrapping around me.

"Uncle Janos, I'm so happy to see you!"

"Well, my dear, I've missed you and your big, beautiful smile. The last time we were together was about a year ago, and now you're growing up. I didn't want another few years to pass before I came to see you. It's harder to travel these days, but I'm here now, and here's where I'll be for a whole week. Where are your grandmother and the boys?"

"They're out by the barn. It's planting time for winter. They should be in soon."

"Good. That gives me time to spend with you before everybody comes in. I've been saving something special for my little girl."

Uncle Janos opened his suitcase and pulled out a small package wedged in between his nightshirt and wool trousers. Without another word—for his smile told all—he handed this mystery to me.

I cut the twine that curled around the pale-blue box and opened it to find more delicate paper. Nestled within it was the most beautiful doll I had ever seen. Standing less than a foot tall, its delicate facial features and peaches-and-cream complexion reminded me of my grandmother's one porcelain figurine, but my gift seemed so much more alive. The cotton mirrored our folk celebrations, where musicians played and girls danced, wrapped in patterns of vermilion roses.

"I found this at a very special doll store and thought, 'I know the perfect home for you.'"

"Oh, Uncle Janos, thank you!" For my first years of life, I had only one tattered doll figure that my grandmother had made for me. I kept it in our bedroom in a box with a few toys. This grand gift, I thought, would go with me and be with me, to sleep with and wake to.

Just then, Grandmother, Sandor, and Josef walked in.

"Look what Uncle Janos brought me!"

My grandmother, always reserved, smiled. "Janos, it's so good to see you. Welcome. Sandor read me your letter telling us about you visiting. Let me put a kettle on for tea."

"It's always good to be here with you and all your family. How long has it been? I think I came last year at this time. Yes, that's the time. I think you were planting then too. As for tea, please don't bother. I brought something a little stronger." He pulled a flask from his suitcase. "Will you have a little brandy with me?"

"Only a little, to celebrate your visit."

Grandmother retrieved two special Czech crystal glasses from the cupboard and set them on the kitchen table. My uncle offered a small sip to her, and, after allowing a more-than-generous pour for himself, he spoke next.

"There's much to catch up on. I'm sure you've heard by now that Peter died. Between his drinking and his heart, I'm surprised he lived as long as he did."

"Yes, I did hear about his passing. I'm sorry I missed the funeral, but I have painful memories of our last years together."

"I know how hard it was on you. So, you may be surprised by what I'm about to say. You know Peter never remarried after your separation and that, except for you, Mary, and the boys, I was his only living relative."

"Mary's been gone for a long time now, but he probably never knew. Peter enjoyed his time with Mary and less so with us. Other than that, he liked working and drinking with his friends and not much else, as far as I knew. And after we left, he never came to see us."

"Yes, I know that too. Then, a few weeks ago, I received a letter. He had someone send me his last wishes. He said he was leaving the house in Hajdudorog to you and the children."

Grandmother was taken aback by this unexpected news. "Why would he leave the house to me?"

Janos placed a hand gently on her shoulder. "Perhaps he still had memories of good times with you. Perhaps he felt guilty all these years. I don't know. But whatever the reason, the house is yours."

I listened impatiently to their talk. I had little interest in this conversation, as I hadn't lived in that house nor spent much time in Hajdudorog, except for school. Once there was a break in the conversation, I jumped in.

"Grandmother, do you see my present from Uncle Janos? Isn't she beautiful? I've never seen anything like her, even in the store in town. I've already thought about a name. I'll call her Mary."

I'd rarely seen such a look on my grandmother's face. The doll—its shape, dress, face, perhaps my mother's name—left her silent. It was almost as if she were seeing through it to something else—a place of hidden memories.

"Yes, it is beautiful, Irene. It reminds me …" Her voice trailed off.

"Maybe I can even take her to school one day."

Ignoring my plea, she turned her attention back to Janos. "It's so nice of you. We have nothing this pretty here. I think even the boys and Johann will like it. Irene, we'll put it on top of the chifforobe for all of us to see and enjoy. You can take it down when you want to play."

I left them to talk about old times, taking the doll with me to the bedroom. As I sat on the edge of the bed, I felt as if my mother were there too. For those few moments, I held her.

When I came back into the kitchen, the topic and tenor of the conversation had changed. "I don't know when I'll be visiting again now that war has broken out," Janos said. "With Archduke Ferdinand's assassination, Austria and Hungary will join to fight Serbia. There's talk about Germany too."

"How could this happen? War? My God, so many of our men have died in so many wars, for what?"

"I don't understand why, but it appears we are there once more."

"We're safe here, though, aren't we? There will be no reason for armies to fight in Hajdudorog."

"I hope you're right, for the sake of you, your sons and brother, and little Irene. Who knows? It's just starting, and no one knows how long it will last. For now, keep in mind that things have changed."

I didn't understand what war meant, but in time I would come to see the scars it would leave on all of us.

We so enjoyed the time Uncle Janos spent with us. He entertained us with his stories of growing up and what life was like in a big city, with its restaurants and cafés, and of going to the stadium to cheer on the new soccer team. My mind drifted. I couldn't stop thinking about his gift. I sat with my doll, studying patterns in the dress, its shape, legs, arms. Weeks afterward, when I would come home from school every day after greeting my grandmother, it was the first thing I saw. It also became my inspiration for a longing unfulfilled.

Perhaps it was my own feeling of loneliness, but I was determined that my Mary wouldn't be alone. I often watched my grandmother as she sewed, stitched, hemmed, and restitched torn trousers, a dress, and a shirt. She often left behind remnants of wool and cotton fabrics, too small to use. One day I gathered these leftover pieces and sat with them. Like parts of a puzzle, I began to put them together in patterns. Then I found straight, short, thin branches that had fallen from trees in our yard. I crossed two and wrapped the cloths I'd made, one by one, around them, then took a needle and thread and stitched two patches so that they draped from the cross stick. Finding a small paintbrush, I drew oval faces on paper for each and pinned them to the top of the sticks. An old box large enough to fit them all became their home, and the space under the bed where my grandmother and I slept was the land where they lived. With my delicate porcelain mother, these tattered remains and what the trees had given up took on their new life as father, grandmother, brothers, sisters—my family.

***

Moving day to my new home was soon upon us when I realized how little I knew of my grandfather. As we prepared to leave for the house in Hajdudorog, my curiosity grew and I began to ask questions.

"All you need to know is that we have a house your grandfather and I once lived in. Instead of spending time asking questions, you need to pack for our move. We'll be there for a while. God willing, we'll have our own farm someday. Once I can save a little and sell that house, we'll move again. It has too many sad memories. But for now, it's a good home for us."

It took only a short time to fill a few boxes and an old suitcase with all that I owned. The only care I took was nesting my family of figurines so that they didn't break and, as my grandmother allowed, carefully wrapping Uncle Janos's gift. After helping my grandmother pack the kitchen goods, and Sandor and Josef their clothes and soccer ball among a few other things, it was time. Johann brought around the horse and cart. As a parting gift to his sister, he had taken the canopy bed apart, assuring us he would return with it after first taking our possessions and us to town.

I knew I'd miss much about our life on Master Kovacs's estate, but the thought of a new home in town and much closer to school lifted my spirits. Sandor and Josef had become bored with farm life and were excited about maybe working and even dining at one of the three restaurants, catching up with friends who lived there, and just hanging out on the steps of the old post office with people their age.

The trip to town passed quickly. As we made our way to our new home, the streets looked and felt different to me. They were now my places to walk, to visit, to be. As for our new place to live, Grandmother had described it before, but now that we had arrived, the house seemed even bigger and grander. Its white picket fence that set it apart from the other homes needed only minor repair. The well-kept exterior, painted a rich yellow, turned golden in the setting sun, offering a warm invitation to enter a new life.

A film of dust had accumulated in all the rooms since my grandfather's death, but there was no doubt that he'd taken good care of his home until the end. In the kitchen, most items were neatly tucked away. Grandfather's skills in craft and repair showed throughout, with simple but strong furniture. Sandor and Josef would have their own small room to share. Another open door led to where we'd put Johann's bed. The door to a third room was locked. My first thought was that I would have my own bedroom, but Grandmother stopped me before I could enter.

"No, Irene. I don't want you to go into that room. Sandor, Josef, that goes for you too." With that, she took out one of the house keys and checked the lock on the door. We understood she would say no more and that questions were not welcomed. What laid behind that door would remain a mystery for some time to come.

All of us were quick to make Hajdudorog our home. Sandor started helping at the supply store, while Josef washed dishes at one of the beer halls in town, hoping to work in the kitchen one day. I stayed close to Grandmother, helping with the cooking and cleaning and always accompanying her to the cathedral on Sunday.

Sunday was a special day of the week. We often had dinner with Johann, as well as Magdalene, Karl, and their children. Neighbors occasionally joined in, and all brought favorite dishes and brandies. Before these festivities began, however, we stopped whatever we were doing when Mr. Katohme, the blacksmith, brought his Victrola record player onto his front porch not far from us. He'd turn the conical speaker so that it faced the street, and for an hour or so, he delighted his neighbors and the town, filling the air with recordings of folk songs and an occasional opera. It seemed that anyone within earshot was there, sitting in chairs or on the ground, sipping whatever they brought from home. Mr. Katohme often joined in the singing and dancing. His bright beaming face, generous body, and long gray beard radiated a joy that warmed all, even on chilly autumn days.

As summer gave way to fall, school became my focus. My grandmother sensed that education for me wasn't just a passing phase one endured until reaching the age for full-time work. She recognized my joy of learning as I told her what had happened in school, how much reading meant to me, and how writing came easily. While the boys quickly moved on from school, I cherished those classroom hours as they took me to lands far away and opened doors to mysteries yet to be discovered. I continued happily with my studies, made that much more rewarding as class time filled my lonely spaces.

Every now and then, I invited a friend from school home with me at the end of the day. We were always greeted with the aroma of Grandmother's baking and cooking. Now that I could spend more time in the company of my friends, I came to see how I was not like them. At school, mothers often greeted their daughters with a kiss and embrace. When I visited them, their mothers were always there. Many times I'd come home and sit in front of my gift from Janos, my Mary, still in its privileged place on the kitchen shelf, and talk to her about my day, imagining what my real mother and I would say to each other.

It was on one of those days that Grandmother couldn't help but notice my tears as she came in from tending her garden. "What is it? Why are you so upset?"

"I love you so much, Grandmother, and I know you love me. But there's something I've never asked you. I know only a few stories of my mother from you. Magdalene told me a little about my mother and father too. But I don't know if he's even alive."

"Your father?" she began and then stopped, as if at a loss for words. Hesitating again, she replied in a distant voice, "Your father was not from here. None of us knew him. He took care of the estate where your Uncle Johann works and where we used to live. But he left."

"What's his name?"

"Eisner. Jacob Eisner."

"Why didn't he stay here?"

"I don't know if you can understand at your age. I don't know if your mother and this man loved each other, but what he did was wrong in the eyes of God."

"Because . . . why?"

"Because he was a married man. Remember the Ten Commandments? Remember 'Thou shalt not commit adultery'? That's what your father did." She drew a deep breath before continuing. "And being a Jew, he didn't practice our faith, didn't worship with us. He kept to his kind."

Startled by what sounded like an accusation, I couldn't remain silent. "I don't understand. What does being a Jew have to do with us?"

"You believe that Jesus Christ is the one true God who sacrificed Himself for us, that he rose from the dead, that He is our savior. Jews don't believe in Him the way we do. They have their own ways. They keep to themselves and celebrate different holy days. They have the money and keep it close to them, giving us only what they can get away with."

"But I still don't see why we can't get along with them, maybe even be friends."

I could tell Grandmother didn't want to continue this line of conversation, but I wasn't quite ready to let it go. "What happened to my father?"

"Your Uncle Johann was so angry that he told your father to leave town. He didn't care that Jacob Eisner had control over his land and his home. Whether your father feared for his life or felt guilt over what he did, or something else, he left and we never heard from him again."

"So I'm part Jew, and I don't have a mother?"

"You do have a mother. She's just not here."

Hesitating and uncertain as I was, I wanted to know. I asked the question that had left me with a sense of loss for as long as I could remember. "Why did my mother leave me?"

Grandmother sat and rested her body against the kitchen table as if to support herself. "I know that your mother was unhappy and didn't like her life. For her, America was a place to begin again. She dreamed of all that she could be and do but said those dreams could never happen in this land. I know it's hard for you to understand how she could leave you, but she has written me letters, and I know in her own way that she loves you. Perhaps a time will come when you'll see her again. But we're here now, and you know I love you."

Her words comforted me and stopped my tears, as they had so many times before, but one yearning question lingered. "I want to ask you something else," I said. "Every morning I hear my friends say 'Goodbye, Momma' when we go to school, and they kiss their mothers when they come home. They talk about going to the cathedral on Sunday, having picnics, and going to the store with their mothers. I'm the only one who doesn't have a mother. Would it be all right if I called you 'Momma' too? It would mean so much."

A tear glistened and ran down my grandmother's cheek. "Yes, of course, Irene. Of course you can."

Her embrace and kiss sealed what I had known to be true all along.

***

My days settled into a pleasant routine with school, helping Grandmother in the kitchen when I got home, and playing with my family of stick dolls. Sometimes Magdalene came by with cakes and children in tow. As time passed, I felt something around me shifting, an unsettling change intruding into our lives. Soldiers with long rifles began to appear in our town. Young men in uniform with medals and tassels rode in on horseback. They'd meet at the center of Hajdudorog, where they'd talk with such animation about their war adventures, fighting for the Austro-Hungarian Empire, and joining forces with powerful Germany to take on the French, British, and others who didn't realize what they were up against.

It was after one of their visits that Sandor came home to announce that he, along with several of his friends, had signed up to join the fight.

"What stories the soldiers told!" he said. "They were all so happy to be off to places they had never been, all for the good cause of defending our motherland. Next week when they return, we'll all be joining them."

Grandmother, who had seen and lived through war before, knew its romantic allure and the horror that followed. "Oh, my son, how could you? Were you that fooled by their words? You foolish, foolish boy."

"But Momma, even Uncle Janos joined. My best friends, Michael and Peter, are going. We'll all join together. I'm a man now, and I want to see the world and help our country. I'll be back before you know it with all sorts of stories to tell. I can see us a few years from now sitting around the kitchen table, having a good laugh about how worried you were."

"Did you tell Josef yet?"

"Yes. He's excited for me. He wants to go too but can't. I told him one of us needs to help you and Irene."

Grandmother knew that once Sandor had made up his mind, there was no turning back. As I sat and listened, the space between them seemed to fill with a sense of dread.

The week before Sandor's departure passed quickly. On his final day with us, he dressed in his new uniform, looking so handsome, trying to be a soldier, but he couldn't hide the innocence and gentleness I had known all my life.

My grandmother cried through that night before he left, but she still hadn't exhausted her tears by morning. Through those tears, she spoke to him with great love and what seemed a sense of loss foretold. "God bless you and keep you safe, my beloved son. I will pray for you every day that you are not with me."

"I love you, Momma. I hope to see you in a few months. They said we might come for a visit then. Bye, Irene! Bye, Josef!"

As we watched him join the troop of soldiers, my grandmother stood there, alone in her silent, stoic grief.

***

Days passed quickly. Now out of school, I spent time by myself and with my family of twigs and cloth, keeping them under our bed until it was time for us to play. While Grandmother was helping at the cathedral, I would bring them to life at the kitchen table. Set before me, I recreated the happy times we had spent with Johann, singing songs in the barn and playing with friends.

Grandmother knew I was lonely, as my few friends, with their days now filled with chores after school, rarely had time to play. Josef, being a young man, didn't want to spend time with a little girl. He was off to work or meeting friends who told tales of the war. In turn, he sometimes read them Sandor's letters of his latest adventures.

On my birthday, when I was putting my "family" away for the day, expecting my grandmother home from the cathedral, she called for me to come outside. In her arms was a wicker basket covered with her black shawl, and it seemed to be weighing on her. When I offered to take it from her, she smiled and waved me away.

As I stood a few feet from her, I noticed something strange. Her shawl seemed to take on a life of its own, moving, although there was no wind to speak of.

"Momma, what is it? Did you bring home some baby chickens from the market?"

With her eyes twinkling and a slight smile present, she brushed my cheek with her hand.

"No, Irene, I brought you a present—actually, two presents. Happy Birthday!" With those words, she removed the shawl from the top of the basket. Snuggled inside were two beautiful puppies: one black as night, one brown and white.

"Are they really mine?"

"Yes, dear. I've been thinking about getting you a puppy for a long time, but when I saw these two, I couldn't make up my mind. They were playing so well together. That's why you have two."

I fell in love instantly. Finally, I had playmates. "What shall we call them?" I said, and then I answered my own question. "I know, Momma. As the rivers are so close to us and I have so much fun there, let's call the black one Körös and the brown and white Maros."

The puppies became my constant companions. They made me forget my loneliness. How could I feel alone with Körös and Maros in constant, affectionate motion around me? I'd call them after climbing a tree and watch as they tried to find me. They loved trips to the rivers the most, especially in the heat of the summer, as they raced me to jump in first. That constant motion was the natural state for my two balls of fur, until exhaustion claimed them. Then they'd collapse by my side. They didn't know it, but their company would lend me much comfort over the treacherous months to come.

CHAPTER 6

As summer faded, the familiar chill in the air heralded the arrival of fall. But this year, these months brought with them the darker reality of the war as it closed in on our world. New words—*Bolshevik, Royalists, Red Army,* and *White Army*—entered my vocabulary as we learned about a revolution that was spreading from Russia to other countries. Hungary had become a nation invaded and ravaged from without and within. News about the war in Europe came mostly from the letters of relatives who lived near the front lines and was shared by neighbors and friends. As the war continued, their words became increasingly tinged with fear.

My grandmother lived for the post each day, waiting for the next letter to arrive from Sandor. At first, there was a certain rhythm to these missives. Once or twice a week we received newsy notes on training and travel, new friendships and camaraderie among those in his brigade. However, as rumors of the war and the fate of our country darkened, so did Sandor's words. Though he spared

Grandmother the details, she could still read the danger within them. Sandor never failed to sign off with how much he missed her and couldn't wait to see all of us again.

Then one week went by with no letters. Then two. Each day without a letter seemed to etch another line into grandmother's brow. Then one early October morning, a grim, stoic courier on horseback delivered a yellow envelope. Grandmother's hands trembled as she handed it, unopened, to me. With a low, straining voice she ordered, "Read it."

I tore open the envelope and began, "His Majesty regretfully informs you that Sandor Szuromi has sustained a serious injury in the line of duty and is now in the army hospital in Vienna, Austria." There was more, but before I could finish, she took the telegram from me, folded it, and retreated to her locked bedroom.

Surprised by the arrival of a government official at a small feudal town, Josef and several neighbors hurried to the house. Josef sobbed over the news, wishing to offer comfort but daring not to intrude.

Hours later, Grandmother emerged from her room, her face drawn, lips taut. She held a letter and once again asked me to read it. It was the last letter she had received from her Sandor three weeks ago, and, like all the others, it spoke lovingly of missing her cooking, longing to see her, and wishing he could hear her voice calling his name.

As I read the letter, Grandmother raised the corners of her apron and dabbed each eye. Then, with a sudden quick motion, as if she had just decided, she drew from that apron pocket a small white handstitched bag. Emptying it, she began to count the change and tightly rolled paper bills that she had saved over the years.

"I hope this will be enough," she seemed to say to no one but herself. Then she said, "I'm going out. Josef, hitch the wagon." We dared not question where or why but just stood by in our own silent sadness.

The sun was setting when Josef and Grandmother returned. She entered the house with two large wicker baskets filled with fruits, vegetables, and other foods. "I'm going to be with Sandor," she said. I begged her through my tears to let me come. At first she told me no, but my gentle persistence prevailed.

The gravity of Grandmother's decision wasn't lost on me. She had never traveled far from where she was born. Now, in a time of war, she was determined to cross countless miles. No obstacle was too great to prevent Grandmother from being with her firstborn son.

That evening the neighbors who had come by left with few words. They feared what we all feared and did not want to say—that Sandor was dying. I waited for my grandmother to go to bed, but she lingered at her prayers for so long that I fell asleep. I awoke the next morning to the sweet smell of her freshly baked bread. I watched my grandmother's wiry body flitting with almost youthful vigor. Her dark eyes, rimmed last night with what seemed the weight of years, looked less heavy this day. As she went about her preparations, her steely focus and determination seemed to lift her spirits. Now and then, she stopped to count on her fingers the contents of her basket, making sure she had everything that Sandor liked. Had she considered that Sandor might be too weak or that he might not survive long enough to see her again? No. Instead she spoke about how he would enjoy this and that and of what she would tell him about home, friends, and family.

＊＊＊

The next morning Grandmother and I boarded the train with our brimming baskets for the two-day journey. Looking out the large window, I caught my first passing glimpse of our homeland's distant terrain: flat lands and fields broken only occasionally by clusters of straw-thatched farmhouses. We passed herds of sheep guarded by bronzed, pipe-smoking shepherds in multicolored overcoats.

The seemingly endless plateau of Hungary gradually gave way as we crossed the border to the hills and mountains of Austria. My grandmother said little throughout the trip, oblivious to the passing scene, occasionally emitting a sigh through tense lips. In her hands, she caressed each bead of her ebony rosary.

We arrived and disembarked at the Vienna station, wandering about, surrounded by words we didn't understand and faces that were foreign to us. After walking aimlessly down this city's streets with its steepled structures rising into the heavens, a passerby took pity on us and, in an oddly accented Hungarian, pointed out where we needed to go. After an hour, stopping from time to time just long enough to set our baskets down, we turned the corner on to Währinger Gürtel Strasse. The Vienna General Hospital loomed before us. Its sheer immensity seemed to drain Grandmother of her reserve. With fatigue overtaking her, she rested her baskets and leaned against the side of the building.

We were truly at a loss for what to do next. Before us were three entrances, each giving no hint of where they led. As we stood frozen in indecision, we looked up to see a young man leaning out a window. "Mother, are you looking for someone?" Finding the direction of the voice, we saw the pale face of a young soldier leaning out a window a few floors above.

"I'm looking for my son, Sandor."

The young man seemed to catch his breath for a moment. "Why, he's in the same room as mine." Then seeing our confusion, he pointed in the direction of the nearest door. "Take that entrance on the left."

Suddenly all the weariness that had permeated my grandmother's body lifted. She rushed toward the door, baskets in hand. A gray-uniformed guard guided us up to our destination. As we climbed the cold stone steps, a sudden gasp escaped her lips. "Why didn't Sandor come to the window? Why didn't he speak to me when he heard me say his name?"

Her pace slowed as she reached the third floor. Before us was a ward lined with beds on both sides occupied by mutilated bodies. Grandmother's searching eyes quickly found the young man at the window. Upon seeing him, she rushed forward and then slowed. Lying in the bed near this stranger was her son. He lay on his back, the top of his head having disappeared under a weave of blood-stained gauze. Placing the baskets by the foot of his bed, she leaned over and kissed him. Speaking with a strong but gentle voice she pleaded, "My son, my son, I have come. Please open your eyes so that I may see them, and speak so that I may hear you."

Her words echoed through the silent hall, but no answer came from Sandor. And yet I could see a faint flush in the deathly pale face, a brief flutter of eyelids and a twitching of lips as if he so wanted to speak but couldn't.

My grandmother cried out for a doctor. Coming quickly, he gave Sandor a cursory examination, and then, turning to my grandmother, spoke gently. "I'm afraid your son can't see or speak. He sustained a mortal head wound while saving the lives of his comrades. What I shall never understand is that he stayed alive this long. To me it's truly a miracle."

Suddenly her face and body relaxed, and I understood. What the doctor said was no mystery to her, as she had prayed that God would keep her son so that she could see him. Sandor had felt her touch, and now knew that she had come. Grandmother's legs gave way slowly as she knelt beside Sandor's bed to pray. The physician's footsteps retreated, and when I looked around, I saw that all eyes had turned to the kneeling figure. I knelt with her to pray in an overwhelming silence, pierced only by her spoken petition: "My Lord, My Lord, receive my beloved son. Thou lovest the meek and pure of heart, and now Thou is calling my son to Thee." With those words, as he took his last breath, she kissed her son one last time.

As we rose, the soldier at the window approached unsteadily. "I'm so glad you came before it was too late."

A soldier in a bed nearby spoke. "Why, only this morning he was restless, almost as if he knew you were coming."

Then another lanky soldier, with his arms in rigid casts, said, "For the first few days before he could no longer speak, he seemed to know the end was near and what little he could whisper was about you. He kept himself alive by sheer willpower."

The soldiers continued to come to Sandor's bedside. Those who could walk surrounded my grandmother, struggling to keep upright, trying gently to console her. She looked up to see their unsteady forms, wan faces, and eyes that bore the weariness of age far beyond their years. Through her tears, she embraced them.

As young as I was, I understood that, standing there with my grandmother for those few moments, they were not alone. She had become for them their own loving mothers, and she, in turn, saw in their faces her dying son's courage. Looking up at those broken and hobbled, she smiled. "My sons, open the baskets. Help yourselves. Everything is homemade."

For those few moments, with the smoked sausages, roasted potatoes, crisp cookies, and an oversized loaf of rye bread, the terror of war lifted as all of their strength and concentration seemed to turn toward living memories of the hearths and homes they'd left behind.

"The bread turned out especially light this time," she said. "Sandor would have enjoyed it very much."

The hospital had known far too many tragedies, and it didn't take long before orderlies came to take Sandor away. They let us know he would be interred at the cemetery the next day, as we had no way to take him home with us. After a sleepless night at a hotel nearby, we were taken to his resting place. There we stood as they lowered Sandor, a place where our prayers and tears flowed as one into that sacred ground.

On the journey home, even fewer words were said between us than on the trip to Vienna. Grandmother's ebony rosary beads seemed her only solace. As I sat in silence, watching the person who loved and protected me suffer so, I understood for the first time the depth of pain in loss. My mother's absence seemed small and distant in Grandmother's tragic presence. As much as I wanted to reach out, embrace, and comfort her, I knew it wasn't what she wanted.

Josef, Johann, and Magdalene, who had become like a mother to me, met us at the train station. Everyone asked about the visit, but my grandmother, unable to speak of what had happened, left it to me. It was only when we arrived home that she turned to all of us.

"As Irene told you, Sandor waited for me to come to him, as he knew I would. I couldn't bring him home, but I want him to have a place here with us."

Grandmother disappeared into her locked room for a moment and emerged with a cross of wood and metal. Standing less than two feet tall, Christ's face seemed to radiate serenity, as if He were at peace. She asked Josef for a hammer and motioned me close to her. "I know where I will visit my Sandor, but I want you to go to the engraver and have a plate made. We'll place it at the back of the yard with the cross."

"What do you want him to carve, Momma?"

"My Sandor's spirit and soul lie here, but he does not lie alone. By the grace of God, my heart is buried with him."

***

Our town became one of many crossroads to bear the scars inflicted by those who fought to conquer, then to defend, but ultimately to plunder. Early on, when the rebel Communist Red Army and white-uniformed Royalists swept through the neighboring country- side, we tried to keep to our routine. I went off to school on those mornings of calm, returning in the afternoon. The only difference was that I could no longer stop by to see Magdalene. We were spared the armies' first waves of atrocities. However, it didn't take long before they made their presence known, detested and feared.

Horror grew as the weeks went by. The staggering Red Army rebels, poorly outfitted and on the verge of starvation, made relentless demands on everyone, ordering families and the farms and towns around us to supply them with sacks of wheat and tobacco. If households failed to meet their orders, they publicly whipped husbands and sons to set an example for others. As the war dragged on, they pillaged what they could. Women were raped, farms decimated. Although the White Armies showed more discipline, they were as ruthless as their enemies in the end.

Grandmother heard these stories of hellfire descending on neighboring towns, knowing that it was only a matter of time before it reached Hajdudorog. So fearful of what would happen to us, she called me to her on the eve of one of these marauding visits and said, "I need your help shredding red and white sheets into strips and hanging them in the trees and yard around the house. We're going to make some ribbons."

"Why, Momma?"

"You'll see when these outlaws come back again."

We cut and stitched neat strands of cloth in each of the colors and stacked them near the front entrance just in time, for in the distance we could see the banners of the Red Army approaching.

"Irene, take the red ribbons and hang them on the acacia tree, the gate, and the porch."

Within an hour, we heard Körös and Maros barking, warning us of unwelcome visitors. Sooner than we expected, the Communist soldiers came by our house, officers on horseback, their infantry marching behind. Seeing the red ribbons, some waved and smiled as they passed, recognizing, in their eyes, a comrade in support of their cause.

As soon as they had departed, down came the ribbons, as Grandmother knew it wouldn't be long before the Royalists, in pursuit, would come along. She then instructed me to display the white ribbons and, as with the Communists, the White Army soldiers passed by and left our home untouched.

My grandmother believed that in this war-torn time, threats to our lives would only grow more dire. Her intuition turned into the reality of the months that followed. With the departure of the Red and White forces came the incursion of the Romanian army into Hungary. At first, we thought their presence would end the bloodshed and restore peace and calm, and many in town rejoiced. But those who wore the garments of war seemed to differ only by the shape of their lapels and their medals. The uniforms of all were stained blood red, and the specter of death and destruction followed wherever they went.

It didn't take long for Grandmother to realize that what was happening was only an early chapter in an unfolding saga of terror. But the fear that consumed her had little to do with her fate. She was an old woman. What would they do to her? Josef, who had lost the use of his left hand when it was caught under the wheel of their cart, was no threat to the soldiers. What they would do to me was another matter.

"Irene, they'll come here, but they mustn't find you. I've been thinking of places for you to hide."

"Under the bed?" I asked.

"No. That is where they'll look first. They will want whatever we have to eat, too, so the kitchen won't be good either, except maybe one place. You're small. Do you think you can fit in our bread oven? If there's nothing baking, there won't be any reason for them to look inside. But if for some reason they light a fire, it will be very dangerous. Still, it's the only place in the house where they might not look."

Time wasn't in our favor. Within minutes, the pounding at the door made our hearts pound as well. Looking out the window, we saw our thirteen-year-old neighbor, Julianna, in tears. "They came to our house and took everything. They beat my father. My mother pleaded with them, but they wouldn't stop. The only reason I'm alive is I heard what was happening and ran out the back door. You must hide me. I know what they do to young girls. They took my friend Katya a few days ago, and I haven't seen her since. I have nowhere else to go. Please."

Trembling and sobbing, she collapsed on the kitchen floor. Bandits were going house to house. Josef and my grandmother looked at each other. "What about the bed?" Josef asked. "What if we hid her underneath the blankets, under me, and I pretend I'm napping on the bed with the quilt and bedspread pulled over? They might still look under the bed, but when they see me, they'll think I'm the only one there."

"We don't have time," Grandmother said. "It's the only choice you have, but you and Irene must both be quiet." Julianna nodded silently and followed Josef into the bedroom just as we heard fists pounding at the door. In an instant, I climbed into the bread oven and closed the door.

Grandmother leaned against the oven. "No matter what you hear, you mustn't make a sound. Promise me."

"I won't, Momma. I promise."

After that, all I heard at first were the muffled sounds of men and my grandmother's voice in response. Then their words turned louder and angrier.

"Who's here with you, old woman? Where do you keep your meat and bread? Do you have any whiskey or beer?"

By now, I could hear them moving about the house, knocking over a table and chairs. Then I heard a shout from what I imagined was the bedroom and, a few minutes later, Josef's voice.

"Well, look who we found asleep in the bedroom."

Josef replied so softly that I couldn't make out what he said, but I did hear what came next: a heavy thud, someone knocking over more furniture, and what sounded like a body falling to the floor.

"You! Hitch up your wagon. We heard about the rich Jew who lives on the hill not far from here. You will take us to his house. We'll need that cart when we separate him from his possessions." Soon after that, the front door slammed shut.

I stayed still, trembling in those seconds of silence.

"Irene, are you all right?" my grandmother cried and opened the oven door. "They're gone. You're safe now. Julianna too. They saw Josef in the bedroom and only looked under the bed. They hit him and made him go to Master Kovacs's house. I pray that he'll return safely to us."

"Are you okay, Momma?"

"Yes, dear. They didn't touch me. They only took what food they found. But when one of the soldiers whispered something to his officer, that's when they ordered Josef to go with them."

Just then, Julianna emerged from the bedroom. In shock from her ordeal, she said nothing as she departed. For the next few hours, we said little to each other as we awaited Josef's fate. It was only when he returned, bloodied and battered but alive, that the anguish in my grandmother's face eased with the fading light of day.

***

That horror, along with Sandor's death and the oppressive threat of war, seemed to hover all around us, but my grandmother bore a greater toll than the rest of us. In the months that followed, Grandmother did something most evenings that neither Josef nor I understood at first. After dinner, she'd pull out a long, shiny key from the pocket of her apron, unlock the door to the room she had forbidden us to enter, remind us not to follow her, and turn the lock behind her. Sometimes I thought I heard her sobbing. Other times I heard her pray, whispering, "Dear Lord, protect us from this war, its evil, and the death it brings."

When we first moved into the house, she had visited that room only on occasion, but now it was a nightly ritual. When she emerged, having secured the door behind her, more often than not Grandmother would emit a deep sigh and slide the key back into her apron pocket.

These occasions left me fearful of what lay behind that door. But my curiosity prevailed. "Momma, why won't you let me go into the room with you?"

Grandmother's eyes gave away nothing. "You shouldn't ask questions about such things. They don't concern you."

Her words rang with finality, and I knew there was no point in pressing her further. Still, her secrecy only fed my curiosity. Then early one evening, just as she had made her visit to that room, we heard a loud pounding at our door. Our neighbor, the elderly Mr. Sos, white-faced, trembling, and gasping for breath, told us his wife had died unexpectedly. Could my grandmother help prepare the body for the journey to the church the next day? She didn't hesitate. Taking off her apron and admonishing me to behave, she left with Mr. Sos and Josef.

Grandmother always made sure she hid the key or had it in her possession, but not this time. As soon as she was out of sight. I reached into her apron pocket. There it was, as I knew it would be. I grasped the key.

Once there, I hesitated. Was it safe to enter? Was there something I shouldn't see? Perhaps priceless jewels meant for me when I married, or some other treasure? These thoughts made it impossible to resist.

I inserted the key and opened the creaking door. At first, I could barely see as the lace curtains and heavy shutters on the two windows blocked any light. My eyes adjusted to the dark, and I found a candle and lit it. What I saw at first held no mystery for me. Off to one side was an old oak table covered with a rose-patterned cloth. But what left me confused was that the table was set neatly for two with grandmother's best dishes—plates with rose-colored borders, a soup tureen, teacups and saucers, knives, forks, and serving spoons.

Puzzled, I turned my gaze to the sideboard where my grandmother had framed a faded photograph of Uncle Janos, who, like Sandor, had died in the war. Draped over a picture of her son was a black mourning ribbon. On one of the two chairs lined up around the table were my grandmother's Sunday clothes—a black satin blouse, skirt, and shawl, all neatly folded.

As I continued my search, I saw a familiar centerpiece, a four-poster canopied bed with a mattress typically high off the floor, topped with intricately embroidered pillows and white starched sheets reaching to the floor that hid the quilt beneath them. I knew from homes I'd visited that these rooms were reserved for special guests, but I couldn't remember anyone ever using it.

As secretive as it was, I was surprised by its ordinariness and turned to go. Then I dropped the key and in the dim light found myself groping for it. Thinking it might have slipped under the bed, I lifted the cover and quilt, and there I found my grandmother's secret. Under the bed was an open coffin of dark wood with a white satin pillow and lining. A new black gown had been carefully arranged within the full length of the coffin. Inside the lid, I recognized Grandmother's crucifix and ebony rosary. Suddenly I understood. My grandmother, who lived with the death of those near and dear, knew her time would come, perhaps soon. Now she was prepared, perhaps even looking forward to that day when, in death, she would once again be with those she had so loved in life.

For many nights thereafter, I couldn't sleep as I thought about the coffin under Grandmother's bed. I lay there listening to the sound of her regular breathing to know she was still alive.

PART II
The Right of Blood

CHAPTER 7

What seemed an endless war came to a tragic end. Wounded men, lost in their visions of death, drifted back to their families. Flowers decorated the newly dug graves at the town's cemetery, now twice its size to accept its new occupants. Our family and all in Hajdudorog did what they could to return to their lives as they had been.

Days, months, and years slipped by, but the routines and world around me were not to be my destiny. One afternoon, after coming home from school, my grandmother called me into the kitchen. "I have a letter today from your mother." Her words carried a tension I hadn't heard before. My mother never wrote unless she wanted something. This time was no different. She wanted me.

"Johann came by and read the letter. Your mother tells me it's time you came to America. She sent some money for the trip and told me where to go."

"America? When are we going, Momma?"

"Only you, Irene. Only you."

My mother was a myth, known only in daydreams, a doll, a few stories, and a faded photograph, living in a faraway land of mystery. Now she was reaching out to take me away. "But I don't know her," I said. "You're all I know. Remember how I asked if I could call you Momma and be like all the others at school?"

"She lives in New York City. It will be your new home. Perhaps your mother believes she can make a better life for you there."

"But I don't want a new home or a new life. This is my home."

Grandmother said nothing. In those seconds, those few words, what I cherished—school, neighbors, family—all were to be left behind thanks to her daughter's demand. My mother had decided for whatever reason that I was to live with her.

My grandmother knew little about making travel arrangements for a twelve-year-old. But with her brother's help and Father Milos from the cathedral, she learned of a ship that would carry me to my new country. She also learned of places of embarkation and debarkation, cost, dates, times, and accommodations. I would travel on the seas alone, but Grandmother made plans to protect me on the voyage. With some asking around, she became aware of a couple from a neighboring town who would be on the same ship. With the little money she had, my grandmother arranged for them to watch over me.

The Nagys were in their twenties, and they, too, were immigrating to America. Zoltan, tall, thin, with calloused hands, was a carpenter. His wife, Margaret, pale and as thin as her husband, worked for a tobacco farmer, helping with the harvest and drying. Like so many others eager to leave, they had saved just enough for passage.

Shortly after receiving my mother's letter, Grandmother, with Magdalene and Josef, went to their home. She came right to the point. "Will you watch over my granddaughter while she's on the ship?"

"How much will you pay us?" was Zoltan's reply.

"Five krone is all we can afford, but for that please take care of her and keep her safe." Both Zoltan and Margaret said they would.

I knew little of what was happening, only what my mother had destined. All seemed unreal. Curiosity excited me, but a submerged feeling of anxiety and dread made it hard to sleep. Only the rhythmic breathing of my grandmother at night soothed my fears.

That last week, I began to pack what little I could take on the trip: photos of Grandmother and Magdalene, Mary, my favorite stick doll, a few pieces of clothing—other items that fit into one suitcase. Along with those things, I had little more than my memories and my life.

"Momma, I don't want to leave you," I said one last time, knowing my protests wouldn't change anything. So, on an overcast day in early June, Johann harnessed the horses and, joined by Magdalene and Grandmother, off we went. The stones and dirt in the road kicked up behind us, leaving a cloud of dust that settled unevenly on the grasses that bordered either side. A light rain in the distance obscured what I knew to be a limitless horizon, dotted with farmhouses. I don't remember the little we said that day. What I never forgot was holding my grandmother's hand, feeling its texture, the roughness of her skin from all the years of working in the soil. My eyes held that look of love she always had for me.

The trip between towns took two hours. When we arrived at Teglag, not much more than a dusty hamlet, Zoltan and Margaret were already packed and ready to leave. "You're late. We must go soon if we're to meet the train in Budapest."

Offended by their abrupt words, Magdalene turned to me. "Your mother has all the information about your travel, the day the ship leaves, how long it takes, when it arrives. She knows that you'll be on a ship, the RMS *Aquitania*, and can telephone their office in New York to find out when the ship will reach America. Dearest, write to us and let us know how you are and how you like your new home. I hope you'll love America and that your mother gives you the life you deserve."

She hesitated for just a moment, as if to isolate and reinforce what she was about to say. "Never forget, Irene, your grandmother and I will always be here for you. If for some reason your mother doesn't treat you well, write, and somehow we'll bring you back home to us."

Although I knew the time to say goodbye would eventually come, I was still not prepared for it. My grandmother made sure I had my belongings: a beautiful headscarf with red and purple flowers as a gift for her daughter, new shoes and clothes to be worn when I first met my mother, and food for the journey. I made sure she knew I understood her instructions, down to her advice about sipping a little brandy she had nested in my dress in case traveling across the ocean didn't agree with me.

I ached for words, comfort, solace, but little else was said. My heart breaking, I watched my grandmother, her chest heaving as if under a great weight, walk away. I stood at the doorway as she left, and I cried out to her, desperate for one last look, one last sweetness between the two of us. "Momma! Goodbye, Momma!"

I waited for what would never come. With her strength and her stride, she never looked back.

***

I paid little attention to the outside world on the train from Budapest to our departure city, Cherbourg, France, determined as I was to commit to memory my life in Hajdudorog. I knew that in the future, my grandmother, home, Uncle Johann, Uncle Josef, friends, and all that was dear would only come alive in what I could preserve. As I sat there, the fields, farms, mountains, and rivers raced by, unfocused and ephemeral. I remained only with what I left behind on that day in the summer of 1921.

Arriving in the mist and light rain of Cherbourg, the Nagys found beds for the night near the docks at a hotel that, by its appearance, seemed never to have seen better days. The hotel's guests reflected what could be found beyond, in the streets outside its doors: a few older men weathered by years at sea and alcohol, and transients like us, passing through to the Promised Land. I ate little of the watery, stringy beef stew dinner, my mind drifting off while my guardians chatted on, seemingly oblivious to my presence.

Anxious about what lay beyond the doors of our hotel, we went up to our room, furnished only with what would get us through the night: three well-worn beds, a dimly lit lamp, two chairs, and a basin. The Nagys drifted off shortly after they lay down, but I slept little that night, listening through paper-thin walls to voices speaking languages unknown but still hearing in them echoes of my tears and fears, excitement, and regret.

Rising at dawn the next day, we ate quickly and walked the short distance to our destination, only to realize that at six o'clock in the morning, the line to board our ship had already formed and stretched far down the dock. But even at that distance, while we waited, I could see the towering behemoth, our home for the days to come. The RMS *Aquitania*, with its four smokestacks belching black clouds that drifted high into the overcast sky, seemed to disappear into the heavens, its size unlike anything of this world I had seen. In the distance, those who boarded seemed no larger than matchsticks against its massive body.

When our turn came, our papers checked, we boarded the ship. We were then directed to stairs that seemed to descend forever. Down we went, passing one level of the ship and then another. A few times I caught a glimpse of what lay behind open doors: beautiful chandeliers, rooms of wood and glass on the first and second floors, a promenade with cushioned chairs on lower decks, people in white uniforms moving furniture, setting tables, carrying food and bottles of wine. Turning the corner of the stairs to our deck, we met a wall of passengers like us gathered on the lower-deck promenade, many waving goodbye to mothers, fathers, family, and friends, while others simply wanted to see the outline of Cherbourg for the last time. So many people speaking words of no meaning to me created a roaring sea of sound. Awed and afraid, I clung to my guardians as we inched past the chairs along the railing to the entrance off the open space.

The corridors too were a moving mass of humanity as people searched for their cabins. We continued to weave our way, passing door after door until we found our room. By then I had seen the interior of several cabins and already knew what to expect. We stepped into a small, barren space with two sets of stacked beds for sleeping four, a wooden table, and a white metal basin resting on it between them. On the beds were mattresses worn down by those who'd come before. The Nagys claimed one set of upper and lower berths as I rested my package of food and nightclothes on the lower berth across from them. As my guardian couple had little to say to me, I went about quietly preparing where I would sleep for the coming days, taking out my sheet, blanket, and pillowcase, plus a book on the history of my soon-to-be new world, which my teacher had given me as a parting gift. Grandmother's bread and a sweater she'd knitted to keep me warm were intimate reminders of the home I'd left behind.

As we settled in, the door opened and the fourth lodger arrived, a woman my height but much heavier, with straight, shoulder-length black hair. She carried an overstuffed bag that befitted her size. An awkward silence followed until I spoke, pointing to the Nagys and myself.

"My name is Irene, and this is Mr. and Mrs. Nagy." Then, pointing at her, I asked in my clearest (but pointless) Hungarian, "What is your name?"

I could see her trying to take in what I had asked, and when she did, a beautiful smile filled her face.

"Elena."

So ended our introduction and first conversation. But even in this spare room of strangers, on this floating city, with the cacophony of the crowds outside our door, excitement, curiosity, and anticipation began to take the place of my trepidation and anxiety. This departure, this journey on the sea, was about to separate me from what I'd left behind. My future was taking hold, lifting me from the past.

I soon understood that my guardians had little desire to chaperone a twelve-year-old girl. They had escorted me on the train, to the ship, and to our sleeping quarters, and, it seemed, their responsibilities had ended there. They went their way and for the most part left me to find mine. They were, however, very curious about a few things.

"So, your mother lives in New York? Does she know where to meet you? Is your father there too? No? Who is your father? You don't know? But your mother paid for your trip. She must have a lot of money if she can afford that. Is she married? Is she rich?"

What little I could say about her life clearly left them puzzled and annoyed, but their prying questions also haunted me. How little I knew about her life! In one of my mother's letters to my grandmother, she'd mentioned marrying a man named Otto Richter. What was he like? He must have agreed to bring me to America, even helped my mother do so. Would he like me, someone he'd never met, someone who wasn't his family? Was he short, tall, thin, round? What will it be like to live there, and where will I be living? What about making new friends? Lost in a whirl of unknowns, after my talk with the Nagys, I finally let my questions go. The answers were waiting thousands of miles across the ocean.

I learned after the first day that being early for everything, from using the bathroom to eating dinner, held simple but great rewards, and failing to do so brought undesirable consequences. I learned this lesson on my first morning when I rose at six and made my way to the toilet, only to discover a long line of humanity stretching down the cabin corridor in wait for the few facilities available. Some gave up, while others remained, bouncing from one leg to the other.

As I rejoined the Nagys and Elena slept, we wended our way to the even longer lines for breakfast. By the time we arrived at the great room, it was already filled with people sitting at long tables opposite each other, their bowls filled with something gray I'd never seen, some crackers, milk, and little else. It was my first onboard lesson: Never arrive late for breakfast. The noise was deafening. I was reminded of our priest's sermon about the Tower of Babel and would recall those words time and again over the coming days.

We inched our way back to the cabin to wash up after breakfast and headed out to explore our home on the ocean. Open sea surrounded us now, with waves gently but persistently pounding the hull and gray skies as far as I could see. My guardians went in another direction, and once I accepted the chaotic din of the *Aquitania*, the majestic waterborne carrier opened to adventures I had never imagined.

I managed to make my way along the promenade to the front of the ship, where I looked at the upper decks and saw what separated our class of immigrants from those above. Women dressed in finery strolled along with their husbands and friends; men in white coats catered to people perched on the chairs overlooking us.

The initial, gentle movement of the ship was soothing to me, as if my grandmother were rocking me to sleep. My fellow passengers seemed similarly taken with the journey, as they crowded into the open areas. However, their smiles and enthusiasm faded within a few days as the rocking movement of the ship became more pronounced, up and down, back and forth, endlessly undulating.

The crowds began to dwindle, until one day, coming onto the deck, I was free to stroll wherever I wished. The solace of the sea, the beauty of the *Aquitania*, and my fascination with this floating world comforted me and left me transfixed by these moments in time. Most others, however, were not so fortunate. The Nagys, Elena, and, it seemed, most of the passengers, had retreated to their rooms, their complexions a seasick green that seemed to reflect the ocean depths.

Within days, instead of the din of languages and voices, I heard sighs and moans throughout the hull. I sat for the midday and supper meals of beef stew, beans, potatoes, pickled fish, and some sort of mixed fruit without worrying about long lines. I still treasured the delicious breads and sausages my grandmother had packed but didn't have to worry about the Nagys hovering over them, as they were too sick to complain.

Of course, the crew of the *Aquitania* continued about their work, as they had been through these rolling seas many times before and had seen the same greenish color among their passengers. Perhaps that was why a young girl wandering the ship by herself, seemingly impervious to these woozy circumstances, intrigued them. At first, a few smiled and went about their work as I walked about. Then, one day, a young man stopped and motioned for me to accompany him. We walked up the stairs and into the ship's galley, where the sight of all the food being prepared and the exotic, delicious aromas were intoxicating.

He left me for a moment and disappeared into a room, reappearing quickly with a freezing canister. He lifted the lid, used a spoon to scoop out something white into a bowl, and handed it to me, all the while grinning from ear to ear. Whatever he had given me was cold to the touch and hard as a rock. I smiled back at him and the few others who were also watching. When I finally broke through the icy mass and ate what was on the spoon, it took all the fortitude I had not to spit it out. Why would anyone take perfectly good, sweetly flavored milk and freeze it so that it hurt your teeth? That's how I learned my first English words: ice cream.

The young man's name was Ivan. By his thin facial hair and complexion still dotted with pimples, I assumed he hadn't yet celebrated his twentieth birthday. As he spoke in oddly accented Hungarian, I learned he'd been a waiter on the *Aquitania* for four years. He introduced me to stewards, chefs, bartenders, launderers, waiters, and watchmen. One would greet me, then another, and with them I came to know the *Aquitania's* beauty and its seafaring human cargo. I was overwhelmed at first, never imagining anything like this world of finery, so alien in its splendor from what I'd known. But by the fourth day I already knew my way around the promenade and all of its detail—its wooden seats and low-ceilinged overhead—and the dining room's three-legged chairs and long tables that seated twenty at a time. We passed the smoking room where I peeked in to see the small, round tables populated by a few men smoking cigarettes or pipes. We lingered in the kitchen, where the platters of roasting chickens, sizzling steaks, baked potatoes, salads, and chocolate desserts left me dizzy with hunger, tempered only by the chef who, on seeing me with my eyes wide and my mouth agape, brought over a platter filled with slices of ham and other preserved meats. Pointing at a mound, he motioned for me to choose from a stack of thick sausages. Ivan and I were to visit this edible paradise of sights, smells, and tastes again and again.

On that fourth day at sea, just as dinner was ending and I was exiting the kitchen, Ivan called me over. I followed him out as he held his finger to his lips, made a *shhh* sound, and led me to the service elevator. The doors closed, and he pressed the button for the upper level. We stopped and walked a short distance into a room stacked with plates and cups. Passing quickly, he pointed at an oval window. I looked through it to see just how distant my immigrant world below was from those above me. Through that glass pane was a dining room whose soaring ceiling displayed a mural painting of a place unknown to me. The room was bathed in electric lights, and the richest red hue accented the woodwork and carved ornaments. Bright paintings adorned the walls. Many well-off diners, able to escape the fate of those below, lingered at their tables over wine and brandy, dressed in white gowns and dinner jackets.

I heard musical instruments being tuned as we left the dining hall, and as we drew nearer, the band broke into a rhythm, tone, and sound that was both alien and hypnotic. We had reached the grand ballroom. Here, through another oval portal, I saw women young and old dressed in gowns and led by handsome and not-so-handsome men across the floor, dancing and slowly pirouetting while others, like an audience at a play, casually cast an eye toward them or were lost in conversation.

Ivan escorted me from there to the window overlooking a smaller room. Here, chairs in rows sat before a small stage where puppets dressed in bright reds and yellows danced and sang, the audience of adults and children laughing along with them. Distance dissolved for those moments: I was back home with my friends and family at the cathedral on special occasions, where a makeshift curtain would open to reveal wooden dancers who brought joy to young and old alike.

Our tour ended with a walk through a lounge area resembling, of all things, a garden, past a winding staircase and a place where I could see a few people huffing and puffing, who, for some reason, were lifting large metal bars with oval plates at the ends.

Ivan and the crew who had known the ship's journeys became my true guardians, my first English teachers, often amusing themselves as my tongue twisted in ways I never imagined. We started with simple words: *ball, floor, boy, girl*. Then, like watching a dog trying to learn a difficult trick, they would say, "Irene, try *promenade*," or, one of their favorites, "*scissors*." Growing up in a world where *s, z, c, h* were as common as *e* and *a* in English, these word games foretold what was in store in learning the language of my new country.

Adventures like these passed the time. As the seas calmed, Elena regained her composure and, finding comfort and company with fellow travelers from her Italian homeland, didn't bother with us. The Nagys too emerged from their ill-born stupor, and their curiosity about me grew greater the closer we came to our destination.

Mr. Nagy, speaking as if to a little child, leveled a question that was also a demand. "You'll tell your mother that we watched over you to make sure you were okay, won't you?"

His wife's demands followed. "And you need to let her know that we made sure you arrived safely in New York and that your grandmother and Magdalene didn't pay us enough for all our concern. She should give us more money." As they had done so little, I smiled but said nothing.

What turned out to be our final day aboard the *Aquitania* began as others had. With calmer waters, the breakfast lines once again stretched down the hallway, the din of languages at the long dining tables like the roar of the ship's engines. After breakfast, as we filed out onto the deck and as the voices subsided, one rose above all. A young man shouted excitedly. His words meant nothing to me, but the expression on his face, bright, smiling, and ecstatic, told all.

We pushed our way to the promenade and looked out on that clear day to see rising in the distance the faint outline of our new world. I watched that speck grow for hours into a shape, an outline, taking on a gradual substance and verticality, as if rising from the earth.

Afterward, I returned to our room to pack what few belongings I had taken out for the trip. It was time to go. By now, travelers gathered and stood wherever they could find space to look outward as the distance between sea and shore had now closed so that faint outlines took on greater definition and distinct structures came into view. The Nagys and I fought through the human sea, making our way to the edge of the promenade.

As America gradually revealed itself, electricity seemed to shoot through us, charged as we were with the hopes and dreams that had carried us across the ocean. Another young man had climbed onto the railing of the promenade and shouted out in a loud voice that sliced through the overcrowded deck. As before, few seemed to understand what he said. However, his body and long, thin fingers seemed to speak a universal language. He was pointing to a small figure gaining prominence by the second.

Pressed against the promenade railing, I looked out and saw that statue, the one I had read about and heard about from my teacher and my ship companions. Looking back at those around me, it seemed all were transfixed and, for the moment, transformed. Some leaped for joy in their small space; others wept openly. No one took their eyes off the Statue of Liberty.

CHAPTER 8

We ended our voyage as we began. Lines to disembark formed as the *Aquitania* docked, only for all to realize that a short boat ride to Ellis Island still lay before us. Of course, to call these waves of humanity "lines" didn't do justice to the chaos that made the embarkation experience seem sedate. The three of us fell in with the masses, all wanting to exit at the same time. As I stood, barely moving, I felt as though I'd been funneled into my grandmother's cake-decorating pastry bag, and that, in time, I would be channeled through a narrow aperture, then poured onto land.

Hours passed, as inch by inch we made our way through the passageway, only to find that the boarding suddenly stopped as the sun began to descend. The trips to Ellis Island had ended for the day, so we would have to wait until tomorrow. After a dinner more meager than usual, the kitchen staff quickly departed, leaving us no option but to return to our empty room. Elena had been one of those fortunate to "cross over," as we called it. Now only three filled our cramped quarters.

I was determined not to spend another day aboard a ship whose accommodations seemed to have deteriorated overnight, as toilets putrefied and debris littered hallways. I awakened the Nagys before dawn, and we made our way to the disembarkation point early. This time we were hopeful, though many had arrived before us. I once again drew on my reservoir of patience, a resource I would rely on beyond anything I imagined over the coming days.

We finally boarded one of the ferries late Friday morning. Upon landing, uniformed individuals directed us toward another line made up of those who had arrived on the previous ferries. This new line led into a building where everyone stood in almost single file, climbing stairs that entered into a large, light-filled hall. We were trapped on those stairs, inching along under the watchful gaze of authorities above us and at the bottom of the stairs. Every so often one of these inspectors approached someone in line and, with chalk, etched a letter on their clothes.

By now, the early morning rush and exuberance had given way to afternoon tension. I didn't know whether to look at or away from these inspectors, and the Nagys offered no help; they knew as little as I did. Eventually, the inspector came to us. He looked at my hands and listened to my heart, then motioned for me to turn left, and then right. Then he raised my chin so that I had no choice but to look into his eyes and at a face that offered no emotion. He lifted my eyelid, then looked over my body and stance one more time.

Another shiver of terror passed through me, as I knew my fate rested in what he saw in me. After a few agonizing seconds, he passed on to the next in line without a word.

The nonstop din in the great hall was inescapable, as was the constant crush of bodies pressed together. The only breathing room, if I could call it that, came by way of the belongings each had carried with them. Every few minutes someone called out a name, and one or two or more would rise and make their way to a door they would pass through. At first, I was frightened for those who were called, but soon I realized it meant that if the Lord and authorities willed it, you would pass from your state of limbo into the new land.

As I sat and stood fitfully and fearfully for hours waiting my turn, I began to see mirrored in the faces of children like me the wonder, anticipation, and excitement of these moments—with one difference: They had the love of their mothers and fathers, who caressed, kissed, and sheltered their beloveds as best they could. I had loneliness for a companion.

As we wound through the building, the Nagys had eased farther away from me. Within the hour, their names were called, and they looked back at me with indifference I had come to know. Now I had no one—except my mother waiting on the other side.

I pulled from my bag the only stick-and-cloth figurine I had brought, one whose painted face brought back my life before. She was my only comfort as I waited my turn. Finally, late Friday afternoon, I heard, "Irene Sormay; Irene Sormay."

It sounded like my name. I ran to the imposing uniformed figure, terrified that I'd be trapped in that enormous space if I failed to heed his call. He looked down at me and held out his hand. No words were spoken, but I knew he needed to see the papers that Magdalene had made me promise to protect. He scanned them and then nodded and motioned for me to come with him. I followed through doors I had seen so many before me pass through. We came to a small room where an officer sat behind a podium. Another officer motioned for me to stand before this man and a desk that partly hid his body yet made him seem like a giant, imposing and forbidding. Even though no words had yet been spoken, I understood my future rested in this room and those within it. Standing there alone, the weight of my fate overwhelmed me. It took everything I had to keep from crying.

The door on the opposite side of the room opened and then closed. A diminutive woman with close-cropped black hair and a plain gray skirt, who seemed to be about Magdalene's age, approached and stood next to me. As the words from the podium came down, the woman translated for me.

"Your name, please?"

"Irene Szuromi."

"What country did you come from?"

"Hungary."

"Did you come with anybody: a relative, friend, someone else?"

"I had guardians for my trip, Mr. and Mrs. Nagy, but I don't know where they are. I saw them go through your doors earlier today and haven't seen them again."

"I see." Then after a moment, she said, "Your papers say that your mother is waiting for you. Is your mother married? Does she have a job?" I knew that my mother had married, but I didn't know anything else.

More questions followed, one after another. How old was I, did I feel well, who paid for me to come, could I read, did I know where I'd live, did I have any money. None of my responses caused the official to change his tone or the expression on his face.

Finally, the questions stopped, and I couldn't hold back my tears any longer. The woman in gray smiled as she gently draped her arm across my shoulders. Without another word, she escorted me out.

By now, the sun was lowering in the late-afternoon sky. After hours of confinement, noise, inspections, and questions, I couldn't wait for this ordeal to end. Turning to the translator and sensing my time with her was about to end, I asked, "When can I go to my mother?"

With that, her smile faded. "Friday afternoon they stop processing for release."

I didn't understand what that meant, so I said, "But where do I go to meet my mother?"

This time, she replied in a stronger voice. "You'll stay here today, tomorrow, and Sunday. You are not allowed to leave."

I understood that I couldn't leave, but I had no idea why. Did I do something wrong? Did I say something the official didn't like that would keep me there or send me back? Had my mother decided that she didn't want me after all?

The translator left me to go to the next applicant. As I reentered the great hall, my fears and tears ran together like two streams merging to become one river of heartache leading—where? Nowhere I had ever been before. I was a person of no particular place, abandoned in a sea of strangers. Like me, all in that room became listless, vacant, and spent. Even children's voices and cries faded with the evening light. So began the longest days and nights of my life.

Officials directed those who had been left behind to a hall for an evening meal of something that looked like bread, its texture the consistency of soft cardboard. A bland mix of beef and potatoes came with it, followed by sticky, stewed fruit. As I sat with the last of Grandmother's sausage, I wondered, *Is this what people eat in America?*

After dinner, guides separated us by sex, leading females to a large dormitory room, once again with bunk beds lined up in rows. Each of us was given a blanket, and our overseers gestured for us to find a place to sleep for the night. Mothers and their children pulled beds together while the rest of us chose from those that remained. After that, loud voices gave way to fading foreign whispers as exhaustion and sleep overtook all in the cavernous room.

Dreams took me back to Hungary that night, into the arms of my grandmother. But not all of them were sweet. In one, I found myself back in my grandmother's secret room of pictures, furniture, sheets, and linens. I moved slowly about, seeing nothing out of place. I neared the casket under the four-poster bed. Someone was in it. I hesitated to draw closer, fearing I'd find my grandmother there. I summoned the courage to lift a lighted candle and take a look. It wasn't her after all. I was staring at myself, dressed in the same skirt I'd worn on the *Aquitania*.

I awakened before dawn in a pool of sweat, disoriented. Only a few of the other displaced persons in the "sleeping room," as I'd come to call it, were shaking off the night's shroud. I didn't know what lay ahead that day or any of the days to follow.

After another bland breakfast, parents with their infants were free to spend time as families outside, but older girls were directed down a long hall. We entered a room where an older woman with a kind, weathered face led us in a sewing and knitting class. As Grandmother and I had stitched and repaired many a fabric, doing something lent me a sense of relief as I sat at a table with others, some older and others nearer my age. At first, we all spoke little, except for two who knew each other's words. They carried on as the rest of us set about our work in silence.

Then something wonderful happened. The girl next to me walked her doll across the table to snatch a piece of cloth. She then walked it back and handed it to me. Soon after, someone else covered her head with her knitting, moaning as a ghost would do behind her makeshift mask. We all seemed tentative at first, but when we saw the smile on our teacher's face, a collective giggle came over us. After that, we were a table of gestures, laughter, and, for a few moments, forgetting.

People in uniforms with red crosses tried their best to fill our time with distractions. Balls, swings, games, and contests occupied the different parts of our day. On Saturday afternoon after lunch, two women led the boys and girls to a makeshift classroom where we were told to find a vacant desk. A middle-aged woman with short, gray-black hair wearing a pretty, patterned skirt and blouse stood before a chalkboard while a few others, who I learned later were volunteers, sat in the back.

"Good afternoon." A few of those in the room knew what she had said, including Katrina, the Hungarian girl I'd just met. I made a point of sitting next to her and repeated the phrase.

I questioned her, and she explained. "Good afternoon. It's the same as *Jó napot* in Hungarian." The phrases and words came slowly but steadily. "Hello. Goodbye. How are you? Here is what you had for lunch," and so on. With Katrina as my guide, I became like a cloth, soaking up precious drops of water, taking in whatever I could hold.

Our second day of lessons was much like the first. We repeated what we'd learned and navigated a few new phrases as time allowed. At one point, the teacher let us relax for a few minutes before moving on to the next instruction. It was then that I sat back and took in the room filled with voices and faces from distant lands, talking excitedly, laughing, and practicing their English. At that moment, I came to understand the common thread that bound us together: It was the immigrant's dream. Although we had spent our lives separated by seas, land, language, and religion, my dream was theirs as well.

In a strange way, I found comfort in our many differences, as I could now see we were all on this journey from our motherlands, across the wide expanse of ocean, to a foreign shore we hoped to call our own. I would carry these moments with me for the rest of my life.

***

Monday started as had the other days. After a few English classes, I had learned the words for what they put before us at each meal. I knew that *bread* was the name for the pasty white squares and that *utmil* was the flavorless bowl of gray cereal with the consistency of paste. As I finished breakfast that morning, another official in gray garb approached and tried to say my name. "Sumi, Suromi? Irene Somi?"

"Irene Szuromi," I replied, quite ready to give up on her mispronunciation.

The official then asked, or rather gestured, for my papers, which I carried with me everywhere I went. After a quick scan, she motioned for me to gather my belongings and follow her.

I found out it's possible for your heart to sink and soar at the same time. Thoughts ran ahead of me. Perhaps I'd been rejected and would now have to return home in disgrace. Or I'd be taken to another building on the island where they house those suspended between two countries. Perhaps my mother would be waiting for me, and I'd finally be with her after all these years, safe in her arms and surrounded by her love.

My guide, clad in that gray attire, ushered me to an area where before me stood three sets of stairs with signs above them. The only symbols I understood were the letters that spelled *New York*. But there were two others that led to places unknown. I slowed, fearing a choice I had no control over, but the official, with little expression, simply pointed toward the sign for the city. I joined a group of women, children, and men who walked down these stairs with looks of joy, and I understood. Hungary was my past; America, my future.

***

The short ferry ride took us to a nondescript building where relatives, volunteers, and friends waited. With my mother's photo in hand, I searched the crowd, desperate to match the image with a face, my heart pounding. After many minutes passed, I saw a strong-looking woman with a complexion similar to mine staring straight at me and knew instantly. I ran and wrapped my arms around her as tightly as I could. Through my tears, all I could say was "Momma, Momma."

My embrace didn't last long, as she pulled back almost immediately. Speaking Hungarian in an accent that reminded me of home, she said, "I came here on Friday and waited for hours. Then they told us that no one would be cleared until Monday. I was very angry, as I knew I'd have to take another day from work and make the two-hour trip again."

I wasn't sure what I should say in response to that, so I didn't say anything.

"Well, now you're here," she said with a frown. "Let me look at you."

Her response belied more irritation than comfort. I stepped back, and so did she. My mother looked as she did in her photo, but older, with a few lines by her eyes. Like me, she was petite, with hair as pitch black as mine. But that's where our similarities ended. Her face was more angular than mine, eyebrows thinner, her body more voluptuous. She also had a very thin waist from what I could see.

"Well, I never would have thought it, but you look like him."

"Who?"

"Your father. You have his nose, chin, eyes. Now you'll be a reminder of him that I'll have to live with."

Once again, I didn't know what to say.

"Do you have everything?" she asked.

"Yes, Momma."

"And why do you call me Momma?"

"Grandmother let me call her Momma. All the children at school had one, and you were far away."

"Call me Mother. Don't use that other name with me."

"Yes, Mother."

"Your last name. It's no longer Szuromi. From now on, it's Richter."

I had no idea what she was talking about. Szuromi was the only last name I had ever known.

"Why do I have a new name?"

"The man I married. His last name is Richter. Otto Richter. My last name is now Richter. Mary Richter. You'll call him Father in our home. He's the one who paid for your trip. You wouldn't be here without him. So show your gratitude when you see him."

"Yes, Mother."

"And another thing. You're in America now. This is your country. From now on you'll speak English, not Hungarian."

I didn't know what to make of what was happening. Would this stranger, my own mother, whose love I desperately needed if I were to live with my utter sense of loss, accept me as her daughter? Was I so unattractive to her that she wanted to change everything about me, including my language? My name? I knew so little about my mother, but without her, I'd be unmoored, at sea alone in this new world.

I had so many questions, but my mother's words left me mute, afraid to speak. I'd had such high hopes for our reunion, but now she left little doubt about her impatience at being inconvenienced and her disappointment in seeing in me a reminder of a life she had left long ago and seemed loath to revisit.

On the trolley, I had so many questions. "Where are we going? Where will I live? What is Father Richter like?"

"Be patient, Irene. You'll find out in due time," was her reply as she stared out the window.

The confusion of this day did nothing to contain my awe as we made our way to a place called the Bronx. People hurried along everywhere we passed. Signs with writing I didn't understand stood atop buildings of all sizes and shapes, some columned, others made of brick, with lettering that I imagined told of what's inside, many with canvas awnings that stretched halfway to the street. All the while the trolley rolled on its iron path, its bell clanging at each stop where people boarded the already-overcrowded car. Walkers dodged across the tracks from time to time, while black cars passed us by, horns beeping their warning to clear the way.

We exited the trolley after coming to a stop and made our way on foot to a large boulevard filled with aromas I knew well. Garlic, onions, sausages, peppers, and spices flavored the air. We passed through a broad street filled with shops, restaurants, and stalls interspersed with houses and apartments and more official-looking buildings and structures. Eventually we turned a corner to make our way down narrower streets lined with two-story houses, each equally distant from the sidewalk, some brick red, others gray with colors accenting their windows. All had basements and a few steps leading to first and second floors.

We came to one with the only green awning and green trim, as if the house itself determined to stand out against rows of conformity. My mother walked up its steps and turned the key, and I followed her into a small foyer. Heavy red curtains hung the length of the front windows while furniture, chairs, tables, and lamps in the sitting room to the left held within their wood an aura from a land not quite left behind. A Victrola, not unlike the one I had danced to in Hajdudorog, sat in a corner by the window.

"Your room's upstairs. Bring your things and follow me."

We climbed stairs that led to two rooms. Much of the space in my mother's bedroom was taken by a double bed, a carved Christ on a cross centered over it. As I walked past, I saw two porcelain dolls dressed in the native colors from Hungary at rest on a small, round table. A few photos of adults and children, none of whom I recognized, hung from small frames. Otherwise, little else adorned the walls.

After walking past a bathroom, we came to what would be my room at the opposite end of the second floor. It had one window that overlooked a small backyard with a patch of grass and a few flowers. Within bare yellow walls, a twin bed, nightstand, lamp, and small dresser awaited my arrival.

"Get your things unpacked. I need your help in the kitchen."

My mother mentioned that her husband would be home from

work in the early evening, and she needed to have dinner ready. Like so much else, she had told me little about Richter. I only knew that, like her, he was an immigrant, having come from Germany well before her. He set diamonds and other precious jewels, and had learned the trade from his father before him. I could see from their wedding photo on the side table with the reading lamp next to the living room sofa that he was older by a number of years, and short like her, with a certain sadness in his eyes.

In the kitchen, Mother asked few questions of me and none about my grandmother. When I told her how well Grandmother had cared for me, Mother made it clear she didn't want to hear more, even after I unwrapped Grandmother's gift to her.

"Johann wrote to me about my brothers. Josef, I guess, is happy and still living at home. But poor Sandor."

"It was terrible. I couldn't stop crying after I saw what happened to him. But I'm so glad we were by his side when he died."

What did pique her curiosity was what had happened to the estate where she had worked.

"Does Master Kovacs still have the property? Does he still visit his property?"

"Yes," I replied. I then told her about how the armies ravaged Master Kovacs's estate. "I didn't think any of us could feel sorry for someone so rich, but what they did to his beautiful house on the hill was horrible. The servants said at first the White Army came through looking for Master Kovacs and his family. Thank God they had already left for Budapest. From the look of blood and death in their eyes, nothing would have saved them.

"Then they took what they could, except the walls, roof, doors, and what was left—the tables, chairs, curtains—they brought outside and burned so that nothing remained for others who came after them. We were afraid he would give up after he saw what they did. But Johann told me he called together his workers and promised them he'd rebuild and renew what was lost."

"When this was going on, did you hear anything about your father?"

"Nothing. No one ever mentioned his name."

"And Magdalene? How is she?"

"Do you remember her husband, Karl? He died in the war. She hasn't married again and lives with her two little ones, who aren't so little anymore. Sometimes after school, I helped her with the children when they were younger, walking them home and playing with them. Magdalene helped us too, after Sandor died. She always looked out for me. I cried when I saw her for the last time."

A moment without words passed between us, the silence laden with tension from what wasn't said or asked. I sensed what it was but couldn't keep it within me.

"Grandmother was so kind and loving," I continued. "She watched over me, making sure I was safe. We did so much together. She taught me to cook and sew. When she could, Grandmother bought me clothes she couldn't make herself and made sure I had what I needed for school. She was always there for me. When Sandor was in the hospital, she—"

"Enough! I've heard enough about her. Now, go set the table."

I had other questions, but her tone told me now was not the time.

Richter came home on the hour, just as my mother had predicted. "Good evening, Mary," was his greeting, but that was all. As in their wedding photo, he wore a dark suit and tie. He had a round face and a well-groomed mustache, his straight but closely cropped black hair flecked with streaks of gray. On his lapel, he wore a small diamond pin, and his vest held a chain attached to a pocket watch. Turning to me, he spoke Hungarian in a soft voice.

"Welcome, Irene. We've been looking forward to having you here with us. I'm Otto Richter." With these first words he reached out, touching me lightly on my shoulder. "We've been planning for your trip and arrival for many months now. I must admit that you look prettier than the pictures I've seen of you. Your grandmother has sent many over the years and with them stories of how well you were doing in school, your favorite things to do, Körös and Maros, and so much more. I feel I know you a little, even though we meet now for the first time."

His greeting set me at ease and seemed to relax my mother as well.

"Oh, and before I forget, I brought you a little 'welcome' present." He reached into his jacket pocket and placed in my hands a small box wrapped in paper decorated with a pink carnation. Inside was a gold necklace with a small diamond pendant attached to it.

"Oh, Otto, do you think that's really necessary?" Mother asked.

"It's a little gift, Mary. I just received a shipment of small stones today and was setting necklaces for two clients. A few were flawed and the clients didn't want them, but they're still quite nice."

I'd never had anything quite like it before. "Thank you, Father. It's beautiful!" With that, the smile on his face broadened. For me, his kindness and warmth, at least for that moment, did much to fill in what I'd missed from my mother that day.

CHAPTER 9

In the beginning, everything was about learning. First came my new language. I tried to absorb every one of my mother's spoken English words and always kept the Hungarian-to-English books of translation on me. Tides of words swept over me, and with my mother's determination that I learn without delay, I willed myself to keep afloat, to conquer the unknown.

To my great relief, Otto Richter became my refuge. When Mother was out of earshot, at the stove or the market, we sat in the living room and talked easily, as I had little trouble understanding his German-inflected but fluent Hungarian. It was during these times together that he told me about his youth in Leipzig and how he came to America at the end of the nineteenth century. He stayed with an uncle who had emigrated before him and who taught him diamond-setting skills. Richter told how he met my mother at the jewelry counter at a department store around the Christmas holidays and wed her after a brief courtship. But that wasn't all about his past. I learned he had been married once before in his early twenties, shortly after coming to America, to a German woman he met at church not far from where we lived.

"Susan and I were so happy to have found each other. I can't tell you how wonderful it was to meet someone from my country. She'd grown up in a town not far from Leipzig. My parents and I had traveled through it on our way to their favorite spa." Looking out the window, he paused only for a moment. "We married six months after we met, and we lived in a small apartment on Olinville Avenue, a nice walk from here. We had to move after a few years because we started a family. Three beautiful daughters, one after the other: the oldest was Katherine, then Dorothy, then Jean. With so many mouths to feed, I worked late almost every night and Saturdays."

"That must have been so hard to do."

"Yes, it was. But I loved being a father to them. When they were young, the girls were a joy. I'd come home, and they'd all meet me at the door. I was quite a reserved person, but they were so affectionate. I'd play with them no matter how tired I was. Those were good days in our house."

"If I may ask, what happened to your first wife?"

"When Susan first came to America, she lived on the Lower East Side of Manhattan in a tenement building with many who had come through Ellis Island. Six others shared a small apartment, living almost on top of each other. All worked hard, came home exhausted, and often became sick from the cold and the damp where they worked. No one could afford a doctor, so whatever they had, they lived with until they got better—Susan too. When we met, she seemed in good health, and we had such good times together. She loved to dance, so we went to nightclubs whenever we had a few spare pennies. We took trips to the botanical gardens and museums. We enjoyed life. But every so often, she had coughing spells. It came to a point where she could barely get out of bed. She'd recover, but each pregnancy took something from her. She became very tired after she had Jean. Where she once enjoyed cooking for us, even that eventually became too much."

By now, he had picked up his pipe, filling it with tobacco but leaving it unlit. "Over the years, those coughing spells came and went, but the time in between became shorter and shorter. She had always made sure the children were healthy, taking them to the doctor for their exams. Susan had never taken time for herself—until she had no choice. One day, after she'd been sick with a fever, she started coughing and couldn't stop. I took her to the hospital. They told me she had the Spanish flu. Susan was so weak before she got sick; she didn't stand a chance. She died in the hospital a few days later."

"I'm so sorry, Father. How did you manage with three daughters?"

"They were all very strong, but I did have my hands full. When Susan died, my youngest was sixteen. I took care of them with the help of my aunt and uncle. Now they're grown up, working, and married with their own families."

"They sound wonderful. Do they live nearby? Do you see them very often?"

He hesitated for a moment, and his face, which seemed lifted by his memories, suddenly sagged as if under the weight of a stone. "When I met your mother, the girls had left home. At first, I saw them quite often, as they all lived together for a time. They invited the two of us over for dinner at least once a month. But it was difficult for your mother. They were the past—my past, not hers—a closed chapter in her eyes.

"Your mother is very strong-willed and determined. She didn't want me to spend time with them and had no interest in making them a part of her life. I haven't seen them since shortly after we married. We keep up with letters—I won't go a week without writing them—but that's all we have now."

These words brought to mind what Mother had said about the days and loved ones in Hungary: that they were the past and we now lived in this present—her present—which left no room for the presence of others.

My mother never liked Richter sitting with me, each of us telling our stories apart from her. Still, these times became a peaceful sanctuary to learn about the lives of others, and a bridge to my new world.

***

By the end of the first month in America, my mother had enrolled me in a special class for immigrants, where I was placed in the sixth grade at PS 41 on Gun Hill Road—a bewildering move, as I was about to be in the eighth grade in Hajdudorog. Still, in my English class I found a microcosm of what I'd met on an ocean. We were strangers, and yet these students and I shared a common fate. On Ellis Island, the swell of alien languages overwhelmed and isolated me. Now, in this one place, together, I took comfort in knowing we were all seekers of learning, assimilation, of moving beyond survival.

School created a welcome routine that I'd been missing. Awake at six, breakfast, off by eight, home by four, then schoolwork, dinner, reading, and bed. However, it didn't take long to realize life with my mother would be far more disruptive and precarious.

My mother's workday started shortly after I left for school during the week and about the time Richter left to drive or take the subway to the Diamond District in Manhattan. From 8:00 a.m. to 2:00 p.m., five days a week, she washed floors and windows, polished furniture, and performed other tasks in homes that were not her own. These menial, mindless days, toiling in the neighborhood apartments and residences of those whose modest means only served to remind her of her own fate and gave little in return beyond an income that helped pay the bills. When I came back after school, my mother greeted me more often than not with things to do before homework and with little to say about the drudgery of the day she had left behind until her tomorrow.

I tried my best to fulfill whatever she required, desperate as I was to please, to gain her approval and her love. Preparing meals eased me into a comfortable role, as my grandmother's lessons in the kitchen often made these tasks a pleasure. Richter's hearty appetite and generous words about my goulash and roasted pork lifted my spirits and often brought a smile to my mother's face. I thought perhaps she *was* very pleased about bringing me to America.

This praise from Mother turned out to be more the exception than the rule, however. Any praise from her meant the world to me. She had little patience for my speaking Hungarian at home. School performance required near perfection from the start. From her days at Master Kovacs's estate, my mother had learned proper table setting, dress, and decorum, all traits I hastened to learn, as she was critical of anything she considered less than acceptable.

As the weeks passed, it didn't take long for my attentive teacher to realize I didn't belong in the sixth grade, nor in the "foreign class," and she recommended that I join the proper grade with after-school help in English. This pleased my mother, as did my care in following her expectations to the point that, one day, as we prepared dinner, a softness in her tone I had rarely heard appeared.

"Irene, you know Otto and I had wanted you to come earlier, but the war had kept me from bringing you here. Otto started saving money for your trip right after we were married. You're my only flesh and blood, and I want you to know how much that means for me, that we are together at last." With that, she kissed my cheek.

Her kind words and gentle touch left me in tears. "Oh, Mother, I love you. I want you to be proud of me, and I want to make you happy. And we still have your mother and brother. They're our family too. I'm not the only one—"

Before I could finish, she cut me off and her smile faded. "I've told you before, they're no longer a part of my life, and they're no longer a part of yours."

Did she not know that I couldn't simply erase my memories? My grandmother's love meant the world to me. I'd been in America for six months, and I'd heard from no one. I'd written three letters to Grandmother and Magdalene and had placed them on the table near the front door for my mother to post. Had they forgotten me? Was I already a distant memory, an abstraction, no longer a part of their lives? I was determined not to let these doubts overwhelm me.

Then, on a quiet Saturday afternoon as I sat at my desk, sun pouring through the open venetian blinds, Mother stopped at my door on the way to her bedroom as I was finishing another letter to Grandmother.

"What are you doing?"

Caught in the moment, I asked, "Has anyone written me?"

"No," was her reply. Then she asked again, "What are you doing?"

"I'm writing a letter to Grandmother."

Her face reddened. "What did I tell you about this? I don't want you writing letters to her!"

"You never said anything about writing letters. I don't talk to you about Grandmother because I know how upset you get. But are you saying I can't write letters?"

"You've left letters at the front door before. I've been meaning to talk to you. I've told you, the past is past. Hajdudorog is the past, your grandmother is the past, your life there is the past. You live here now with Otto and me."

I was speechless. Tears welled up, but I didn't want her to see them, afraid they would only feed her anger. I needn't have worried. Having made her demands, she turned and left my room. I knew then that memories would have to remain locked within, a forbidden knowledge never to be opened in her presence.

This exchange left a question that haunted me for days to come:

What happened to her that drives her to erase all that had gone before in our native land as if it had never never been?

***

School and home became my life's divide, and the corridors and classes my immersion into cultures, races, and prejudice. I entered Evander Childs High School after eighth grade, and it didn't take but a few days to understand I had stepped into a world filled with those like me, from distant lands. Heavily accented English mixed with alien languages echoed down the hallways. Rosy-complexioned girls and those with darker skin like mine, fair-haired boys and others with jet-black hair, and a few Black boys who kept to themselves, filled classrooms. Among us were "the natives," those whose parents had lived in America for a generation or more. They, more than the others, kept their distance from the rest of us. Passing them by in the school halls between classes or in the cafeteria, we'd hear words meant to cut, to belittle, to hurt: *kike, wop, Jew-boy, mick.* These slights only created bonds among those of us who were new Americans. We sought shelter in our diversity, welcoming to new people, new adventures.

Still, I didn't expect what happened in the lunchroom one gray, wintry afternoon. As I sat daydreaming of Hajdudorog, I overheard two girls talking about a crush one had on a boy in her class. There was nothing unusual about their broken English, until one of them shifted into the rapid dialect I knew so well. They were speaking Hungarian. Except for Mrs. Szalagi at the bakery, Mr. Orzag at the grocers, and my stepfather, I'd rarely heard my native language. From then on, Ursula and Kalmina became my lunchtime companions—friends I would never invite home, as I knew my mother wouldn't approve.

I awoke each day curious about the adventures awaiting me. Teachers were my beacons. Classmates became my journey's companions, the school my ship where I set sail. And the public library not far from where we lived became a daily destination. I would choose a new adventure each day: history, science, biography, literature, or poetry. I would lose myself in these worlds, and when I had visited them all, I began again. I stayed as long as I could, then picked which book-bound friends to take home. I traveled wherever they carried me, absorbing language, thought, action, consequence, and lives lived.

Education became a narrow bridge across all that divided us. Mother prided herself on how, unlike her mother, she could read and write. The novels I brought home, *The Adventures of Huckleberry Finn*, *The Wonderful Wizard of Oz*, *Anne of Green Gables*, and *The Wind in the Willows*, created a common language between us. Each evening I read the poetry of T. S. Eliot, E. E. Cummings, and others. Tests, grades, teacher comments, visits to school were grist for dissection and discussion, especially for my mother, who was quick to pass judgment. I excelled in school, as my love of learning propelled me forward. Doing well became the currency to possess my mother's praise and love.

Still, from time to time my mother let me know ways I could never please her. I had heard about her beautiful singing as a little girl. The three of us attended Mass on Sundays at the Church of the Immaculate Conception on Gun Hill Road, favored by Richter as its roots lay in serving German immigrants, especially those who had arrived toward the end of the last century. Its twin towers and Italian-style architecture stood out against the elevated train and small shops that lined the street. My mother came to love the church for a different reason. A natural soprano, she had joined the church choir, leading the congregation whenever she was asked to do so. Songs from the Catholic hymnal came naturally to her, and members of the congregation told her they appreciated how her voice penetrated all corners of the church. During Catholic holidays, her "Ave Maria" even attracted some non-Catholic neighbors. Her singing became part of our life beyond the church, as the American patriotic tunes she had learned filled our home on many Saturdays and Sundays.

Grandmother had told me stories about my mother's singing and how it captivated parishioners week after week at the cathedral. She had adapted that talent, born among the fields and furrows of her native land, to her new land. Even her heavy accent became part of a lyrical charm I could only admire. Richter and I hummed along as best we could. My mother was resigned to her husband's muted accompaniments but did little to conceal her disappointment in my atonal refrains.

"I had hoped you'd follow in my footsteps at church," she said, "but you sing just like your father and grandmother."

Her criticism didn't end there, not by any measure, but took turns I did not see coming. Once, walking home from a good day at school, it started to rain, and then pour. There was something about it—the clouds, drops touching my face, and the wet feel of my clothes—that transported me back to the afternoons in Hajdudorog when I'd return home soaked, having danced through every puddle along the way. My grandmother was always there, waiting for me, sweets on the table. She'd smile, grab a towel, and run it through my thick curls until they no longer dripped onto the floor. Then I'd change my clothes and sit with her, telling her about my day.

I was lost in those happy memories and moments as I approached our house. Then I looked up and saw my mother there, standing on the stoop, umbrella in hand, with an all-too-familiar look. As soon as I reached the bottom step, she started in. Glaring at me, she said, "What are you doing walking home like that in this rain?"

When I tried to say something about my old school days, she interrupted me. "You're such a stupid peasant girl. Simple and stupid."

As soon as we stepped inside the house, she turned the umbrella around and with the curved wooden handle landed a blow to my head that sent me reeling. As I struggled to steady myself, I didn't realize she wasn't done venting her venom until she retreated to the kitchen and returned with a rolling pin.

"I'll give you something to help you remember what not to do!"

That strike landed with such force upon my lower back that I ended up flattened on the floor. My mother raised the pin again, but seeing me lying there grimacing made her hesitate.

"I hope you have learned your lesson." With that, she left me with my pain.

I didn't dare say anything. I only cried behind the door to my bedroom. Little did I realize at the time that this was only the beginning. Through the pain and confusion came my first sense that fault may not lie with me but with my mother and a past that she considered irredeemable.

***

Mealtimes were a refuge, especially as I took on more of the cooking for my mother and Richter. Often exhausted after her workday, Mother, at first, appreciated my preparation, and soon came to expect it. Early on, we shopped together for dinner. Before long, I visited the butcher, the vegetable stand, and baker's shop alone. Everyone seemed to enjoy this new girl with her heavily accented English. Speaking of sausages, chicken, legumes, fruits, and pastries, their aromas and displays became yet another gateway to all that America offered.

Days and dreams didn't allow me to follow my mother's admonition and prohibition about Grandmother. Not only did I enjoy my time in the kitchen, but I also often felt Momma's presence there. The two of us were safe in our own world without words. The smells, recipes, and tastes kept my grandmother close to me. These memories, clear and potent in recalling loving times, warmed me through. They became my staff of life. Some days I was so lost in them that my mother would catch me with eyes crinkled from the breadth of my smile.

"What's so funny?" she would ask.

"Oh, nothing," I'd say, or "Just thinking about a friend at school."

The shelter of the night at times brought the greatest comfort. Sleep became the portal, and those memories were the lure that tugged me back to Hajdudorog and home. I never knew where those dreams would take me. Sometimes I drifted above, looking down on the rivers, forest, and fields where I played. I'd see Körös and Maros fetching a stick or chasing each other through tall grasses. Then I'd see the landscape changing from autumnal gold and brown into the white of winter. At other times, I played with Sandor and Josef, teasing, talking, and laughing at their silly jokes. But I most awaited those moments with my grandmother. Some happened over and over again, as if each night I were donning an old coat. I'd come home from school, and she'd wrap me in her arms, or I'd read a story or a letter from Uncle Janos, or sit across from her at the kitchen table with her freshly baked bread between us, the aroma so real that it seemed to fill my head.

As the months passed, dreams took me to the world I had left, a world that I hoped would help me to understand the mother I had never known. Many of those nocturnal conversations began with the same questions: *"Momma, what can I do to make my mother love me? Why does she seem so unhappy with me?"* Others tumbled out as I searched for some meaning that would help me to understand. *"Why did Mother want me to join her in America? What really happened that made her leave all those years ago? Why does she seem to hate you so?"*

"Don't blame yourself, Irene," Grandmother in my dreams told me more than once. *"Your mother doesn't know how to accept the love that you give. She does not realize it is one of life's true gifts."*

Many mornings I awoke saddened to leave the comfort of those dreams. With them had come warmth and tranquility, a peace of mind, and a growing acceptance of who I was.

As much as my mother's distance and eye for imperfections were constantly present, Richter became a gentle counterpoint. Although he never said so, I felt the spirit of his daughters present in his words and in our moments together, in how he protected me and how we enjoyed each other when we were alone. I said nothing about what had happened between my mother and me, fearful of the pain it might cause the two of us.

Then there were the gifts. "Irene, how was your day?" he would ask as he walked in the door. I'd tell him the latest stories we learned in school, about teachers and friends. He'd smile in response to my tales of mispronunciations in English class—especially words with an *s* or *z*, as Hungarian had so many ways to pronounce these letters, depending on their pairings—which elicited giggles from the other students. He was always curious about how my classes were going, praising me when I had good news about a test and encouraging me to do well.

"Oh, one more thing before you go off to the kitchen," he'd say, and then I knew a surprise was coming. "I was making something at work today and, well . . ." With that, he pulled a small, simply decorated package from his briefcase. I'd throw my arms around him and plant a kiss on his cheek, as I knew what I'd find within the little square: delicate earrings, necklaces, a brooch, and once, a ring. All were made from diamonds he couldn't sell. To me, they were precious jewels I wore proudly whenever I went to the markets, to church, and, when I was older, the world.

Uplift and downdraft flowed through my days at home. Richter's kind ways buffered against the disappointment that Mother never failed to impress on me. Still, she was my true and only family in America, and although she'd abandoned me when I was an infant, I was finally with her. Above all, I loved my mother, as I was her daughter, her flesh and blood. Feeling truly accepted and loved, as much as I tried, remained out of reach, appearing before me for an instant, only to vanish like snowflakes in the wind.

Still, something about her relationship with Otto held a key. What was it that drew my mother to a man who seemed so different from her? He was magnanimous in spirit, attentive, and, when she allowed, affectionate. At first, I couldn't make sense of their marriage. Yes, my mother was still very attractive, carrying a subtle sensuality in the way she walked, her smile, and even in her occasional flirtation. But more than that, she held within her a desire unknown to me, to reach some pinnacle, to prove to herself and, as I came to understand, to her mother that she'd achieved a life so much better than what she'd left behind. Her life with Richter had allowed her to take a step up, but I sensed it wasn't enough.

What she did to earn a living was a constant reminder of the life that remained out of reach. The only work she'd known in America came from her experience in Hungary, but my mother's ambition prevailed just as it had in her motherland. While in her first few years she took whatever housecleaning work came her way, marrying Richter opened new doors and homes. Among many of her husband's clientele were the well-off, residing in elite homes on New York's Upper East Side and Park Avenue. Upon learning of his reputation as a diamond setter, they sought him out for his expertise as well as his knowledge of who among the merchants in the Diamond District had the highest-quality stones. He didn't reveal the names of his clients to my mother right away when she asked about them—he respected client privacy. But Mary persisted, and eventually Otto relented. Shortly after these revelations, she made him promise to ask if any needed a housekeeper.

At first, none showed any interest. Then one day, the Raskins, frequent customers who lived just off Fifth Avenue, complained to him that one of their "hired help" had suddenly departed. When Richter mentioned my mother's interest, they were eager to learn if she could start right away.

That evening, as we sat for dinner, Richter told my mother what had happened. "You had asked me to see if any of my clients needed a housekeeper. Today Mr. and Mrs. Raskin came in to set a ring. They happened to mention they need a housekeeper, as theirs had just left a few days ago. They seem nice enough, so I said you might be interested in working for them."

Mother's eyes lit up. "Where do they live?"

"Their address is not far from Central Park. I know the street. I've had to drop off merchandise for customers. They live on streets with some of the most expensive homes and mansions in the city. I have the address."

I had rarely seen my mother appear so animated. "Yes. Tomorrow's my day off, and I can take the train to see them."

"The Raskins have a butler, a cook, and someone to look after their three children. The maid who left lived with them. I told Mrs. Raskin that would be impossible for you. She said that would be all right for the time being, until they can find permanent help."

"Maybe we can work something out, even if it's only for a while. Besides, once I meet the Raskins and they like my work, maybe there'll be other homes."

I learned that the visit was a success the following evening. As it turned out, Richter was right: The Raskins did live in a mansion not far from Central Park.

For my mother, their home was more than just a new place to work; it brought her back to the world of the privileged she hadn't been a part of since her time in Hajdudorog. So began my mother's return to a world of wealth, but not of it.

As the months passed, I began to see another side of my mother. Word got out among the Raskins' friends about her reliability, diligence, and experience. When she came home in the early evening and, frequently, with Richter, she spoke in admiration more than envy about the lives of her clients. Pride and a certain charm came through when she spoke of the way she won over another family. More than anything, these places of the well-to-do rekindled her ambition.

Even their relationship seemed to take a subtle turn toward each other with gestures of affection, a touch, a glance, and a kiss no longer hidden. The pleasure of simple things—talk of small events of the day, gossip about the people who lived in regal homes—now filled their time together.

My mother's curiosity carried over to my stepfather's day. "Otto, the other day I saw Mrs. Raskin leaving for some fancy lunch with her friends. She had on a gold necklace with a pendant of blue stone surrounded by diamonds. It was so pretty."

Otto smiled. "Oh yes, I know that. Lapis lazuli. I just set it for her a few weeks ago. She was so taken with that stone that both she and Mr. Raskin came in. I think it's a family heirloom."

"And Mrs. Berman. Did you set her diamond and ruby brooch too?"

"Yes, but that came from a store not too far from me, well known for high-quality merchandise."

When they came home together, I often found them continuing their conversation only to realize that supper was more than ready. "Your mother and I stopped for a beer at Pete's Tavern downtown. We just got carried away. Sorry we're late. What's for dinner? It smells so wonderful."

During this time, a lightness eased the tension that seemed to drift through each room of the house. I'd been mystified about their attraction to each other, as they were so different, but I'd always hesitated to ask. Now these times of seeming contentment inspired my curiosity. One Saturday afternoon, as we sat at the kitchen table peeling carrots and dicing onions for the evening's beef goulash, my mother hummed a hymn she was learning for church. I felt at ease and happy with her.

"Mother, Father is such a wonderful man. He's always there for me, interested in what happened at school and wanting me to do well like you, bringing me little presents that always surprise and make me so happy."

"I think he spoils you."

"Well, it's just so nice of him."

After a few minutes, I continued. "How did the two of you meet? Father hasn't said much about it."

As she finished peeling the last of the potatoes, she looked up at me. "Unlike you, I didn't know anyone when I came here. People I met on the way over told me about a place to live downtown. They said maybe we could save some money if we all stayed together at least for a while, until we could find work. I knew what money I had would run out soon, but most of the work was terrible, especially for women: factories for making clothes, sewing, stitching, not so different from sitting around in the barn in Hajdudorog with the tobacco harvest. Just like I'd avoided that type of work in Hungary, I promised myself I'd find another way to earn a living."

She paused to take a sip of coffee, by now cold. "On Sundays, our one day off, I'd go to St. Mary's Church on Grand Street. People there were always nice to me, and when they learned I could sing, they asked me to join their choir. I got to know the rector and everyone in that choir, some struggling like me but others a little better off. At one of their Sunday breakfasts, one of the women, Mrs. Gilhooly, if I remember, said she was looking for someone to help clean their house, only a few blocks from St. Mary's. Well, I did it, and she spread the word about how good I was. Before I knew it, there was enough work from church members that I was able to quit the factory. Most of my earnings went to room and food, but I did manage to keep a little spending money. That's when I'd go to one of the big department stores downtown, Wanamakers. I'd get little things there, a few plates and cups, some candy. I'd look at the jewelry and other finery too while I was there, and think about what it would be like if . . ." Her voice trailed off before she continued. "One Saturday in December, I decided to go for a stroll. I remember thinking I looked very pretty. I'd just fixed my hair, put on a little rouge, and wore a lovely dress perfect for a beautiful and unusually warm day. You may not believe this, but I even turned a few men's heads and got a whistle from time to time."

"Was Father one of them? Is that how you met?"

"No. I'm coming to that. I felt so good that morning. I decided to spoil myself and see if I could find a pair of earrings I could afford at Wanamakers. It didn't take long at their jewelry department to see that everything cost too much. It was all so expensive! Then, just as I was getting ready to leave, I overheard this man talking with a saleslady about repairing earrings and setting stones. He was older, dressed in a navy-blue suit, white shirt, and tie, and looked as if he might even be rich. We were at the same counter, almost as close as the two of us sitting here. He didn't seem to notice me at first, as he was so wrapped up in some business conversation with the saleslady. Then he looked up and saw me. I'll never forget his smile. It was so warm. And he had the kindest eyes.

"Otto said hello, and even with that first word, I could tell he was different, not so full of himself as other men I'd met in the city. We talked for a while, and I found out what he did and that he'd lost his wife a few years back. Otto was supposed to meet a client, but before leaving, he asked to meet for a coffee the next day. Then he asked me to dinner. We were together all that winter and spring, and then on October 10, 1919, as we sat on a park bench in Central Park, he reached into his vest pocket, pulled out a little box, and laid it in the palm of my left hand. In it was an engagement ring, a circle of little diamonds with a ruby at the center. That's when he asked me to marry him."

"That's such a sweet story. What about your wedding. What was that like?"

"We married at St. Mary's. Almost all the choir came, plus a few others. Otto's daughters were there, and that was all. The priest said a few words before we took our vows. That was it."

"You must have been so happy."

Her subdued response wasn't what I expected. "Happy? Yes, but I always imagined I'd find a rich man to marry, and we'd live in a great big house, and I wouldn't have to work anymore. But at least we're not poor."

"It must have been hard to bring me here."

"Yes. I'd never have been able to pay your way. Otto and I talked about all it would take to bring you here after we were married, but it didn't take long for him to say he wanted you to come. We just had to work out how to make it happen, what time of year, the money, tickets, and so on." With those words, my mother turned her attention to the pot on the stove. "We have to finish the vegetables. They're not going to peel and cut themselves."

I now knew what seemed obvious all along: Without Richter, I wouldn't have come to America. That revelation only made me more curious about this man and his dedication to find a way for me to be with them.

A few days later, coming from school on a Friday afternoon, I was surprised to see Richter home early, busy fiddling with some brown box and its knobs. "Oh, hello. I hope I didn't startle you. Your mother's not back from work yet. Come; come here. I know your eyes are open. Now open your ears."

With a slight twist to one of the knobs, a faint light from inside the box began to glow. Then, after a minute, sound, actually a tune I'd heard at school, filled our living room. "This, my dear, is what's called a Rogers Batteryless Receiver, the newest radio that you can buy. From the look on your face, I guess you've heard 'St. Louis Blues' before. Isn't that Prince's Band wonderful?"

I had heard a few students talk about radio shows at home, but they complained about the crackling reception or when the signal was lost. But as I listened to the saxophone play its clear, soulful sound, it all seemed perfect. In his own way, Otto had once again brought joy into our home and into my life.

At first, my mother complained that we couldn't afford such a luxury or that she didn't like the music. Then, within a week, she too was seduced. Richter, ever aware of her predilections, knew how to assuage her. "Mary, tonight our favorite station is broadcasting a live concert of Béla Bartók's 'Kossuth.' It's one of his first works for orchestra."

On those evenings, we all gathered around, transfixed by what we heard. At other times, especially when my mother was at evening vespers, Otto sat listening to one of his favorite shows, *Rambling with Gambling*, which broadcast a seemingly endless stream of news and chatter about everything from the price of gasoline to President Coolidge's fight against corruption. If I wandered into the living room from the kitchen, he'd more often than not silently beckon me to come listen with him.

On one of those lazy Saturdays with Mother at church as usual and just as *Rambling* was ending its evening program, we sat together, just the two of us. "Father, I'm sorry I never thanked you for helping bring me here. Without you, I might never have seen my mother again. And I never would have met you."

"I can't tell you how happy I am that you're here with us. For as long as I can remember, I always wanted a family. I had one. Now I'm a father again." My stepfather paused, collecting himself before he spoke again. "I didn't know what to expect when you came here. Would you like New York? What would you think of America—or of having a stepfather? Of course, I also wondered how it would be with your mother, whom you hadn't seen in so many years. But from when you first walked in that door and greeted me with that great big smile, I just, well, from those first moments there was something about you that reminded me of my daughters, especially the youngest, Jean, who is so sweet and affectionate. And here we are sitting together, just like I used to sit with her and her sisters."

"I'm sorry that you never see them," I said. "Something I haven't told you is that Mother has forbidden me from writing to my friends and family in Hungary."

His smile faded. "No, I didn't know that. I don't know what it is about your mother, what happened before she came here or since, but whatever it was, her way of dealing with her past is to put it behind her and not look back. That goes for your past and mine. Yet, I don't know. Maybe you—not your grandmother or anyone else from those days, for that matter—are the exception. Perhaps you're the one reminder of her past, the world that she isn't quite ready to give up."

"But what about you and your children?"

"You know how charming your mother can be, and she was like that when we'd get together with one or all of them, usually over dinner and conversation. Her demand came only after I fell in love with her and we were married. I had to choose. We both love your mother and want to please her. It makes me terribly sad, but that's the price I pay, and now I find that you pay it too."

What I felt was true. My stepfather and I were bound by separation from those we held dear: his sacrifice for a wife's love and my sacrifice for a mother's.

CHAPTER 10

One evening before a Friday school holiday, as we sat after dinner, Mother made a plan for me. "You'll come with me tomorrow," she said. "In a few years, God willing, you'll have a good job or be in college. You may be smart, but because of that public school you go to, you know so little about the beautiful things I saw before you were born. The great rooms, the grand paintings that lined the hallways and led to bedrooms as large as our first floor. You'll see places that remind me of some of my happiest days when I was young."

The next Saturday we awoke and left the house at about the same time I usually left for school. We boarded the elevated train into a part of the city I hadn't seen since my trip from Ellis Island. Our train stopped at a station that my mother called "The East Side." We walked past names I remembered from my American history class: Madison, Lexington. My mother led the way across intersections and down streets. The homes we passed, fleeting though they were at our pace, left me in awe. A number of them filled half a city block; they were structures with elaborate details, some with turrets and many with arched entrances. We arrived at only slightly less prominent, four- and five-storied homes populating side streets off the main avenues. They were less dramatic and ornate but still imposing.

It was before one of these buildings that we stopped and rang the bell. A thin, middle-aged man with a pale complexion opened the door. He wore a black suit with a dark tie and very starched shirt, and he greeted my mother coolly but respectfully.

"Good morning, Mary."

"Good morning, Arthur. This is my daughter, Irene. If you remember, I asked if it was all right for me to bring her to work today."

"Yes, I recall." With those few words, he let us in.

Stepping into the entranceway, it was all I could do to keep my mouth closed. A brilliant crystal chandelier cast rainbows from a vaulted ceiling over an entry hall of oak and mirror. To the right, the marble staircase formed a semicircle to the second floor, where an oriel welcomed light inside. French doors at the back of the home flooded the through floor with light and offered views of the garden.

At fifteen, I had never even dreamed of the finery that appeared before me.

We descended a staircase at the rear that led to the servants' quarters and the kitchen. There I met Inga, a younger woman who, I was to learn, had been the live-in au pair for the Raskins since the children were born. Emerging from the pantry was Agatha, a round, large-breasted woman who oversaw the kitchen and, like Inga, had been with the family for years. My mother, the lowest in their hierarchy, was given daily tasks to attend to, including cleaning the four bathrooms; cleaning the oven, the stove, the trash containers; washing and wiping the marble floors; and polishing silverware.

I would perform these tasks with her that day while Inga took on lighter work and minded the children.

We left at one to fulfill the same role at the Morgensterns' home. I was once again wide-eyed at the size and scale of the riches before me, from the wood-paneled library and dining room to the stained-glass windows and marble mantelpiece. I bore witness to a fragment of my mother's past at each of these homes. It was as if she had stepped into and returned to a world she had committed to memory. Charm, decorum, social graces, polite gestures of careful deference to authority, and knowing her place were her routine. I could see how she became, if not indispensable, at least someone who fit well into her role within their lives.

That day with my mother wasn't meant to be idle exercise. She started in almost immediately after we left the Morgensterns', as we headed to the El. "So, how did you feel about what you saw today?" Her voice and tone hinted at something beyond an innocent question, as if she were testing me.

I fell back on what I thought she wanted to hear. "The homes are so beautiful. I saw things I had never seen before and never dreamed of."

She pressed further. "Yes, but that's not what I asked you. How did you *feel* about what you saw today?"

I was unsure of how to answer, not sure what she was looking for.

"Well, I was happy that you took me with you today."

I sensed her patience wearing thin as we approached the El. "Irene, I didn't take you along just for you to see how the rich live. Did anyone in Hajdudorog ever tell you where I worked and for a time lived before I had you?"

"Only a little."

"I worked and for a time lived in a mansion with beautiful furniture, linens, chandeliers, and crystal not so different from what you saw today. I belonged in that world. Your father lived surrounded by beauty. As soon as I stepped into his home I thought, *This is where I should be.* It became my dream to make it so. As you know, that's not what happened. But it hasn't stopped me. It will happen. If Otto can't give me the life I deserve, then I will make sure you will. This is your first look, but it's far from the last."

She looked at me and smiled. "I'll tell you something I've never told Otto. Only a few weeks ago, I had a dream about a mansion where you and I lived. It had French windows with lace curtains from floor to ceiling in the living and dining rooms, pewter figurines on the hearth's mantle, a wood-paneled library with a roaring fire, high-backed chairs, and bright-white light streaming through on a cold winter's day. In that dream I had the strangest feeling, as if we were home."

"What about Father Richter? Was he in the dream too?"

"No. Only you and me."

My confounded silence didn't seem to bother my mother. For the moment, she was lost to me.

From then on, when school didn't interfere, I went to work with my mother, helping her without pay, but with a singular, focused purpose: to know this wealth and luxury in all its dimensions so that one day I would live it. In fulfilling that dream—her dream— little did I know just how much a part I was to play.

***

As much as my mother intended to indoctrinate me on the means and manners of high society, it only made my love of learning and school that much more vital. However, it was my teacher, Mr. Kapinsky, who opened a door that would forever change my life.

On the first day of science class in my junior year, Mr. Kapinsky stood by the door. Here was this balding, stout man, perhaps in his late forties, wearing a white shirt with a tie, and a dark suit that looked as if it had become one with its owner after years of wear.

Once we had all filed in, he shuffled over and sat at his similarly worn wooden desk, which held only a paperweight and a small globe of the world.

"Good morning, students. My name is Mr. Kapinsky. I'll be your science teacher this year."

He paused, scanning the classroom, eyes resting on no one in particular but seeming to take us all in at the same time. We fidgeted in our seats as we waited to see what he would say next. Then, speaking with an accent, he continued. "For those who have been at Evander Childs as freshmen and sophomores, this will be your first year-long science class. In this room and beyond it, you'll learn about the wondrous things science tells us about ourselves, the world we live in, and the worlds beyond our planet. By the time you leave here, you'll have taken trips to places you can't see with your naked eye, places you've never imagined. Like me, many of you have come from distant lands. In what we study here, you'll see not only the differences between here and there but also how much where you've been and where you now are—and who we are—have in common. This won't be an easy course. You'll work hard in my class, but I'll be with you every step of the way."

It didn't take long for me to understand what those words meant. Biology, anatomy, astronomy, horticulture, the microscopic worlds of animate and inanimate objects, the composition of planets and the universe beyond our solar system—nothing was beyond this teacher. To Mr. Kapinsky, our class was only one of the places we would gather to learn—to assemble, discuss, and test. Class trips to the world just outside our doors on wintry and spring days—to the Bronx Zoo and botanical gardens—all became our playgrounds. On the days he came to school with his microscope, we took turns exploring our physiology and the plants and animals around us.

He didn't stop there. Mr. Kapinsky guided us on journeys into our immigrant and native memories and made our lands, our histories come alive again. Inspired by his words, I turned to the library to revisit my roots, the flora and fauna and events of my past. How did tobacco leaves come to be? What happened when Momma made bread? What is rabies, and why did Körös die from that disease? So many questions, so many doors to walk through. Grades reflected my drive and determination to do well in all classes. But there was something special about science—and Mr. Kapinsky.

Then, one day toward the end of March, before the Easter holiday, he came up to me as we were leaving class. "Do you have a few minutes after school that you could stop by?" No teacher had ever asked me such a question, and sensing my hesitation, he quickly added, "I want to talk with you about your work in my class."

"Yes, Mr. Kapinsky. I'm meeting with some other students about the English test next week, but I can come right after."

I had no idea what I had done that made him want to see me outside of class. His words left much to my imagination. I had lunch and the entire afternoon to fret about them. Test scores? Raising my hand and answering questions in class? Experiments? He was my favorite teacher, and science was my best class. Had I missed something? By the time the end of the school day came about, anxiety had crept in and taken hold. I knocked tentatively and entered, standing just inside the classroom door.

"Come in," he said. "Come, sit."

A moment of silence passed between us, as I seemed to have caught him in mid-thought. "I've wanted to speak with you for some time now. You've done very well in my class so far. In fact, I daresay you're my best student, and after seeing your work over several months now, one of the best I've had in my days of teaching. It's not just your grades and assignments; it's your natural curiosity and the way you work with other students. I've seen how your love of science rubs off on them. And you always do it with a smile."

I could feel my cheeks turning red from his compliments, and

I, unaccustomed to them, was at a loss for words. "Thank you, Mr. Kapinsky" was all I could manage.

"You're welcome. But that's not why I wanted to see you. Each year, the junior and senior classes participate in a citywide science fair, with each school featuring the best student projects. Your project on photosynthesis in the tobacco plants you grew up with was excellent. Your presentation was clear and written in a way that we could all understand. I'd like to enter it in the fair. Having been to many, I think it may even win you a ribbon. What do you think?"

"I don't know what to say. If you really think so . . ." My voice trailed off.

"Yes, Irene. I do." We sat across from each other, not saying a word, which, by now, I knew meant that there was something else.

"You may remember that in the first week, the first day of class, I mentioned that we have something in common. Well, I was just a bit older than you when I came to this country. I don't know about your family, but I'd imagine that like many Evander Childs students, you probably didn't have much when you came here. We were without much too, but my father was determined to make a better life for us."

"I imagined you growing up in a city, maybe, like me, studying, reading, spending time at your library," I replied.

Mr. Kapinsky smiled and rolled his eyes. "Oh, hardly, Irene. We lived on a farm not far from your Hungary, in southeastern Poland. We got by. Like you, school was a place I loved. I tried my best at our little classroom and did well in my classes, such as they were."

"It's funny—I saw you as so accomplished, attending a city university, graduating at the top of your class."

"That's a nice thought, Irene, but no, that's not what happened. Fighting broke out between Poland and Russia, and things turned very dark. Many people died; others starved. Then the Russian army started to take boys and young men to fight for them. That was the last straw. My parents knew it wouldn't be long before my brother, Michael, and I would be taken from them. Not long after that, we made our way to America."

Mr. Kapinsky paused for a moment, looking out the window as if to collect his thoughts.

"Coming here with almost nothing, my parents worked hard. My mother did laundry, and my father learned to turn what he knew about working with his hands into working on the new buildings that were going up around New York. They knew that going to school and getting an education was the way to a better life. I made sure I did well in high school for them. When I had the chance to go to college, I didn't hesitate. I saw what learning could do, and that's why I became a teacher."

He paused for a quick breath and then continued.

"I tell you this story not merely to have you listen to me go on and on. It's because of what I see in you. So, here's a suggestion. In a little over a year, you'll graduate from high school. I don't want to speak for the other teachers, but I'm well aware of how well they think of you. Mrs. Mulvaney, especially, feels the same way. I'd encourage you to talk with her too."

Mrs. Mulvaney's English class had been another beacon, showing a way to my future. She knew exactly how to take what I had written in my freshman and sophomore years and help me form and unite my learning with what my life could be.

"Have you thought at all about what you'll do when you leave here?" he asked.

Conversations with my mother and Richter around the dinner table, signing my report cards this year, discussing what I was doing in school, all seemed to exist in both present and future time. "Yes, Mr. Kapinsky. We talked a little about what I would do next. We'd talk about college, but I've wondered whether I could get in and if so, could my family even afford it."

"I'm glad to hear that you've talked about it. I know you've done well through your years here, especially for someone who came to this country not that long ago. If you keep up your good work, I have no doubt that you'll be a strong candidate for college. As for help paying for school, I have some experience with that too. At the very least, I can help you apply, and I'm sure that Mrs. Mulvaney will too."

I sat there taking it all in.

"I've given you a lot to think about, and of course I'm not expecting you to make a snap decision. But promise me you'll think about what I've said."

"Yes, Mr. Kapinsky. I promise."

Like the billowed clouds on that unusually warm spring afternoon, I drifted out of Mr. Kapinsky's classroom, lost in thought and in the day's promise. I daydreamed about a future that in those few moments had opened before me. As I reached our street, my pace quickened at the thought of telling my mother all my teacher had said.

I heard her moving about in the kitchen as I walked through the door. "Mother, I just had this wonderful talk with Mr. Kapinsky. Remember my science teacher? He thinks I have a very good chance of getting into college. He even had some ideas about how to pay for it."

As usual, my mother's unreadable look gave nothing away. Finally, she managed to turn the corners of her mouth into a slight smile. "Is that so?"

"Yes. He said I am one of his best students. He told me that other teachers think the same." I knew better than to say too much about myself, as my mother wouldn't take it well. So, I waited for her to speak.

"Good. Did he say anything else? About what you need to do?"

"Not yet, but he said he'd help me plan."

"All right. As you're late coming home, we need to get dinner on the table. Otto will be home soon."

***

As much as I had hoped this good news would help distract my mother from her disappointment in me, it offered little protection from the madness to come. Not long after I told my mother about my prospects for college, I returned from school another day and she started in again.

"You spend so much time studying that you don't have any friends, do you?" she asked.

I thought about my Hungarian classmates but knew better than to say anything about them. "Actually, I do have a few friends. They don't live near us, so it's hard to see them outside of school, but we're in two classes and study hall and almost always have lunch together. We've even talked about going to the same college in the city."

"You should have friends around here. There's a girl about your age, Diana. She lives just down the street. I see her and her mother at church. You've met her there. You should invite her over for cookies sometime."

This wasn't simply an opinion but a command. "Yes, I remember her," I said. "Next Sunday I'll see if she wants to come over after services."

Diana's Greek family, like so many where we lived, had emigrated to America around the time I came. She was almost my height but rounder, with straight black hair and a light complexion. We had little in common, and not only when it came to our looks. School didn't come as easily for her; she struggled through her courses to the point that working in her father's shoe repair shop had more appeal than the thought of graduating. Still, we made the best of our time when she visited, talking about boys, teachers, and what we remembered of our homelands. My mother seemed pleased with herself for her "suggestion" about Diana.

Then, on one of her visits to our home, Diana confessed that she was failing English. "Oh, that's one of my favorite subjects," I told her.

"Would you help me with my homework?" Diana asked. "I have to write a story, and it's due in a few days."

"What's it about?"

"Coming to America. I'm supposed to talk about what I remember about Athens and my thoughts about being here. What's the same, what's different, you know."

Her assignment was so familiar to me. "Sure, I'd be happy to help. Can you come over before school tomorrow?"

"Oh, that would be great. Thank you!"

The next morning, Diana came by at seven, just as we finished breakfast. We pulled up chairs in the living room and went over what she'd written so far. We had barely begun when my mother came in.

"What are you doing?"

"Diana was having trouble finishing her homework for her English class, so I said I'd help her." I was telling my mother about the assignment when she interrupted me midsentence.

"I need you in the kitchen now."

I excused myself with my mother trailing me, ordering me in a forbidding voice, "Stay there." With that, she left, closing the door to the kitchen and leaving me dreading what might come next. I then heard her ask Diana to leave. On returning to the kitchen, I recognized her all-too-familiar look of fury. It was in her penetrating silence, a venom that poured forth from her fixed stare.

"So you were helping her with homework, were you? How long has this been going on?" As if she knew the answer to her own question, my mother didn't wait for a reply. "Don't you see that she's using you? You help her get ahead, and what do you get out of it? What has she done for you? Nothing. I have such a foolish, stupid girl for a daughter!"

My mother clenched her fists, and the tension in her words terrified me as I felt she was coiled and ready to strike. Without warning, she grabbed my hair. It was all I could do to keep my balance, but that didn't deter her, as her nails dug into my face, scratching lines of red down my left cheek and just missing my eye. I pulled away, then grabbed a tissue and held it against the swelling rivulets. I stumbled into the living room, tucked my books under my arm, and ran out the door.

I dried my eyes as best I could, hoping no one would notice, but when I entered Mr. Kapinsky's class I knew immediately that he saw right through me. As class ended, he rose from his desk and said, "Irene, I'd like you to come by my class during your lunch break today."

"Yes, Mr. Kapinsky." I wasn't about to say no to him, as it took everything to keep my composure at this point. The morning passed. Class after class, my peers whispered around me but said nothing to me.

A few minutes after noon, with little appetite, I made my way over to Mr. Kapinsky's classroom, where I caught him in the middle of a sandwich. As I opened the door, he swallowed quickly and waved me in.

"Irene, it may be none of my business, but in my class today I could see something happened to you and wanted to ask if you might want to talk about it."

I didn't know how or even whether to start. I couldn't make excuses for my mother's cruelties, and I didn't have any way to make sense of them. As much as I wanted someone to help me understand, I wasn't prepared for what I felt would leave me raw and exposed. I couldn't betray my family.

"Thank you for asking, but I don't want to talk about it."

Mr. Kapinsky's pursed lips seemed to keep the words he wanted to say locked within. Instead, he simply nodded. "I know how hard it can be. There were times that my father took out what he was going through on me, and no one ever knew. I'm not you, but I may understand more than you think. If there ever comes a time you want to talk, I'm here." Coming over to where I sat at my desk, he placed his hand gently on my shoulder.

It took everything to not break down before him. Holding back tears, I spoke softly. "Mr. Kapinsky, your words and your offer mean more to me than you may know." Just then, the bell rang for my afternoon history class. "And now I must go, or I'll be late." Little did I know at that time what his understanding and caring would mean for what was to come.

***

The trauma of that time left its scars but steeled my resolve to find a way out. College became my focus, my obsession, my means of escape. My teachers at Evander Childs nurtured that promise of possibility. Mr. Kapinsky had been right about Mrs. Mulvaney. As the spring term started, my fascination with literature and the fiction and poetry I had written found a welcoming home in her class, where I was happy to revisit novels and stanzas, plots and poetic forms, and immerse myself in classics that were new to me. Her encouraging words during the school year took on an intimacy of sorts, from the elementary scrutiny of sentence structure and grammar to what lay within and beyond my storytelling. Like Mr. Kapinsky, my few moments with Mrs. Mulvaney after school and after class opened worlds of possibility, helping me navigate the relative calm waters of that time and the swells and treacherous seas at home.

She often began our meetings by saying, "I was thinking about something you'd written . . . "—her Irish brogue in full bloom. Then after a few criticisms and repairs, which sometimes consisted of a reconfiguring of my creative immigrant misunderstandings, she started in on a short story I'd written about silliness or loneliness or love and longing for the past.

Her parting words at the end of the school year were what I carried into the summer to come. "You've come a long way in my class," she said. "Your grammar has improved, as has your grasp of language and vocabulary. It even seems you've overcome your shyness about speaking up. When you do speak, you usually get right to the point. What's really impressed me are your stories. You have such a passionate voice. And there's something else that comes from within you. Hungary and home, sweetness and sadness. Many of my students come from different countries and write about them too. But what you say, what you feel, what would I call it? The way your express yourself, it's as if you share a certain understanding, an honesty and openness that speaks to them, and me, all of us who have traveled a long distance to come to America."

She rose from her chair now and stood before me.

"In your senior year here, you'll have Mr. O'Hara for English. I've already spoken with him about you and shared some of your writing. You've been a great student to teach, and I'll miss your intelligence and passion for learning. But my advice to you is to not neglect those gifts, as they'll carry you through life."

She was right. My senior-year teachers, especially Mr. O'Hara in English, as well as my science teacher, Mr. Jacobs, took me further down the path set by my junior-year mentors.

As my final year came to an end, I became more determined to apply to college, a decision that set me apart from all but a few of my classmates, as parents and relatives pressured them to carry on the only life they knew: marriage, family, and work. For those about to finish high school, even that success was oftentimes met skeptically unless and until they could draw a direct line from what was considered a waste of time to a good-paying job.

My mother saw education differently. Continuing my studies, graduating from college, and having a successful career were now a part of *our* future. She often laced her encouraging words with more than a tincture of expectation, an assumption, if not a demand, that her wishes, as well as mine, come true. Richter, in his kind and gentle way, never doubted me and supported me as best he could, but he was no match in the presence of such a dominant force. As for me, I came to understand the bitterness born of her unrealized dreams that lay not far below the surface of my mother's words, and I accepted it as the way it would be until I could leave home.

CHAPTER 11

The snow and slush of New York City in December of my senior year cast its gray pall over the concrete-and-brick landscape of our neighborhood, but it failed to distract me from what I needed to do. When I wasn't in class or doing chores or studying for semester finals, I was reading about colleges at the library. Mother continued what she referred to as my lessons in etiquette and sophistication, as I accompanied her to the regal homes of her clients whenever time and tasks allowed. I learned how to set tables with exquisite china and crystal; to observe art, architecture, and haute couture; and to be less intimidated in the company of those with unimaginable wealth. Although these trips took time away from my scholarly passions, I felt the seductive tug of privilege pulling me far beyond the humble places I had known.

Mr. Kapinsky was true to his word, and his intuition about who I was and what lay hidden inside guided me in thought and deed. "Have you decided where you would like to go to college? Your grades are excellent. Your arithmetic, comprehension, and logic scores on that new Scholastic Aptitude Test were among the highest here. You and your family need to decide what's best, but if I were to advise you, I'd suggest aiming high. I'm convinced you have what it takes to do well in any college you choose. As a matter of fact, I have a few ideas in case you're interested."

"I have been thinking about it a lot, Mr. Kapinsky. My mother wants me to stay close to home, but if a very good college somewhere other than New York accepted me, maybe she'd change her mind."

"Well, I'm not surprised that's what your mother wants," he said tersely before continuing. "Have you read at all about the Seven Sisters schools?"

"I read a little about them at the library."

"I mention them because they're the best schools for women. They're not easy to get in to, but you stand a good chance, and I think you'd excel if you were to go to one of them."

I was so happy to hear this. "Do you really think so?"

"Yes. By the way, this doesn't come out of the blue. There's one more thing that I haven't told you. My wife, bless her, went to one of these colleges: Mount Holyoke. It's a great school for women in a very pretty area in Massachusetts. Woods, ivy-covered buildings. Like me, she came with her family from Poland as a little girl, with nothing but the clothes on her back. However, she did have something in common with you: She had a great head on her shoulders—much smarter than me. Her parents were raising three children on a butcher's salary, but they saw the light in her too. They'd saved a little money so she could continue her schooling but not enough to pay for all of it. So, she did something I never thought of doing. She wrote to the three schools where she had sent applications and asked whether they had a way to help poor students who wanted to attend. Mount Holyoke replied, saying that they did."

By now, Mr. Kapinsky was smiling from ear to ear as he reminisced about his wife's good fortune. "To make a long story short, she applied and was accepted. The school covered part of the tuition as well as room and board. To this day, she says those were some of the best years of her life."

Mr. Kapinsky's cheeks had now taken on a reddish glow.

"Irene, you have what it takes. Mount Holyoke would be a great place for you, a great community. It might not happen right away, but I think they'd help you find a way to pay for your schooling once you've taken courses and proven what a wonderful student you are."

"It would be a dream come true for me, but I wouldn't know where to start."

"Not to worry. I'd be happy to help with your application."

Thrilled as I was by Mr. Kapinsky's words, my mother's strong will tempered my enthusiasm. "Thank you, Mr. Kapinsky. I don't think I could do it without you. But I don't know what my mother would say."

"I know your mother wants you to go to school here, but there comes a time for you to make your own way. Aim high, Irene." Then he added, "Please don't take it the wrong way, but I think it would also be good for you to be away from home for a while."

As I rose to go, I nodded in agreement. "I know you're right. I promise to talk to my family, and I will let you know how it turns out."

Mr. Kapinsky had become as familiar and comforting to me as an old coat with little treasures in its pockets, little gems that pointed to a way to fulfill a dream I never imagined possible. Over the following days, I gathered the courage to tell my mother where I would apply, in the hope that she would agree that it was a good idea. A week later, over dinner, I related every detail of my conversation with Mr. Kapinsky, then took a deep breath.

"Mother, I know that you want me to go to a college in New York, and for a while I did too, as it's where my friends are going. But now I don't know. After talking to Mr. Kapinsky, I'm excited to think about Mount Holyoke and all it has to offer."

As my enthusiasm grew with my description, Richter's lips curled up into an expansive grin, a smile that needed no words. Mother sat silently, her face, once again, inscrutable. Richter and I waited for her response.

"So, Mr. Kapinsky thinks you can get into a school like Mount Holyoke?" she asked.

"Actually, he didn't say 'like' Mount Holyoke. He wants me to apply *to* Mount Holyoke. His wife went there and knows it well. He feels I'd do better there than at some of the others. I talked to him about the New York colleges, but he said most don't compare. It's a lot of money, over a thousand dollars, but Mr. Kapinsky thinks I could get a job there after a while and pay for some of it."

The smile remained on Richter's face as he listened. When the words finally came, he spoke with confidence. "I knew this time would come," he said. "I'm so proud of how you've grown into a lovely young woman. I've come to love you like my own daughters. Listening to you now, I can see how excited you are. Just like my three girls were when they set out on their own. I was determined to help them make their futures as bright as could be, and I'm just as determined to do the same for you."

He continued. "I want you to know I've been saving up for just this sort of thing. There's enough to get a good start paying for your four years at Mount Holyoke. And for what remains, I'll work to make sure you get the education that your mother and I didn't have."

His confident words took my mother aback, and she stared at him in disbelief. "Really, Otto?"

"Yes, Mary," he said, with a tone intended to end any questioning of his decision.

My elation and overwhelming gratitude prevailed over these

worries about what she might say or think. There, in that moment, I saw my future setting out before me, emerging from shadows cast by years of doubt and fear.

I sat on my bed that evening, staring through the windowpanes into the darkness outside, revisiting the words Richter spoke at dinner. With his gift, I felt an electricity of possibility coursing through me. For the first time, the future and what I would make of it would be in my hands.

Still in my reverie, I heard Richter climbing the stairs as he made his way to the bedroom, stopping at my door for just a moment. "Irene, dear, I now know I'm blessed with not three but four daughters. You've become not just part of our home. It's as if you've become a part of me." His final words seemed to catch in his throat. "As with me, they would all love you too."

Whatever disagreements my mother and stepfather had, they kept to themselves, behind closed doors. I sensed that ever-present yearning my mother felt in her life and hoped that my Mount Holyoke application might help fill what was missing.

On an early spring afternoon, I sat in my room as I had for the past few weeks, nervously awaiting the mailman. As my mother climbed the stairs, she stopped before my door.

"I haven't said much to you about college since that time over dinner with Otto. I've thought about this Mount Holyoke. I would've liked you to stay in New York, but this school, well, it'll show the neighbors that we're as good as they are. Better, even." Without waiting for a response, she turned and left.

She said nothing more about it over the following weeks. Studies still filled my days, but as the end of my time at Evander Childs neared, school dances and events brought welcome relief and distraction from the anxiety of waiting to hear from Mount Holyoke. It was during one of these school evenings in early March that Joseph Tarini asked me out to a movie. He was nineteen and a senior, taller than I was by a few inches, thin, with olive skin and straight auburn hair that fell across his face, lending a little mystery to his dark-brown eyes.

I was so excited to tell my mother when she came home that evening. I thought she might help me choose a dress, fix my hair, and even have some ideas about what to say and how to act.

"What do you know about this boy, this . . . what is he, Italian? How old is he? Where does he live? What does his father do?"

I answered as best I could. "I think he lives near us, on Underhill Avenue. Joseph doesn't say much about his father or mother. He's a nice boy. He sits behind me in English class. I've talked to him before. A group of us even had lunch together a few times."

"What do you know about boys? You're too young. They can get you into a lot of trouble."

These and other excuses came one after another. Having heard the stories of my father, the estate, the affair, I knew that what Mother said had little to do with me and more about her own regret.

I wanted to say, "That was you, Mother. Don't put what happened to you on me," but I resisted, sitting in silence as she carried on. By the time this "talk" ended, I was more determined than ever to see Joseph, with or without her help.

Up until this time, my mother's opinion about how I looked and dressed ruled the day. Prim and proper, certainly. Ankle-length skirts, frilled blouses, dresses that revealed little were my common attire, as if I were clothed in body armor. At school, my girlfriends and I talked about weight, shape, and styles from head to foot. I thought about such things day and night, along with my ever-present insecurities. Will he think I'm too fat? Will he like my hair and my dress? Am I pretty? Do I really look like my father? Mother thought he was attractive, so maybe I am too? Excited as I was, no encouraging words about my looks and social etiquette from friends or strangers could relieve my anxiety.

Finally, Saturday came. Joseph called on me, and Richter answered the door. I heard the hellos from the top of the stairs.

I continued to listen, relieved that my stepfather alone had greeted him. Richter eased into a conversation with Joseph about the walk to our house, the weather, and the movie we were going to see, a Western. I pulled down on my wool skirt, brushed back my black curls, and looked in the mirror. Far from the models in the magazines, my wide face and hair as dark as pitch made it impossible to hide my Eastern European roots. Pretty? Maybe. Exotic? Perhaps, but my reflection was, for that evening, the best I could do.

Just as I entered the living room, my mother came from the kitchen, her expression nothing more than a polite smile. Joseph's outstretched hand and his smile that had so disarmed and charmed me did nothing to change her lack of enthusiasm. Tension radiated from these moments of silence. I was unsure that any words would ease the awkward exchange, and so I moved to end it.

"Mother, I don't have a scarf to wear that matches my blouse. Can I borrow that pretty red and violet scarf of yours, the cotton one with the frills?"

"Yes, but you'll have to get it yourself. I left the beef tongue stewing on the stove, and if I don't take it out soon, it will fall apart. It's in my closet, on the shelf above where I keep my shoes."

"This'll just take a minute, Joseph," I said as I hurried up the stairs to Mother's bedroom closet. The scarf wasn't where I thought it would be, so I searched in the drawer, pulling out one item after another. Just as I was about to give up, I felt something that didn't belong there. Reaching under some folded sweaters, I pulled out a stack of plain white envelopes tied together with twine. At first, I thought my mother might have been writing home after all and these were letters from my family. I turned them over to see who had sent them and stood, frozen. They were my letters to my grandmother and Magdalene. The emotion I had poured out to them on those pages. None was ever sent. My mother had been true to her word.

Stunned, I forgot about the scarf. My only thought was to leave, afraid of what I would say or do if I were to face my mother at the moment. Once downstairs, I took Joseph's hand and walked toward the front door. "I'll be back after the movie." We left with those few parting words.

Sensing my distress, Joseph took only a few steps before he stopped. "Are you all right, Irene?" he asked.

"I'm fine," I said with a forced smile. There was no way I could tell him what had just happened.

"It was good to meet your parents. Your stepfather is really nice."

I said nothing. My mother's coldness had chilled me. It took a moment before I relaxed enough to speak again. "Thank you for being so nice, Joseph. Now I just want to see the movie with you and not think of anything else."

I left the pain of the moment behind. Forgetting about my mother for a few hours was all that mattered.

***

My evening with Joseph offered only a brief respite from the shock of my discovery. Now I understood why no one had written, but it left me distraught. *Did they think I had forgotten them? That they were no longer a part of my life, just as my mother had wanted?* Yes, Mother had made sure to sever any lingering ties to my past, not caring what those lives meant to me. But what could I do? Trapped in the depths of despair, my application to college had now come to mean a chance to exit, to escape.

Not long after that revelation, an envelope came from Mount Holyoke. With my hands trembling, I fumbled opening it and grew impatient. Grabbing a knife from the kitchen drawer, I finally tore open its contents. There, written on embossed stationary with the college's seal, was Mount Holyoke's answer:

This letter certifies that Miss Irene Richter has fulfilled the entrance requirements and is entitled to admission to the Freshman Class without condition in September 1929. Please notify the Board of Admissions promptly if you do not intend to enter Mount Holyoke in September.

Along with the acceptance came notice that a copy of the final course catalog would follow with a request that I submit a list of preferred courses before school starts.

Pinching myself in disbelief at my good fortune, I raced downstairs and found Richter relaxing in his easy chair with his morning coffee. I didn't need to say a word. He knew exactly what had happened just from the look in my eyes, as big as saucers, and a smile that danced within me.

"I'm so happy for you and so proud."

Our embrace almost toppled him from his chair.

"I feel like I'm floating above the ground! I am so excited!"

I looked at this man and remembered all the faith and love he'd bestowed on me over the years, and I knew my joy would have been impossible without him. "Thank you for all you've done for me. You mean so much to me."

Just then, my mother walked in, sensing the room somehow wasn't how she'd left it.

"I got my letter from Mount Holyoke," I said. "They accepted me for the fall semester."

She stood there, and I studied her, searching for something that would give me a sense of what she was thinking, what she might say.

"Good. Well, then it's settled."

With that, she approached the hall mirror, fluffed her hair, and walked straight out the door to run her usual errands.

CHAPTER 12

Joseph and I continued to see each other over the spring and summer. He worked in his father's carpentry shop as I spent my free time in the library when I wasn't helping my mother. That left Saturdays, which we kept all to ourselves. Van Cortland Park was our favorite destination on temperate days when the heat didn't bake us. I'd prepare picnic lunches of roasted peppers, sharp cheese, freshly baked bread, roast beef, and, when I had the patience, kolaches filled with sweet homemade apricot preserves. We'd walk the length of the park after lunch, making our way over the stone bridges and to the fountain, stopping to take in the beauty of the marigolds and crocuses in the Colonial Garden.

On blisteringly hot afternoons where the concrete seemed about to catch fire, Joseph would treat me to an Italian ice at Firenze's on the Concourse. When the owner, Lorenzo Tancredo, nicknamed "The Tank," a fellow Italian, was at the machine, more often than not, he waved off Joseph when he tried to pay.

Then one evening, Joseph and I each let the veneer that hid the scars of our youth fall away. We had just come from seeing *The Great K & A Train Robbery*. Tom Mix once again foiled the bandits and got the girl. As we walked out, I asked Joseph, "Do you think he ever fell off his horse when it reared up?"

"He's ridden that horse so many times, I bet it's second nature by now."

A few minutes later, as we waited for a car to go by to cross Olinville Avenue, Joseph said, "It's only five o'clock. Luigi's is around the corner from here. Could we stop for a pizza?"

"As long as I'm home by eight," I said.

"Oh," he said, smiling widely, "I'll have you home in plenty of time."

A short distance later, we stood in front of the restaurant. "This is my favorite place to eat. Luigi has been working the pizza oven for years. The whole family came from a town outside of Naples not that long ago, so his English is a little rough, but his pizza is the best."

Entering the restaurant was like stepping into a different country. The pungent aromas of garlic, oregano, and tomatoes seemed to waft over the red-and-white-checkered tablecloths on the ten small wooden tables that took up most of the floor space. Posters and pictures of Italy displayed a bell tower in a town square, a vineyard heavy with grapes ready to harvest, and a view of Naples from on high. On the wall by the cash register were pictures of what looked like several generations of family, great-grandparents on down to a pretty, young woman and handsome man holding an infant. Joseph noticed my gaze fixed on these portraits.

"That's Luigi's family, a mix of those still in the old country and his father and mother, who came here. Oh, and that's Luigi with his wife and son, who he hopes will take over this place someday."

Luigi, now with a number of years and several pounds added

since that photo, came out from the counter that separated the oven from the customers. *"Buonasera, Giuseppe!"*

He greeted Joseph with a full-on bear hug and launched into Italian, with Joseph responding in kind. I understood little other than *madre, padre,* and my name. Then, with a smile from ear to ear, Luigi turned to me. "Welcome, Irina. Come, sit," he said as he pronounced my name in his Italian accent and then led us to a table by the window that looked onto the street.

We sat for a few quiet moments, gazing out, watching families and couples go about their business. Just as the Cokes that Joseph had ordered arrived, I said, "You seem to know a lot of folks in the neighborhood. I'm impressed. Did they know your family?"

"My father loved the little town where he was born. Since I was a young boy, he made a point of bringing me around to his favorite places, run by people like him who had come from Italy, speaking Italian, and making me say hello. At first, I was bored, but now that I'm older, I've learned that it wasn't such a bad idea. They know me as Alfonso's son, but that's okay. It makes me appreciate a little more about where we've come from."

"You haven't told me much about your father, or your mother, for that matter."

"They're from the old country, hardworking but set in their ways. Life hasn't been easy for them, but what they want for me isn't what I want, and that makes it hard sometimes."

"How?"

"For one thing, and it's a big one, the idea of me finishing high school doesn't sit well with them, let alone me going to college. They've started to ask when I'm going to get a job." He hesitated before continuing. "It's led to some arguments and some not-so-pleasant dinners. They talk about my uncle's son, Daniel, who's about my age, how he dropped out in tenth grade and now works with his father as an apprentice for the New York Railroad.

'He's already making two dollars a day,' they say. And so it goes around and around with us. I've stopped trying to change their minds. I just know that there's more for me."

After feeling so wounded by my mother and living in solitude with my pain, I felt oddly comforted that I wasn't alone after all. "I'm sorry, Joseph," I said and reached over to take his hand in mine.

"Yes, it's been tough, but so am I," he replied. "I know what I want, and nothing they say will keep me from it. But what about you?"

I stifled a laugh. "It's funny. School's about the only thing my mother and I agree on. It's as if she knows that's the way to make a better life than the one she's had. She's smart, but I wonder sometimes if . . . if it's a way to relive her life through me."

Joseph was about to ask something, but then Luigi showed up with a piping-hot pepperoni pizza large enough to feed us twice. "*Grazie*, Luigi." After our first bites, as Luigi hovered over us still, Joseph smiled. "*Bene. Multo bene!*"

"*Sei il benvenuto, Guiseppe*," he replied, grinning ear to ear. He could see my delight as I eyed another slice. "I'm so happy you like it," he said, and with that he took his leave.

We ate our way through each delicious piece, leaving only a few crusts and two slices. "You can take that home to your mother and stepfather if you like."

"Thank you. I know they'll love it."

As we sat in a slight stupor, Joseph said, "I'd love to go to a Hungarian restaurant. Do you know any?"

"There's a restaurant not far from us, but we only go there on holidays."

"Don't you ever miss it? I mean, do you miss where you came from?"

"It's a long story. Let's just say that my mother wanted nothing to do with her past, and she's told me that's the way it should be with me."

Taking my hand, he leaned in close to me. "Now I'm the one who's sorry."

"So am I, Joseph."

During the first times we were together, I revealed little about my mother. When the time came that I couldn't hold back my preoccupation, he listened, his words, his friendship comforting, never pressing. And when he took me in his arms a month after our first date, after our latest evening at the movies, what had consumed me eased and fell away for the moment.

Just being with Joseph stirred feelings I'd never known before but seemed so natural. We held hands and shared our first kiss. I had no idea what would come next for us as desire, passion, and anticipation mixed with unsteadiness. At first, this potpourri of emotions left me reluctant to steer our time together into any waters that might leave us adrift. Gradually I felt safe to venture further out, pouring out what I had kept within about my distraught home life and the hope for a future that college offered.

These weeks and months didn't go over well with my mother. Her distant but distinct doubts turned darker, her questioning sharper and ominous, like clouds gathering on the horizon. "You and Joseph see a lot of each other," she once said. "Don't tell me that you just go on walks or have a Coke at the diner and that's all. And those movies you say you're going to. What do you do all those times?"

My attempts to allay her suspicions came to nothing. Then, one August evening, my mother made it clear she had no intention of letting it go.

"I see the way you look when you go out, dressing like you do. You're asking for trouble if you haven't gotten into trouble already."

"Mother, I'm not in any trouble. And as for the way I dress, it's what my girlfriends wear and what's in the fashion magazines these days."

"It makes you look cheap, with the makeup and showing your legs like you do. I see how tight your dresses are. You're asking for it. Don't think you're fooling me."

"I don't know what to say to you other than nothing has happened between us. But when you talk like this, you frighten me."

"Maybe that's what you need. I don't trust that boy. I know what boys and men want, and if it takes you being scared, maybe that will keep you out of trouble."

Although my mother's love still meant everything to me, I was once again realizing the high price I would pay for it. Even if I paid that price, what would that love mean? What *was* her love, and would it even last? Or would there always be something new, something I would have to read into her gestures, words, and the way she looked at me? As she doubted me without any reason, I began to see a window into her life—her infinite distance from Grandmother and how, once again, what she was saying had more to do with her own life than mine.

Her suspicions grew more intense over the summer months and left me fearful but defiant. I knew these months with Joseph would end with me going off to college, but I had no intention of giving up our remaining time together.

On one of those last days of summer, Mother unfurled the fury that, by now, she barely hid. On a sultry August evening, Joseph walked me home as he had done many times before. Usually he took me to the door and no further, but that night he hesitated.

"What is it, Joseph?"

"I don't know. With what you've been telling me about your mother, I feel funny about not coming in with you."

"That's so kind of you, but I can manage. It's fine."

"Just this one time, let me bring you in," he said. "Who knows—maybe she'll want to wish me well."

We kissed and went in. Part of me was relieved that he stayed.

Mother had been expecting me and looked as if she had built up a head of steam. Alone as she was, with Richter working late, she sat at the kitchen table, a dour expression on her face.

"Mrs. Richter, I wanted to say hello and also maybe goodbye, as Irene will be leaving for school soon and I may not see you for a while."

Mother nodded. "Sit, Joseph. I've been wanting to talk to you."

Joseph pulled out a chair opposite Mother at the kitchen table. I sat in the middle. The usual cookies and sweets were nowhere to be found.

"You and Irene have seen a lot of each other this year. For . . . how many months has it been?"

"Going on six months, Mrs. Richter. I like your daughter very much. I'm sorry to see her go away to school. I'll miss her."

My mother dismissed these words, as they were of no interest to her. She spoke as if she had prepared for this moment. "Just what are your intentions with my daughter?" she demanded.

Joseph looked stunned. "I'm sorry, Mrs. Richter. I don't understand."

"I mean, Joseph, that when two people have spent as much time together as you two have, most respectable men would make a commitment to the woman."

"As I said, Mrs. Richter, I like your daughter very much and hope—"

My mother was just warming up. "Let me finish. As you know, Irene's twentieth birthday was in July. She was expecting at least a commitment from you, if not a ring. And what did you get her for her birthday? A book. You gave her a book!"

I couldn't sit by silently any longer. Joseph and I had never spoken about the future, as we had known months ago that I would leave for Mount Holyoke. Whatever was going on with my mother was of her own making and had nothing to do with us.

"What are you talking about?" I asked. "I didn't say anything about wanting something from Joseph. I like him very much, but I'm leaving in a few weeks." *Was she thinking he was supposed to wait for me? Or was it something else?* What I was about to say, that what had happened to her when she was young is not what would happen to me, caught in my throat. Instead, I said, "This isn't the time" and hoped that would be the end of this inquisition.

My words meant nothing to her. Her inquisition had already taken hold and would now play out. Glowering, with her elbows on the table, she leaned in closer to Joseph, pointing her index finger at him.

"Did you have sexual intercourse with my daughter?" she said, her eyes narrowed and teeth gritted.

Joseph struggled to respond but then answered with his quiet but firm voice. "No, Mrs. Richter. No."

His answer seemed to leave her flustered but not finished. "Well then, Joseph, tell me: What would you do if Irene were your daughter?"

He seemed to regain his composure with that question. Looking directly at my mother, he replied, "At this age, if my daughter were as bright and mature as Irene, I don't feel I could tell her what to do any longer, but I would want her to know that I loved her and that I was there for her, to help her if she asked me."

My mother's face turned crimson before she blurted out a curse in her barely stifled rage. "I wish on you all daughters. I hope you have all daughters!"

She was at a loss to say more. Joseph stood and said goodbye. I followed him outside. My eyes brimmed with tears as I said "I'm so sorry."

He kissed me gently but followed with a warning: "I don't know what's going on with your mother, but she scares me. I'm glad you're leaving for school soon, but I don't know what these last days will be like with her."

As we parted, I tried to assure him as best I could. "I can't tell you all that's eating at her, Joseph. But please don't worry about me. With Father Richter there, I'll be okay."

I was shocked and humiliated by what had happened and expected my mother to continue her tirade after he left. I locked the door, and by the time I went back to the kitchen, she had disappeared into her bedroom. Minutes later, Richter let himself in. As soon as he saw me, he knew something was wrong. Trying to keep from crying again, I only said that we'd had a disagreement. I didn't want him to be caught in the middle, but I knew he would ask my mother what had happened.

The next morning, as he was leaving for work, Richter stopped me just as I was getting ready to leave for school. "I don't know what comes over your mother. Maybe your leaving for college really is for the best. Maybe once you're gone, she'll feel differently. Just know I'll do what I can to help and protect you."

His words didn't ease my pain, but I knew they were my hope and the truth.

In the days that followed, no one spoke of that evening, but the words hung in the air like ashes drifting from an unquenchable flame. I busied myself with packing, goodbyes to friends, and last visits to the library to learn what I could about what to expect in the coming weeks and months. Richter tended to whatever I needed: train schedule, finances, things for school. I agonized as time's door began to close. The day before leaving, I gathered the courage to speak to my mother.

"I don't want to go without talking with you about what happened that night with Joseph."

She continued to stir the goulash on the stove, but I was determined not to let it go without trying.

"I don't think there's anything I can say that will change your mind about what I did or didn't do, and about Joseph and me. All I can tell you is what I know to be true and that I've told the truth. Please trust me. Believe in what I say. I've never given you any reason not to."

She turned away from the pot and pointed the ladle at me. "You don't think you've given me any reason to doubt you? You're the one who decided against my wishes to leave me and go away to school. I'll make the best of it. As for your Joseph, I was suspicious when you told me about the boys you liked at school. When you spend so much time with one boy, I know what that leads to. I'm surprised you're not pregnant."

I slouched into the understanding that this was going nowhere.

"Okay, Mother. You win. I know you've sacrificed for me, to bring me here to be with you. I know Mount Holyoke wasn't what you wanted for me, but you seemed okay with it. Now that I'm going, I want to make you proud of me. It's such a good school, and so much of what you've taught me about how to hold myself, how to act, what to do—I owe all of that to you. I am grateful to you, Mother, more than you know."

She replied in a voice tinged with doubt. "I guess we'll just see how this works out. Won't we?"

***

The next day was a whirl and flurry of last-minute tasks before leaving, as I was so caught up in not forgetting all I needed for school. I didn't know my mother would come to see me off until that morning when she asked about the train schedule.

"I picked up some things if you get hungry on the train or when you get to college," she said, gesturing to the kitchen table.

I smiled. The bag's contents held their own truth: that even for my mother, severing all ties to me was impossible. In it were sausages, bread, cheese, fruit, and sweets, just like Grandmother's last gift to me.

"It means more than you know," I said. "Thank you."

As we spoke, Richter appeared at the door of the kitchen with my suitcase. "It's time for us to go. Is your suitcase ready for the car? It'll take some time to get to Grand Central."

"Yes, Father. I only need to get my purse and a small bag upstairs."

My mother grabbed a scarf, looked in the mirror, and followed him out.

On the ride to the station, I promised to send a letter soon after arriving at Mount Holyoke. "We'll write too," Richter replied, "and perhaps mail you a little something. Let us know if you need money. You should have enough for the first few months."

"I will, Father."

After parking the car, we entered the noisy chasm of Grand Central, purchased my ticket, and waited. Richter sat quietly, asking only if I had forgotten anything or if there was something I needed. My mother sat silently, observing the rush of people around her. Then the announcer let us know the train was ready to board.

"Goodbye, Father. Thank you for everything."

He smiled, and I kissed him on the cheek.

No smile came from my mother. When I embraced her, she offered only the stiffness and reticence I knew so well. No words would make a difference, so I turned to go, waved, and soon lost sight of them.

Part III
Learnings

CHAPTER 13

I had never before thought of a school as a salve, an elixir for body and soul. My first memory of Mount Holyoke was feeling overwhelmed and entranced: stone, stained glass, moss-covered bridges arching over a stream that flowed into waterfalls. Wrought-iron gates opened into a semicircular driveway. An ivy-covered wall rose with a clock tower in a row of buildings set flat against a walkway. Plinths with statues set upon them stood for stories and history I would come to learn. Trees! So many trees! Birch, oak, maple; their bark, branches, leaves, strength unknown. I came to learn all their names. I was to sit under and among their boughs with the feel of grass and earth beneath me for the days and years to come.

I found my way to the registrar's office, awed and anxious about what would come next. Office staff directed me to Cowles Lodge, my home for the next four years. I followed a long wooden walkway and crossed a footbridge with a single lamp overhead and water gently flowing below. Passing around another grove, I looked up. There, in a clearing, sitting atop an incline behind a gated wooden fence, was my destination. Its bright-white siding contrasted with the verdant surroundings, and the structure, with angled roof and sides, had a familiar shape, like a barn, except that a slatted porch ran its length. A second connected building, also with an angled shape, sat farther back.

I entered an open foyer and lounge. Many Cowles Lodge students had already arrived and sat around in a makeshift semicircle chattering away. I stood there only a moment before a blonde girl bounced up from her chair and greeted me.

"Hi, my name's Ruth. I'm, I guess you could say, the unofficial meeter and greeter."

"I'm Irene, Irene Richter."

"Oh, so you're Irene," said another, taller girl with straight brown hair, who broke into a smile and joined us. "I'm Esther, your roommate."

"Nice to meet you, Esther."

My first impressions of the Cowles girls? Some displayed the kind of elegance I remembered from my visits with my mother to the Upper East Side. Others dressed more like me, in plain skirts and blouses and sensible shoes. While clothes may have set them apart, their animated conversations, and even where they sat, blurred lines of class. They quickly drew me into their den of curiosity and camaraderie, asking question after question. Where did I come from? How was my trip? Was I related to Claire Richter, a senior in Wilder?

The warmth of that indelible moment melted away the anxiety I'd carried to the Cowles front door.

I had little sense of what was to happen before arriving at Mount Holyoke, but I somehow knew the world would be different, foreign, unknown but waiting to be discovered: from the intimacies of friendships and social life to the classes and curricula. Good fortune started with Esther.

"At Cowles and the other lodges, it's not typical for upper-division students to room with freshmen. I wanted to try something different, though. I was asking our head of Cowles, Mrs. Kennedy, about our new Cowles residents, and she told me about you coming from Hungary and living in New York. My father has an office there. I thought, why not? I don't know anything about Hungary, and I could learn about a new country. As for New York, I might like to live there sometime and maybe she can tell me if she thinks it's awful, great, or somewhere in between."

"Thanks for taking a chance on me. I hope you won't be disappointed."

We entered our lodge room, nondescript but for what was on the walls. "I hope you don't mind, but as I'm in my third year here, I've accumulated a few things. I've always liked to take pictures, and so what you see above my bed is all mine."

"I'm amazed," I said as I stood before them. "Your photos, they're beautiful. Are they scenes from around the school?"

"I'm so happy you like them," Esther replied, smiling. "Some are from around here, although, as pretty as Holyoke is, wait 'til you see what's beyond the campus . . . See this one? Last semester a few girls from the house hiked to Bare Mountain. I took that from the top looking over the trees and river. And this one? My zoology professor was on the hike with us one time, and I got a chance to take a picture, of all things, of a bear. I was scared but so excited."

"I don't have much to hang on my wall, so if you want some extra wall space for them, I'd be happy for you to use it."

"Oh, that's great. We can look through my scrapbook, and you can pick out some. Much of the rest you see is basic stuff for the room. I did buy the floor lamp between my bed and desk when I first got here, and then a friend of mine who was graduating gave me the one by your desk. If you don't want it, that's okay."

"That's so kind of you. I didn't even think of what I would need for my room other than a picture of my family, an old doll I grew up with, and a few books."

Esther, being a junior, was a font of knowledge. She regaled about teachers, events, clubs, the other "Cowles girls," and the boys at the international college nearby. Esther's family, unlike mine, had been in America for generations. The Hammersmiths lived in Boston, and her father was in banking. She told me about where she grew up, her home life, her maid, and her favorite person, James the butler, who had been with them since she was born. Otherwise, Esther rarely spoke about her inherited wealth. The trinkets, picture frames, and other possessions she'd brought to school were modest. Only her closet, with its fur coat and silk dresses rich in color and texture, revealed that part of her life. But I never felt class differences in what we said and did together. And as we grew closer, I felt that in time I had found someone to trust, to reveal what I had hidden away for so few to see, what I had carried with me across waters, and what I lived with now.

Swept up in my first few weeks at Holyoke, I hadn't yet written Joseph, but somehow his letter found its way to me, addressed only to the school. His words were as warm as ever, weaving stories about his first days at school with how much he missed me. After classes that day, I curled up on the sofa by the fireplace at Cowles that cool autumn evening and wrote about my immersion into another world so far from what I had left behind. I wanted to tell him everything: about the lodge and its residents; demanding assignments even in these first days; and the beauty of the campus. Closing the letter, I wrote:

I miss you too, Joseph. I smile when I think of you and all you've meant to me.

***

Those early days with Esther and the other girls at the lodge gave way to the first classes of the term. English, the sciences, history,

German, and math allowed little time for distractions. Esther was of no help, as we'd spend much of the night talking and laughing about all things. The library, with its rules for silence and its surrounding stacks, rescued me from diversion. Each night, after lectures and dinner, I'd gather books, papers, and assorted pens and pencils, walk to the library, and find an empty desk. Once there, I quickly came to understand all that Evander Childs didn't prepare me for and what it would take to stay afloat at college.

My first-term courses absorbed as much of myself as I could give them, with some professors fussier when it came to assignments and their coursework needing even more time, care, and feeding. Some classes, such as physiology with Dr. Bennet, I took to immediately. Her smile disarmed me, and her patience seemed limitless as I stayed after class, time after time, asking questions about that day's content. Our math professor, Dr. Russell, seemed annoyed with us most days as she wrote imponderable calculations on the blackboard and I, along with many others, at first sat with my head in my hands. Even our opaque textbook, which she authored, was written in what seemed a foreign numerical language, and that was a point of pride for her.

"Look at my section on derivations. John Kerrington's textbook takes ten pages to explain what I cover in two paragraphs."

Concise? Yes. But it took what seemed endless hours of study to decipher the algebraic hieroglyphics she laid before us.

Then the weekend arrived. As one of only a handful of upperclass women at Cowles, Esther used her powers of persuasion on our "resident adult," Mrs. Kennedy, to organize hikes off campus, where she could indulge her love of photography. One time, Mount Sugarloaf was our destination. Another time, it was a climb up Mount Holyoke, and another, a boating trip on the Connecticut River. We visited this land of beauty often, always finding something we'd never seen before. A world of landscapes I'd only imagined took me away from study, from the Bronx, and from the roiled sea of strife at home. Only a letter from Joseph in early October brought me back. He wrote that classes were harder than he had expected. But at least he was finding time for weekend parties with a new group of friends, and one, Gina, whom he had known from his English class at Evander Childs. I had spoken with her a few times during lunch at school, but we'd never spent any time together. Still, I asked Joseph to say hello for me.

***

New friendships opened new worlds to me. Everything before seemed small, confined. In the expansive world of Holyoke, the school nurtured and encouraged women to pursue knowledge and find a place to progress and lead. Faculty and administration at the college had embraced the protests around the right for women to vote and continued to pursue the hopes born from the suffragists. While social calendars, dates, and the latest fashions were always in play during our weekends and evenings, so too were conversations about current events. Talk about the lingering effects of the Great War and the dark clouds gathering on the European horizon mixed with animated discussions of favorite books and least favorite professors. Even the president of the college, Mary Woolley, wasn't off limits.

"Do any of you have Professor Marks for English lit?" Sarah, a freckle-faced freshman with flaming-red hair, asked as if she knew something we didn't. I had Professor Foster, but three freshmen girls at Cowles were in her class. Susan, tall, slender, with ruddy cheeks, was the first to speak. "She's pretty good with Donne, Byron, and other poets, but I'm not crazy about her. You're not in her class. Why do you care?"

"Well, I heard that Professor Marks and President Woolley are, let's just say, *together.*"

I looked around the room. We in our first year all seemed to register the same astonished look. The upper-class girls didn't change their expressions.

"What?" almost all seemed to say at the same time. Sarah picked up the cue. "You know that Professor Marks came to Holyoke right after President Woolley took over. They spend a lot of time together. They're not married, and they don't have boyfriends."

I didn't know what to say, but I looked over at Esther, as she grew more agitated with Sarah's gossip. Finally, she'd had enough. "What's your point, Sarah?"

"I'm just saying, don't you think it's peculiar?"

"Are you saying they're homosexuals? Is that it? Listen, Sarah, Professor Marks is the best poetry teacher here. As for President Woolley, she's done some great things for this school. She's raised a lot of money for classrooms and other buildings. Do you know some people say that our college is one of the most beautiful in the country? She made sure of that. I know you've been to New York. You know how beautiful Central Park is. Well, guess who was hired to help design Holyoke. Mr. Frederick Olmsted, the same person who designed Central Park. After Mr. Olmsted died, President Woolley worked with his sons to make sure their father's dream for Holyoke would become the beautiful place it is today.

"Oh, and a few other things," Esther added, becoming more animated. "If it weren't for her, the great education we're getting would take a back seat, if that, to finding a husband, having kids, following whatever the man of the house would tell us to do. So, to answer your question about President Woolley and Professor Marks, I don't care to know, and even if it were true, which no one really knows, what difference would it make?"

Silence fell over the room. No one said anything else about it that evening, and I never heard it mentioned again. Esther's words rang true for me, an immigrant like many others, who only wanted to lead a good life but who knew what it felt like to be seen at times through the suspicious eyes of others.

These conversations about students, professors, and Holyoke absorbed my attention early on in my first semester. But one particular day and its aftermath left an indelible mark. At first, I didn't think much about what happened on October 29, 1929. The front-page headline announcing the Wall Street Crash came up over coffee, and a few of the professors mentioned it in class. However, it didn't disappear like other headlines. Its devastation didn't come all at once but spread like a virus that slowly took hold. It was crippling for some and fatal for others.

Corinne's tragedy administered the first shock at Cowles. We had never talked much about money or gone into detail about how much one's family had. For Corinne, there was no need to, as her ease in social gatherings, the way she dressed, and her demeanor spoke volumes. Then, one cold day in early November, as we sat around the fire at the lodge, enjoying an evening of nothing unusual, Corinne's mother phoned.

Corinne excused herself and went into the other room.

We didn't pay much attention to her absence, absorbed as we were with upcoming social events at the school, until a scream cascaded down the stairs into the heart of the house. We sat frozen as if the sound had strapped us in. A minute later, Corinne flashed by us and ran out the door. May, one of the juniors, jumped up and disappeared after her. Neither of them returned, and no response came from the other side of the closed door. Then, as if we all understood the gravity of the moment at once, we rushed outside. There, on a browning patch of ground not far from the lodge, lay Corinne with May sitting by her side.

Mrs. Kennedy approached the girls. Whatever words she spoke seemed to infect every bone and muscle in Corinne's body, as she fell almost in a faint.

We didn't know what to do. We wanted to go to them but were unable to move. Finally, May came to us, as by now Mrs. Kennedy was hugging Corinne as she shook and sobbed.

"Some of you know that Corinne's father worked in New York

for a company that bought and sold stocks," she said. "He and his clients lost all their money. Today he jumped from the thirtieth floor of the building where he worked. The only other thing her mother said is that he didn't say anything to anyone about what he was going through. He just ended it."

It was as if a knife had pierced us all at once.

Many of us remained on edge, knowing that Corinne's family wasn't alone in its anguish after that day. Everyone was relieved that none of the other Cowles girls ended up suffering as she had, but changes followed the crash of 1929. Weekend shopping trips to the high-end shops in Boston dropped off. Gifts from home, perfumes, jewelry, and care packages stopped coming for many of the girls. Tears and tension followed phone calls. Some whose lives weren't quite as upended adjusted to the new reality. Others were at a loss as to what to do. Where they hadn't taken much of an interest in how I got along on so little, how I managed suddenly drew considerable interest at the lodge.

Sarah was the first, cornering me one cold, snowy afternoon when I was alone in the library. We hadn't talked much since the exchange about President Woolley and Professor Marks, so when she approached my desk, I was a bit surprised.

"Hi, Irene," she said with hesitation. "Are you studying for the math test tomorrow?"

Lost in an equation, I nodded absently.

"So am I." Then, breaking a moment of awkward silence, she continued. "Can I ask you a question?"

"Sure."

"I was wondering. I've never seen you go shopping with the other girls. And you dress so down-to-earth."

"I can't afford to go shopping. It's no secret my family doesn't have much money. So some of the things that you and other girls at Cowles have, well, it's just not possible."

"Is that okay? Don't you wish you could?"

"Oh, it'd be nice, but I really don't mind. I'm used to it. Just like home. The only difference here is that I have to be more careful about what I spend. But before I left, my stepfather sat me down and showed me how."

"Really? What did he show you?"

"He made me write down what I'd need to get by each week and for the semester. Food, toiletries, and things to wear that I didn't have at home, like boots and socks for hiking and the snow. We figured out how much each week and what else I'd need, but not more. We made up a sheet, a ledger for expenses, filling in what we thought they would be, and that's what helps me manage. My mother wrote just this week to say that my stepfather doesn't have as many customers as he did before the Great Crash, so I'm trying to spend even less, and I've started to look into earning money earlier than I'd thought I would. But so far our plan's worked pretty well."

I sensed that Sarah's interest was more than idle curiosity. "Why do you ask?"

"I've never had to do that. My mother and father seemed to have all the money they needed. It's the way I grew up. So, when I came here, they just said 'Let us know what you want and what you need.' That was it. Then something changed after that time at the end of October. I got worried sick about my father after what happened to Corinne's dad. He's okay so far. But my parents told me they lost a lot of money, and now it's different. I don't have a clue as to how to do with less and to, as you said, 'manage money.'"

Now I understood. Not wanting to make it any more difficult than it already was, I tried to lead where I thought she wanted to go. "Can I help in any way?"

That broke the ice. A flood of questions followed, but that wasn't all. Sarah spread the word, and before long, others at Cowles in similar situations came calling for advice, and in a small but singular way, the need to manage their funds became a window into their lives.

There was Janet, tall, aristocratic in her poise and posture, always proper in dress and demeanor, who, up until then, had kept to her own circle at the lodge. Tapping on my door one day, she came right to the point.

"Hi, Irene. I know we haven't spent much time together, but Sarah said you've been a real help to her."

With that, she told of her father's bespoke tailor shop, which had served the rich and almost famous—and a few infamous—clientele of Newport, Rhode Island. Shortly after the end of October, however, his business crashed, leaving little save a diminishing savings account. All that tumbled out of Janet's mouth as we stood at the door.

"Come in, Janet."

Like Sarah, Janet was a quick and eager learner. Leaving late that afternoon, she touched my shoulder, smiled, and said, "Irene, I don't know what I would have done without you."

Others followed. Christine, whose father, the chef and owner of Le Boutonniere in New York, a restaurant she quickly let me know was the finest in the city, had lost everything and was selling off the tables, chairs, kitchenware, and even his priceless collection of French wine.

I listened and quickly understood she was in the same boat as the others.

"I never thought about money or what they call 'cash flow.' Or keeping a list of what I spent and what I had."

Like the others, Christine was so grateful for my simple guidance.

Through it all, Esther was a good sport about yet another knock at the door. She would simply say with a smile, "Here we go again."

Beyond that, the Great Crash did something I hadn't anticipated.

Class differences, subtle but still present from the start, fell away. A common plight became common ground, lessening the distance between where we came from and who we were.

CHAPTER 14

I spent hours still learning the nuances of English grammar and sentence structure not quite mastered in high school. Science demanded equal time, which I was happy to give to it. Laboratory assignments and quantitative experiments often absorbed late afternoons and evenings. I hadn't heard from Joseph since his October letter and was surprised and pleased to see an envelope with his name and return address. His letter began with the latest about grades, tests, and the weather. I read through it quickly on my way to history class, until I came to the last paragraph, which froze me where I stood. He had saved his upending news for the end. He and Gina had been dating since meeting at a party. They had spent most days together and had fallen for each other. He didn't know if it would last, but he felt it was unfair not to tell me. In the very last line, he wrote:

Dear Irene, I never thought this would happen, and I'm sorry. I'll miss your smile, your eyes—so alive with love and compassion—and the stories of our lives we have shared. I hope you can understand and forgive me.

I remember little from classes that day, lost as I was in reminiscence and regret. Returning to Cowles, I could no longer hold back my tears. Esther rose from her desk as soon as I entered.

"What is it, Irene?"

"It's Joseph," I sobbed. "I know I haven't said much about him to you, but now that he's met someone else, I feel such a loss. It's something that I half expected when I left for college, but now that it's happened, it just hurts."

Esther wrapped her arms around me. With her eyes welling up, she spoke softly. "I know nothing I say will make up for your loss. I'm just so sorry this happened to you."

"I feel as if I've lost a part of myself—lost someone who helped keep me from falling apart, who made me feel I wasn't alone."

"I know it's not the same, but you aren't alone, Irene. This may not mean much now, but I'm here for you."

No words could erase my anguish. But somehow I sensed that her kindness would see me through these dark days.

***

When Thanksgiving arrived, most girls went home to join their families, but papers were due, so I, along with more classmates than I'd expected, celebrated Thanksgiving at Cowles. During the break, we drank tea or hot cider by the light of the fireplace every night. And on Thanksgiving Day, we all feasted on a traditional turkey dinner in the dining hall, squirreling away leftovers for the days that followed.

I missed home, but the warmth of company and the beauty of Holyoke, with its trees, paths, clock tower, and our lodge nestled in snow, more than filled that empty space. Tests, assignments, and final drafts left no time to think of anything but what the teachers required. Then, what seemed to never end was over. We'd all be celebrating Christmas and New Year's in just a few days.

I made my way to the station and boarded the train home. I had hidden my past away from others with all that school demanded but now was about to return to it. Would things be different? Mother's letters, filled mostly with news of well-worn routines and rituals—work, church, neighbors—had given few clues.

My stepfather was at the train station alone, waiting for me as I arrived late Saturday afternoon before Christmas. As I approached, I couldn't help but notice he seemed paler and more stooped than before. Still, his smile and embrace set me at ease.

"Welcome back, Irene. It's so good to have you with us again. Your mother wanted to come, but she's working. She should be back by the time we get home. What about you? How is college? I've loved your letters. You seem so excited and happy."

"I am. I've made so many new friends, and it's such a beautiful campus. You and Mother must come and see it sometime. It's not easy. I'm still catching up a little in English class, but the science classes have been great. It's early, but I do know I want to take more next year."

Once we were in the car, questions I hesitated to ask tumbled out.

"How is Mother?"

"The same."

"Has she said anything about me coming for the holidays?"

"Oh, she's been bragging to anyone who will listen about her daughter going to one of the best schools in the country, better than sons and daughters of her friends, and she wants to show you off."

"Do you think she's missed me?"

"Yes. We both have."

"And you? How are you doing?"

Richter hesitated as if he didn't know what to say next. "Work's been a little harder to come by these days. I lost more than a few clients this year, and few have come back. Diamond setting is a luxury many people can't afford. Even some of the places where your mother worked stopped asking her to come. I still have savings. I was smart not to invest in the stock market, but I did put money into the banks, and they're a hard luck story too. We live on a little less these days, but we get by."

"I've started to look for a job at the school. I may work in a lab. By next term I should know more."

"Money isn't your concern. I told you I planned for your education."

Knowing his pride, I changed the subject.

"Remember Joseph?"

"I do. How is he?"

"He's good. He's going to New York University and is doing pretty well. But as for the two of us, it's not the same. When I first got to school, we wrote and said how we missed each other. But then, in his last letter, he told me he'd met someone at school. Since then, I haven't heard from him."

"I'm sorry, Irene."

"I am too. I miss him terribly. But I'm not surprised after the way Mother treated him."

By then, we were home. As Richter carried my suitcase from the trunk, I stood at the bottom step of our home. Taking a deep breath, I opened the door and entered. I knew my mother was back, as the lights were on in the kitchen. Before she could say a word, I wrapped my arms around her just as I had eight years ago on Ellis Island. Her body once again felt stiff and stolid, and in that instant I was twelve again. Still, I took heart in her slight smile.

Stepping back, she eyed me up and down. "I see you haven't starved at school. What happened to your curls?"

"They feed me well, but we get a lot of exercise hiking and even mountain climbing every once in a while. As for my hair, shorter styles are what girls are wearing these days."

Sensing more scrutiny, I shifted the conversation to stories about teachers, courses, the dining hall, the outdoors. I told her about making new friends, evenings around the fireplace, gossiping about the day, and, most of all, my roommate, Esther.

Then there was Cowles Lodge. "Mother, there's something special about Cowles Lodge. I guess you could call it a spirit and a history we've all come to know. There's even a rhyme we have for it:

Cowles is a castle that's most picturesque,
In a style neither Gothic nor true Romanesque.
Those who would storm it find entrance a task;
Those who are in it have nothing to ask.

Isn't it lovely?"

"I don't understand those words," my mother said. "What do they mean?"

"The first part says it's a very pretty place that sits like a castle, though I will say it's not as beautiful as some in Hungary. Gothic and Romanesque are building styles from the olden days. The third line reminds me of when I saw it on a hill in the distance. Not easy to get to but very imposing. The final line is about those who live there: that for me and the other girls, Cowles has all we need."

"I still don't understand most of what you're saying."

"I had to learn all about ancient times, and I've come to love poetry much more too." Seeing her curiosity as an opening, I smiled and rose from the table. "Just a minute." I grabbed my history text, came back, sat down with her at the kitchen table, and opened the book to Greece.

"Since you seem interested in the poem about Cowles Lodge, let me tell you a bit more about it. Remember when we became citizens, and we had to learn about the US Constitution? Remember the words 'We the People'? Well, in many ways we have Greece to thank for that since that's where democracy began. I learned that the word *democracy* actually comes from two words: *demos*, meaning people, and *kratien*, meaning to rule. You know how when I came here, you wanted me to learn English and to live as an American? I never forgot those words, as they meant something so different where we came from. I could never imagine anything like that in Hungary."

My mother was taking it all in. This little history lesson, with its great significance for her adopted country, brought that slight upturn to her lips.

"While I'm home, maybe I could tell you more about what we're learning about Rome, the temples, and what life was like in ancient times."

As she cast a suspicious eye, I could tell she was thinking about it. "With all I'm doing around the holidays, I won't have time," she said coolly.

***

I wasn't sure what to expect that first evening, but my parents' curiosity about Holyoke, my adventures, and life away from home left little room for admonition or censure. Even Richter stayed up well past his usual bedtime. I went to bed that night thinking maybe things *had* changed for the better. Perhaps I had become an independent young woman in Mother's eyes, deserving to do well in a world of my creation.

We all were off to church Sunday morning. My mother always preferred the eleven o'clock High Mass, as it was the weekly occasion when she performed with the choir. Just as before, she climbed the stairs near the entrance and assumed her place among the others, leaving the two of us to find our pew. For the next hour, organ and voices joined in songs of worship and praise. And when "Ave Maria" and "Christ Be Our Light" echoed throughout, her soprano soared above all.

I expected to see my mother waiting for us near the holy water font as we filed out after the final blessing, but we only caught up with her when we stepped outside. She had corralled three women, two of whom I recognized as our Italian neighbors down the street and another whom I only knew from the church choir.

"Irene," she called out and motioned for us to come join her. "You've met Mrs. Berudi and Mrs. Di Paolo. You also know Mrs. Szalagi. I was just talking with them about you, telling them that you go to one of the best schools. Isn't that true?"

Not waiting for me to answer, she continued. "A lot of rich people send their daughters there. Irene, you were telling me about all the girls you live with, the nice furs and expensive jewelry they wear and trips they make to all the fancy stores in Boston. Oh, and how pretty the school is, the trees, old buildings, even where you live. I don't know anybody whose daughter is going to any school like it."

The three women stood silently, each sharing the same wan smile. However, my mother wasn't finished. "Mrs. Di Paolo, your daughter, Anna, where does she go? I know you told me once, but I forgot. Isn't it one of the local schools?"

Mrs. Di Paolo answered in a soft but proud voice. "Yes, she goes to City College and is doing very well there. She wants to be a social worker and help people. It wasn't something she set out to do, but after what's happened since October and all the suffering she's seen in the city—the bread lines, people with no place to live—she wants to find a way to help. My husband and I and our two other children also love that she still lives with us. She takes the trolley to school each day. As hard as she studies, Anna still helps us at home too."

My mother's smug expression fell away, as I could tell she hadn't expected this woman's reply. Instead of the envy she had antic-ipated, my mother, along with the rest of us, felt Mrs. Di Paolo's defiance and certainty about her own daughter. She had turned my mother's vanity around on her.

"It must be hard not having your daughter home with you. Irene, what about you? Isn't it hard being away all the time? You haven't been back since you left, if I'm right."

I wasn't surprised that my mother didn't respond, but I was secretly pleased with how well things were going for Anna and with how her mother had stood up for her.

"Oh, yes, I do miss my family and friends very much," I said kindly. "Sometimes it's hard not to be here with them. But I'm so happy to know about Anna and her school. Please say hello to her for me."

The other women drifted away. Mrs. Di Paolo wished us all a Merry Christmas, leaving the three of us alone on the church steps, the snow falling around.

Christmas vacation was blessedly uneventful. Mother went about exchanging sweets with the neighbors and decorating the house with wreaths and other reminders of the season. My stepfather spent long hours at work, as this was a peak earning time of year. He'd come home exhausted, spending evenings slumped in his chair in the living room, a paler shadow of the cheerful man I remembered. I fell back into my routines, stopping at my favorite shop for cookies and breads, helping in the kitchen, and seeing a few friends when they weren't visiting with relatives. As I strolled the snow-covered avenues, their shimmering and sparkling holiday lights stood against the gray that stretched in grounded harmony to the stars. All the while, the snow muffled the sounds of the street, seeming to calm the city and me at the same time.

We decorated our tree with the same ornaments we used every year: mostly painted orbs, a manger scene, and a delicate star that adorned the treetop. Only Richter honored his younger days in Germany, unwrapping and draping a small, fragile wooden sled, a cherubic Santa, and a few other trinkets from his childhood. Presents were modest that year. I had saved just enough to give one present to each parent. Knowing my mother's love for things

American, I had bought her Fannie Farmer's *The Boston Cooking-School Cook Book*, with its recipes for Thanksgiving pudding, Waldorf salad, cakes, and pies; for Richter, I had purchased a wool scarf from Mount Holyoke, its rich green the color dedicated to my graduating year. Otherwise, mittens, stockings, and practical gifts ruled the day with one exception: my small yellow diamond bracelet from Richter.

As with holidays past, Mother cooked a typical American Christmas dinner of turkey, potatoes, green beans, and cranberry sauce. This time, she indulged in one New Year's Eve ritual from her Hungarian past. "What's for dinner?" I asked, but I knew. The aroma brought the memories flooding back. "So you're serving New Year's Eve lentils?"

"These are tough times for us. Otto works very hard for much less than what he used to make. You're away at school, and he wants to make sure you have enough. Since October, I haven't had as much work." She paused there. "As for the lentils, remember each one's a coin, so maybe we'll have good luck and not have to worry about money next year."

She didn't have to remind me. My grandmother always served this meal on New Year's Eve. For an instant, I was back in her kitchen—the sights, smells, the pot on the stove, soup bowls on the wooden table, even the drifting snow I could see from the window on those cold winter nights as we kept warm around the fireplace—all this unfolded before me in a landscape of the past.

"Yes, I remember it well," I said. "I know these are difficult times, but I'm so glad to be here with you and Father Richter." Kissing her on the cheek, I felt for that moment we were together in time.

My stepfather ate early that evening, wished us a happy New Year, and labored up the stairs, leaving the two of us alone.

"It's good to be home," I said, "but I'm excited about the next semester at school. I thought I'd be terribly lonely there, and for a while I missed being here, but my new friends and the school were so welcoming. Oh, and I told Father that I was going to ask one of my professors about working in her physiology lab next term to help with my room and board."

"I'd hope you'd be able to find a job sooner rather than later. It's good that you're looking now, with all that's happened."

She rose from the table as if that were all, but I didn't want our conversation to end just yet.

"There's one thing I haven't had a chance to talk with you about. It's Father Richter. He doesn't look well. He doesn't seem to be himself."

My mother's face dropped, but her response told me there was no use in asking anything else. "He's just tired. He worries about business. There's nothing wrong with him that a few more customers wouldn't cure. Now, help me clean the dishes before we go to bed."

As I lay in the dark that night, my new life pressed against memory. Leaving home and finding my place at Mount Holyoke had eased the grip of haunting insecurity and anxiety that came from living under my mother's dominance. We both seemed to be on good terms during this holiday season. Even so, I felt the pain of the past eight years lurking in the shadows, always there, waiting to spring unannounced, triggered by a word or gesture.

My grandmother visited me as I drifted off. We hadn't met for some time now, but the setting was the same: the kitchen table in our old house. Nothing else. Just that table, my grandmother, and me. For a moment, she sat silently, looking through me.

"Momma, what is it? Why do you look at me that way?"
"I worry for you, Irene. I know your mother. I know how deeply you feel for her, but I also know all too well how she can use those who love her to get what she feels she deserves. She feels your love, but that's something she'll use too, and I'm afraid it

will hurt you in ways you can't imagine. Be careful, Irene. She'll
never change."
"What is it that makes you say this about Mother?
What happened to the two of you?"
No answer came to the question. All my grandmother would say
was "Look, learn, and protect yourself. And don't be fooled, as it
will cost you dearly."

As she spoke these words, my grandmother's image became one with the dreamy, indistinct haze that surrounded us. *"Momma, don't go!"* I cried. *"Don't leave me."* When I awoke, my pillow was still moist from the tears of the night.

I was prepared the next day to take a trolley to Grand Central, but Richter insisted on driving me to the station. He packed my bags into the Model T he had owned since I'd arrived in America, its seats worn to the springs, rust peeking out from underneath, eating into the baseboards, and fenders dented from wear, tear, and the occasional unwanted touch. Still, it ran well.

"I'll drive my car to work today, so it's no trouble to drop you off," he said.

My mother had fewer reasons to venture downtown, as the Great Depression had upended even the lives of many of her well-off clients. She said goodbye before I left, her cool touch and reserve the same as always. "Good grades, Irene. And let us know as soon as you can about work."

My stepfather tried his best to hide what was consuming him all the way down the slushed streets. "I still don't want you to worry about money for school. I've made sure what I set aside for you is safe. It was there before the Crash, and it's there now."

"But what about your business?"

"Some of the folks who came to me lost everything, but there are a few longtime customers who still need their diamonds set and reset, and repairs to jewelry keep coming back too. The couples who didn't have much in the first place have stopped coming. They'd saved over the years for a special time. Now they need that money just to get by."

His words didn't allay a fear I couldn't shake. As we neared Grand Central, I knew the time was short. "Father, what about you? How do you feel? I asked Mother, but all she said is that more work is all you need."

He hesitated as if he were trying to decide what to say. "I come from a family where we don't talk about things. Even as a child, if I fell and scraped my knee, I knew better than to cry or complain. Your mother doesn't have much patience for what she might call 'whining.' And God knows you have so much to do as you go off to school. But I've seen you watching me. You don't hide your worry well."

He let me know what he had hesitated to say as we arrived at the station. "I've had a pain in my chest for the past few months and had trouble climbing our stairs, so much so that instead of going to work one day, I went to a doctor. He said I probably had a heart attack—and that it might happen again at any time. He said I should rest and not work as much, but I can't do that. For now I feel all right, except sometimes it's a bit hard to catch my breath."

"Does Mother know this?"

"No, and please don't tell her."

I sat there, afraid to leave. I looked at this man who had been my saving grace. "Father, I feel so helpless. What can I do?"

"I'm still here. The best thing you can do for me is to make your dreams come true. You have already meant so much to me, and if I know you're happy, that will be your gift to me. That's what you can do."

The train would be arriving soon, but I couldn't move.

"You must go now, or you'll be late. I'll get your bags."

As his car door creaked open, I jumped out and ran around, throwing my arms around him. I held on, afraid to let go. "I love you, Father."

He looked down at me. His smile and the warmth in his eyes were all I could feel and see. Everything around us—the noise of the street, the buildings' facades, and snowflakes gently descending— disappeared into that moment between us.

"Your love has meant the world to me, Irene, more than you may ever know. Now go before it's too late."

I took my bags from him and said goodbye. But unlike that moment from my past when I waited in vain for one last glimpse of my grandmother, this time I turned around to see him standing there, not moving from where we had parted.

***

All during the train ride, I kept going over what had happened. Outside, the hustle of the city and its people, the boulevards and avenues, offices and shops, soon gave way to fields and farmhouses. Cattle and sheep wandered aimlessly, taking the place of the cars and pedestrians of just an hour ago. I looked out the window at the changing landscape and the gray and white of a winter's day, lost in what I had left behind.

Had anything changed between my mother and me? I had avoided what I had come to expect. Still, by the time I returned to Holyoke, I realized this holiday had filled me with a familiar feeling of unease, tinged with melancholy and foreboding.

I made my way along the familiar but now snow-covered path to Cowles. The lodge was quieter than usual, as many girls hadn't yet returned. When I opened the door to my dorm, I found Esther already back and settled in.

"It's great to see you!" I cried.

She rose from her bed and kissed me on the cheek. "Welcome back. I was hoping you'd come back today before the craziness started." Then she sat back on the bed and lifted her cup of tea. "I have lots to tell you. Seeing my mother and father again made me realize how much I missed them. I even missed my little brother, still annoying as ever. And presents! I can't wait to show you my new dress for our spring fling. We even went for a sleigh ride on Christmas Eve that almost toppled us into a snowdrift. But what about you? How was New York and your family? What did you get?"

"It was okay, I guess. It did feel good to be home. I didn't do much. Shopped for dinners and saw some of the same folks who've been there forever. Did a lot of cooking and helped my mother around the house. Our Christmas was quiet. Got a few things for school. But my stepfather, bless him, did give me this."

"Oh, your bracelet's so pretty!"

Then my facade gave way.

"What is it, Irene?"

"It's my stepfather. I may not see him again. He's very ill. All the time I was home, I knew something was wrong. But it wasn't until he drove me to the station and we were alone that he told me he'd had a heart attack."

"Did he see someone?"

"He went to the doctor, something he never does. They said there wasn't much they could do. And the one thing that might give him more time he won't change, and that's working as hard as he does."

"What about your mother?"

"I don't think she knows. Maybe she suspects something, but the only thing she's said to me is 'If only he had more clients,' which is the last thing he needs. And he told me he didn't want her to know."

"Really? Why would he say that?"

"I haven't told you much about my mother."

"Only that she came from Hungary before you and that being an American was very important to her and for you, once you came to live with her. You did talk about how good Hungarian food was and how much you enjoyed her cooking, plus a little bit about your stepfather. Other than that, you spent more time telling me about high school. I kind of understand. There's stuff about my family I haven't told you either."

Suddenly the floodgates opened, and out poured what I'd kept inside, the things I'd not told a soul, not even Joseph. How I came to be, my grandmother, the *Aquitania*, passing through Ellis Island alone. However, when it came to my mother and father, some things—how my mother hated my grandmother, the abuse she inflicted on me over the years—were left unsaid, as they would have left me naked and raw.

Still, as the evening gave way to early morning, Esther sat there, at times leaning over to touch my shoulder or arm, or shaking her head.

"God, Irene, you've been through so much. How did you manage to keep your sanity? I don't know if I could've kept mine in the same situations."

"Those first twelve years were far from perfect. We were poor and lived very simply. What's here at school and what others have I couldn't even imagine in Hungary. I lost two uncles in the war. Armies came through, put a torch to our land, and stole as much as they could, but my grandmother protected us and made sure we had what we needed—not much more, but never less. Esther, she was so strong raising her children and me. Most of all, I never doubted how much she loved me. She held me when I cried, was there for me when I came home from school. She was my savior, and those years with her were my blessing. More than anything, that's why I'm here with you now. Without her I don't know what would've happened to me, what I would have become."

After I told her as much as I dared, Esther took a deep breath and, for the first time in hours, leaned back on the bed. "When I think of what you've been through, my life seems so ordinary."

"You haven't told me much beyond what it was like growing up in Boston."

"Well, I don't feel there was anything special. Dad worked, and Mom stayed home and raised my brother and me. I was bored through most of high school. Of the boys I dated, most just wanted to score and the rest were kinda goofy. Then in my senior year, just when I thought I'd wasted four years, I had Mr. Heinrich for art class, and that changed my life. That was where I learned about photography and fell in love with it."

"It's funny, but I had the same thing happen to me. It was Mr. Kapinsky's science class where I found something I loved. He kept on telling me to aim high. 'You have it in you to do this,' he said."

"Then you know what I'm talking about. Mr. Heinrich made all the difference to me. My mom and dad could see it. They said it was like I'd found a true love. I was upset when December came because the class came to an end. Then something wonderful happened. That Christmas, sitting under the tree, was the only present wrapped in bright gold-and-red paper. It said *To our Esther. May you come to love and learn about the world all around you.* My father, I knew he was the one, had given me a Leica. A few months later, he picked up a Kodak when he was in New York. That's the camera I mostly use now."

"What a great story!" I exclaimed.

"But that's only the beginning. I started seeing things differently." By now, Esther couldn't keep her hands still. Making them into the shape of a camera, she pretended to snap the shutter as she circled the room. "I started paying attention to everything around me: houses, furniture, animals, ants, and people. I took pictures for the school yearbook. That photo of my family by my bed? I took that too. When I came here, I learned about a woman at Cornell, Margaret Bourke-White. Her photos of her campus and beyond were an inspiration for me to do the same at Mount Holyoke."

We sat in silence for a minute, but I sensed she wasn't quite through. "You know how you told me about your teacher and your family, and that's how you ended up here?"

"Yes, Mr. Kapinsky got it started. My stepfather wasn't far behind, and while it took longer, my mother was eventually okay with it too."

"Well, it was kind of the same with Mr. Heinrich. But for me, it's my mom who made the difference. When I told her about wanting to go to school here, she gave me a big hug and said she'd be with me all the way. She's very artistic, loves the Impressionists, especially Monet. Mom majored in art at Bryn Mawr but dropped out to get married. My brother and I came along soon after that. Taking care of us, cooking, doing the laundry, getting together with her girlfriends—that's pretty much been her life. Now that we're older, she's taking up painting again. I'm happy for her. I just know there's more she wanted to do, and now she can. But, like you once told me about your mom, I still think she's living part of what she wanted but never had through me."

"Sounds like a happy ending now that you're here and have your cameras and are doing what you love."

As she finished, her body sagged. Esther stood and started to pace back and forth.

"What is it, Esther?"

"Not quite the happy ending it sounds like, actually. Far from it. Something my dad said when I was home." Her face reddened, and tears and mascara ran together down her cheeks.

"The day after Christmas, he asked me to go for a walk with him, just the two of us. It was kind of unusual, but I was happy to get outside, as we'd been eating our way through that day and the day before. At first I thought he wanted to ask me about school or if I had a boyfriend. Instead, he started talking about how great it was that we were all together. Then he started talking about the details of some conference he had gone to in New York a few months ago. It wasn't like him to talk about work. He went on about who spoke at the conference and the sessions he went to, and much of it I didn't understand, but after a while, I got the feeling there was something else.

"We came to a bench in the park near our house and sat down. So, here's this beautiful, crisp winter's day, sun shining, snow covering everything, peaceful. We sat on that bench for a few minutes, not saying a word. Then he turned to me and said, 'When I was in New York, I met someone. Actually, I'd seen her a few times before at similar meetings. We talked about work, family, kids, the usual things. Well, this last time we saw each other, we met over drinks, then dinner.'"

Here Esther started shaking as if a chill had passed through her. "He stopped for a moment, but I was already preparing myself for what was to come. He said, 'Esther, I don't know how else to put this to you. We spent the night together. And since then, we've continued to see each other.'"

"I'm so sorry," I said, not sure what else I could say.

"My father then went on about how he still loves my mother and doesn't want to leave her, but he felt he needed to tell somebody and thought he could trust me to understand."

"My God, that must be so hard."

Esther's fists clenched as she pummeled her pillow. "I was in shock and couldn't move. My first thought was, *Why are you telling me this? Why me?* What was I supposed to understand? That he's, what, in *love* with someone else? Having a crisis as he turns fifty? Once the shock wore off, I jumped up from the bench, stood in front of him, and started screaming 'How could you do this? What were you thinking!' He just sat there shaking his head and saying 'I don't know.' Back and forth we went. Finally, after I calmed down, I asked him, 'Do you love her? Are you going to leave us?' Those questions seemed to snap him out of whatever other world he was in. 'No,' he insisted. 'I don't want to do that. You all are too important to me.' By now, I was shaking but had the sense to say to him, 'Then just end it! End it before it's too late, for God's sake!'"

"Then what happened?"

"He said he knew I was right and that he loved us."

"So, you think that's the end of it?"

"I don't know. I really don't know. I believed what he said about us. I just hope he has it in him to do the right thing. I did ask my dad to write me and let me know. So, now I wait for his letter."

I found myself waiting for that letter along with Esther in the days that followed, knowing it would decide the fate of her family and those she counted on the most in her life. I felt something within me had changed too. That shared intimacy had chipped through the wall that had kept my secrets locked within. In the days to come, I knew I no longer had to be alone with them.

CHAPTER 15

January brought with it new snow that by now piled high and deep across campus. Shovels had carved out narrow paths, with walls of white silencing everything except the sounds of our boots crunching against the hard surface as we made our way to our classes. Winter's days brought such a chill to the old stone buildings that we often sat at our desks cocooned in our coats, with fingers naked and stiff pencils in hand, recording in stop-start what was said and written.

The cold did nothing to temper my enthusiasm for Cowles, the school, and my learning. Mr. Kapinsky and his science class remained my North Star as physiology, with its experiments, study labs, and out-of-class discussions in Clapp Hall, held my attention most of all. Fewer students registered, unlike many of the other classes, creating a smaller, resolute circle.

My professors' commitment to and love for their work extended far beyond the subject matter. We learned about the legacy of

Dr. Cornelia Clapp, who was determined to take physiology at Mount Holyoke from a course on nutrition and diet for women in preparation to be good future wives and mothers to basic and applied scientific research with concentrations in biomedicine and biochemistry. Dr. Abby Turner picked up where Dr. Clapp had left off, delving into experimentation and studies in circulatory efficiency, blood serum, and respiratory response, seeking to raise the integrity and prominence of women's investigation by publishing in the *American Journal of Physiology* and elsewhere.

I'd been introduced to this world during my first months of school, and the more I learned, the greater was my desire to work for the department, with Dr. Turner, and in that way, to find a home within the walls of Clapp Hall. And there was one more thing: Richter's heart condition embedded within me a personal dimension beyond a career. Perhaps I could learn something that would help me to understand what he was going through.

After physiology class on a Thursday in February, I went to see Dr. Turner. I had practiced with Esther what to say, but now as I stood before the office door, my heart raced, nerves on edge. No response came from my first hesitant tap on the door. After a moment, I tried again, this time with a firmer knock.

"Enter."

I opened the door and understood why she had ignored me. Her desk was piled high with papers, journals, and reference books. More of the same had collected on bookshelves that reached to the ceiling. Dr. Turner sat behind her mahogany desk, hands to temples, poring over something. A student test? A manuscript? I couldn't tell, other than whatever it was held her undivided attention.

"Just a minute" was all she said initially. Eventually as I sat there, still nervous and impatient, she rose from her chair. She was bespectacled in nearly rimless glasses that were perched below full, dark eyebrows. Her smallish face was framed by full hair that held a slight wave. A modest white blouse and tan skirt outlined her body but gave few clues as to what lay beneath them. One look at her face, and I knew I had little time—I had to get to the point. I had prepared as best I could for my visit by reading up on her research into the circulatory system in women, but in her presence it felt inadequate.

"You're Richter. Irene Richter. How can I help you?"

"Dr. Turner, thank you for seeing me. I took your class in the fall, and now I'm enrolled for the spring semester."

"Yes, Miss Richter, I know that."

"I really liked your course, and it's made me think that I might want to major in physiology."

"Oh, is that so? Beyond liking the lectures and the topic, do you have any other reasons you're interested in physiology?"

"I've wanted to know more about nutrition, exercise, and the body. In your introduction to physiology, I've already learned a lot about organ systems and what you called 'bodily functions.' In my time at Mount Holyoke, your class has been the one I've most looked forward to."

"Is that all?"

I could already feel her patience thinning. I was a distraction from what had been absorbing her time and attention. "There's one other reason, Dr. Turner. My stepfather. He has a very weak heart. I don't know how much longer he'll live. You're an expert on the circulatory system, blood flow, and how the body works. I've read about your research, and although it's not exactly what you do, I think that physiology could help me to understand my stepfather's condition and maybe even help him."

She stopped shuffling the papers on her desk as I finished my confession. "Where are you from?"

"Hungary. I came to America not that long ago, about eight years. That's where my accent is from."

"We don't have many students from your country at Holyoke.

Have you looked at the curriculum for this major? Do you have any idea of the work involved?"

"Yes. The courses, lab work, experiments. At the library I looked up what's involved."

"You also know, then, that very few students here graduate with a degree in physiology."

"Yes. But it's something I want to do."

"Well, let's see how this semester goes. Come back and see me at the end, and we'll take it up then."

"Thank you, Dr. Turner." I sensed my time was up but couldn't leave before asking one more question.

"Is there anything else, Miss Richter?"

"Dr. Turner, is there any work I could do in your lab? I'm trying to find a way to help my family pay for school."

"Not now, no. But we do sometimes take on students in their junior and senior years to help with courses and for laboratory research."

"I understand."

I left Dr. Turner's office lifted by what my academic future at Mount Holyoke might offer but also adrift about how I could support that future. I knew Richter would understand, but I dreaded telling my mother. My letters home highlighted the usual topics—meals, outings, and the cold, wet weather—as I had no desire to incur her irritation. I dared not write my stepfather directly, as Mother wouldn't like that, but I did ask about his health and hers every time I wrote. On the rare occasions that she replied, news from home told only of neighbors, church, and work. Nothing much about my stepfather.

I settled into where I had left off before the holidays: class and homework, lectures and quizzes, and evening meals at the dining room. We cherished our weekend hikes to locales that took us far from the books and walls that preoccupied our Mondays through

Fridays. We followed the trails as best we could, naked as they were except for winter's white blanket. Ingrid, Sarah, and others from Cowles tried their hands and feet at skiing Prospect Hill. Once, and only once, Ingrid pressed me to go with them.

"Didn't you ever ski in Hungary?" she asked.

"Not exactly, Ingrid." I thought better of trying to explain that flat, feudal lands don't make it a promising sport, but they insisted.

"Oh, come on," she said. "You're petite, close to the ground. Your center of gravity makes it easier than for someone like me, although coming from Sweden I did start when I was three. Give it a try."

By now the other girls were chanting in unison, "Go, Irene! Go, Irene!"

With a wan smile and unsure feet, I borrowed Ingrid's skis and clamps. Ingrid laid down the basics: "All you have to do is point the skis downhill and use your poles to balance. It's a straight run—no hills and no trees. Easy! Okay, Irene, good luck!"

"I have no idea what I'm doing," I said, but she paid no attention, just helped me point downward and let go. I knew in an instant that only by shaping my skis into an inverted V would I stand a chance. Instinctively, I knew after that one act of downhill desperation, skiing held no hope for me. With one scream in the ten feet traveled and one face-freezing fall, it was over.

Ingrid ran over and wiped my eyes clear of snow. "Well, Irene, at least you tried. Wasn't that exciting? I bet you can't wait until next time."

All I could say was "I don't know about that." While few things in life were certain for me, I held one sure truth: My days of downhill adventures were over.

The cold and wet had penetrated even the hardiest of the Cowles girls by the end of that afternoon. Mrs. Kennedy waited for us as we staggered into the lodge. She ladled out hot chocolate to all, and we sat in the great room and sipped by the hearth's fire, our amber liquid casting its own radiance onto rose-colored cheeks, our warming glow seeming to fill the room, leaving behind the chill of the day.

Ingrid and I had rarely spoken before my Prospect Hill adventure. She was hard to miss, standing a head taller than most, with her peaches-and-cream complexion and hair the color of silk. We didn't attend any of the same classes, as she was a sophomore art major, but we often saw each other in the dining room. I never assumed we had anything in common, but as I was to learn, we shared more than I'd imagined.

One day as we came to dinner, Ingrid sat next to me, a first, as I usually ate with others from Cowles or with a classmate to talk about a lecture, test, or homework for that day. Now here she sat with a disarming smile, talking as she took a seat across from me. "I hope you didn't mind my teasing you about skiing. I thought it would be fun for you to try. You were a good sport about it."

"I never would've done it if you hadn't insisted. I'm glad I did, even if my cheeks were half-frozen!"

"Well, don't give up. If you'd like, I'll take you out to the hill again sometime."

"Maybe," I said politely. "I can tell you that I'm in no hurry." We sat for a few minutes, not saying anything, and I suspected skiing wasn't the only reason we were having dinner together.

"Where did you say you're from?" she asked. "I've never heard an accent like yours."

"Do you know anything about Hungary? The eastern part, near Romania?"

Ingrid's blank look encouraged me to continue. "Well, it's nothing like here, except for the snow. It's farmland. We used to grow crops that you never see around here. Tobacco was the largest of them all."

"What was it like? Do you miss it?"

Until now, few students had asked me about my life before America. "It was pretty simple," I said. "Up at dawn, help make breakfast, off to school, then back home. Sometimes I'd play with my dogs, but I spent a lot of time at home with my grandmother. Most of the time it was peaceful, and we'd go about living day to day. Then there was a war, and terrible men came to our town. Two people I loved died in that war."

"That's so sad. Where I lived, we had nothing like a war. The small farming community where I came from, not too far from Stockholm, was in some ways not so different from where you lived. Actually, it was quiet and kind of boring. I was excited when my father and mother decided to come to America, even though I was only eight. Coming to Holyoke, I thought I'd be the only person not from America. Over time, I found out there are many more like us. That's one of the reasons I wanted to talk to you. Have you ever heard of our Cosmopolitan Club?"

"No, I haven't."

"It's great. Most of the Club members were born somewhere else and came to America not that long ago, like you and me. We come from all over the world, but the Cosmopolitan Club, or 'the Club,' as we call it, is open to anyone who's interested in, I guess you might call it, getting along with others. I think some of its ideas around world peace came out of the end of World War I, the League of Nations, if I remember. There are chapters in other schools too. Cornell has one, and so do some schools in New York, all around the same ideas. The Club actually has a motto: 'Above all nations is humanity.' We hold events to bring together students and faculty across campus to learn about what's happening in the world and about each other, where we all come from, what we like about America, and sometimes what we don't like. I found out about it as a freshman and never had second thoughts about joining."

"What do the Club members do?"

"We get together once a month, sometimes more often. We started off in September with each of us talking about ourselves, where we came from, what we miss, and what's easy and hard about being here. A lot of the time it's just fun. We take turns cooking meals from our countries. I found out I like Boston baked beans as much as I like pasta! Sometimes we introduce others to our clothing and jewelry at galas that are open to the college. Other times we tell stories about how mean people have been to us, people who look down on us as foreigners, making fun of our accents or the ways we're different. Not so much here on campus but where we lived, in high school, on the streets. Many things that others at college never have to go through. It's, what would I call it? Almost like a community of different people come together. If you're interested, we're having a meeting next week."

Her words about these new Americans, settled in their new land but bound by their roots, touched something I had felt but was still struggling to understand. "Yes, I'd love to go with you."

***

A week later, on a cold, snow-flaked evening in February, Ingrid met me downstairs at Cowles and we walked over to the hall where Cosmopolitan Club members met.

"Are you nervous?" she asked.

"Just a little. This is the first time I've ever joined a club here."

"Don't be. They're so nice. No one's going to bite your head off."

As we climbed the stairs, I slipped on the sheet of ice that caked each step outside the building and, for a moment, imagined my first impression, standing before a room of strangers bruised and soaked. Ingrid grabbed my arm just in time.

"You okay?"

I nodded, and we went in.

The meeting room was nondescript except for a few colorful tapestries and photos of places unknown to me adorning the walls. Students stood around in clusters, some drinking tea or coffee and nibbling on sweets that came from a box on a folding table. I could have been with any group at school. But, looking and listening, I knew there was something different from other campus get-togethers: accents from worlds unknown to me; words heard in Bronx stores and kiosks; skin tones, some a beautiful bronze, others rich brown or paler white. While a few students had come from class wrapped in woolen sweaters and skirts, others wore rainbows of vivid colors. I felt transported in that moment to a familiar place of people I'd known before. Voices, dress, complexions, all so different. From where? Then it came to me: those days on Ellis Island.

Ingrid slipped her arm into mine and led me to a group of five women. They widened their small circle to make room for us as we approached. Ingrid greeted the group in a pronounced Swedish accent. "*Hej!* I want to introduce a prospective member. This is Irene. She's from Hungary, a new country for the Club!"

The conversation stopped, and each took turns welcoming me, some speaking in their native tongue and others with a simple "Hi." While I recognized a few from my classes, I'd never had a conversation or spent any time with them. Here was the world in miniature hidden among the students of Holyoke. Some words in German, Italian, French, and Turkish I'd heard on the *Aquitania* or in the Bronx, and many I'd never heard before: Yu Lee from China, Mercedes from Uruguay, Vimala from India, Takako from Japan, Maricel from Spain. Others had ancestors who had been here for generations—some had descended from pilgrims or lived through the American Revolution and the Civil War.

***

I never thought that the Cosmopolitan Club would become what I cherished most about the rest of that first year. When it came to classes, physiology was my home. When I needed to know I wasn't alone, nothing felt as true as the Club did. I wrapped myself in a blanket of comfort and conversation among kindred spirits on the cold days of winter. After a few weeks, I came to understand that the Club wasn't just a social gathering place.

I caught up with Ingrid as she approached the Club building one Thursday evening in mid-March. "Do you know what we'll be talking about?"

"Felidia is very organized. She'll have her list. My guess is it'll be continuing to plan our annual celebration. What's happening in Europe will come up too."

By now we were climbing the stairs to the meeting room. Rows of folding chairs filled much of the modest space. Members and a few faculty had already settled in. We sat in the back just as Felidia called the meeting to order.

"Welcome to all. Another cold evening on campus, but still a good turnout tonight. I've listed the agenda on the blackboard. During the last meeting, we had decided on the *when* and *what* for our fall festival. For those of you here for the first time and others who may have forgotten, it's October 1 and our theme is, to quote Alexander Dumas, 'All for one.' After our opening speaker, we'll have a talent show, music, and dancing. We'll host a food fair that will start about two hours in. The evening will end at nine. Now to fill in the missing pieces, the *who* and *how*."

One after another raised their hands. Vimala was the first to speak. "Felidia, when you say 'dancing,' does that mean from our countries?"

"Yes."

"Great. I'd like to propose that a part of the program include traditional folk dancing. I'd be happy to perform. I even have a native costume from Ceylon. For me, it's so important that people learn about the land I come from. We want our independence, but no one knows or seems to care. Maybe I can help change that here."

Felidia looked around the room. "Are there any questions about Vimala's idea? If not, we'll make room for it in the program as we have for dancing in past years. Maricel?"

"Is there space on the program for a bullfight?"

The room erupted in laughter.

"I don't mean bringing a bull to Holyoke, but I've been to many bullfights in Pamplona, and I could show what one is like."

Mercedes didn't wait to be called on. "Do you need someone to be the bull?"

"You're pretty good at shooting the bull, Mercedes," Maricel said. "Why don't you volunteer?"

Giggles swept through the room. "I didn't mean me," she protested. "Oh, okay. I'll do it. But please don't run a sword through me!"

Others followed with more ideas, and within the hour, the entire program was set. They'd have Turkish music. A display of Japanese and Chinese porcelain and scrolls. Clothes from everywhere. As for our menu, members promised pasta, egg rolls, paella, New England clam chowder, Spanish ham.

I wanted to contribute to the day, but in what way? Singing and dancing were out of the question, as I was too shy. I had no heirlooms to show, as I'd left Hungarian mementos behind. Then I realized one way to bring Hungary to Holyoke: through recipes from my homeland.

"Irene, you've had your hand up for a while."

"I'd like to prepare a Hungarian dish for the evening, perhaps a sour cherry soup."

"What kind of soup? Sour cherry?" Felidia asked with a smile. "Great. That'll be a first for us." Then she brought her gavel down. "Well done. Let's move on."

Dr. Aldis, a faculty member who sat in the front row, spoke for the first time that evening. "During this term and the last, I devoted part of my political science class to the rise of fascism in Europe. Threats against Jews, Roma, and Slavs in Italy and Germany are on the rise. Newspapers have been firebombed, and freedoms we take for granted taken away. I'm asking that the Club work with me to hold a meeting, perhaps in the spring, on what all of this means for the future of democracy in the world."

A student in the front row added, "Dr. Aldis, let's not forget what's happening here too. America isn't a fascist country, but some of the horrible things being done to people who came here not that long ago aren't so different from the racism in Europe. The other day I read about some Irish boys who were beaten up just because of where they came from."

She paused for a moment. "I look around this room and see a lot of heads nodding."

Dr. Aldis picked up where this student left off. "I know many of you have stories to tell too. There's no doubt we face some of the same dangers in this country that are happening abroad. We must discuss it further at the meeting."

I looked up to see Felidia wiping tears away. "This means more to me than any of you know. Italy is my homeland, and I'm very frightened about what's happening there. My brother was arrested in Rome just a few weeks ago for protesting Mussolini and his thugs. I don't know where he is now or what they'll do with him."

"I fear that your tragic story is one of many happening all across Italy and beyond at this time," Dr. Aldis said as he reached over and took her hand for a moment.

Recovering her composure, Felidia added, "Thank you for your offer, Dr. Aldis. Yes, the Cosmopolitan Club will work with you. Let us know how best to help. Maybe we can make the program part of an international day."

Silence settled over the room. The festival planning and the emotional moment had drained the evening's momentum. "I know there's more to discuss, but I think it best that we call our meeting to an end," she said. "Thank you all for coming tonight. We'll see you next month, if not before."

As I walked back to Cowles, the sting of frigid night air heightened my excitement over the events to come. Purpose and passion coursed through me like the shock from a surge of electricity. I didn't know what to expect from the evening and still didn't know where it would lead. I only felt that my sense of this school had changed, as had my worth and place in an unchosen country.

The Club and the new bonds formed within it absorbed my attention over the term, to the point where I had to find a balance between studies and social life. I quickly learned that lingering over coffee or at dinner took a toll on coursework. Determined to secure a place in the physiology department, I once again settled into the solitude and soft sounds of the library. Surrounded by books and aisles of knowledge, the distractions of the day flickered and then vanished. I knew my future lay in the pages before me and those to come in this hallowed setting.

Midterm exams had gone well enough, except English grammar, which remained a constant challenge. I just couldn't seem to set aside old Hungarian habits of the word. As hard as I studied physiology, the formidable Dr. Turner gave no indication of my standing, and that uncertainty only made me more determined not to fail. I took no chances with finals bearing down, visiting, revisiting, and memorizing the course's areas of concentration: organ systems, functions and maladies, hygiene, women's reproductive systems, and especially Dr. Turner's laboratory research on the circulatory system.

As I left the final exam on a fateful spring morning, one of my classmates turned to me and said, "Whew, I'm glad that's over. That was one of the hardest finals for me. Hey, I know you're hoping to major in physiology. What did you think?"

"I'm hoping all my studying might have paid off, but then a little voice says to me, *Nothing you can do will meet Dr. Turner's approval,* so I don't know what to think. I guess I'll know by the end of the week. I'm waiting for that grade before deciding whether it's worth making an appointment with her to talk about next year."

I awoke Friday morning to Esther shuffling around our room, looking for a lost sock. "Morning. I'm going over to the dining hall for breakfast. Coming? If so, I'll wait."

As soon as I sat up, nerves took over. "No, thanks. Today I find out how I did in physiology. Last night I was so wound up, I hardly slept. But oh, what nightmares! I dreamed that I walked into my final test and didn't know a thing, and then Dr. Turner said my grade was an F. I don't think I could keep anything down right now."

"This is *the* day? I'm so sorry I forgot." Then, abandoning her sock search, she left.

I gathered my courage and hurried past the blossoming birch and oak trees, over the quiet stream that wended its way through campus to Clapp Hall. I ran up the stairs to Dr. Turner's office to find more than a few students eager to know their fate. I scanned down the list of names, passing by lower letters of the alphabet next to them: C, C+, C, D, and few Bs and fewer As. Finally, I found my name: Irene Richter, Final exam, A, Final grade, B+.

One of the other students, clearly disappointed, turned to me. "Irene, you did okay. Actually, better than okay. Dr. Turner is one tough grader. I'm glad this isn't going to be *my* major."

I felt a sense of relief that all wasn't lost. But then I thought, *Was this good enough?* I decided then and there to find out. I didn't have an appointment, but her office light was on, so I knocked on the door.

"Yes?" the voice behind it said, more a question than an invitation.

"Dr. Turner, it's Irene Richter. May I come in?"

"All right."

Upon entering, I found Dr. Turner just as she was when I left her the last time: bent over a desk piled high with papers. "Dr. Turner, I'm sorry to bother you without an appointment."

She looked up from what absorbed her and motioned to me. "Yes, yes, come in. Sit down. I know you want to find out how you've done and what it means for a major. I'll be candid with you, Miss Richter. Your early work this semester left a lot to be desired. Understanding organ functions, fundamentals of anatomy, and basic physiology were an uphill climb for you."

"I know, Dr. Turner. I don't want to make excuses, but some of my difficulty had to do with learning some English terms and phrases."

Dr. Turner nodded. "I did see that. I also noticed that you became more comfortable with terminology as the semester went on. You've made progress, but your final grade also includes those assignments early in the semester, and they weren't at the highest level."

"But I want to do well, and my work shows, as you said, improvement. And in your class and laboratory, I realized how much I like the subject."

"I could see that. It comes across in your attitude and your work habits. As much as you struggled at first with the class, I've been impressed with your approach in the laboratory. You take your time, sometimes too much, but you're exacting, methodical, and reliable." She paused. "Next term we're adding a very talented professor to the department, Dr. Charlotte Haywood. Between us, the department will continue to build on our areas of expertise. We'll focus on respiration, metabolism, circulation, and reproduction. All will require considerable laboratory time. We'll need students committed to our experiments and studies. With the addition of Dr. Haywood, we hope to make Holyoke one of the major schools for women to study physiology, not just in Massachusetts but across the country."

Dr. Turner let these words sink in for a moment. "Miss Richter, we accept a very small number as physiology majors, perhaps five or six students. I'd like you to take time to think about the commitment you will have to make if you join them. If you do decide—"

I couldn't wait for her to complete the sentence. "Dr. Turner, I have thought about it. I don't need to think about it any longer. If you'll accept me, I would love to contribute and to have physiology as my major."

Dr. Turner allowed a small smile. "Then I welcome you to our department. You'll need to come back to school earlier than other students. I haven't decided exactly when, but you should plan to be here before the end of August. Now I must get back to a manuscript."

Even as I thanked her, Dr. Turner was already at her desk steeped in reading, nodding absentmindedly. I rose and gently closed the door.

My first year had finished on a high note. I had done well in most of my classes. I hadn't yet found a job on campus, but now the physiology department had accepted me, and with Dr. Haywood's pending arrival in the department, perhaps I'd have another chance at gainful employment.

The whirlwind around departures left little time for goodbyes. Bags were packed, cars arrived to whisk daughters away for the summer, and arrangements were made for trips to the rail station. Esther and I were among the last to leave.

"Are you looking forward to getting out of here for the summer?" she asked.

"To tell you the truth, I'm wondering what I'll return to. I'm worried about my stepfather. Mother's letters didn't tell me much over the past months. What about you? How are you feeling about going home?"

"I don't know. I really don't. I've kept you up on all the correspondence from home, but, like your parents, mine haven't told me much either. Remember that letter Dad promised to send after our talk? Never got it. So now I wonder if we're still going to be a family and, if we are, what it's going to be like."

"Maybe it's worked out, and he didn't want to go into it in a letter. Maybe he's too embarrassed. And it might be good news, too, that your mom hasn't written to say anything."

"I hope you're right. It's bad enough to know what he's told me. I just hope he's figured it out."

"I'll be thinking of you and will write over the summer. Do let me know."

CHAPTER 16

I sat alone on the train all the way back to Grand Central. Things were different this time, though, as I'd left school filled with the promise that lay ahead. As I came closer to home, however, thoughts of Holyoke receded. I didn't expect my mother to be any different, but I wondered if her love for me would come more easily with all I'd accomplished at school. I had changed, but what would I be like in her presence? How much would I put up with what Mother said or did to me?

This flood of the unresolved filled space and time all the way to the city. My mother had written that Richter wouldn't be meeting me at Grand Central, so I made my way to the subway and then took the trolley to Gun Hill Road.

I stepped off at my stop and was met with the sultry blast of the city's early summer. The neighborhood haberdashers, meat markets, and vegetable stands all seemed locked in time but more tattered than I remembered as the Depression's grip took hold. I'd been away less than six months, but Holyoke's streams, greenery, and open spaces had heightened my sensitivity to the clatter and crammed quarters of the streets. As I walked the last blocks home, one sound seemed to knit together part of what I'd left behind. The accents of people who spoke to one another as I passed by, those in doorways or leaning out their windows, and the signs in languages from other lands, even the occasional hand gestures, brought to mind the Club at Holyoke and, with it, a comforting familiarity with the world I had come to love. Then I turned onto our street and knew the time had come to turn to what was about to unfold. I stood outside our house for a moment, hoping for the best but steeling myself for what awaited me.

The lateness of the afternoon meant that my mother was at the stove, hovering over a pot of chicken whose pungent aromas of garlic and paprika filled the foyer and living room. Entering the kitchen, I waited until she turned around. As she did, I put my arms around her and kissed her cheek. "It smells great in here."

"You startled me. I didn't expect you home until later."

"I was lucky. The train was on time, and I made perfect connections once I left Grand Central. Is Father at work?"

"Yes. He'll be home in about an hour, as usual."

I was relieved that he was still going about his business. "How are you doing?"

"I have a few more aches and pains. It's getting harder to mop floors and clean for a living. And Otto's slower. His work has picked up a bit but still not to where it was. What about school?"

"I did pretty well in my classes this semester. Mostly As and some Bs. The great news is that I've been approved to major in physiology. I'm one of only a few students. I'd have written you, but it happened just before I left."

"I don't understand. What's physiology?"

"It's science. You learn about the way your body works. Your heart, kidneys, lungs, blood, eyes, and all the things you're made of. We do experiments, some on animals and other times on each other to learn about how we live." I could tell from her puzzled expression that this conversation wasn't sitting well.

"What's it good for? What do you do with that?"

"Oh, there are lots of ways I can use it. It teaches you about what happens with the food you eat, what's good and bad for you, how to stay healthy, what makes you sick. I have a long way to go before I graduate, so I don't know where it will take me yet, but I could see working in a hospital or clinic, or some job that helps people."

"If it helps you get a good job when you finish school, that's what you need to do. Your stepfather won't be around to support you forever." I could tell she was ready to move on. I breathed a sigh of relief that she hadn't asked about my plans to help pay for room and board.

"You're always writing about your friends. Have you been invited to any of their homes? From what you've told me, some very rich people are sending their girls to that school."

My mother's question didn't surprise me. Status and class, whom I knew and where I went, were never far below the surface and gave her stories to tell the neighbors and churchwomen. "No, not yet. A few of us have talked about holiday trips. Maybe next fall."

"You're not getting into any trouble with boys? You never say anything about them when you write."

"For good reason. Between classes, studying, the Cosmopolitan Club, and weekend hikes and outings, I haven't had the time to meet anyone. They did have dances at the school that boys from local colleges came to. We had a nice time with them but pretty much just talked. I'm a bit shy about getting out on the dance floor, so being with my friends at these dances just made it fun."

"Do you hear any more from that neighborhood boy? What's his name? James? John?"

"Joseph, Mother. His name is Joseph. And no. He met someone at his school."

"Well, that's for the best. I saw where the two of you were going and didn't like it one bit."

Just then, I heard the front door open. Relieved of answering her questions, I left my mother by the pot on the stove. "Father Richter, welcome home!"

His appearance had changed markedly since I'd left. The oak cane in his right hand steadied his gait. He eased his frail body into the lounge chair, where with a heaving sigh, he reclined in exhaustion. As I bent over to plant a kiss on his pale cheek, his blue eyes, bright as I had remembered, came to life.

"Welcome back. I must say, school's worn well on you. You look even prettier. And I love the way you've cropped your hair but kept your waves and curls."

What I'd held back just minutes before in my mother's presence gave in to the warmth of his voice. "Father, there's so much to say. The good things I told you about at Christmas, they've just gotten better."

I abandoned the kitchen, sat at his knee, and filled in the unwritten lines of the letters home: the joys of friendship, the Club, nights at the library, and my interest in physiology. I also let him know that I hadn't yet found a way to help pay for school.

"Don't worry about that, dear. I wasn't planning on it. I want to talk to you later about the rest of school, but for now, why don't we see what your mother is cooking?"

I held his arm as he rose from the chair, and we joined my mother at the kitchen table. Words between us would wait for another time.

***

I returned to memories of high school in the summer of 1930, and of Mr. Kapinsky, the prime mover in creating the life I had come to cherish. I wanted to see him before school let out for the summer, so I made my way over to Evander Childs one warm afternoon the second week in June. School had ended for the day, but I knew he would still be at his desk, perhaps planning the final exam or having a talk with a student. I stood before this citadel of memories, thinking back on how much of my life came to pass within those halls, some only fleeting and fading friendships or idle cafeteria conversations, but others, like the teachers who guided and believed, forever fixed within me. It took only a minute to reach room 105 on the first floor. I knocked gently. Hearing nothing, I tried again, this time with more force. Footsteps approached, and the door opened. For that moment, time stopped. There Mr. Kapinsky stood before me quite as he had before, rounded and balding in his rumpled, slightly tattered suit and frayed blue tie.

This unexpected visit caught him off guard, taking him away from wherever he had been in his thoughts. Quickly reorienting himself, he exclaimed heartily, "What a surprise!" his face lighting up, from upturned lips to his high forehead.

"Hi, Mr. Kapinsky," I said, smiling from ear to ear. "I hope I'm not interrupting anything."

"No, no, not at all. Please come in and sit down. I'm just touching up the last lessons of the semester, but by now I know them by heart. How was your first year? I hope Holyoke has been good to you."

He pulled out his chair from behind the desk and brought it around to the front row, where I had sat so many times. "I can't think of another place I'd rather be than there. What your wife said about Holyoke, how much she loved it? It's the same with me. The campus is beautiful. I've made such good friends, and my best friend, my roommate, is a great photographer. We go on daylong hikes to take pictures. The walls of our room are covered with them. But mainly I spend my evenings in the library studying. There isn't anything easy about the classes, but the professors are there to see us through. It's all been wonderful, and I have you to thank for it."

He moved on, ignoring my words of gratitude. "So, tell me. Does science still interest you?"

"Yes, even more so."

"I hope it works out. You've got a talent for learning and a passion for it. Do you have a major in mind? Botany? Biology? And what about all those times we studied the galaxies and planets?"

"Actually, physiology."

"Why physiology?"

"Part of it has to do with my professor, Dr. Abigail Turner. That's her field of research. There's something else too. It has to do with my stepfather."

"Is he ill?"

"It's his heart. School is teaching me things about the body that might help him. I do so want him to get better, to live a long life."

"I'm sorry to hear he's not doing well. I know what he means to you. And speaking of your family, how does it feel to be back home? What about your mother?"

Although I had rarely spoken with Mr. Kapinsky about my family, he knew that my home life was far from tranquil. "She's okay. More worried than before the Crash because many of the people she used to work for stopped hiring her to clean their houses. Father, bless him, has made sure we have enough to get by. As for the subject of Holyoke, my mother seems to have made peace with what we decided, at least for now."

"I hope it stays that way. Now you must excuse me. I promised I'd meet my wife. We're going out to dinner for the first time since New Year's. We've been married twenty years tomorrow. It's a surprise. She thinks we're just going for a walk, but I made reservations at La Romagna, our favorite restaurant. We'll enjoy tonight. Then it's back to doing what we all are doing these days: saving our pennies."

I stood, came around as I turned to go, and kissed his cheek. "Mr. Kapinsky, you'll never know what your faith in me has meant."

His pale cheeks turned rose. "Just be happy in what you do."

I was buoyant after visiting with Mr. Kapinsky, surrounded by a warm nostalgia, comforting and nurturing at the same time. However, walking through the neighborhood dispelled that serenity. I felt the slower pace of life. The sidewalks, like concrete kilns, captured and held the heat of the day, making the air heavy with humidity, becoming one with the sweat from human traffic. Yes, much was as it had been, but as I went about my errands, I saw more hardship and tragedy. While away at school, the 1929 Crash and what followed had taken a toll on this world. Many of the shops lining the avenues not far from where I lived had closed, and fewer customers visited the butcher and the bakery. Where businesses had once thrived, now bread lines drew the most attention, streaming down the street as long as the food lasted.

My stepfather had always been careful with money. We kept to a budget. Restaurants were out of the question these days, travel was only for school, and clothes were sewn at home and purchased from shops only when needed. We ate more beets and potatoes. Soups and stews for dinner. Meat three or four times a week instead of every day. We didn't have to depend on soup kitchens or church charity, unlike many of my mother's fellow choir members. In that way, we were blessed.

Still, neither our circumstances nor my being home lifted my mother's spirits. I tried as I could, helping around the house and taking over much of the cooking and cleaning. Worry lines had appeared on her face, and what she saw on the streets and heard from her neighbors disrupted the certainty of the daily routine she had known. Though my mother didn't speak about it, she couldn't deny my stepfather's decline. It helped me to understand that her words seemed to come from the fear of being forsaken once again. I felt her immense pride, and how she lived for and through my dreams and future, although I sensed that wasn't all.

A few days after my return, as the two of us were coming home from church, she asked, "When do you start your job at school?"

I prepared for her question but dreaded what would follow. "It didn't work out. I had hoped they might need me in the lab or to help with paperwork, but all those positions go to juniors and seniors. The school, like everywhere and everyone, has less money with all that's happened. I really wanted to help with my expenses, but I can't do it now. I'll keep trying."

I expected irritation with what I didn't do. That's not what came next. In a voice speaking beyond her words, she turned to me. "You know your stepfather won't be around forever to help."

She'd warned me in the past, but this time it came tinged with an urgency I hadn't heard before. Suddenly I understood. As my stepfather could no longer hide his fate, my mother could no longer deny it. Yet all of us would continue to dance around what was to come.

***

I visited the local library, intent on preparing for new classes. After a futile sift through card catalogs for reviews, manuscripts, and research on the curricula content for the next year, I decided that only the central branch downtown would do.

The next day I took the trolley and subway into Manhattan and exited a few blocks from Central Park. Dodging traffic, walking past store after store, I reached my Forty-Second Street destination. Pictures of the main branch had given me a sense of its size, but those representations didn't do justice to the grandeur of the New York Public Library. Standing on its steps for the first time, its gray marble, Beaux Arts beauty, and true enormity took my breath away. After making my way between the imposing stone lions flanking the entrance, I found the Rose Main Reading Room and its line of long wooden tables. The soft glow from rows of table lamps and natural light pouring into the hall through the arced windows left no doubt about where I would spend my summer days.

I found the card catalogs and requested recent journals and publications by the American Physiology Society, sifting through them for anything that touched on the work of my professors. Most of the articles were written by men, but I also began to understand the importance of Dr. Turner's circulatory system work, so much so that shortly before closing time, I already had a sense of what lay ahead on the return to school. I also sensed that in the not-too-distant future I would learn about my stepfather's heart.

At home that evening, my stepfather shared my enthusiasm, even though he didn't understand the content. My mother listened with more patience than usual about what my new routine would mean for helping out. "You still need to be here for dinner, shopping, and housework," she insisted.

"I know, Mother. I promise to do all of that too. Chores on the weekends, and as for the groceries, I'll come home as I need to."

"Well, good. As long as you can keep that up." So ended my mother's interest in that part of my life.

She knew my schedule well: up at seven to make breakfast and my own lunch, out the door by eight, home by four in time to prepare dinner. Once at the library, I found a corner with little distraction, choosing my topics and texts each day during the week, saving the weekends for everything else. It wasn't long before life took another unexpected turn.

On a quiet Saturday afternoon in June, with Richter dozing in his favorite chair, my mother came down the stairs, hat in hand, wearing a bright summer skirt. "I'm off to church. The choir is practicing a new hymn for Sunday Mass. I'll be home in a few hours, in time for dinner. I hope you remember to cook the leg of lamb at 350 degrees. Any higher and it will burn and dry out."

"Yes, Mother. I know. See you then."

The sound of the door creaking closed startled my stepfather from wherever his dreams had taken him.

"Father, that was Mother leaving for choir practice."

Speaking through a groggy yawn, he nodded. "Yes. She does this every once in a while. She'll be there until at least six. It's a chance for her to gossip too."

I went back to the physiology text I had borrowed from the library.

"Is this a good time to talk to you?" he asked. "I hope I'm not interrupting your studies."

"Not at all," I replied. "I could use a break anyway."

"Good. Remember when you first came back from school, there was something on my mind I wanted to go over with you?"

After I nodded that I recalled, he continued.

"I appreciated you talking to your professor about work, but I've always told you not to worry about earning money for school. That hasn't changed." He stopped for a moment, coughing into his handkerchief. "Remember that talk we had about my health at the train station at Christmas? Well, things haven't gotten better. Now the doctor says I have something called heart failure. The disease is making it harder and harder to breathe. I still go to work, but I don't know how much longer I can."

I focused on him and his every word, dreading what was to come.

"They don't know how much longer it will be before I have another heart attack or a stroke. Could be tomorrow or months from now." He took a breath and sighed. "As before, I haven't mentioned this to your mother, only that I get a bit winded from time to time. I think she knows it's more serious than that. But that's not why I wanted to talk to you. Wait here."

He rose from the chair and disappeared upstairs. He reemerged after several minutes, carrying with him a weatherworn wooden lockbox, ordinary looking except for the pale curvature of inlaid mother-of-pearl that adorned its corners. He sat before the living room table, inserted a key, and lifted the top. "I keep my valuables here. There are even a few things I have from when I was growing up in Germany."

I came around to his side of the table. The box was filled with trinkets from a lifetime ago: an old pocket watch, a few German marks, what looked like a ribbon awarded at school, a locket with a photo faded with time. He gently moved them aside and lifted out a small envelope. He pulled back the flap and poured six small diamonds into his hand. "I've been keeping these for you. If you wish, they'll make a beautiful ring when you get married. But no matter what you choose to do with them, they're yours."

A larger manila envelope was just beneath the packet of diamonds. He untied the string and laid its thick contents on the table. "I've been keeping a will for the past several years. I was so pleased to see how well you did at Evander Childs and that you wanted to go to college. I've estimated the cost for the next three years, as I have a good sense of what you need from your first year. No matter what happens to me"—he stopped there as if catching himself before continuing—"no matter what happens, that money will be there."

I had known such kindness and generosity over the years from my stepfather. Here he was once again, this time making sure my future was secure. I realized he wasn't quite finished. The box contained one last envelope. "Irene, there's one more thing: call it insurance in case something comes up." He opened it to reveal small stacks of twenty- and fifty-dollar bills tied together with string. "There's about five hundred dollars here. I've been adding to it as I can, a little less in these times, but I had gotten a good start before October of last year. Use it at Mount Holyoke if you need it. If you don't use it during college, you'll have some money to start you on your way afterward."

He placed all the contents into the box and locked it. "I keep this key in an eyeglass case I don't use, in the back of my closet. Only you know that. Your mother is also provided for, but you'll need to help her in the reading of the will."

I tried my best to keep my composure. "Are you sure, Father?"

"I'm very sure, dear. I wouldn't have it any other way."

"You've meant so much to me. Have I ever told you that your heart condition is why I chose physiology? That I want to learn about how the heart works and maybe help you?"

"Irene, I don't know what to say."

"I wanted you to know how you've been an inspiration to me. I don't know where I'd be without you."

"Your smile and happiness are all I want. Now, I hear your mother coming back. Keep this between us for now."

"Don't worry; I will."

CHAPTER 17

My few friends from high school had moved on with their lives, which helped me stay focused on preparing for my sophomore year. By the end of June, I had eased into my weekday travel to Forty-Second Street, where I often lost track of time, immersed in what seemed a journey along endless paths of my choosing. At some point, around midday, I'd step outside into the heat of the summer and find an empty bench for lunch in nearby Bryant Park, then watch people go about their business as the pigeons pecked at the morsels left behind. Every so often, I strolled along the avenues window-shopping and daydreaming about the fashionable dresses, so different from my *practical* wardrobe at college, but well beyond my means.

But then the earth gave way beneath us.

Returning in the afternoon as I had for each of the past four Fridays, I found Mother at home well before the usual time. She stood as I walked in, her hands shaking, her face ashen, tears glistening at the corners of her eyes. "Otto's in the hospital. The doctors are with him. I'm going to see him now. He's at Lebanon Hospital on the Concourse."

I froze for an instant but then, without waiting for my mother's response, told her, "I'm going with you." She didn't protest.

We sat in silence in the hospital emergency room beside those whose faces mirrored our fear and anguish, and where the soft sobbing of friends, families, and loved ones were the only sounds amid the bustle of staff. After an hour, a man in a white coat approached us.

"Are you Mrs. Richter?"

"Yes."

"I'm Dr. Tomkins. I've just come from seeing your husband. He's had a stroke. He's not conscious, so as of right now we don't know how serious it is. We've made him comfortable. All we can do is wait."

My mother froze, words lost to her, but I wasn't about to let him leave us just yet. "Is there anything we can bring him or do? Can we see him?"

"You can visit for a time now, if you wish. You can bring something familiar from home too. If he wakes up, it might help. What's best is for you to speak softly to him, so he can hear your voices. It can be comforting."

Dr. Tomkins pointed us to the nurses' station. After a few minutes, a nurse's aide escorted us down a long, brightly lit corridor, eventually stopping before a wood and glass door. She nodded for us to enter and left quickly. I didn't know what to expect. The room's barren beige walls, divided by a curtain, gave off little warmth or comfort. We walked past an empty bed to the other side of the red drape that separated the patient areas. My stepfather lay colorless, eyes closed, mouth open, with tubes attached to poles inserted into his veins. For just a moment my mother took my hand in hers, held it tightly, and stood with me at the foot of the bed.

I let go of her and came around to the side of the bed, where I sat for the next hour, talking, willing Father to heal, holding his hand, feeling the warmth, the lifeblood I had known all those years coursing through him.

"I will never forget when we first met," I told him. "How kind you were to me from that very first time. How much you enjoyed my cooking, and our trips to the train station. I always knew you'd be there for me."

With my stories, I gave him tales of school, both heard and unheard, all the time never letting go. During this time, my mother sat, listening and watching for any stirring, any sign of recognition, of life. It was only when we were about to leave that she stood and went over to Father. With a tenderness I'd rarely seen between them, she leaned over the bed railing to caress his left cheek gently with the back of her right hand. "*Isten megtarthatja Önt.* May God keep you."

Once in the corridor outside his room, I knew what to do. "I don't want to leave him alone. Will you stay here while I go home and get some things for us?" I asked. "We may be here for a while."

"Yes, you go home and rest for a bit. I don't need anything now."

I left the hospital and ran to catch the trolley, tripping on the curb just as it was about to pull away. Afraid that the driver would close the door before I could board, I screamed for him to stop. As the door opened, I looked up to see all the passengers staring at me, some with blank expressions, and others with squinting irritation. In that moment, they meant nothing. Only my stepfather's life mattered.

When I reached home, my head and heart were racing against time. *What should I take to comfort him? What would he like to see when he awakens? Does he need clothes or a comb?* I scanned each room in the house, searching for bits and pieces of his life—*our* lives. I hurried back to the hospital after packing a photo from his and my mother's wedding, a small statue of the Blessed Virgin Mary from a table in their bedroom, his favorite pocket watch, toiletries, bread, and cheese.

The hospital halls were empty in those early morning hours except for the nurses at their stations and a janitor mopping floors. I entered my stepfather's room to find my mother softly snoring and my stepfather as he had been, except that his breathing had become shallower than when I'd left.

My mother stirred from her sleep. "How long have you been gone?"

"A few hours. I tried to close my eyes at home but couldn't. It's almost four now. I brought something to eat. Why don't you go to the cafeteria? You can get a cup of coffee there. I'll stay here."

"All right."

Alone with my stepfather, I now heard a slight rasping as he took in what little air his lungs could hold. I sat as before and took his hand in mine. By now, the warmth had drained, and his cool fingers and palm signaled a prelude to a final act. I wouldn't let go, helplessly hoping that my warmth, my life, would somehow flow into him and give him the strength to stay a little longer.

A few more minutes passed before my mother returned. "Mother, please get someone."

A look of panic came over her. "What is it?"

"Something's changed. I think we're losing him."

She ran out of the room and returned with the doctor on duty. He listened for a few seconds with his stethoscope and then lifted my stepfather's eyelid. "Your father is dying. If it's of any comfort, I can tell you he's not suffering. But there's nothing more we can do."

My mother collapsed into the chair. Turning to the doctor, I asked, "How much longer?"

"Today. This morning. Not long. I'm sorry. I'll come back after I check another patient." With those words, he left.

Within the hour, shortly after sunrise on an ordinary day in the middle of summer in the city, an end came to what was to me a generous, loving life, my guiding spirit. With one last kiss, I bid him goodbye.

***

I soon learned that as much as my stepfather had tried to hide his condition, my mother had prefigured his funeral. She had spoken about a Mass and arrangements with the parish priest, Father Avila. My stepfather had planned for almost anything that involved money and had set aside enough to cover the expenses.

The funeral, on a brilliant, sunny day in July, was a simple affair. An open-casket viewing at Crestview Funeral Home drew a few neighbors and parishioners. In the hushed quiet of that space, over coffee and cookies, I spoke to those who had gathered.

"I wanted to say a few words about my father. The poet E. E. Cummings once wrote that, like life, 'Death is no parenthesis,' and that memory creates new ways of knowing and new ways of loving. What I've written for him is what I know in my heart.

Thank you, my stepfather,
For without you I would not know how strong I can be.
For telling me you loved me.
For all you did and sacrificed.
For being human, for being there.
For pushing me to do more and to set my aim high.
For loving my sausages and cabbage.
For allowing me to bring joy into your life.
For letting us know about the pain of life and living.
And for letting me hold your hand as your life slipped away.
Above all, thank you for all you were and all you have
shown me."

I had been standing all this time, but as I came to the end, I felt as if my legs were about to give way. I grasped the back of a chair for support, moved past my mother, and sat down next to her.

Mrs. Kokas, who lived a few doors down from us, stood and shuffled slowly to the front of the room. Turning to us, she dabbed her cheek with a tissue before speaking in her Hungarian-inflected English. "Your stepfather was such a gentle person. I never heard him say a mean word about anyone. We will miss him. There aren't enough people like Otto Richter in this world today."

A few neighbors walked the short distance to the church. Once there, only Father Avila spoke, but his New Testament words were a fitting epitaph: "Blessed are the meek, for they shall inherit the earth."

My mother and I were alone with him on his last journey. The hearse wound its way through the streets to Woodlawn Cemetery. We inched our way along a narrow dirt path past tombstones, some standing as erect monuments while others were lost in moss. All of them marked the end of time for young and old, those known to many or no one. After a few minutes, we stopped before a plot of newly dug earth. There my stepfather would be, beside others new to this resting place. I looked to his gravestone to find one final gesture: My stepfather had reserved a place for all of us to be together.

During this trip to the cemetery and afterward too, my mother's rosary never left her hand. She said prayer after prayer while whatever grief she felt went unsaid. I wanted us to share our loss, but I knew not to breach that wall, just as I knew not to breach the one that held back my grandmother. Home didn't lessen that separation. As my mother retreated to her bedroom, I remained downstairs, feeling the oppression of my stepfather's absence as if a vacuum had replaced air. I sat in his chair, taking in what residue of him remained, the sweater that still hung over the back, the pipe he smoked on rare occasions. I sat as he did and let my senses touch a vestige of our past and what he had been. It was only then that I came to realize what was missing in the waning days of his life: My mother had never let his daughters know of their father's passing.

***

I tried to move on in the days that followed, but the thought of my stepfather's daughters not knowing about their father's death haunted me. I didn't understand the force that drove such a never-to-be-forded separation between them. But I knew that my mother had conjured a similar fate that he and I endured and that while I wasn't yet free of the ties that bound me to her demands about leaving behind my past life in Hungary, I wasn't about to let it rest with his family.

From my conversations with Richter, I knew that Dorothy and her husband had moved to New Jersey and Jean's husband had found a job working on oil rigs in Texas. Katherine, though, still lived in the Bronx, not far from us. I made a vow in his memory to find her.

On a Wednesday morning after breakfast, I walked out of the house in search of my stepfather's past. It didn't take long to find where Katherine lived. Her home resembled ours, a row house with a flowerbed of daisies wilting in the summer heat. Walking up the six steps, I heard the cries of an infant coming from behind the green-and-gold-painted door, then heavy steps approaching. I knocked, and a tall blonde woman with a little one in her arms greeted me. I said, "Hi. Are you Katherine?"

She appeared quite puzzled at the stranger standing before her and hesitated for a moment. "Yes, I'm Katherine. What do you want? If you're selling something, you can see I'm very busy."

"I'm Irene. Your father is my stepfather."

Her eyes widened. "You're Irene? Oh my God. Come in. Come in."

I stepped into a living room and navigated my way around a floor littered with children's toys and trinkets. "I apologize for the mess. This one, her name's Martha, keeps me going all the time, as does her brother, Otto. He's in his room upstairs. Please, sit down. Can I get you a cup of coffee?"

"No, thank you. I'm sorry to surprise you, but I didn't have your phone number."

"Oh, not at all. Otto wrote about you, so although we've never met, I feel like I know you. He always says the kindest things, like you're one of us."

"He told me all about you. Dorothy and Jean too. He missed you terribly."

With those words, Katherine's eyes filled with tears. "Seeing you just reminds me of the lost years. This separation has been awful for all of us. I don't understand your mother keeping us apart all this time. How lonely he must have been after our mother died that he'd allow it to happen." Then, turning her attention to the infant in her arms for an instant, she asked what she most wanted to know. "Are you here to tell me that maybe your mother has had second thoughts?"

"Katherine, it's not that. It breaks my heart to tell you: Your father died two weeks ago."

She gasped, and her tears became a stream. "No! No! No! It can't be!" she cried out.

"I'm so, so sorry that this is what brings us together for the first time. But I couldn't go on with you and your sisters not knowing." I rose to embrace her, but she turned away, swaying as she did. She steadied herself, placing her left hand on a side table, then falling onto a well-worn sofa as her infant bounced in her arms. At that moment, her composure and welcoming words fell away. When she spoke again, it was from a place she seemed to have carried with her for years.

"I hate your mother. I hate her! We'll never see him again because of her." Rising from the sofa, she motioned me toward the door. "I must ask you to leave. I know you're not to blame, but you being here reminds me of why he's lost to us."

"I understand. I really am sorry. I'll go."

I knew no words would comfort her, so I simply left as quickly as I could.

Katherine's bitterness wasn't what saddened me. It was a sense that someone who might have drawn me even closer to my step-father's memory was now lost to me. Still, I was determined to keep his spirit alive as well as who he was, what we were. I was desperate to forestall the fog of forgetfulness. Any hope that my mother would help was lost, as she said little to me and seemed not to have any wish to recall what was now her past. Instead, the present and future—her present and future—dominated our conversation.

"I don't know if there's enough money for me to live on," she said.

"Mother, we've been over this more than once. I know you worry about it, but Father Richter did a lot to make sure you're okay. The house is paid for. His life insurance policy, all five thousand dollars, goes to you. You should continue working to make sure you have enough for the future, but you will be fine for now."

She said she understood, but her look belied her words. "But who's going to be here for me now?" she said. With an ominous resolution, she came to the point. "I want you to transfer to a school here and live at home with me."

What bitter irony! My mother, abandoning her mother, now telling me it was my duty to be with her. I had no intention of giving up Mount Holyoke but knew better than to attack her demand head-on. I tried to assuage her fear, hoping she would feel differently in time.

"This is such a difficult time for us. It's still only July. I'll be here a few more weeks, and we can talk about the future, but it's too late for me to transfer now."

"What if you took a semester off? That way you could stay here and start school in January."

"Mother, as you know, I've started some things at school that I can't get out of. I'll be extra careful with what I spend and come home, maybe for Thanksgiving and, of course, Christmas."

My suggestion didn't sit well.

"Let me be clear, Irene. I want you here. I don't care how you do it. Figure out a way."

As much as I didn't intend to give in to her, I understood it was pointless to continue, so I tried to smile, and then said, "We'll talk about it later."

Some weeks had passed since I dreamed about my grand-mother, as less-troubled times had set my mind at ease. With all that had happened, though, uneasiness and a sense of foreboding had returned. One night, soon after Richter died, she came to me. We were sitting together at Cowles Lodge, in the great room. *"I'm scared, Momma,"* I told her. *"I don't know what Mother will do, and I feel if she has her way, who I am will disappear."*

At first, my grandmother didn't say anything. In my dream, her gaze moved around the room, landing on the fireplace, the photos on the walls, a few girls talking and laughing nearby. Taking it in, she smiled. *"This is where you belong now."*

Her words became my fortress for the days to come.

Esther's friendship had sustained me during this time. I didn't respond to her earlier letters, but she paid it no mind, as if somehow she understood what I was going through. They continued to come until I finally found time to reply. We held each other in our words as I relived my stepfather's death and she relayed the uneasy truce that had settled over her parents' marriage after her father had confessed his breach of trust to her mother. The love and loss I couldn't express at home poured out on paper, and her consolation returned to comfort me.

Our letters seemed to reveal an awakening within each of us of what life had wrought. It was as if we were emerging from a protective shell to face the realities of our lives more fully, if not fully prepared.

An epiphany of resignation and resolve began to crystallize through these writings to my friend: that all the love for my mother might not be enough to overcome what bitterness my being, my existence, had conjured up within her. For Esther, her family's trial eroded the security of a childhood she realized was gone forever. There were no easy answers for what would come next for us, but we knew our bond would help us through.

Time passed quickly. By August, the tone of our letters grew more lighthearted, as we knew the new school year wasn't far away. When I asked Esther what meant the most to her in this world, her reply was the same as mine: the beauty of Holyoke and our Cowles Lodge. My mind was already drifting away from the city and preparing to return to school. I had made a point since my stepfather's death to defer to my mother's wishes within reason, offering to attend her choir sessions at church, shopping and cooking her favorite dishes, and picking up around the house before she returned from work. These and other gestures seemed to lessen tension over my plans and her financial worries. Still, as my day to depart approached, I knew that she hadn't forgotten her plan for me to move back home.

"I see you've started packing as you said you would. What about finishing college here? When will you transfer?"

I had given quite a bit of thought to what I saw as her ultimatum, and I was determined not to give in but to explain why completing my education at Mount Holyoke should appeal to her and quiet her fears. Easing my anxiety was the knowledge that Richter had secured my future, and there was little my mother could do to sabotage it.

"Mother, do you remember our conversation about where I might go to college? Schools in the city were a possibility, but what I'll never forget is how you felt when I was accepted at Holyoke. You were so proud of me that you told our neighbors, the parish priest, the choir, even the butcher and the shopkeepers. You know what else? Thanks to all your etiquette lessons, I've never embarrassed myself at college. And one more thing: My college is still one of the best in the country for women. It'll put me ahead when it comes time to get a good job, especially in these days."

Before I'd made my case, I sensed that my mother had come to a decision that wasn't to be denied, but my words seemed to stop her premeditated train of thought. I had struggled to assure her that what *I* wanted would please her: to leave the exalted impression she wanted to make to others and to right some injustice not known to me but that she felt life had dealt her.

"We'll see. I'm alone now, and you're my daughter, and daughters take care of their mothers. You have three more years of college. That's a long time not to be here with me."

There it was again. My mother had no sense of the hypocrisy that rang out in those words.

"I'll do what I can to travel home more often," I reminded her.

I wouldn't say my mother was at peace with what I'd decided, but for that moment, she let it rest.

I breathed a sigh of relief. Now I could concentrate on what the coming months had in store. Although I was still at home, my time, attention, and thoughts turned to Holyoke. I collected notes from my days at the public library, put together essentials for school, and made sure tuition and other finances were in order. When it came time to say goodbye, my mother allowed a kiss and a gentle embrace. Her words were few beyond wishing me well, reminding me to write often, and urging me to return for Thanksgiving at the latest.

My eagerness to return to school made my journey by train seem to last forever. Fields, towns, and trees crept by as if teasing my thinning patience. I dozed off from time to time, drifting into classes and campus as if my dreams were setting scenes of what was to come. Classmates and teachers passed before me, resuming what they were and did when last I saw them, everything in order as they and the school anticipated a return to a life suspended.

I awoke with thoughts of another time and place. Nine years had passed since I'd left Hungary. I had never written to my grand-mother again, as there was something so forbidding about Mother's words. Now, my year away at school and all that had passed over the summer had loosened her grip. Fear of the forbidden no longer restrained me. I didn't want to defy my mother, but I no longer would tolerate her rule. I reached into my bag, took out pen and paper, started writing, and didn't stop. I channeled my life with and without her on page after page. Tales tumbled out like beads of precious memories upended from the box long hidden. Final words echoed my affection and yearning:

Momma, you are never far away, as I travel to you in my days and nights. As I search for who I am and what I might be, you are there beside me with your wisdom and love. You are my strength and my guiding light. I pray for you and that we may be with each other again.

Love always,
Irene

Holyoke loomed before me at the end of twenty pages. More than one journey had just ended. In rereading what I'd written, I was surprised to see that, in all those lines and paragraphs, I'd left no room to embed my mother's words about the life she'd left behind.

I arrived to a quiet campus that evening. Cowles was deserted except for a few students who, like me, had returned to prepare for the semester early or to work with professors on projects. My room was as I had left it, empty of possessions and awaiting its residents once again. I unpacked my suitcase and sat on my bed. Esther had written that her summer vacation would delay her return but that she couldn't wait to see me. Remembering that sweet sentiment, the room didn't seem quite so bare.

I had returned to school with little time to spare. After a restless first night, I awoke early the next morning, dressed quickly, sat alone in an almost empty dining room for as long as it took to down a scrambled egg and cup of coffee, and made my way to Clapp Hall. As expected, Dr. Turner was already at her desk, her door slightly ajar. I knocked and leaned in.

"Good morning, Dr. Turner."

"Good morning, Miss Richter. You're the last of this year's students to arrive, but your letter explained why. I'm very sorry to hear about your stepfather. From what you wrote, I understand he made it possible for you to be here. Well, let's make the best of it, then, in his memory. Later I'll introduce you to the other students, but for now, let me take you to Dr. Haywood's office. She's met everyone except you and wants to get started working with all the students."

Dr. Turner rose and escorted me a few doors down from her office. With an impatient knock, we walked in.

The department's newest professor sat behind stacks of unopened boxes at a desk piled high with papers and unopened containers. She came around from behind her desk as soon as we entered and stood before us, a woman younger than Dr. Turner by some years, petite and pretty, with a warm smile, rounded features, and short straight hair that fell between a darker blonde and brown.

"Good morning, Dr. Haywood. I'd like to introduce you to the sixth and last of our students for this year, Irene Richter."

"Nice to meet you," she said in my direction. "I've read your file, and now I can put a face to it."

"Good morning, Dr. Haywood. I've been reading about your

research and look forward to helping you. I'm very excited to be part of the physiology program."

With a distracted goodbye, Dr. Turner left us alone.

"Before we begin, I wanted to say Dr. Turner and I spoke about your sad news and why you were delayed in returning. I lost my father a few years ago. I miss him, as I imagine you do your stepfather. All I can say is my sadness has lessened, and my memories of him are a source of great solace to me."

"Thank you, Dr. Haywood. Yes, I feel he's still with me."

"Well, in that case, his spirit can keep us company as we plan your future. I know you've spoken with Dr. Turner about your interest in physiology, but I'd like to hear why you chose it as your major."

There was something so disarming and open about her. I relaxed in those cluttered surroundings and spoke briefly, telling her about my growing interest in nutrition, what makes our heart fail, and what keeps it and our other organs well.

"Thank you. Let me fill you in a bit on my background and the research that you'll be helping to further. I don't know whether you're aware, but this isn't my first time at Holyoke. In the early 1920s, I was an instructor in this department and came to love this school and my students. The legacy of Dr. Clapp and the research that Dr. Turner began here were so important because they elevated women's studies beyond the subordinate work to men in the field. President Woolley instilled it in all of us, then and now. You may know one of her sayings: 'How uncomfortable to be a static woman in a world where all the men are moving.' She was truly inspiring and a great part of the reason I left to attend the doctoral program at the University of Pennsylvania. Now that I'm back, I intend to fulfill that promise."

She gestured to some boxes that surrounded her. "What you see here is much of the work I started and plan to continue. For some time, I've been interested in the research that Dr. Turner has undertaken on respiration, heart, and the effects of carbon dioxide. In addition to studies conducted here among students, I've focused on species such as trout and frogs. In some ways, it complements Dr. Turner's work, but it also takes it in another direction. Irene, have you heard of a new organization and site called Woods Hole?"

"No. I've read up on some of your research, but I haven't come across it."

"I'd be surprised if you had. Woods Hole is a research center located on the coast, about four hours from here. It was founded this year, and I intend for it to become a center for my research. The lab work you and your fellow students will be doing will help me not only here but also in the research I have planned for Woods Hole."

I sat and listened, letting her words sink in.

"This is a very exciting time to be part of an emerging field," she said. "Class, studies, and research will require full commitment. I'm here to support and encourage you in what you choose to pursue and to make it fulfilling at the same time. Somewhere in this sea of boxes, I have a little desk plaque that reads 'A model of virtue I must confess, you can have fun nevertheless.' That's my intent: to conduct and produce honest, inspired, leading work we can be proud of and have a great time doing."

I smiled and nodded, barely able to contain my enthusiasm. I kept my mouth closed as I hung on her every word, feeling that she wasn't quite finished.

"Now that you have an idea of the work and program, at least as far as your involvement with our research will go, I have a question for you. What I've told you might seem a different place from where you started when you decided on your major. Do you still feel you've made the right decision?"

The question took me by surprise, as I was so taken by her passion and sensitivity.

"Before I walked in, I knew that physiology was what I wanted to pursue. Listening to you has only made my commitment stronger. It will be a privilege to work with you."

"And what about your stepfather's passing?"

"This is a tribute, a dedication to him."

"Good. Then it's decided. Now, please excuse me," she said, raising her arms. "As you can see, I have a lot of unpacking to do."

***

When I dropped into fall, I fell into the land of the familiar: classes, study, library, welcome weekend diversions, and meals with fellow Cowles Lodgers. My school concentration and all academic demands took over my life. I quickly became dedicated to tasks in the physiology lab, the gradual, meticulous fulfillment of class assignments and helping Drs. Haywood and Turner, and other faculty, with their research and experiments. Upper-division students kept watch over our work but had little desire to socialize, leaving our small cohort—Adelaide, Gertrude, Marjorie, Carolyn, Louise, and me—to commiserate and find our way together. That we did, relying on each other to help navigate our science courses. This bond, built on books, papers, and seminars, seemed to exhaust the desire for anything outside our studies. We knew what we had to do, and most everything else fell away.

My friendship with Esther assumed its natural rhythm without pause, helping me to navigate these days and find what had been an elusive peace of mind. Our conversations picked up where our correspondence left off. "My stepfather was the voice of calm in our house," I told her. "Sometimes, when my mother was so hard on me, so hurtful, I felt trapped and thought that if it continued, I'd lose my mind. Then he'd come home from work, and most of the time things settled down. Now I don't know what will happen when I go back."

"Do you have someone there you can talk to? I ended up seeing the minister at our church about what happened with my dad. I've known him since I was a kid. He really helped me, at times just by listening. Things are still not quite right at home, as I feel my dad hasn't settled what happened with my mom. But I realized what happened wasn't my fault, and there's nothing I can do about it. I loved my father before he told me, and I don't want to lose that."

"I've been thinking about talking to the priest at our church when I go back. I have to tell you, coming back to school is like stepping into a different world. I don't have to worry about home life right now, and it's great. I can just sink into my work, what's going on here, and my friends like you."

"That about sums it up for me too," Esther said. "I couldn't have said it better."

CHAPTER 18

Although my schedule granted me little freedom, I still found time for the Cosmopolitan Club. I had come back to school determined to support it in whatever way possible. I had arrived late that evening to the first meeting after a chemistry lab, just as Felidia gaveled the meeting to order and posted her list of topics and to-dos.

"I want to pick up where we left off with planning our gala, but first I want to welcome one of our new members. Angi, if you'd start us off. Please introduce yourself."

"Hello, or *Szia*, as they say in my homeland, Hungary. I'm Angi, a freshman, and I'm so glad to be here. Mount Holyoke was my first choice, and I feel very lucky to be accepted."

I smiled. Another Hungarian. She was dressed in typical school fashion, had a similar broad face to my own, and dark hair in curls, but she was a bit taller and slimmer than me. At the break, I offered a greeting in our language.

"Oh, Irene, it's so good to meet you! I thought I'd be the only one!" she cried.

Students standing next to us giggled as words in my native language tumbled out in rapid fire. I told her about the school, Cowles, and New York, and Angi readily kept pace as she told me about living in Albany after her family emigrated and how she had wanted to attend a sister school and Holyoke was the first to accept her. The gavel fell to reconvene the meeting just as our conversation hit yet a faster gear.

Felidia let us know that to broaden the appeal of our event, the school had urged the Club to make our activities part of Holyoke's annual May Day celebration. We now had a longer time to organize what we had already laid out to do. Responsibilities turned toward managing tasks and time and assuring that we remained truly international in displays, activities, and capturing worlds beyond our shores.

Felidia then called on Dr. Aldis to speak about his upcoming sessions. "For those who were here last term, you may remember that I'm putting together a program on the threat of fascism both here and abroad. I'm asking for your help, as we're seeing its effects across the world in hate speech and violence against immigrants and others. Recalling the words of the Cosmopolitan Club motto, I'm thinking of calling the event Humanity in Our Times. While I want our day's discussions to explore how we can make things better, we'll need to talk about threats to democracy here and abroad. I think the work of your club and clubs like this around the country are good examples of how we can bring people together not only to see what we need to do but also to understand how far we have to go." He paused there. "Any questions so far? Ingrid?"

"Do you want Club members to talk to attendees about our experiences and what they've meant to us?"

"Absolutely. It's critical that all at the college, students and faculty, know what people of different heritage have faced. Maricel?"

"Will it include others who for one reason or another are not at Holyoke?"

"Possibly others. Are you thinking of any people or place in particular?"

"Well, in Spain, where I'm from, Jews are such a big part of our heritage, and they're the ones who seem to suffer most of all. They've been beaten up on the street and had their synagogues burned in Germany. By the way, I don't think America is always a great place for them, either. Take our school. Holyoke has a reputation of, let's just say, not admitting many Jewish students, if any. How many of you know any Jewish people here? Do we even have any here now? There may be a few, but they're afraid to let anybody know. We need to talk about why that happens here and what, if anything, we should do about it."

No one at the school knew about my real father. Suddenly the stories my grandmother, Johann, and others had told about my father's exile and threats to his life came flooding back. To be silent, I felt, would be to forsake those few memories of him.

I raised my hand. "I just want to second Maricel's suggestion. It's very important with all that's happened to Jews and is happening now in Germany and other countries."

A few murmurs rippled through the room. After they died down, Dr. Aldis continued. "Does anyone have any questions about this?" Waiting a moment, he continued. "As I don't hear any, we'll plan to include it in the day's program. Felidia?"

"Thank you, Dr. Aldis. With that, I move to adjourn—"

"Felidia, I have one more request," Dr. Aldis interrupted. "I'd like to ask for volunteers to help plan the sessions and logistics."

Maricel, Ingrid, and I raised our hands at the same time.

"Great. I'll let the three of you know when we can meet. It should be by the end of the week."

As we left the meeting, I caught up with Angi on the way to the dining room. "I have quite a story to tell about how I came here. Do you want to have dinner?"

Angi nodded eagerly, and we took off for the dining room.

"So, tell me. What were your travels like?" I asked.

"Where to begin? I came over with my mother and father about ten years ago. We had a really nice house in the Buda hills across the river from Pest, not far from the Budavári Palota castle. My father made it through the war without dying, unlike so many of his friends. He had worked at a bank before and had been so hopeful that the new government wanted Hungary to be a democracy like America, so he took a job in the finance ministry. It was soon after that everything started to go wrong. Communists wanted to take over the country and fought with people who didn't want them to. Some wanted a king to rule like we'd had before the war. Riots broke out. Many people died. Even at my school, my friends wanted to know which side I was on. Neighbors turned against each other. It was awful. Did this happen where you lived?"

"No, but there were very frightening times," I replied. "In our small town, not too far from Romania, we didn't have riots, but we had something you probably didn't have: roaming armies, Communist, Romanian, others. It was almost as if they took turns killing our people and destroying what little we had."

"How terrible. Like you, we were very scared. My father said if we stayed, he'd probably end up in prison or worse. My mother knew that would be the end of us. It wasn't much later that they made plans for us to leave. And that's why we're here."

Absorbed in stories about what we'd left behind, it seemed that neither of us had any desire to stop. "Do you miss home?" I asked.

"Oh, yes, very much. Have you been to Budapest? It's so beautiful. Where we lived, almost everywhere we went was a steep hike, but when I could, I'd make my way down to that castle, walk over to the wall that overlooked the Danube and Pest on the other side, and get lost in how pretty my city is. Every once in a while, our family would take the funicular down the hill to the chain bridge and cross into Pest. Those were such wonderful days. We'd start out at the museum, then have a pastry and take the bridge to Margitsziget Island, which sits between Buda and Pest. My mother would prepare a picnic for us, with bread, sausages, carrots, potatoes, and a plum or apple tart. After playing in the park, we'd have dinner in Pest at my favorite place, Mátyás Pince. It was always a special treat. We'd all stuff ourselves on roast goose and dumplings and then waddle home like ducks. Oh, Irene, you must see it sometime!"

"You make it sound so wonderful. I've only been to the train station."

"Well, if we're lucky, maybe we can one day go together, but it won't be for a while. Things aren't so great there now. When things get better."

"When that time comes, I'd love to."

We had stood before the dining hall for some time talking but now hurried, as service would end soon. Others had drifted in from the Club meeting, dining later than usual. We joined them just as Carol, a tall, bespectacled senior from the North Rockefeller Lodge and a member of Delta Sigma Rho, the debating society, posed a question to all seated nearby.

"Do any of you know any Jews?" She elongated the last word for effect.

Carol's question unnerved me. Her tone seemed to say more than her words. Like the others at the table, I said nothing, but I felt a distinct foreboding about where this was going. After a few seconds, Eunice, a pale, small-boned sophomore who I only vaguely remembered, was the first to respond. "No. Someone said there's one here now, but that may be wrong. I would think not."

"I don't know about now, but Mildred told me there was one here a few years ago."

Mildred, from South Rockefeller Lodge and old money, who wore only the latest fashions even for dinner in the cafeteria, had spoken with pride about royal lineage in my history class, so Carol's source of information didn't surprise me. I had no intention of letting the question go. "Carol, why do you ask?"

"I just don't think it's a good idea to have them here," she replied, with a tone of cocksure arrogance.

"But why?" I ventured to ask.

"They just don't fit in. They're different. They stick to their own. From what I hear, it's the same at the other sister schools. We're pretty much like them."

"Really?" I said incredulously. "You really think that?"

"Yep. And it's just as well. I don't know any, but I've heard they're greedy, always about money. You've read *The Merchant of Venice*, haven't you? Remember Shylock, before he saw the light and converted? Well, there you have it. Oh, and one more thing. We go to church on Sunday, don't we? We might be Protestants or Catholics, but the bottom line is Holyoke is a school for Christian girls. No one goes to a synagogue. Can you imagine one here? No baptism, no confirmation. Do I have to go on?"

"No, you've made yourself pretty clear." By now, I was building up a head of steam.

"It's pretty obvious that they just don't belong here," she continued. "And I get the sense the school feels the same way."

"How can you feel that way about Jews and not students who come from other countries?" I asked.

"That's different. You see how well everybody gets along here? I don't have a problem with that. You try to fit in. You're Christian. You speak English, not, what do they even speak? Hebrew? Yiddish? I like to meet people who are Americans. I see you and the others sitting around this table as Americans. And besides, do you know of any women Jews who are worth their salt?"

"What about Gertrude Stein?" I said with a laugh. "She's brilliant, a great writer. And, oh, you don't happen to have your portrait painted by Picasso like she does, do you?"

Carol raised her voice, bristling and losing patience because someone dared to challenge her. "An exception. There's always an exception. Congratulations—you found one."

Carol had been talking to all at the table, only glancing at me from time to time. Now she turned her gaze and, with a trace of wariness, addressed me. "You've sure asked a lot of questions. How come?"

I felt exposed in that instant. What would they think, knowing my father was a Jew? But I wouldn't let that fear take over. "Actually, Carol, I think of the Cosmopolitan Club as having no cultural limits. What if we said we wouldn't accept people from Africa because they have different customs and they look different? Or Russia because they might be Communists?"

"Maybe the Club, which was here before you, knew better. In any case it's a moot point we don't have to deal with, unless there are some Jews here now who won't say so."

By now Angi, and everyone else for that matter, was staring at me. I realized the conversation wasn't going to be settled tonight and so turned it back to the Club plans. "Well, I for one am glad that Maricel raised this at our meeting tonight. And Dr. Aldis's seminar will be a good place to discuss it."

Carol picked up her tray and left in a bit of a huff but without a final word. Those around the table, though, weren't ready to let it go. "Well, that was something," Ingrid said. "No matter what, what you said about the Club is true. It's not the place to close the door on anyone because they're different or people have preconceived notions about them."

Others around the table nodded in agreement, all except Eunice, who once again seemed to disappear.

As Angi and I walked out after this exchange, she turned to me. "Is this a typical topic for Club members? It's not what I expected."

"No, Angi, not at all. Why some people single out Jews, I'm only beginning to understand."

"I don't get it either. Jews were everywhere in Budapest. We bought our clothes from them, some taught at my school and the university, and others worked in government with my father. I even went to a friend's house for Seder once. I do know that when the riots and fighting started, people blamed them for the rising cost of food, shortages, everything. It made me wonder if people felt that way all along and just didn't bring it up or if they needed someone to point the finger at and say, 'It's their fault.'"

Maybe it was her warmth and understanding, or that we shared a common motherland, but I hesitated for a moment before saying what I said next. "That was more than a dinnertime disagreement for me. It was personal."

"I know what you mean. I didn't like what she said either."

"No, no. That's not what I mean. My father was a Jew. I never knew him because he left the town where we lived, but I do know it's part of who I am. Tonight gave me a window into my own past. What Carol said, all you told me about Jews in Budapest, what's happening in Germany, even the things I'm reading about eugenics, Jews, and inferior races, where did this all come from? Why them? And what would Carol and others say if they knew about my father?"

Angi's eyes widened, and for just an instant, I thought my revelation might have been a mistake. "I'm so happy you told me! Growing up in Budapest, Jews were a part of the world I lived in. Coming here, I thought it would be the same. I don't understand Carol either. Maybe the Club's the place to bring it up. That way we could decide what to do about it for the school."

"You're right. But even with the support at the table tonight, I'm not ready to let people know."

"Not to worry. It'll stay with me until you're ready. That's totally up to you."

We stood outside in the cold a little longer. When we parted, I still wasn't ready to return to Cowles. I took in the cool of that October evening, finding the path over the stream that ran through the college, stepping softly over the carpet of fallen leaves that cushioned and covered the stones. I was lost in thought about how far I had come from the land of my birth through the sea of humanity at Ellis Island to where I came to live with a mother I had never known—and a Jewish father, who would always be unknown—to Holyoke. I couldn't see what was next but now understood that chance and choice had destined my life and were setting an uncharted course for what was to come.

That unsettled feeling stayed with me through the days leading up to the meeting with Dr. Aldis. The Club discussions and encounter with Carol had opened my eyes to the ignorance and racism that festered beneath the surface on campus, and they left me with a sense of urgency about what we were about to undertake.

We all arrived on time at Dr. Aldis's office that Saturday morning to find him in a chair at his desk, staring at a map of Europe on a wall nearby. "Good morning. I've been looking forward to our meeting. Please sit." He motioned us to a round table with papers that now lay in a pile on a chair and quickly made the importance of our task clear.

"I'll get right to the point. What's happening in countries across this continent these days is adding a sense of urgency to what we are about to undertake. Just this week, I read about the growing numbers of Nazi Party Brownshirts terrorizing Jews in Berlin and how that party is on the verge of bringing down the Weimar Republic administration. The conference can be our way of educating students and faculty about this danger. I know you and other Club members have a lot to contribute to setting our day's agenda. I've sketched out times for the day's events but wanted to hear from all of you before filling in the content."

Maricel spoke first. "I've been thinking a lot about what's

happening in Europe right now. It may not be so different from all that's happened in Spain over the years. Muslims, Jews, and Catholics used to live in harmony, but over time so many were killed or told to leave because of their beliefs. Now democracy seems lost.

"Our last leader, Miguel Primo de Rivera, was a dictator through and through. His motto, 'Country, Religion (the Catholic church), Monarchy,' didn't leave room for differences of opinion and the way people lived. This new person, Francisco Franco, has been around for some time. He looks like he'll continue that legacy, especially the dictatorship. And what I see happening in Italy and Germany, I feel like it's a movie I've seen before."

Dr. Aldis nodded. "I agree, Maricel, and while I hadn't focused on Spain specifically, what you've told us captures what I think should be one of the major sessions. Perhaps we could call it The Rise of Dictatorships in Europe and the Threat to Humanity. We could even have a second session on the dangers of religious intolerance."

I had been waiting my turn. "I agree. As I said at the Club meeting, we need to pay as much attention to all that's going on in America, like laws passed to keep people from other countries out, except for what they call 'desirables,' like you, Ingrid. They seem to really like your part of the world.

"Did you hear about the law that passed when Calvin Coolidge was president? The Immigration Act of 1924 is still with us now. They may as well have called it the anti-immigration act. No Mexicans, not letting in people from places like Japan or Eastern or Southern Europe. But if you came from England or Scandinavia, you were, as I said, a desirable. President Coolidge's slogan kind of summed up what he and I think a lot of others in this country believed: 'America must be kept American.' I can tell you this: If I tried to come here now, I'd be one of the unclean undesirables and wouldn't stand a chance at getting in. I don't even know if I would have been allowed to try."

Ingrid smiled. "That would've been our loss, Irene."

"I'm well aware of these actions and have been paying attention to them for some time," Dr. Aldis said. "Again, it's a topic for another session. We could call it Government, Immigration, and the Policy of Exclusion."

Ingrid then added, "As we talk about programs, laws, and government, let's not forget what this has meant for all of us who have come here. As for our personal stories, they should be part of each session. They need to be heard."

We all looked to Dr. Aldis. "It's critical that your voices are heard," he replied. "I will ensure it's a core part of the day."

By now, all in our small group were leaning in, eager to hear what turn our conversation would take next. "I want to come back to what some have called 'the Jewish problem,'" I said. "It seems no matter where we look across much of Europe and now the United States, the Jews are envied, hated, or seen as greedy or as the source of the country's ills. Even my family in Hungary believed these myths. Dr. Aldis, some of the students have also wondered why Holyoke has so few Jewish students. Is it by choice? From what I've read about how some colleges are finding ways to keep them out, I doubt that's the only reason."

Maricel jumped in. "Exactly my point, Irene. That's what I have been seeing in Spain too. There, it's 'Jews are money grubbing,' but funny, at the same time, many are labeled Communists."

Dr. Aldis didn't offer a session title but instead addressed us directly. "You've given me a lot to work with as I pull this day together. As a professor at this college, I've thought about who's here, who's not, and why. And yes, Irene, from what I've heard, when it comes to Jewish students and even faculty, Harvard, Yale, and other Ivy League schools have taken steps to limit what they see as those who 'don't look like' Americans or don't have the right 'character' to fit in— whatever that may mean in their eyes. I'm certain that immigrants from the so-called 'less desirable' countries are affected too."

"Dr. Aldis," I asked, "what is it that makes one person 'right' and another undesirable because of their character?"

"In this case, I think the term is just a way for justifying prejudice," he replied. "Why do people do it? Ignorance, fear of those who are different, the need for someone to blame for their troubles. Sometimes just being a member of a religion that's not yours can do it. I'll give you an example. On a recent trip to Boston, I passed a retail store that had hung a sign that said 'Help wanted: Irish need not apply.' They lose on two counts, in emigrating from another country and being Catholic."

"As if we needed reminding, your example tells us we will find these attitudes in our own backyard," I replied.

Dr. Aldis reached out and tapped me on the shoulder. "Exactly. I think there's a line of continuity that runs all the way from Europe to America. I'll make sure our sessions reflect that. Let me work up an agenda and get back to you. Now, try to enjoy what you have left of your Saturday."

As we walked into the cold, Ingrid turned to us. "Maricel, your idea was great. Irene, you've been doing some homework, haven't you? All of your suggestions were right on target."

Something had indeed come over me, as if the patches of my history, my various lives, had created something of form and substance. "Yes. The more I thought about all of us coming to America, including my stepfather, my mother, me, I realized that we owned little but the clothes on our backs. And many of our neighbors were, I guess you could say, in the same boat.

"Coming here, we were given a second chance. What have we done with that chance? We've opened businesses, helped other people live their lives, gone to college to help make the country even better. And yet, what do we hear now? More and more talk about foreigners taking jobs, and the opposite, undesirables or ignorant people who just freeload. Or the Jews who are rich and fat from the work of others. You know, coming to this country, I'll never forget seeing the Statue of Liberty for the first time and what it now means for me. Since I've been in America, I've come to know how rich a land it is.

I don't mean dollars, no. Take where we are now. Just being here at this school, coming from a place so far away, I'm being given a chance to learn in ways I could never imagine. I don't want all that opportunity to be lost. Those laws are a symptom of something I'm afraid is more deep-seated here."

Ingrid nodded and said, "You two might think that coming from Sweden, it has been all sweetness and light for me and my family, but more than one person has told us to go back to where we came from too. And they have said things like 'You don't sound like an American, and you don't look American; you're not one of us.'"

"Try having a Spanish accent," Maricel said. "I bet we all have stories about what people have said about how we talk and why don't we learn to speak English the way it's supposed to be spoken."

"I can't tell you how many times that's happened to me," Ingrid said. "Whenever that happens, I just smile back at them and say a few words in Swedish, like 'You smell like pickled herring.'"

"I'm sorry I didn't think of something like that in Hungarian," I said with a chuckle.

We were about to go our separate ways, but I could no longer keep hidden the truth that had remained unsaid that morning. What I had revealed to Angi had freed me from the tyranny of shame and separation. Taking a deep breath, I gathered my courage. "There's one more thing about our meeting today that hit closer to who I am than just talk about international day. My father is a Jew. I never knew him because he left my mother before I was born, but whoever he is, I am too."

The lightness of Ingrid's last words vanished suddenly with my revelation. Her eyes glistened, and she took my hand in hers. "Irene, I am so sorry you had to keep this bottled up. God knows I can see why you did after Carol's rant and all that's happening. You know, it brings everything we talked about today home. Telling me this makes me feel that much more determined to do something about it."

"It just makes me angry," Maricel added with fire in her eyes.

"We talk about the hatred we hear about in other countries when it's happening right here in America—and I'm sorry to say, it's probably right here at Holyoke too. Prejudice against the Jews is part of our international day, but we have to be on guard for this sort of evil every day. Thank you, my friend, for making it that much closer to all of us. What you said brings home the work we need to do."

We had reached a fork in the path, and it was time to head back to our dorms. With that, we went our separate ways, our lives not quite as we had left them prior to the meeting.

***

A few weeks after that meeting, on a cold, crisp Friday in October, Esther took charge of gathering us before dawn. The school had canceled classes to honor Mountain Day, an annual tribute to the land that surrounded our campus, and she was determined to take us on a hike to her favorite Holyoke hills, far from academic classes, papers, and tests.

As we sat in the lounge, Esther prepped us for the trip. "Listen! This is the perfect time of year. Not too hot, not too cold. The oaks, birches, and maples are practically on fire; the colors are so bright. The paths are still in good shape, but they won't be for long. My guess is the snow will be here before we know it and that will be it for hiking until the spring, unless you like trekking uphill in two feet of the white stuff."

Her enthusiasm elicited what seemed a collective yawn, as we were no more than almost awake.

"I know, I know. It's still dark outside, but unless we get going, we won't return until after dark, and coming back at night isn't a good idea."

At that, movement began to happen. Girls returned to their rooms to gather what was needed. For all the groans about the hour, almost all were there: Corinne, Sarah, even the housemother, Mrs. Kennedy, blinked herself awake and took Esther's lead, appearing in her well-worn laced boots, cardigan, and wool knickers.

Esther called on me to help her marshal the troops. "Irene will make sure everyone is ready for our trip, right?"

I shook off what remained of my night and nodded. "Yes. All of you heard Esther. Please make sure you have your snacks, and be ready to leave in ten minutes," I replied, which is what we did in random disorder.

It didn't take long before we appreciated the early hike. The mountain's beauty, rich in the rainbow of autumn colors, drew us in and seduced us into wanting to see what nature would reveal around the next bend and the next. Deer and fox crossed our paths from time to time, warily keeping both pace and distance, perhaps waiting to see if they could make a midday snack from our picnic remnants.

I caught up with Ingrid and Angi, who had heard about our outing and were tagging along with the girls from our lodge. "Each time we're here, it reminds me of how far I've come from Hungary—or the Bronx, for that matter," I said. "And this time of year, there's no place like it."

Ingrid smiled. "Yes, it's beautiful. But if you ever get to see the fjords of Gullmarn in the fall, as the first snows cover the trees or when the winter light reflects off the land, it's different but just as breathtaking."

"I can tell you that Budapest has nothing like this," Angi replied.

The three of us walked along the dirt trail in easy silence. Then Ingrid said, "Irene, I've been really impressed with what you've been saying at the Cosmopolitan Club."

"Oh, thanks. It's made me think about who and what I left behind. Ever since the day I came here, my mother has told me that I'm in America now and that I should forget my past. 'Speak English; act and dress like everyone else,' she always says. You and my other friends have made me feel there's room for where I came from *and* where I am now. But when I hear the hateful things people say about immigrants and Jews, I want to do something, and the Club is a good place to try."

Ingrid had slowed her pace. "That comes through loud and clear, and that's why I want to plant an idea. The Club will need new committee members soon because this is Felidia's senior year, and an officer position—secretary—is opening up too. If it's okay, I'd like to nominate you for secretary. It won't come up until we leave for the semester, but it's not too early to start thinking about it."

"Really?" I asked. "Surely there are others with more experience."

"Experience? Yes. Passion, smarts, and dedication? No one I know. You don't need to decide anything right away, but if it's a possibility, I'd like to bring it up with a few others."

"Thank you for thinking of me. I'd be honored, but I won't be disappointed if someone else is elected."

"We'll worry about that later."

As the sun was setting, we made our way back to campus, quietly shuffling into Cowles exhilarated and exhausted, trailing in clumps of dirt and grass. Mrs. Kennedy, who had returned early as her daylong hikes were well behind her, greeted us at the door, then frowned at the evidence of our day. "You *will* be cleaning this up as soon as you take your showers."

"Yes, Mrs. Kennedy," those of us who had the energy replied as a group.

Esther had gone ahead of me and had left the door open to our room. I had expected to find her undressed, a towel in hand. But she was sitting on her bed, an envelope in her hand.

"This letter's for you, slipped under the door. I stepped on it coming in. I was going to put it on your desk but then looked at the address. It's from Hungary."

Weeks had passed since I'd written. "Esther, I had just about lost hope that I'd hear from anyone, as it's been weeks," I said excitedly.

It took me a few minutes to recall some of the Hungarian words, as I hadn't read in my native language in several years. I knew right away that Uncle Johann had penned the letter by the uneven handwriting and misspellings. He had always been direct, and this letter was no exception.

In the first few lines, he told of my grandmother's death the prior year. There wasn't much detail, just that, at sixty-eight, she'd had a stroke, was bedridden for a few weeks, and then passed away. He and Josef had kept vigil during those days. She was unable to speak but a few words at that time, so they placed near her bedside photos of our family.

"I held each of them before her," Johann wrote. "The look on your grandmother's face changed only once. When I was sitting at her bedside, she looked over at all the pictures on the nightstand. I could see that she wanted one of them. One by one, I held them up to her. She nodded only when I held up a photo of you at nine or ten, dressed in a skirt, in front of our old barn. I could see she wanted to hold it, and when I gave it to her, your grandmother just looked at you and smiled. It wasn't more than an hour later that she passed away. Irene, I was at her side, but so were you."

The rest of his letter merely glanced over other lives, as he was a man of few words. He had married and had a five-year-old son. Josef was still living in our Hajdudorog home. He too had married and was awaiting the birth of his firstborn. Magdalene lived by herself, having raised her children. Johann made a point to stop by every now and then to see if she needed anything. His words softened at the end. "I don't know if we'll ever see you again. We all miss you and hope you are well. But don't forget us here, the farm and the land where you were born."

Esther read in my distant gaze what I couldn't hide, as I was lost in the past. "I'm so sorry, Irene. I'd hoped your letter would bring better news."

"I so wanted to hear all the things my grandmother was doing and what she thought of my life. But in the past few days, I've had such a feeling of sadness. Now I know why. Oh, God, to live knowing I'll never see her again just leaves a hole in my heart. She was so strong. I just never thought of her not being there. Oh, why didn't I find a way to see her one more time?" By now, my tears melted into the letter, as if my grief was now married to the message on the page.

"Irene, please don't torture yourself over what might have been. From what Johann wrote, you were always with her, even at the very end."

As we sat, the only sound was the rhythmic ticking of Esther's clock. By now, it was very late. Esther rose from her bed and sat beside me. "This probably means nothing right now, but your grandmother would be so proud and so happy for you. That and her love will be with you the rest of your life."

"I know. But I feel as if a part of me has broken away and is now forever lost." We said little more that night, but those truths were to shelter me through what was to come.

CHAPTER 19

C lub, class, exams, laboratory. Once again, they took up whatever time I had. Planning for Dr. Aldis's seminar, however, upset the delicate balance I had managed to keep during the fall. We filled in the details for that special day during nights and weekends, extending invitations to speakers, preparing background materials for each session, and finalizing all that fell in between. Felidia added to our planning by deciding that the Club would integrate our international festival's events into the late afternoon and evening of the same day.

Conference day finally came. Dr. Aldis and our small group of advisors gathered nervously as the time for the opening address drew near. At first, we worried that no one would come. About a half hour before the opening, a few people trickled in, then a few more, and gradually, ripple after ripple began to fill and then flood the room. As the auditorium filled beyond capacity, Maricel said what was on all our minds. "How will we manage this number?"

I looked over at Dr. Aldis, who was standing at the entrance to the auditorium, smiling from ear to ear. "This is just what I had hoped for. Stop worrying. When you put these meetings together, you never know who or how many will show up. Let me just say the size of this crowd tells me that there's great interest in what we have planned. I know it's early, but I would call it very promising indeed." His words took the edge off my anxiety, and looking over at Ingrid, I saw her smile for the first time that morning.

So many students and faculty attended that the auditorium was standing room only. In his opening address, our featured speaker, Dr. Robinson from Dartmouth, set an ominous tone for the day, painting a stark portrait of Europe after the Great War, the uncertainty around the League of Nations, and what he saw as the rise of nationalism and something called "nativism" in Italy, Germany, and other places.

His talk set up the next speaker, Professor Pettis from Yale, who'd been studying the history of immigration in America from the end of the last century until now. Most of his lecture was on how the Ivy League and sister schools like Holyoke had changed with the times. It wasn't all pretty by any means, he pointed out. Quotas and "special" screenings kept the number of Jewish students down. As it turned out, our school had been following the lead of Harvard and the other Ivies, and that's why so few Holyoke students were Jews. Others spoke of immigrants and eugenics, how some who came through Ellis Island were considered "mongrel races," inferior people who were infecting the white Americans who had been here for years. A professor from Harvard, Dr. Bolton, said some people called it "race suicide" and that even some professors at the Ivies thought intelligence depended on what you looked like or where you came from.

During these sessions, I waited pensively for how the audiences would respond. A number of the male professors sat quietly stroking their beards and mustaches, looking thoughtful. Students, however, didn't hesitate to ask questions, and for me, a few stood out. Shy Eunice, who had remained so quiet during our tense dining room conversation, asked Dr. Bolton, "What are you doing as a professor to fight this at your school? And what suggestions might you have for us at Holyoke?"

"I am so glad you asked that question," he replied. "Read and learn about the history of our country and the immigrant contribution. Have those who have changed their minds for one reason or another speak to those like them who hold bias close. And don't forget just being in the company of those not like you, here at Holyoke and elsewhere, can help dispel prejudice."

As Eunice thanked Dr. Bolton, the audience erupted in applause. I listened eagerly to several students probe for answers and suggestions during other sessions but held my breath when Carol raised her hand after Professor Pettis's speech.

"Thank you for the stimulating presentation," she began. "But I wanted to ask you about these quotas. Might there be a good reason that some of the great schools felt it was good for them to do?"

Professor Pettis was shaking his head even before he spoke, and his reply echoed our words. "There's no good reason to do so. Immigrants and Jews have made such contributions to science, medicine, literature. That is indisputable. But I think resistance comes from fear of those who seem different in some way, someone forever cast as the 'other,' never to fit into my world. And I believe some in our country seek a scapegoat, a person or group whom they can blame for society's ills or their own. Even those good schools are not immune from these distortions and may embrace them as a way to reflect our society at this time."

Adding to these conversations, Felidia, Maricel, and I spoke of the personal insults we'd weathered and what people had said behind our backs about our looks and accents. My friend Angi told a story about having a conversation with two students from Boston University whom she'd never met before. After a bit of small talk, one of them looked suspiciously at her and said, "I was just wondering what your nationality is. If I had to guess, I'd say Africa or maybe Greece?"

"I knew the point he was trying to make," Angi added. "It's that he thought I came from a country whose citizens, in his eyes, were not smart, were crude or primitive, even though, by language, Hungarians are closer to the people of Finland and Estonia. In other words, Northern Europeans."

Dr. Aldis closed the session praising the Club's contribution to the day and extolling our mission as a bright light during these times.

After the sessions ended, all who came were ready for the evening's festivities. Maricel made a great matador, but Mercedes, playing the bull, couldn't stop laughing, taking a bit of the drama out of their program. As for the food, every bit of it was devoured, even my sour cherry soup.

***

I kept my mother up on my classes through that fall but didn't mention much more, afraid it wouldn't sit well with her. Her few letters repeated time after time: *When will you be home for Thanksgiving? Have you decided on what school you will go to here?*

As the weeks came and went, I could no longer put off my decision. I wrote to say that as much as I had planned to return at Thanksgiving, studies and the lab work for my physiology professors would keep me at school until Christmas. She stopped writing after that early November letter.

What I had told her was the truth. Dr. Haywood's research and Dr. Turner's experiments demanded constant attention. Our small group depended on each other's work to complete assignments. This immersion also became my escape, a way to put off what was to come.

Esther and I wished each other well for the December holidays as the term wound to its end. It was in those final days that she could no longer hide her growing concern. "I worry about what's in store for you," she said. "I don't like that your mother hasn't answered any of your letters for a month now. Remember what I said: promise me that when you get back, you'll talk to someone about your mom."

"Thank you for looking out for me. I've been thinking about it too. Yes, I promise."

"Do write to let me know how it's going."

"That's a promise too."

The demands of school had kept my unease at bay through the entire semester. As exhausting as the final days had been, I was returning with pride in all I'd done. My classes had gone well, Dr. Haywood was pleased with my help in carrying out her experiments, and my grades, while not perfect, continued to improve.

And yet, as soon as I took a seat on the train, that familiar foreboding descended upon me like a well-worn shroud once again darkening my life. The hope I had brought with me on past visits had given way to anticipation of the familiar reality I knew would unfold. This time, my stepfather wouldn't be there to protect, to buffer, or to mend. I was anxious but determined to stay at Holyoke whatever she might demand. Still, I hoped Mother could share in a budding sense of pride over all that I'd done and what it might mean for securing a future where I could earn a good living so that she wouldn't have to worry. Perhaps that would please her.

I turned these thoughts over and over, all the way to the city. Stepping out from the shelter of Grand Central into the drifts of snow on that gray December day, I made my way to the subway, passing through unnoticed landscapes. What little remained of the afternoon light gave way to twilight before night descended, and I realized that moment was like my life—that I existed in a between time of a tethered but untenable past and present, fated to play out within me over and over again until resolution or dissolution.

I slipped on the ice-packed sidewalk as I turned onto our street but grabbed a lamppost and managed to steady myself. Stepping slowly the rest of the way, I once again stood before our home, taking a deep breath before climbing the few steps to the front door, which was now decorated with a Christmas wreath and a postcard-sized portrait of the infant Jesus at its center. Not wanting to surprise my mother, I called out to her as soon as I entered.

"Mother, I'm home." I stepped inside and pulled off my gloves. "Mother, are you here?"

Still no answer. I balanced my suitcase on the bench in the foyer and walked into the kitchen, surprised to find no pots simmering on the stove nor anything on the table but for an empty jam jar my stepfather had recommissioned as a water glass, an empty bud vase, and a notice announcing the yuletide Mass schedule.

I returned to the hall and heard the rapid click of shoes across the floor above me. My mother appeared a moment later, dressed in her church skirt, blouse, and sweater.

"Hi, Mother. I just got in. Didn't you hear me calling?"

"I have to go. This evening is the sixth night of the Christmas Novena, and I'm already late. A few leftovers are in the refrigerator."

"What time will you be back?"

"After nine, maybe later since the priest asked about songs for High Mass on Christmas Day." With that, she was out the door.

I sat next to my suitcase on the foyer bench, startled by the suddenness of her hasty exit and breathing a sigh of relief. Whatever was to happen between us was put off for the moment and hopefully for the night. Having little appetite for what there was in the refrigerator, I made my way upstairs to my old bedroom, unpacked, and undressed. I lay under the covers, taking in the delicate frost etched onto the window, and waited for my mother to return. Drained from the trip by my all-consuming anticipation, a deep, dreamless sleep took me safely away.

***

The next morning, I heard my mother clattering pots and pans in the kitchen. I made my way downstairs.

"How was church last night?"

"All right. Father Avila—you remember him? He's the priest who's been there forever and gave the sermon at your stepfather's funeral. He's been a great source of comfort to me for all that I've been through. I'm happy to do what he wants, as he's asked me about singing at Masses during the holidays. That's why I stayed late last night."

"Of course I remember Father Avila. I'm so glad he's been there for you, and I imagine your friends in the choir have been there for you too."

"Yes, they've all been very good to me, especially since you aren't here."

Here it comes. I had hoped we might go a bit longer before this. I tried to change the subject, as I had so much to tell her about school, but knew it was best to follow her lead, to keep the conversation about her. "It sounds like this time of year your singing is so much in demand, and it's great to know that Father Avila is relying on you. I bet the others in the choir are looking to you too."

"Yes, they are. We're learning three new songs for the season and still have to practice the four from last year. They really depend on my soprano."

"Well, I can't wait to hear you, Mother. I'm sure Mass on Christmas Day will be something. I'll go with you during the week too."

Pressing further with this diversion, she filled me in on her world. Mrs. Kokas's husband passed away in October, the Martinis had a new granddaughter, Jablonsky's meat market closed, and the early morning bread lines had become an almost daily ritual for more than a few of her neighbors.

"So many people are finding it hard to make it," I said. "I just thank God Father knew what to do to make sure we were okay."

"It still hasn't been easy," she said, narrowing her eyes to make sure I got her point.

We sat at the kitchen table sipping our coffee until I thought it was safe to talk about Holyoke. "I tried to keep you up on so much that was happening at school. My physiology classes and teachers, the Cosmopolitan Club—did I tell you they're thinking of nominating me to be an officer?—and the outdoor trips to the beautiful mountains—"

She cut me off. "You wrote me about these things, but you didn't come home as you said you would. And what about starting school here? Not a word."

"I'm sorry I couldn't visit during the term, but it was impossible with all that was going on. I wasn't the only one. A lot of girls were in the same boat as me." She took little interest in my story. Instead, it seemed to lead to what she'd been saving up for some time.

"So you have time to go hiking, spend time with your friends, do any number of other things, but you don't have time to come home? I've told you many times I want you here. I can always tell people that you went to Holyoke. I'm proud you went there. But that doesn't matter anymore. You're my daughter. You need to be with me."

There it was yet again. That irony coming from a daughter who had left her own mother, never to return. It took everything I had not to confront what I had now come to know all too well. "Yes, Mother, I know you want me to come back, but I told you that I couldn't get the same courses and education from a college in New York. I have to stay at Holyoke. And if all goes well, it will be the best for both of us when it comes to finding a job."

Ignoring my point, she continued expressing her disappointment. "You're an ungrateful girl. Do you have any sense of all that I've done for you? Taking you away from that, that place with nothing, raising you, making a good home for you. This is the way you thank me? Well, this is not the end of it, not at all." With nothing more to say, she stormed out of the room.

My mother had been this upset on a few occasions—with my boyfriend, coming home from school in the rain—and I didn't know what would come next but understood that I would at some point bear the consequence of an unremitting rage. Esther's words came back to me. I had to find help.

That afternoon I set out to see Father Avila. I had never spoken with him outside of confession but felt my choices were limited. He had come to know my mother well over the years as a member of the church choir, and I assumed he would keep what I said between us.

It was well before evening Mass, and I hoped Father Avila would be available. Arriving at the church, I knocked on the sacristy door. After knocking a second time, he opened it, registering a look of mild surprise at this unexpected visitor. In a vaguely affable but distracted voice, he greeted me. "Oh, hi, Irene. What a surprise. Come in."

The priest was as I had remembered over the years, but my recollection came from far-off pews that I occupied near the church entrance on Sundays and holy days. Seeing him up close, his face seemed fuller, cheeks and nose redder, and body rounder. A few fallen strands of his gray hair stood out on the shoulders of his pitch-black cassock. We exchanged a few pleasantries about school, the holidays, and plans for Christmas, but he seemed eager to get back to an oak desk covered in papers, wrapped presents, and an empty brandy snifter.

"I'm sorry to bother you, Father, but I need your advice and, maybe, help. It concerns my mother."

"Is she ill?"

"No, nothing like that. It's about what happens when we're together and what she expects from me." I recounted the mounting tensions in our relationship, how unhappy she seemed, and her insistence that I leave school and live with her. I spared him the more disturbing cruelties.

He listened politely before speaking. "Your mother means well, Irene. I've known her for many years. She's been through a lot with the loss of her husband. Perhaps you could try harder to get along with her and to please her, and with time, she'll be more understanding too. You could take on more responsibility around the house, take her out to the movies, and spend more time with her. I know you want to return to Holyoke, but what about taking a semester off? I'm sure your mother would be very happy to have you here."

"I can't do that, Father. I'd fall so far behind, it would be impossible to catch up. Besides, the work I do with the other students in my lab would suffer. As for spending more time with her while I'm here, that's a good idea if we can avoid our disagreements. I'll try."

Father Avila had little more to say, so I took my leave, feeling a bit better about airing my concerns but uneasy about where to go from there.

***

Coming home the next day from choir practice, my mother stormed in and called out to me. Descending the stairs, I knew a grim fate awaited. "Irene, when I was at church today, Father Avila told me all about your little talk with him. You told him how unhappy I am. Whose fault is that? And what you said to him about school and how hard it is at home? I spoke to him about how you're a selfish girl, thinking of no one but yourself. As for your boyfriend, Joseph, and who knows how many others, I told him you're a whore who would sleep in the gutter with any boy who wanted you."

Her face had turned crimson. She raised her hand to strike but held back at the last minute. Leveling a Hungarian curse, she left me standing alone in the living room with a final threat: "You'd better change your ways—or else."

Selfish? A whore in my mother's eyes? Father Avila had betrayed my confidence. I stood there in shock, frozen in place, once again terrified by what my mother might do. I followed her into the kitchen, desperate to talk, to explain. "Mother, please believe me. I was only hoping to make things better. I've tried to please you as best I could. It hurts to think that in your eyes I'm such a disappointment."

"This is how you show your love for me? Well, until you change your ways, I have nothing more to say about it." She donned her winter coat and left.

Distance and distraction filled what remained of my winter break. My mother often left the house before I awoke, returning most days only at dinnertime, preoccupied as she was with choir practice and ceremonies. Tension ruled our time together, relieved only by an occasional afternoon get-together with neighbors and church dinners on Christmas Eve and Christmas Day.

I felt as though there was little I could say or do to relieve that tension and so made plans to leave well before the end of the year, using my professor's research as an excuse to return to school early. In the end, I knew it was for the best. My mother was true to her word. I packed my bags and a few things from the pantry to tide me over, knowing the school dining room wouldn't be open. Mother went about avoiding me. When it came time to say goodbye on that frigid, gray Saturday after Christmas, no kiss penetrated the wall between us.

***

Home and school. School, home. I had always seen them as distinct in what they were, what they wanted and gave. As I walked the snow-covered campus path to Cowles, the warmth I felt dwelling within the college confines left me confused about what I'd assumed. Was my grandmother right? Had Holyoke taken the place of a home that could no longer provide? Was it where I felt safest and where hearts were kind? Had distance, cruelty, and peril made a charade of my dream of a mother and daughter's life together?

I came back to my room, lost in these questions. To my great relief, there stood Esther, head down over her desk, absorbed in photos laid out on every inch of available space, with others strewn about on the floor.

"Oh, Esther! I didn't expect you'd be back so early. It's wonderful to see you."

She turned and, with her great smile, embraced me. "Hadn't planned on it, but something a bit strange and wonderful happened over the holidays. What's here might look like a mess, but when I was home, my mother gave me boxes of family photographs, almost all of them tracing parents, grandparents, and great-grandparents through the years. For the first time I can put faces to names I've heard so many times and others I've never known."

She took my hand and walked me over to her good fortune. "Here are my great-grandparents, stiff as boards and dressed as if they'd just come from a haberdasher that specialized in starch. This is an early photo of my mother's parents with my mom at the beach, all dressed in outfits that look like they belong in an old secondhand store. Mom was only seven then, but I could already see that her dark curls and dimples were there. Here's one of my mom and dad on their first wedding anniversary. They were so in love. Maybe whatever it is keeping them together is in that photo."

And so it went for the next hour, with Esther taking me through her history, introducing me to lives from her past, many lost up until now. As we stood before them, I was grateful for the distraction that took me away from where I'd just been. Yet I couldn't help but feel such regret for what I might have left behind forever.

Then, as if coming out of a trance, she stopped suddenly. "My apologies. I haven't asked you about your visit. How'd it go?"

I shook my head. "I'm so sorry I didn't write. My mother is

obsessed with me moving back in with her. And as for my going out with Joseph, a very nice boy whom I dated for a while before coming to Holyoke, well, that just set her off. It's all become pretty scary at times."

"Did you talk to anyone?"

"Yes, but that only made things worse, as the priest ended up telling my mother everything, including how I thought she needed help. She blew up."

"Oh, God, now I'm so sorry." Esther draped her arm over my shoulders. "I was thinking of you all through the holidays. I even talked to my mom about you. Both of us feel that you need help. She's friends with a psychiatrist who knows someone practicing near campus. I've got her name."

"I don't know what else to do. I worry that what's going on with us will one day become something I can't bear."

"School doesn't start for another week. If you've got some time outside of your lab responsibilities, then I think you should see her sooner rather than later."

"Okay, I'll call her."

First thing Monday morning, I called the local number of Dr. Ernestine Kiley. At first, the receptionist replied that her appointment calendar was booked, but when I mentioned the reference from Esther's mother, she paused. "Dr. Rogers? He's an old colleague of Dr. Kiley's. Let me see." She came back on the line after a moment. "Dr. Kiley can see you at ten tomorrow morning."

The next day I borrowed a bike from Cowles and traveled through slush and snow to the town of Holyoke. What would otherwise take about thirty minutes stretched to an hour, thanks to the New England winter and the difficulty I had keeping the bicycle wheels straight. Approaching the town on that frigid December day, I passed the massive Albion Paper Mill on the banks of the Second Level Canal, a testament to the Industrial Revolution, its smokestacks belching gray vapor that took the shape of billowy clouds as it ascended.

Without the usual distractions of my friends from school, I entered the town of Holyoke as if seeing the people and place for the first time. High Street, which stretched through the center, was still dressed in festive lights and decorated wreaths for the holidays, its shop windows draped in necklaces made of pine cone and tinsel. Couples and children drifted lazily down the block, stopping at store windows from time to time. A few cars skidded and spun their wheels as they motored about.

I followed the rough sketch Esther drew for me as I made my way down High Street and turned at the corner grocer. Within a few blocks, stately homes replaced commercial establishments. Making my way farther along, I came to matched sets of Victorian residences and stopped, as I saw in one bay window Dr. Kiley's name and professional plaque in the window. Its four stories, front door with intricate beveled glass, and coned turret top reminded me of Upper East Side ventures with my mother.

A moment after ringing the bell at the top of the stairs, a woman appeared dressed in a white blouse, modest skirt, and hair up in a bun. "Good morning. You must be Irene. I'm Mildred, the woman you spoke with yesterday. Please, come in."

As I closed the door, she noticed the bike leaning against the railing. "You didn't bicycle all the way from Holyoke, did you?"

I nodded.

"My, my, that must have been trying."

"The roads weren't that slippery. I actually enjoyed the ride. Not many people out, and the countryside was so pretty."

"Well, we're glad you made it in one piece. You're a few minutes early. Please sit, and let me take your coat. Can I offer you a cup of tea while you wait? Dr. Kiley should be finishing up with a client momentarily."

"Yes, hot tea would be wonderful. Thank you."

As I settled into a high-backed Queen Anne chair, the tea gradually took the chill out of what had turned out to be a longer ride than I'd anticipated. That and the warmth from the living room fireplace in full glow calmed the restlessness I had felt all morning. Just as I finished my tea, Mildred reappeared. "Dr. Kiley will see you now."

The design of Dr. Kiley's office was the same as her living room. Rich crimson drapery, dark wood panels, and a bookcase filled with no room to spare set a warm backdrop to a large oak desk populated with several folders neatly stacked. A pen-and-pencil set sat at the front next to another plaque with her name. Degrees from several universities and what looked like an award encased in glass hung on the wall behind her. Two high-backed chairs like those in the living room were positioned in front of but turned away from the desk. Next to each chair were two small square tables with lamps, their light softly radiating through Tiffany shades. Dr. Kiley, dressed in a pine-green shirt and light cashmere sweater, welcomed me from behind her desk.

"Hello, Irene," she said. Her shoulder-length hair was more gray than black. "I understand you bicycled in all the way from the college this morning. That must have been quite a trip, but I must say it's something I would have done in my heyday too."

"Dr. Kiley, I'm very grateful that you made room in your schedule to see me on such short notice."

"Well, let me come around and greet you properly." As she did, I heard a slight squeak. Dr. Kiley approached but never rose, as the movements of her arms propelled the wheels of her chair forward. She spoke with a pronounced accent that was familiar but not one I could place, and she pointed at the high-backed Queen Anne. "Please sit. As my day is very full, it would be best that we save any casual talk for another time, should there be one."

I took that as a cue not to waste a minute. "It's about my mother and our relationship, Dr. Kiley." Lost at first as to where to begin, I told of the words and warnings from our Christmas together. Then, what I'd kept within poured out like water overflowing a dam. Hungary, my grandmother, separation, my love for Mother unrequited, her threats, the all-too-brief time with my stepfather.

Dr. Kiley's hazel eyes never strayed from me, taking a few notes without looking down and never interrupting. Only when I stopped did she speak, almost as much to herself as to comment on what I had said.

"Trauma."

"Trauma?"

She nodded. "You've been through a lot. Was it truly like this from the beginning? And did you ever speak to your mother about these feelings and what her words were doing to you?"

"There have been good times. When I've done something that she could brag about to her neighbors, like when I was accepted to Holyoke. There's once when I felt a little closer for just a while, when my stepfather died. What it was, I'm not sure. That she had only me now? Grief? I thought maybe we'd be the way a mother and child—my mother and me—were meant to be. That didn't last. I just get a sense his death affected her in ways I've yet to understand, although whatever that is has fallen on me."

"My guess, Irene, is that whatever is going on with your mother has been there for a long time. Your stepfather's passing only brought it to the surface."

Only then did the doctor glance at the grandfather clock. Before I'd realized it, an hour had passed. "I have many questions and after this visit some thoughts about what you may have to do. But our time is up. I do think it best that you come again."

"Dr. Kiley, I don't have a way to pay you beyond this visit."

She thought for a moment. "There's something you could do for me. I've kept personal papers over many years and plan to write a book about my life, my work, perhaps submit a manuscript for publication in a psychiatric journal. The problem is that I have had no time to put them together. If you're willing, perhaps you'd help me organize them on the days you visit. I'd accept it as a sort of payment."

I had opened a door and would do anything to walk through it. "That's very generous of you, Dr. Kiley. I'd be happy to." I didn't know it then, but what began on that day would last a lifetime.

Part IV
Resolution

CHAPTER 20

S pring semester's demands were immediate and consuming, and my immersion into physiology complete. The department professors stressed that we had chosen no ordinary path. The survey course, with its lessons and lectures on human anatomy and invertebrates, brought home the significance of my chosen field. Drs. Turner and Haywood, and other faculty, also made it clear that our learning mustn't stop at the steps of Clapp Hall.

Any doubts about my major vanished shortly after my return. In the early days of January, I had restarted my work with the seniors assisting Dr. Haywood in pursuing her laboratory research. Now, as my advisor, my appointment was with her alone.

On a blustery, frigid day, anxious yet excited to meet with her again, I came to her office early morning, as was her preference, and tapped on her door.

"Come in, Irene, and please sit. We have much to discuss."

My first thought was about assignments and initial impressions of me from her students, but she quickly brushed that aside. "I hope you're settling into the work with the others. I know it can be overwhelming at first, but I assume you're getting used to it. Now that you have a semester behind you and you've gotten past most of the basics, there's something important to consider, and that is the coursework you're planning to take during your junior and senior years."

She leaned back in her chair, her features bright and open. "You recall when we first met that I talked to you about Dr. Clapp's vision for education and that by grounding that vision in this department, Dr. Turner has made it unlike other schools of higher learning. Dr. Clapp realized early on that the future of women in science lay in knowing the world we live in and our place in it, and her leadership has charted the path you and the students here will undertake."

"I've read about Dr. Clapp and all that she had done, but I'm not sure what that means for me."

"Well, now we come to that. You already know that majoring in physiology carries with it an obligation to take courses that connect with other sciences. Chemistry, zoology, and botany at the very least."

"Yes, I've already signed up for chemistry this semester, and the others will follow."

"Right. What else?"

"Oh, I thought I'd continue with German in junior or senior year. But I haven't thought much beyond that with all I'll have to take for physiology."

"That's fine. We want all our graduates to be ready for the world of science once they leave here. Part of preparing is being able to see where what you learn can help you understand how people live, how they become ill, and what can help them be well. That kind of information isn't found only in our labs or texts. For that to happen, you'll need to explore, to take the opportunities that this campus offers."

"It's funny you bring this up. As much as I'm looking forward to the science courses, psychology is a subject I plan to take too."

"Good. There's much that happens in our minds that affects the body's responses. The opposite is true too. There's an area of study, psychophysiology, which shows how the body's responses can cause disruptions or pathologies. While we're on this subject, let me ask you a question. Where else is physiology in our lives?"

"Could it have anything to do with where I live?"

"Exactly! Think about who you grew up with, your neighbors and friends, how what they thought was good for them affected you. Take food, for example. What's available and what your family thinks you should eat can affect your heart. The air you breathe affects the health of your lungs. What does that come back to? Our laboratory. Our respiratory system research. I remember the conversation we had about your stepfather. Blood, circulation, and flow all connect to how and where we live. Remember that when you're in the lab or studying trout and their circulatory systems or carbon dioxide absorption or, for that matter, our furry white rats and vitamin intake."

I sat there for just a minute, eyes wide, smiling at my good fortune, captivated as I was by Dr. Haywood's passion for her chosen field. "Yes, Dr. Haywood. You said a number of things I've thought about. It reminds me of Dr. Woolley's address to us at the start of my freshman year, where she told us that service and education of—what was her term?—the 'whole woman' was the mission of Mount Holyoke. Now our conversation and your advice make me realize even more that I made the right decision when I chose physiology for my major. I promise to do my best in my classes and in the lab."

"It's not going to be easy. That's why we accept only a handful of students each year. There are many courses to take, the lab work is demanding, and while we professors are here to help, you have to take a lot on yourself."

"I understand."

"Well, then, best of luck this year and for the ones to follow."

That was it. I'd been accepted! I stood and walked to the door, but the gratitude I felt wouldn't allow me to leave without one final gesture. "Dr. Haywood, thank you . . ." The words caught in my throat. "Thank you for accepting me."

***

After my conversation with Dr. Haywood, a new horizon appeared before me. I now realized that a true commitment to my major demanded that I take courses across the campus. After I had fulfilled daily assignments, my late nights at the library were given over to perusing the course catalog, indulging in my love of learning. Where to? Everything seemed connected to physiology classes, and I was determined to follow those connections wherever they would lead.

I was excited to tell Dr. Kiley about my conversation with Dr. Haywood, and so a few weeks later I made my way to a Saturday morning appointment. Entering her office, I found her gazing out her French doors. Two massive birch trees laden with snow from the night before set the boundaries of a property with little distinction other than a few bushes that poked through the white blanket covering the grounds. She seemed lost in thought and, as it turned out, those thoughts had very much to do with me.

She pivoted her wheelchair in one fluid motion. "Good morning, Irene. I'm glad you're here, as I've been thinking about our last conversation. I'm also looking forward to your help with my papers. Now, please sit. Where would you like to begin?"

Leaving my past behind for the moment, I filled her in on my Club involvement, Dr. Haywood, and lab work. "Dr. Kiley, it's been a great start to the term. It's as if I've stepped into a place that I had hoped to find when I first came to America. Mount Holyoke has almost become like a . . . home."

"It's as if you've found what seemed out of reach until now?"

"Yes. I don't mean to say that life before I got here never felt like home. When my stepfather was alive, he did all he could to create that place, loving me as I was and am. Once in a while I've felt it with my mother too, but those were fleeting moments. I found myself always expecting the other shoe to drop, and when it did, it fell on me. Once my stepfather died, I felt so alone. There was no one for me to turn to."

The questions Dr. Kiley posed that morning prompted my outpouring of hopes and heartaches, drifting between Hungary, New York, and school, my life continued and condensed into our time together, told as part oral revelation, part soliloquy. I didn't know what to expect from her. Sympathy? Guidance? Admonition? What she did say I never saw coming.

"There's something you and I share. Kiley is not my maiden name. It's Comescu. I was born not too far from you, in Romania, near its capital, Bucharest. It turns out we were almost neighbors. My family took trips around the Carpathian Mountains into Hungary several times. I came here well before you, but like you, I left my country behind. I only traveled back once, when I was younger and before my husband, Paul, passed away. It made me realize how much I missed the land, the people. I always thought of returning, but then, well, what happened to me"—she tapped her wheelchair—"has made everything more than difficult, to say the least. The point is, I know a little about separation. Fortunately, my marriage and the life we created became the home I had lost. Paul has passed, but what we had remains with me."

I smiled. "So, you know about where I came from?"

"Yes, indeed. Although it was a long time ago, that part of the world is never far away. And Irene, there's one more thing we share."

"You and I?"

"Yes. I don't know if you remember, but toward the end of our first session, *trauma* is how I described what you've been through—the separation from your grandmother, how you were abandoned at Ellis Island, the difficult home life you've described. Paralysis has been my trauma. It's different, of course, from your experiences, but the effect is similar. When I was young, I thought about all the paths I could take, and where what I loved to do might take me. Sometimes, though, life takes a turn and something you never expected or wanted happens. And you try to understand and live with, as you put it, what fell on you."

"So, you understand."

"I don't pretend to fully know what you feel. One should never assume that of another. But your uprooting as well as the trouble with your mother don't seem that far from my personal experience in their effect."

She glanced at the grandfather clock. "Once again, an hour has passed very quickly, but we can continue on your next visit. If you have time, can we turn to my papers?"

"Yes, I'm open for two hours this afternoon."

"Good. My receptionist left ham and cheese in the refrigerator, and rye is in the breadbox. If you make sandwiches for us, we can eat, and I can fill you in on what I need you to do. There should be a few Cokes too. I'll take one, and do help yourself."

I made my way through her living room, catching glimpses of some framed photos on her side table: wedding pictures, older photos from what might have been Bucharest, a picture of Dr. Kiley at what looked like a swim meet. Even her swim cap couldn't hide her beauty.

Returning with two sandwiches in hand, I asked about it.

"Oh, that old photo. It's from college. I used to be a competitive swimmer. Won a few medals in high school and college but was never quite Olympic caliber. It's my favorite sport. I'd swim anywhere: quarries, city pools, lakes. Even when I traveled for work, I'd ask the hotel staff about the nearest body of water. You'll find a few newspaper clippings about those days mixed in with my professional papers and talks."

"Are your materials all on the same subject? It'll be good to know as I'm organizing them."

"No. What I wrote in college is so different from where I am now. In those early days, students were taken with Sigmund Freud—you may have heard of him—and psychoanalysis. I imagined my shingle: Dr. Ernestine Kiley, psychoanalyst. Once in medical school, I became interested in other schools of therapy. And after my accident, I became committed to studying the effects of trauma and applied that focus to my research and through my private sessions with patients."

"May I ask what happened?"

She turned away from me, focusing on the bookcase nearest her desk. "About four years ago, at a party at the home of a colleague, I wandered out on the third floor of a patio, martini in hand. As I was chatting with friends, I leaned against a wooden railing that overlooked the estate. It turned out that others had been on that patio, too. They had been having quite a good time, but in their exuberance, they had loosened the railing supports. When I leaned against it, the railing gave way and I fell three stories. As I fell, I remembered thinking in midair that I have to protect my neck as if I were in a curl. I twisted into a curling position. You see the result. My neck wasn't injured, but I broke my back."

"Oh my goodness—I'm so sorry."

"I was so active before, exercising, always full of energy and moving, moving, moving. That all came to an end. I was so depressed for the first months. I was lost. Then I had a talk with myself and decided there's much more to live for. Paul took such good care of me, making sure I attended my physical therapy sessions. And from all of it came my interest in trauma and the great richness in experience and people I've come to know."

She paused there, looked back at me, and smiled. "Now, let's see if we can get started before I take up all of your time. There are so many presentations I've just put into boxes, academic papers and notes on my accident too, and even a few manuscripts I'd started before I fell. You'll find all and more in a jumble, but I know where I want to go now, what I want to write. With your help, I'll get there."

I left her office late that afternoon. We had made our way through just two of the half-dozen boxes filled with the passions and trials of the person she had been and became. Dr. Kiley's idyllic life had been broken and lost, then reformed and reborn. Knowing that she was able to rise again went to the heart of my past, present, and by will and good fortune, what I was to become.

***

Like a ship's captain navigating treacherous waters, Dr. Kiley was there, her keen insight bordering on premonition, letting me know what the future might hold and what it might take to survive my first visit home since the terrifying Christmas trip. "Dr. Kiley, I've promised my mother over and over again that I would see her during the school year. I can't put it off any longer. Easter seems like a good time to do it. With all the pageantry around that holiday, she'll be busy with her choir events at the church. Besides, she's always loved Easter Sunday for the songs and attention they bring her. Who knows? Maybe with the uplifting message of Christ's resurrection, we can find some peace."

She wasn't convinced. "I hope so. I must say, though, after all you've told me about her life and what she wants from you, you need to steel yourself for whatever may happen. And for heaven's sake, be careful. Your intentions are good, but past life and profound discontent with what she sees as how life has cheated her of the happiness she deserves are what's driving your mother. And that may be well beyond what you can do."

As much as I wished for more encouraging words from Dr. Kiley, I knew she spoke the truth.

On the train ride to New York, I opened a letter from my mother that had just arrived before I left school. It seemed rather serene for Mother, so I tried to read between the lines. I convinced myself that the time she had taken to tell me all about the upcoming Holy Thursday prayers, Good Friday observance, and Saturday ritual anticipation through High Mass on Sunday was an encouraging sign. She even included what the choir would be singing. I prayed yet again that her dedication to the Easter holiday might buffer and soothe our time together. My mind drifted to the beauty that was passing outside the window on this cool but brilliant spring day. Budding trees emerged from winter's grasp, their leaves just beginning to decorate the spindles of their branches, stems of flowers by the side of the tracks poking through and upward. All seemed to hold the promise of renewal and rebirth. Still, as I traveled home to that place of freighted memories, scars from recent and distant pasts tempered my hope. What took their place were Dr. Kiley's ominous words: *For heaven's sake, be careful.*

After I arrived home, Mother met me with a brusque greeting. "So, you found the time to visit me for a few of your precious days, have you? Well, as it's Thursday evening, are you coming to church with me? I'm already late. You have just enough time to put your suitcase upstairs."

"Of course I'm coming with you. I came home to be with you, and I knew this was a busy time. Give me just a minute."

We walked without a word between us all the way to the church. I knew it was pointless to bring up my school stories now, as they would only annoy her. My mother's narrowed glare and pursed lips warned of something else, as if once again she'd been building up a head of steam.

I was grateful for the prayer vigil. But as the services came to an end, my doubts crept in. Did I do the right thing coming back at this time? Should I have just stayed at school and put off what was to come? We left the church without socializing on the steps the way we usually did. Instead, we walked home, my futile efforts to bridge our worlds coming to nothing.

Once back home, I draped my coat over the tree at the door and went to the kitchen, as I hadn't eaten since leaving Holyoke. After heating soup from a tureen in the refrigerator, I sat at the kitchen table. My mother came in moments later and sat across from me, veiled in the same expression that had met me at the door.

She spoke with a grim determination of what had clearly been on her mind for some time. "I've been doing a lot of thinking. Just the other day I was talking with Mrs. Berude. You remember her and her daughter, Agatha? Such a nice girl. You never did play with her or invite her over, I'm sorry to say. Well, Mrs. Berude's husband fell from a building where he was working and died several months ago. You know what her daughter did? She came back from college in New Jersey to help her mother. Now she's transferred to City College and lives at home so she can be with her mother. Mrs. Berude is so happy now that her daughter's at home again. Agatha knew what she needed to do and did it. It's what you need to do too."

This was what my mother had been holding back since I arrived. "I'm very sorry to hear about Agatha's father. It was good of her to come back. But I'm not Agatha. We've had this conversation before, and if anything, I'm even more convinced that Holyoke is where I belong. I'll be home for summer, and maybe I'll find a job in New York after graduation. So please, Mother, let's enjoy our time together. I'll be with you again in just a few months after the semester ends."

"I don't think you heard me. I'm saying you should live with me, not in two or three years when you finish at that school, and not just for the summer, but now."

"Can't you be happy with what I told you? I promise I'll be here whenever I can. What you're asking for is impossible."

Her rage filled the room, radiating from lips taut as a harp string. "Don't you tell me it's impossible. You're my daughter. I brought you into this world, and you'll do as I say or, or . . ."

Mother raised her hand and then lowered it. Her daggered glare cut through me. With blind anger as her compass, bitter words continued to spew. "You will be here with me one way or the other. And if you don't obey me, I swear that one night when you're asleep, and you'll never know when, I'll come into your room and I'll cut your throat."

She left me with that final threat, once again terrified and alone in the dimming light of the night.

***

Lives can turn in an instant. An accident can cripple a future full of promise. Illness can snatch health for days, weeks, months, forever. Soldiers fight, not knowing if each new day will be their last. Now I knew what they knew, felt what they felt. Nothing would be the same. Sleep would never be restful. Nights would no longer grant me peace. Fear filled every corner of my bedroom. I felt the panic of a foreboding that had hovered over me for so long and had now descended. Wrapped in its suffocating grip, I felt myself gasping as I struggled to catch my breath. But then, just as all seemed lost, I recalled the courage of Dr. Kiley, how she had overcome the tragedy of loss to find her way. I willed myself to step away from the consuming trauma. In the horror of those moments, I knew my life was at stake and now I must act to preserve it. I placed a chair against the door, wrapped a scarf around my neck, and laid my head on the pillow. Sleep became an ordeal to pass through—and survive.

We didn't speak of that night for what remained of the Easter holiday. I was desperate to leave, but the Easter holiday and my time-restricted ticket made an earlier departure difficult. To my relief, choir practice for Good Friday's Stations of the Cross, Holy Saturday observance, and the celebratory Sunday Mass took my mother away each morning and returned her mid-afternoon when she retreated to her bedroom to rest. Goings-on with choir and idle neighborhood gossip kept our dinner conversations distantly civil. Through those evenings, however, portent lingered in the air like ashes from a still-smoldering fire. In these fraught hours I looked to Dr. Kiley's words, to recognize my peril, escape from it, and above all, remain resolute not to be overrun by my mother's warped and perilous preoccupation to get what she deserves.

Sunday came as a blessed relief. College beckoned, as did the train that would take me there. I awakened early and was determined to set the day off with something I knew she would enjoy and not to provide her with any reason to threaten me. I prepared Mother's favorite Easter breakfast of hard-boiled eggs, ham, challah from the bakery, tea, and a bowl brimming with freshly cut slices of apples, pears, and bananas. Hearing footsteps, I put on my bravest face, removed my apron, quickly flattened a few wrinkles in my skirt, patted my hair into place, and turned to the open kitchen door just as she came into view. "Good morning, Mother. Happy Easter."

After scanning the display of delicacies, she said, "You've been busy this morning, haven't you?"

"I hoped you might enjoy it. It reminded me of all those Easters when Father was alive. The three of us would sit down after church and have so much to eat that we'd be too full to have lunch. I know you're off to church soon, and I'll need to catch my train, so this was the only time for us to have breakfast together."

My mother seemed on the verge of a smile, but then her lips flattened. "Yes, I know you're leaving today. As for this meal, I can only have a bite since Father Avila wants the choir in place well before the start of Mass at nine."

"I knew that, but I wanted to have everything ready. You can eat it when you come back from church. You could invite friends over. There will be more than enough food, even after I take some for the train ride."

"You prepared too much for me. I'll see if Mrs. Berude and Agatha might want to come over."

Without another word, she sat and quickly peeled an egg, placed challah on one of the two dinner plates, and poured a half cup of tea. Moments later she rose. "I must go."

"Yes, I know." For once, I couldn't embrace my mother as I'd done so many times before. For however it would be taken, I said, "I know you may not believe me, but I do want you to be happy."

The sentiment elicited little more than a fixed stare. With nothing else said, she left me standing alone, my wistful words drifting into silence.

I found a seat alone on the train, where thoughts of Holyoke fought for space with all that had just happened. The world of classes, the Club, and Cowles was the escape from the dread that perforated my sense of self. Once I reached the lodge and took refuge in my room, I poured out the poison of that chalice to Esther, whose embrace I needed to help me stop shaking.

"Oh, Esther, I felt so trapped and alone. I don't know what to do."

She held me as if I'd fall apart if she let go. "I'm no psychiatrist, but to me your mother is sick, and if you're not careful, she'll do something terrible. When's your next appointment with Dr. Kiley?"

"I didn't make one, but I know she wants to see me."

"You must make an appointment as soon as you can."

I was desperate to visit Dr. Kiley, but school left little time to dwell on what had happened. Dr. Turner and her assistants were readying findings from her "tiltboard" research, an experiment in circulatory system changes. We needed to resolve the remaining questions as soon as possible to be included in an article for a journal.

Everyone in my class took turns reading and then retyping draft pages to correct misspellings and other errors. We knew that less than perfect was out of the question, so we paired off, each checking the other's work. Once corrections were made, we forwarded our final typed pages to Dorothy, the student who was coordinating all reviews. Then it was off to Dr. Turner.

As texts and tests vied for attention, my delicate balance of class assignments began to fray. Physiology and chemistry experiments took up weekday evenings, while weekends at the library became essential. As May began, I could no longer contain what I had done my best to hide. I was losing weight, and sleepless shadows around my eyes worried my friends to such a degree that they could no longer be silent. Esther reminded me to see Dr. Kiley.

"If you're not careful, your mother may have her way after all," she said.

On my first free Saturday in early May, I made my way to Dr. Kiley's office. Though reserved and professional in her demeanor, she smiled up at me upon my arrival. "I'm glad to see you again. It's been about a month since we last met, hasn't it?"

"Yes, Dr. Kiley." I glanced around her office, which was the same, except that a board with rollers in the middle like a seesaw sat in the corner.

"I see you've noticed my little addition. The doctors said if I worked hard, perhaps one day crutches could be my companions. That, my dear, would simply not do, as I'm determined to make the very best of a bad lot. So as part of my physical therapy, I arranged for this strange contraption, a 'tiltboard' they call it, to help with circulation. Every other day, my neighbors come by and lift me onto the board. I've already noticed a difference. A little more feeling in my muscles and legs. I'll be damned if this accident is going to keep me in this chair. It's very difficult, but hard work is a price I'm more than willing to pay."

"Dr. Kiley, you may find this hard to believe, but that contraption, as you call it, is part of our experiments at Holyoke for my physiology class! And we measure, of all things, circulatory response. I'm so happy you're using it."

She smiled. "Well, isn't that a coincidence! It's another step on my road to recovery. But there's more. In my papers, you'll see I've been thinking about starting a new organization, Courage to Live, to help people in similar circumstances."

"Please tell me about it. Perhaps I can help."

"Well, that's very kind of you. It'll be a while before I can make it into something, but I'll give you a short version. Very few organizations try to bring handicapped people together to help each other. It could mean helping when they need to get to the store or being there when they are depressed. I imagine it as a mutual help organization for people who have gone through what I have. I hope to meet with some possible donors in the near future. When there's more to tell, I'll tell you. But enough about my trials and hopes. What about you? How did your visit go?"

I found Dr. Kiley's story a welcome distraction from what I had left in New York. My composure fell away over our hour together, recalling, moment to moment, what had become a living nightmare. As before, Dr. Kiley said little, jotting a few notes, her countenance moving fluidly between gravity and empathy.

"With what you've told me before, I must admit I'm not greatly surprised. There's a familiar path here, a trajectory of escalating words and deeds. Her actions over the holidays, I'm sad to say, seem to me part of that pattern, extreme to us, but to your mother, retribution for what happened in her life and preservation of what she now feels is rightfully hers to control and command."

"Is there anything I can do? Should I give her what she wants: quit Holyoke and move back?"

"No. Her course is set, and if you give in to her will, it will be your destruction."

"So what are you telling me?"

"What I'm telling you is to get as far away from your mother as you can. There's nothing you can do for her."

"I can't just give up. She's my mother. And now you're saying . . . "

"I'm saying you can try and try again. I fear the end will be the same, if not worse. Let me put it bluntly, Irene: I'm worried for you. I know the end of the semester is around the corner. Should you choose to return home over the summer, it would be best to have a plan in case things do take a turn for the worse with your mother."

"Take a turn for the worse? As in what, Dr. Kiley?"

"Honestly, I don't have a good feeling about this. I don't want to alarm you, but you must have a plan to leave. Perhaps return to school for the summer? Or, if nothing else, call me. I might be able to help."

My heart raced as she fell silent. "I promise to think about what you've said, and I'm so very grateful for your offer. I pray to God it doesn't come to that."

I could no longer deny what had become plain to Dr. Kiley.

Returning to Cowles, I found that Esther agreed wholeheartedly with the doctor. "Nothing Dr. Kiley said surprises me. I hate to say it, but I've thought for a while that your mother is just plain crazy. Let me correct that. Not just plain crazy but dangerously so. I'm worried about you and what might happen when you see her again."

"But I'm not ready to give up. I've lost my grandmother and my homeland, and she is my only family . . . At the same time, I don't want to live the way I've been living, not knowing what she'll do to me or when."

We sat for a minute, both of us gazing out the window that overlooked an early budding sugar maple, its skeletal limbs otherwise bare this time of year. Then Esther rose from her chair and came over to where I sat on the bed.

"I have an idea," she said. "When I graduate in June, there's a very good chance I'll end up working for my father's New York office."

"You will? Oh my gosh."

"Yes, and that means I'll need a place there."

I couldn't believe my good luck. Esther would be nearby!

She went on, adding, "We've already talked about what kind of place to rent. Both Mom and Dad said they want me to have a place big enough for them to stay, although I don't think they plan to make a habit of visiting. I'd be happy to know they were thinking of things they would do together and for them to come see me. That got me thinking of you. So, keep this in mind. If things get too much for you over the summer, you can stay with me. As for my parents, they're flexible. I know I can just tell them to put off coming until the fall. What do you say?"

"That's so generous of you. I did hope to see you over the summer if you're in Manhattan, but staying with you? This is too good to be true."

"Just know that there will always be a place for you."

I rose from the bed and put my arms around her. "Thank you, my dearest friend."

CHAPTER 21

The cold of early spring fought to keep its grip on Holyoke toward the end of May, but gradually the warming days returned. Rain and rebirth were in the air. Mists rose from the grasses on campus, buds slowly gave way to the violet beauty of lavender and the early bloom of columbine, and oak and maple canopies emerged to cover our well-trodden paths. All were signs of semester's end, but with them came the reality of what lay before us: Finals and papers loomed. My nights at the library, already long, extended into early morning. I'd sit, always at the same table, taking in all I could from those texts, nodding off from time to time or staring vacantly at the leatherbound and clothbound books that populated the shelves from floor to ceiling.

My understanding of English had improved over the semester, but a number of idioms and colloquial phrases still escaped me. Angi and I traded papers on the poetry of Henry Thoreau, and Felidia volunteered her seasoned critique. Dr. Sherrill's chemistry class hadn't come easily; I struggled with learning the terminology. My Austro-Hungarian roots, however, did help in my German class with Dr. Held, as the words came more easily to me.

And then came my major. Our small flock huddled together, offering each other support through our assignments. Dr. Haywood allowed her upper-division students to manage routine requirements as research and manuscripts absorbed more of her time, so as our semester drew to a close, fewer opportunities arose to schedule an appointment or meet after class.

I had one last visit with her. Tapping lightly on her office door, I waited to be invited in.

"Hello, Irene. What can I do for you?"

"I'm sorry to disturb you, but as the semester is ending, I wanted to ask whether there might be a way for me to work in the department. I'd do anything: copying, filing, organizing papers. I can come back early this summer if you need me to. It's just that, with my stepfather's passing, helping with expenses would mean a lot."

Dr. Haywood leaned back in her chair. "Dr. Turner and I did talk briefly about your request a few weeks ago. You say you could come back early? This will be a very busy summer for my experiments at Woods Hole. Could you be here in early August? There's much to do at that lab."

"Yes, I can. As a matter of fact, that would be great timing," I said, thinking I would have a few months at home to come to some peace with my mother.

"Good. But we'll have to see how you did on your final exam first."

"I understand, Dr. Haywood. And thank you."

The Cosmopolitan Club held its closing meeting in the waning days after finals and just before I left for the summer. Our nerves were on edge as grades had yet to be posted. Small talk about summer and travel filled the air as we waited for Felidia to gavel us to order.

"I know all of you have a lot on your mind these days, so I'll move us along. First off, I want to congratulate the Club members on the success of the conference and festival. Dr. Aldis now wants us to hold a conference with him again next year, making this an annual meeting. I especially want to thank our committee—Ingrid, Irene, and Maricel—for all the work they put into it."

Applause filled the room. As it subsided, I raised my hand.

"Yes, Irene?"

"I wanted to say our committee was nothing more than you, the Club members. What we said and did came from who you are, your words, your lives. You know, many of us here have something in common that will be with us after we graduate. We traveled across oceans and borders. On Ellis Island, I sat and waited for my turn to set foot in America, not knowing what my future would be. Now, among all of you who come from places all over the world and as different as we are, I know how blessed my future has come to be."

Felidia quieted the background conversations. "Thank you, Irene. I suspect many of us feel the same. Now, on to some business we need to conduct. As you know, I'm graduating this year, if the grading gods smile down on me," she added. "My departure will leave open the chair, and as Mercedes will depart our hallowed halls as well, we have the position of secretary to fill. First, at this time, I'll entertain nominations for the position of chair."

I was the first to speak again, nominating Ingrid after listing all that she would bring to the position. No other names were offered, and when it came to a vote, all agreed.

Ingrid didn't hesitate in putting forth my name for secretary. "I know how this may sound like a mutual admiration society, but I'd like to nominate Irene for Club secretary. In my junior year, I've seen her grow over time to become a person with such intelligence and dedication. As for a passionate commitment, well, you just heard her words."

Felidia waited for a moment. "Any other nominations for that position? No? All in favor?"

A collective "aye" rose up. Angi, sitting on my left, leaned over, squeezed my hand, and whispered, "You've made me very proud to be Hungarian."

We looked to Felidia for her parting words. "Congratulations, Ingrid and Irene. Best wishes to you and all Club members. As for my time as chair, this year has been exceptional. More members than ever before, all we've done together, and taking our annual meeting much further than it's ever been."

She paused for a moment. Tears glistened in the corners of her eyes. "Much work lies ahead for all of us, my friends. I may be gone, but I'll be with you in spirit, watching over all you do in the coming year."

With that, her gavel came down for the last time.

***

A few uneasy days passed as we all waited for the posting of our final fates outside each classroom. Esther made a point to visit each of her professors to learn if she had passed, not that I harbored any doubt. She returned to the room at the end of her walkabout and didn't need to say a word, as the light in her eyes and her smile said everything. "Irene, I did it! I was pretty sure, but knowing it now, I'm just so happy."

"Congratulations! All that hard work for four years. Your parents will be so proud of you. *I'm* so proud of you."

"Thank you, my dear roommate, who's kept me company these two years. Now, it's graduation in a few weeks, a little time to relax, and then off to New York. It'll be a whirlwind, but right now I just want to remember these moments."

"As well you should."

"And what about you?"

"I think most of the grades will be up today. I'll let you know as soon as I make my rounds."

With a "Good luck" from Esther, I walked into uncertainty.

I made my way to each professor's office and found that I had survived my sophomore year with surprisingly good grades but had saved my greatest trepidation for last: physiology. Walking into Clapp Hall, I fought to keep scenes of dancing Cs or Ds at bay.

Once on the second-floor landing, I heard Carolyn's voice. "Hey, Irene, we're over here." I walked over to where she was standing with Gertrude, Marjorie, and Louise.

"Adelaide was too scared to come," she said. "She wanted me to break the news to her." Just at that moment, the department secretary came out with two single sheets of paper. Her wan smile as she tacked them onto the bulletin board gave nothing away. Afraid to look but knowing I must, I found my name. *Irene Richter: A.*

I quickly scanned the other names. We had all passed with at least a B. Gertrude—or Gertie as we had come to call her—had the only other A. Barely muffling a scream, Louise spoke for us all: "Well, I'll be. I did it. We all did it." Turning to them and grinning from ear to ear, I echoed her words. "Yes, we did. Here's to all of us, together for another year. See you in the fall."

Walking back to Cowles, the campus beauty came back into focus. Spring was now in full bloom, a spectrum of color covering the land. Even the grass seemed more verdant, fuller, and soft as a plush carpet. The air felt light; I felt light for these few moments. All the heartache and anguish that lurked in the shadows of my memory, my life, I kept at a remove, a distance I knew would have to be forded one day, but not now, not in this splendor.

I returned to my room to find Esther already packing. "My father's coming in later today, so most of whatever I'm taking with me has to be ready. I don't think there's much you would want, but there's one thing I'd like you to have." She reached into her desk drawer and pulled out a flat box. "I didn't have time to wrap it, but as they say, it's the sentiment."

I opened the box flap and pulled out an eight-by-eleven-inch photo she had taken on her Leica. It was of the two of us standing on the porch of Cowles Lodge when we first met. I remembered her fiddling with the timer, but otherwise I had forgotten all about it. Those days seemed far away. We hadn't changed much, or had we? Esther exuded the same confidence she'd possessed all along. She was so tall in the photo standing next to me, almost statuesque. I seemed so small, with a sadness hidden behind my smile, an innocent deceit I recognized but no longer felt.

"Thank you. Thank you for this memory. And may there be many more." Just then, Angi came bounding into the room. "Irene, did you see today's *Holyoke News*? You made the paper. Our Cosmopolitan Club secretary!"

***

The term had ended on high notes. My grades had turned out better than expected. I'd weathered physiology and landed a job for the following year. I didn't yet know how but sensed that perseverance, skills, and, above all, being part of something, some place, would stay with me far beyond these years.

Before I left, one promise remained. I scheduled a visit to Dr. Kiley. Walking into her office on my last Friday at school, I found her strapped to her tiltboard, straining, with eyes closed as if willing herself to heal. "I hope I'm not interrupting your exercise, Dr. Kiley."

"No, I've done my time today with this contraption. Please ask Mildred to come in. I think the two of you can help me back into that two-wheeler."

It took some time to lift her up and out, but I could see even over these past few months she was making noticeable progress, slowly gaining partial control and movement in her limbs. She settled back into her wheelchair, breathing heavily. "It's my least favorite part of the day, but I'll see it through, no matter what."

"Take your time, Dr. Kiley. School's out, and I don't leave for home until Sunday. I was hoping we might pick up with organizing your papers."

"Yes, I'd like that. I've been thinking about using my earlier presentations to write a paper on my accident and how I came to understand and overcome the depths of depression and despairing disability. Your work with me has helped me think about my professional life in a new light. Now I must bring it to others."

Dr. Kiley dabbed her forehead lightly with a hand towel and positioned the wheelchair closer to where I sat. She reached over and patted my knee. "We can talk about that another time. As you'll be gone for the summer, I'll use the time to outline my manuscript. When next semester begins, you can help me research authors and materials on the subject. That's for later. You must have a lot on your mind these days."

"It's funny, but in one way I feel a huge amount of relief and accomplishment because I did well on finals and in my classes too. But there's more—much more. My friendships have—how shall I put it?—they're richer, deeper. I feel safe within them. And the Cosmopolitan Club has become my gathering place, my commons. It's where I talk with others who've come from faraway places about what we love and fear and regret as immigrants."

"So, what does that mean for you?"

"It means a greater sense of who I am, and more confidence too. That's not to say I'm set and ready to move on. Far from it. But for the first time, I feel so much less insecure. And as much as I still want to please others, I'm beginning to understand that wanting to please my mother comes at a steep cost, especially if I let it rule my life."

"That's a valuable lesson to learn. But what does this mean for you as you return home?"

"I don't know. Nothing I do seems to make a difference. The one thing my mother wants me to do, to quit Holyoke and move back, I can't do. I feel that it would be the death of me, of who I am. I have the school, my friends, you, and memories of my stepfather to thank for where I am now, and one other person . . ."

"Your grandmother."

"Yes. Her devotion to my first twelve years lives in me to this day. The love my grandmother gave me taught me what it means to be loved, and her love still visits me in my thoughts and dreams. I've tried so hard to please my mother so that someday I might feel that same acceptance, that warmth and embrace again. I want to continue to hope, but I just don't know anymore."

As was her way, Dr. Kiley sat and listened, speaking sparingly. "I know you still want that love. Our desire, our craving for a mother's love, is embedded within us, and to give up on it, to suffer that loss, is devastating. Still, there may also come a time when, as you put it, your very survival is at stake. Let your insight and intuition guide you. You may find that you already know what you have to do. As a psychiatrist, I can tell you that what you've told me about your mother is not unfamiliar. Over the years, I've met and treated people who see the world only through their eyes. In your readings of Greek mythology, did you ever come across the story of Narcissus?"

"No. Please tell me."

"Narcissus was the son of a god who fell in love with his own reflection and was eventually destroyed by it. In psychiatry, people who feel they're always in the right find it hard to see other points of view. They're obsessed with control, and their anger can be severe when things don't go their way. These people have what we call 'narcissistic personalities.' It's hard to say for sure, because I've never met your mother, but from the way you describe her, she may very well be a textbook case."

"But what about all she does for the church? And she did bring me to America. She didn't have to do that."

"These behaviors fit a pattern. Yes, she does volunteer for the church, but from what you tell me, the priest applauds her talent and singing in a way that feeds her sense of self-importance. As for you, she expects nothing less than obedience to her will, and that includes being cared for as her will demands. She feels it's her right. In her eyes, disregard or disobey and you get what you deserve."

"But what are you saying? What should I do?"

"I know you'll be leaving school in a few days, and you'll go home and try again, try with all your heart and your being, to find the love and acceptance you desire, the love you had in the past with your grandmother. I'm sorry to say that I don't think you will find it. And I believe you'll proceed at your own peril."

CHAPTER 22

From Dr. Kiley's office to the bus ride, to the station, to the click-clack of the train on its ironbound journey and up to the walk home in the Bronx, I felt her words gradually taking up residence within me, haunting my thoughts and intentions. It didn't take long to understand just what those words meant.

My mother's and my greeting, like an old, tired song, replayed the same sad refrain. The scene was as it had been, the sentiment too familiar, but seeing my mother now felt different, as if a fog of confusion I had lived with for years had receded. Dr. Kiley's insights had crystallized what I already knew but was fearful about acknowledging.

"I thought you were coming in on Monday. I'm leaving in just a minute, as Father Avila is expecting me for Sunday evening vespers."

"I wrote you a late letter about the change in plans. As for vespers, of course I'll go. Just give me a minute."

"Oh, and you'll see I changed a few things around in your room."

A "few things" was an understatement. My last few mementos from the motherland were gone: my stick doll, old ribbons the color of the Hungarian flag, Grandmother's wool sweater she'd knitted for me, even the small wooden box with its keepsake contents of reminders of where I was born. A dime-store print of the Blessed Virgin Mary now hung in place of the photo of Esther and me in the Holyoke snows. Next to that was a picture of my mother and Father Avila. Gone too were magazines, personal papers, and letters from Esther that I'd left on my now-barren desk. It was as if my mother wanted to steal my memories, as if by removing what meant something special to me, she had hoped to nullify their existence.

I knew better than to confront her. My mother's self-satisfied grin greeted me when I returned. "I hope you like it, Irene," was all she said.

I did what my mother expected me to do during these summer days—shopping for necessities, cooking, and cleaning—but the New York Public Library downtown once again became my escape. She grudgingly tolerated my routine: up by seven to make breakfast before leaving to catch the trolley, returning home late afternoon to cook dinner. We shared church and meals. To my relief, familiar neighborhood gossip once again filled the void between us, as I feared where talk about the future would lead. Little did I realize in those early days of the summer of 1931 that my life would never be the same.

I had loved my freshman-year visits to the public library. College had opened doors of opportunity that I happily walked through. Sophomore year had revealed more of what was behind those doors. Classes had demanded more depth of field, depth of thought. Friendships, so bright and fresh from my first days, had become richer, deeper in their shared intimacies. I had come to know comfort and conflict through the eyes of others as an immigrant at Holyoke.

Now, with a major declared, my time at school had taken on a greater sense of direction and importance.

I delved further into our amphibian research to support Dr. Haywood's work at Woods Hole that summer but also expanded into the effects of diet and nutrition on health. I prepared for what lay ahead in other courses, having pored over the contents of the junior-year catalog: psychology, the languages, and art.

My thoughts never strayed far from the disturbing events unfolding in Europe. Each day the *New York Times* and other papers carried increasingly grim news on riots, fascism's grip on Italy, and the rise of Adolf Hitler's Nazi Party, all of which struck at the core of the Club's goodwill and intentions. Thoughts once again turned to the land of my birth and the lives known and forever lost to me. Rising anti-Semitism and hatred of all things Jewish, my father, and my heritage left me lost in the land of what-ifs. Had he seen me, met me, might he have loved me and never abandoned us? Might we all have lived happily together? Might my mother and I never have left Hungary? What had become of him now that rhetoric and reality were turning against him simply for being alive? I was his flesh and blood, yet separated from him over continents. Perhaps he would be proud of what I had become and all that I had come to value in the richness of immigrant lives and my life as an immigrant to this new land. These questions stayed with me as I sat with my lunch in Bryant Park, keeping the company of pigeons as well as those rich and poor who found relief in the cool green on those warm days.

It was on one of those days that a tall young man sat next to me. He was dressed casually in tan wool slacks and a white cotton short-sleeved shirt. He opened his brown paper bag and unwrapped a typical American lunch: two slices of white bread with some gray-brown matter in between. My lunch was especially fragrant that day, as I had packed roasted long red peppers and dark rye bread, along with a very aromatic smoked Hungarian sausage.

I noticed that he had lost interest in what he had brought and was eyeing what lay in my lap.

"Excuse me, but I was wondering what you're eating. It looks and smells delicious."

"It's just something from home—a few leftovers."

"Well, it certainly beats my slices of baloney and white bread."

"Would you like to try some sausage? It's easy for me to break off a piece."

"I don't want to impose."

"I don't mind at all. Here."

Taking the slice, he inspected it for an instant before eating. As he chewed, his eyes lit up. "That's very tasty. We never have anything like that at home. For us it's cabbage and boiled beef."

"Really? Where I come from, what we cook is always so tasty. And as I do a lot of it, I'm always adding garlic and spices to what we eat."

"May I ask where that is?"

"Hungary. Do you know anything about my country?"

"A little. I could find it on a map of the world but not much more."

"And you?"

"My parents and I came here from Ireland when I was very young. That explains my diet and the accent I can't seem to lose."

"Well, as you can hear, mine's still there, but I haven't been in America as long as you."

"What's your name?"

"Irene."

"Mine's Thomas. Last name O'Keefe. Nice to meet you."

There we sat in Bryant Park on a typical summer day. Hours later, lost in conversation with Thomas, I had hardly noticed the heat and humidity. He talked about how he was so taken with his art history major at Columbia and that he was about to begin his senior year. He'd fallen in love with the Impressionists, especially Degas's dancers and Van Gogh's vivid colors, and dreamed about visiting

France to trace the lives of his most revered artists. His father had worked as a department store manager but had lost his job shortly after the Crash. He had taken on odd jobs but recently had a part-time offer at Gimbels. Thomas had a job as a busboy at a downtown restaurant to help support his mother and father and four younger siblings. His school was in Manhattan, though he too lived in the Bronx, not far from my street.

"Do you like museums? I've been to the Metropolitan Museum, oh, I lost count of how many times."

"I've never been," I said.

"Would you like to go with me sometime? It's a magnificent place. I'd love to show it to you."

"That would be wonderful."

Thomas took down my address and agreed to come by Saturday at one o'clock. I realized that school, studies, and my responsibilities at home had taken up all the space in my life for the past two years, and male companionship was something I'd sorely missed—and greatly welcomed. My mother, however, didn't greet my news with the same enthusiasm.

"You don't know anything about this boy. How old did you say he is?"

"He didn't tell me, but it's his last year in college."

"You know how much trouble you almost got into with that Italian boy."

"I know you don't believe me, but I didn't get into any trouble with him, and you humiliated me when you made him sit with all your questions."

"It was for your own good. I don't trust those Italian kids. When are you meeting this Thomas?"

"Saturday afternoon. He's taking me to the Metropolitan Museum."

"Just be back for supper."

Her tone and temperament didn't bode well. Still, I knew this wasn't the time to go against her command. "Yes, I'll be back then."

Thomas came by precisely at one on that early June Saturday, just as he'd promised. Although we differed in age by just a little over a year, I felt so much younger in his company, impressed as I was by his sophistication and knowledge of art. He seemed to have memorized the Metropolitan Museum's floor plan, as he knew just where to go and what he wanted to show me.

We stopped midway through the Impressionists' hall and sat on a bench, both of us silently lost in shimmering palettes of starry nights, Paris streets, water lilies. Marveling at all the beauty before me, I turned to Thomas. "Just how *did* you come to know so much about art?"

"When I was very young, my mother kept a small collection of art books. Some of them, like Gustave Dore, drew these fantastic images of heaven, hell, the blessed, and the damned. Other books had paintings of these beautiful landscapes or portraits with eyes that seemed to look into and through you. Sure, I read mysteries and the comics. The Katzenjammer Kids and their trips to different countries and crazy adventures were so funny. But my mom's art books were what I liked the best. So, when I went to school, I wanted to find a way to keep learning about it, and a few teachers helped me. I can draw and paint, but not very well. To stay close to what I loved, when I started in college, I chose to major in art history. What about you?"

"My mother and stepfather wanted me to go to a good school, and so did my high school teachers, especially my science teacher, dear Mr. Kapinsky. He helped me when I was applying. That's how I ended up at Mount Holyoke."

"So Mr. Kapinsky was your guiding light."

"Absolutely. I wouldn't be here if not for him. As for my major, it's physiology. I know that's not what most women choose. It's hard, but I'm very happy with the choice I've made. And there again, I have Mr. Kapinsky to thank, as something he told the class stayed with me: that virtually all that we are and do has something to do with what we're made of and what we do with it. But enough about me. Where are we off to next?"

With that, Thomas continued his tour through the great building and its treasures, lingering over the works he knew best, detailing the techniques used to make them, their origins, what the artist was thinking. His infectious energy and passion carried us through the day all the way back to my front door.

"I hope I didn't overwhelm you today," he said with a coy smile.

"Oh, no! Today was such a good time. I found out how little I know about art."

"Could we get together again? Next Saturday, maybe?"

"Yes. Maybe we can go somewhere else that's closer to home."

"How about the Bronx Zoo?"

"What a great idea! I've only been there once, on a high school outing, and enjoyed it a lot, especially the elephants."

"Then it's a date. If you're up for it and the weather is good, we can walk there. And we could have dinner after we see what the animals are up to."

We said goodbye, and I went into the house without so much as a kiss.

Mother, as I had suspected, had been at the living room window watching the whole time. There was nothing for her to see but the two of us talking and smiling.

"Hi, Mother. How was your afternoon at church?" I said as soon as I walked in.

She ignored my question, as I could tell there was something else on her mind. "So, did you two really go to the museum?"

"Yes. Where did you think we'd go? It was just as I said. We took the train downtown and spent the entire day there. Thomas knows so much about so many of the artists and their paintings. Maybe you and I can go there sometime."

"Next Saturday there's a wedding and a High Mass, as well as a party afterward. I told the priest that you'd help set up before and pick up after the reception."

"I can't. Thomas said he'd take me to the Bronx Zoo and dinner."

"What do you mean you can't? I promised them you'd help. And what do you know of that boy?"

"I'm sorry, Mother, but you should have asked me first. And please don't start in again like you did with Joseph."

"Don't start in again? Don't start in again? Now I wonder what you do at that school too."

"Mother, I've told you. Between my friends, the Cosmopolitan Club, and studying, I don't have time to do anything else."

Raising her voice, she stopped mincing words and came to the point. "I've seen you flirt with boys at church. I have a good idea what you're up to, and I know you think you can just walk out on me into the arms of your boyfriend. Well, there's a way to fix that. Some night when you're sound asleep, when you least expect it, perhaps after a good time with one of your lovers, I will fetch my bottle of cleaning acid. You'll see what it will do to your face. After that, no one will want you."

These words from my mother froze me. Sensing that any response to her threat might escalate beyond control, I said, "I don't want to get into an argument with you. If Thomas comes by before you leave next Saturday, you can meet him, and you'll see how nice he is. Now, I have to start dinner."

That night, I barricaded my bedroom door once again. Fear had become an unwelcome presence standing just outside that door, waiting to enter and destroy my peace of mind, to destroy me. Harm was no longer an abstraction. What I understood from Dr. Kiley's words rang true: "Your unrequited desire for conciliation will give way to a primal drive to survive."

***

I continued to see Thomas over lunch at the park, and as June's warmth gave way to the heat of July, we spent Saturday afternoons and weekend evenings exploring the life of the city.

Coming home from the library on a sultry Friday afternoon, I showered and changed into my favorite rose-colored skirt and a white blouse with a ruffled collar. A look in the mirror showed me what I hoped to see, what Thomas had told me: I was a pretty young woman.

I found my mother standing at the doorway as I came down the stairs. "You're not going out tonight, are you? I've told you once, and I'll tell you again. People see what you do. I've talked to Father Avila about you. The neighbors see you going out with men. They know what you are: a whore. I have a daughter who's a whore."

I'd had enough. "What is it, Mother? What happened to you? I'm your only daughter. All I've ever wanted was for you to love me. Instead, you cause me humiliation, pain, and fear. I can't stand it anymore. What's made you want to hurt me? Why do you want me to be terrified of you?"

She narrowed her eyes to razor-thin slits, a look that I felt could penetrate skin. "You have no idea what I gave up when you were born with a Jew for a father. Do you know what your father said to me? When it came to being a father and husband and taking care of us, he would have nothing to do with you. He said that if I gave you up, he would take me away with him. I was tempted, believe me. Then he told me the truth: He would never marry me and leave his wife. What he really wanted was to set me up in a nice apartment so I could be his mistress. His mistress! Hah! That's what you did to me."

Mother caught her breath. For an instant I thought she had finished. But no, far from it. A cascade of cruelties continued to pour from her bottomless well of bitterness.

"Because of you, he could never see me as his wife, and I could never have the chance to make him see I was the woman for him. Oh, you might think that I could stay with you in Hajdudorog. Remember, I was unmarried and had a child with a Jew. The priest wouldn't even let me sing in church. People whispered behind my back when I walked by. Don't think I didn't notice all the looks they gave me. Is there any wonder why I left home, why I left you and your precious grandmother? Yes, she loved you, so it didn't take long before I thought, *Well, you love her? You can have her.* So, I saved and saved, got your father to send me some money, and finally left for America."

She stopped for a moment, sipped water from a chipped glass, but still wasn't done. "After all that, you may wonder why I bothered to bring you to me. When I came here, I had very little money, and unlike your grandmother, who at least had Josef and Johann, I had no one. I met Otto and married him even though he was much older. A few months later, when I told him about you, he came up with the idea of bringing you here. I hadn't thought much about it, but he kept bringing it up, saying how nice it would be to have a child with us in this house.

"It took me a while to warm to it, but I finally agreed. I also began to think about my future, that Otto would probably die before me and that I'd be left alone. I have no one: no sisters, brothers, aunts, uncles. So, that's why I wrote to your grandmother and told her to send you here. Otto planted the idea, and you came. And as you *are* my flesh and blood, it's your responsibility to take care of me."

For years, I had dreaded knowing this answer. Now I was certain that my love for her offered no redemption from her torment. I finally understood that the demons that haunted my mother would remain with her for the rest of her life and that if I stayed with her and her demons, I would eventually be destroyed.

While her words scalded me, I withstood the pain, my skin having grown tough and scarred over the years. I drew on strength from all the knowing voices past and present determined to save my life.

I willed myself to stop shaking. "Mother, I'm sorry your life didn't turn out the way you'd hoped it would. I now know what I suspected all along: A part of you wishes I'd never been born. I also know I can't stay here anymore, or I'll be eaten up by what you can never have. It didn't have to be like this here in America. You're still young. You've had a good life in many ways, a loyal husband who died caring for you and me, and as much as you may find this hard to see, a daughter who's loved you since she first saw you at Ellis Island. And I have wanted to love you ever since. You've made it impossible to be loved, at least as you are. Maybe you'll come to be at peace. God, I do wish that for you. But I also know I can't be a part of your life now, if ever."

I hesitated for only an instant, knowing the less I said the better. I moved toward the stairs, turning back to her as I did. "I have nothing more to say to you. I'll pack my bags and be out of this house as soon as I can."

"You were always ungrateful, Irene," she said, her face filled with spite. "So this is how you pay me back, by leaving me?"

"It's not payback. You've just threatened me, and not for the first time. You've made me afraid for my life. And more than that, I'm afraid if I stay, I'll lose my soul."

I left my mother at the bottom of the stairs glaring at me, seething in her silence.

***

No rest came that night, terrified as I was that my mother would extract retribution for my betrayal and abandonment. I was desperate to leave but knew that few if any buses or trains were running at that late hour. Once again, I wedged a chair against the knob and lay in bed in pitch-black darkness, listening, waiting, in fear of the fury that lurked on the other side of the door. Minutes took hours, hours an eternity. As the first rays of morning light seeped through the venetian blinds, I rose, knowing I'd pay dearly if I made a sound. I packed one suitcase with clothes for school and my stepfather's box, with his blessed gift securing my school years to come, that lay hidden under the mattress, and little else. In the smaller bag I carried across the sea—was it my imagination, or did it have the faint hint of the sausages from my grandmother?—I placed the few mementos that had escaped my mother's purge: a picture of my grandmother and Johann I'd safely hidden in the closet all these years, my first A on a test in Mr. Kapinsky's class, and letters from Esther and Johann.

There wasn't much time, as my mother would be up soon. I removed the barricade and said a prayer to St. Christopher, turned the knob ever so slowly, and opened the door to blessed silence. Tiptoeing to the stairs, careful to avoid the creaking banister, I took one step at a time all the way to the first floor, quickly opened the front door, and once again stepped into the unknown.

CHAPTER 23

I was severed from my last vestige of family but now knew that Mount Holyoke, a place of those native and new, had anchored me to where I belonged. Still, in that fraught August before my junior year, Esther carried me through.

I called her from a phone booth early that morning, letting it ring until she picked up. "Esther, I'm so sorry to wake you at this ungodly hour, but—" and before I could finish my sentence, she interrupted me.

"I was expecting to hear from you, Irene," she said in a voice that quelled any doubt. "Your room awaits. I can't wait to see you!"

Carting the contents of my life, I labored up the stairs to the elevated platform at the Gun Hill Road station and, after a brief wait for the train, found a seat on the IRT Seventh Avenue Line. My only company was workers dozing as they headed home after their night shift and a few others staring blankly out the car windows as they traveled downtown. Preoccupied and weary, none of them paid attention to this new passenger with her life's possessions.

Exiting at Christopher Street, I made my way to Esther's West Village address, a small red-brick building nestled on a quiet street. It didn't take but a minute after ringing the bell for Esther to appear, greeting me at the door with a warm embrace that almost took my breath away. We descended to the basement, where I stepped into an apartment not unlike our college room, sparsely furnished and decoratively plain except for her black-and-white photos of Holyoke and her parents and brother. She had made the small bedroom inviting: a twin bed with pale-blue sheets and a matching light blanket, a lamp on a simple wooden nightstand, and four pictures of us around Cowles, one for each season. We sat in a small outdoor area with space just for two chairs, a small table, and her flowers, and talked through the night and into the early hours, tearful at times, but most of all, happy, safe, together.

A week later, I introduced her to Thomas, who arranged for Sean, a fellow Irishman and friend from school, to join us for a double date with Esther and, as fate would have it, many others over the remaining days of summer and beyond. As for Thomas, what he'd seen me through brought us closer as the days of August drew down. It was on one of those last steamy days in the city, sitting together on a bench in Bryant Park, that we could no longer avoid what lay ahead.

"There's only the rest of this week before it's back to Holyoke. As much as I'm looking forward to school, it's hard to leave you, Thomas. Your kindness and understanding have meant the world to me. *You've* meant the world to me."

"I feel the same way. But does it mean the end? Won't you be returning for the holidays and next summer?"

"Before this summer, it would have been crazy for me to think I wouldn't. Now, I just don't know. My professor's work is going to take up much more time than before. And I no longer have a home to come back to."

"What about Esther's place?"

"She'll be very busy come fall, when her work picks up. Her parents have put off visiting. There's Sean too. My guess is what they've started, thanks to you, has, what might I call it? Let's just say quite a story with what looks like a great ending. It reminds me of that wonderful, funny movie we saw, *Trip to the Moon*. They seem to be so in love."

His sweet smile faded. Taking my hand in his, he asked, "Will you write me?"

Letting go of his hand, I pulled him close to me and kissed him. "There's nothing that could stop me. I'll write you again and again. That I promise. As for coming back to the city, who knows what the future has in store for you and me."

***

Those romantic days in August would not last forever. Before Thanksgiving of that year, Thomas wrote me at school to say that he had taken a position at an art gallery in Buffalo. In that same letter, he embedded on the page his humor and the wishes of his heart.

Dear Miss Irene Richter,

I am keenly interested in applying for a long-term position with you and respectfully beg to call attention to what I believe are excellent qualifications for that position.

I am a practiced dishwasher after years of experience at the home of Mrs. O'Keefe, my mother. As you know, her menu included boiled beef. I can iron shirts and neckties, mop floors, and make beds. I've even mastered a turn in the kitchen: icebox salad is my specialty. As for school, you know whereof I've been. But did you also know I can discuss happenings in places like Ethiopia and artifacts from Mongolia?

Unfortunately, I can bring little capital beyond what I earn to this offer. But between my domestic experience, my "work of art," so to speak, my devotion, and your professional skills to be, blissful domesticity is assured.

Please consider my offer in the coming days (although, as of now, it has no expiration date).

Respectfully yours,

Thomas

I'd been standing by my desk when I opened his letter but had to sit by its end, so taken by what he had written and the life he wanted for the two of us. But I also knew I couldn't turn back from the path I'd chosen, wherever it would take me. I kept my reply to Thomas brief.

Dear Thomas:

Your letter made me giggle, and I felt a bit embarrassed, as I opened it at the library and those around me seemed a little put out!

I'm very happy you found something that you love to do.

However, as beautiful as your offer is, finishing my education means everything to me right now. It's something I must do for myself before anything else. It's my present and, for the time being, my future.

I hope Buffalo is treating you well and that your art gallery appreciates the smart and wonderful person you are.

With love and fondest wishes for you,

Irene

***

My last days with Esther in New York were what kept me true to who I was becoming. We sat on her patio, the evening sun casting dappled light across her pots of brilliant purple and pink hydrangeas.

"Nothing I say can tell you how much your friendship has meant to me, Esther."

"Nothing needs to be said, my dear friend. It's amazing to me. We came from such different worlds, and yet we have so much in common in what we love, all we've shared, what we feel is important in life. You've always been there for me."

"And that's where I'll always be."

After sipping her tea, she pointed to her flowers. "I never told you why I planted these."

"They're beautiful. They remind me of Holyoke, and you've always loved flowers."

"Yes, there's that, but much more. The hydrangeas are special. Pink is for how our friendship has a special place in my heart. The purple flowers are about the depth of our friendship, of knowing someone and caring about you as much as I do."

I listened quietly until I could no longer hold back my tears. I said, "It's true what you've said about those flowers. I'll miss being with you more than I can ever say."

Esther smiled and we embraced. Then she released me and took a small step back so that we stood face-to-face. "I know you're worried about all that's happened with your mother and leaving Thomas."

"And you."

As her smile receded, she reached out with both hands and held my shoulders. "I've seen you come so far. You went through so much with your mother. Even after all that, you blossomed at school. You found a home at Mount Holyoke and, I'd say, a purpose. Then there's your major, something I could never do. You may get lonely or down, but never forget that you've come out the other side."

Dear Esther had seen in me what I'd longed for and felt: an affirmation of my life not only as it had come to be but as I *wanted* it to be. I took both her hands in mine, held them to my face, and kissed them. "You know me so well, my dearest friend. And with God's good grace, what you say will come to be."

***

I returned to Holyoke in September 1931 keenly sensitive to endings and beginnings, as if chapters in a book had closed and others had yet to be written. Trepidation for what lay ahead filled my days, but visiting Dr. Kiley strengthened my resolve.

On a crystal clear, cool autumn Saturday, Dr. Kiley greeted me not in her wheelchair but standing with the help of a walker when I arrived at her office. "Dr. Kiley, you're walking!"

"It's so good to see you again, Irene. I must say, you were on my mind all this time. Yes, it's been a busy summer for me, as I imagine it's been for you. I must admit that confounded tiltboard has helped me regain at least some of my strength. Just a few weeks ago, I took my first steps in years."

Careful not to upset her balance, I embraced her gently. "I'm so happy for you."

"Yes. As you know, I've had quite a journey. But what about yours?"

I could see that her progress was still tentative. Taking her arm, I guided her to a chair and then sat beside her. "I'm sorry I didn't write to you, but there was so much going on. I've only been back a week but wanted to see you before classes started. Oh, where to begin?"

"Why don't we start with how you are?"

"I feel as if I've lived so many lives in just a few months. I met a sweet young man, lived with my best friend, Esther, in the city, and of course, kept up with my studies." Exhaling deeply, I continued. "As for my mother, what you warned me about came true. Thank God for Esther and her apartment. That's where I spent the rest of the summer."

"And now what? What comes next for you?"

"I can't think, and actually don't *want* to think much beyond being back at college. My present is my future now for at least the next few years, and that's where I'll stay. Dr. Kiley, I feel I've moved on from the terror. You've made that possible. And, of course, I have my friends at school and in New York."

"I'm so happy to hear it," Dr. Kiley said as she broke into a smile. "Irene, I don't know if you sensed it, but as you were telling me what you've been through, your body shifted—became more upright. You have a brightness in your eyes I've not seen before now. I know you'll never forget what you've been through, but it seems to have lost control over your life. Now you can go about just being who you are and become who you want to be."

"What you say is very true: I'll never go back. And now please tell me about your writing and your organization."

"Well, that's a story too. I was quite busy this summer, and that work has paid off. I've been invited to lecture at the University of California at Berkeley, the University of Chicago, and Tufts. It seems that little seed of an idea, Courage to Live, has flowered. Along with my research on trauma, a few foundations are very interested in meeting with me about dedicating a national organization to helping those who, as you've said to me, are on unchosen paths."

"That's wonderful," I said.

"Now that I'm a bit more mobile, I'll be away for a while. That's all the more reason I'm glad we had this chance to meet—I'm not sure when I'll return."

Taking her delicate hand in mine, I kissed her cheek. "I have to tell you that is my gift too, thinking I played a small part in it."

"It may seem small, but what you did helped me get to where I am."

Seeing her glance at the grandfather clock, I knew our time was up.

"And now we must stop, as my next client has been waiting, I suspect quite impatiently."

I stood, but as I turned to leave, we both seemed to have the same instinct. As I leaned down to where she sat, we embraced.

"I don't know how to thank you for all you've meant to me," I said as the words caught in my throat.

Echoing my stepfather, she replied, "Seeing who you've become is all I need, Irene."

On my way back to school, I turned over all that had happened. I sensed, yet again, another chapter closing but this time with an uplift to its ending.

CHAPTER 24

Cowles Lodge was just as it had always been, with one major difference. My room wasn't the same without Esther. But then Angi moved in shortly after I'd returned, and with her Hungary came alive.

We talked long into that first night, teetering back and forth between English and Hungarian. My native language was halting at first, but it didn't take long for the hesitant words and phrases to tumble out. Along with our reminisces, Angi planted an idea.

"Irene, what do you think of decorating our room with what we have from the old country? Thanks to my parents, I have all sorts of mementos: dolls in beautiful dresses, a painting of Budapest, the country flag, and photos of swimming at Lake Balaton."

I didn't hesitate. "I was wondering how to replace Esther's beautiful pictures. I don't have much to put up, but you are welcome to use anything you have. Maybe before we decorate, we should bring what we have to the next Cosmopolitan Club."

"What a great idea!" Angi exclaimed. "We could also share them at the next international day. My mother has some personal heirlooms that go back to her great-great-grandparents, Anna and Oskar. They even have Oskar's saber and his officer's uniform from when he fought in the Great Patriotic War."

"I have nothing like that but my memories. Still, I'm sure that we have members from many other countries who have brought pieces of their past with them to Holyoke. We've never decorated the walls of our meeting room, except for a few pictures. What do you think of creating a great international room of memories? We could invite all the members to bring mementos from their native lands and give them their own wall space to hang them until we run out, which I suspect we will. Then, every month, they could take turns exhibiting things from their countries. As far as I know, the Club has never done that. I'd have to run this by Ingrid, but knowing her, I think she'd love it."

As I spoke, Angi smiled and patted my hand. "No wonder you were elected the Club's secretary. Your idea would do wonders for our drab meeting room. Count me in!"

That inspiration was to become part of the Cosmopolitan Club for my junior and senior years, offering voices to our pasts and honoring intimacies we had carried within.

***

My good fortune didn't stop with school, Dr. Kiley, Angi, and the Cosmopolitan Club. I continued my studies through my junior and senior years, eventually earning one of the coveted positions as Dr. Haywood's teaching aide. Helping grade the quality of students' laboratory experiments and tests created an unexpected bond between us, such that when my four years at Holyoke were coming to an end, something I had never expected happened.

Two weeks before the graduation ceremony, Dr. Haywood asked me to meet at her Clapp Hall office. I will never forget that bright spring morning, sun shining, daffodils and lilacs lining the path to Clapp Hall, unfolding their blossoms in the warmth of the day while squirrels clambered across the grass, still wet from mist. All were reminders of Holyoke's beauty and what I'd miss when I left.

Her office door was already open.

"Hi, Irene. Come in and sit. Would you like a cup of tea? I only have Earl Grey in the pot, but it's quite good."

"I'd love a cup. Thank you."

She placed a finely patterned Limoges cup and saucer before me and then began. "I know you're aware that the work at Woods Hole is showing great promise. I'm planning on presenting and submitting several papers by the fall, which means that the summer months are going to be hectic, to say the least. I've also come to see that we are understaffed."

"In some ways I'm not surprised you need more help with all your work, Dr. Haywood. I've enjoyed being a small part of it."

"Well, it's interesting you say that, because that's why I've asked you here. I'm very pleased with your detailed work. It's that kind of attention I'll need in the coming months at Woods Hole, analyzing data, assuring the accuracy in numbers and narrative, and of course, writing papers. I'll come to the point. If you're interested, I'd like to offer you a research assistant position at Woods Hole. I can guarantee a year's salary, but if all goes well with my submissions, there'll be much more to come. I know this offer is out of the blue, so go ahead and think about it for a few days."

A grand gift. In just a few words, her offer had lifted the fog of my future to reveal a lovely landscape of learning before me. "Dr. Haywood, I don't need any time to think about it. I would be honored to work with you."

A broad smile elevated her wire-rimmed glasses. "Very good. Please plan to join me no later than June 15. I will already be into the summer work, but we can make up for a bit of lost time. I'll arrange for transportation to Woods Hole from Holyoke as well as accommodations there, spare though they will be."

"I'm used to living with little. As for timing, I can start as soon as you wish."

"Ah, all the better. Then let's plan our trip for the first week in June."

Only then did I realize that I was so taken into the moment my teacup had tilted so that a small pool had collected in the saucer.

Seeing what had happened, she mused, "I think your tea is no longer warm. Would you like another cup?"

"No, thank you." As I stood to leave, my words spoke for my heart. "Dr. Haywood, what you've offered means the world to me. I can't thank you enough. I'll be ready and waiting."

***

Woods Hole became my refuge. The first year stretched into two, then three, offering new ways to be part of something important, attending conferences, writing research papers, and supervising undergraduates new to the rigors that Dr. Haywood demanded of us all. Education was the linchpin that kept me sane in my youth, and now it had secured my future. What may have seemed trivial or silly to some—I still remember Angi's puzzled look when she asked, "What is it about those fish and frogs that you find so fascinating?"— was titanic in its importance to Dr. Haywood and her assistants. More than that, I became a mentor to those new to America. I saw in them what I'd once been.

My time at Woods Hole also brought a newfound joy and purpose, reducing to memory the tragedy that my life had become. I had emerged from the darkness of those adolescent years with a path to *my* future, no longer fearful of being consumed by another's illusions. I knew my recent past was indelible, just as the sweet days with my grandmother had nurtured who I had become. But what had eluded me was that bridge of reconciliation I had so wanted to build between my lived and lost lands, between a love forever held only in hope unrealized and that nurturing love of so long ago.

Still, I had discovered the intimacies that would sustain me: my friends, my grandmother, my stepfather, the professors who offered life lessons, and Dr. Kiley, whose words and wisdom saved my life. With them, I'd etched a palimpsest, a rebirth that effaced the horror that was. Within the memories of those beloved lived my salvation from the inconsolable.

ACKNOWLEDGMENTS

I have many people to thank for helping bring *Motherlands* to life: my wife, Lisa, for her infinite patience and keen critique through the many drafts; my son, Stephen, for his insights in review and essential contribution to the *Motherlands* website; Susan Leon, Kim Catanzarite, and Carolyn Cohagan, for their ideas and suggestions; Amy Megill, for her tender loving care in editing; my friends Jan Rothschild, James Medlin, Mike Shefman, John Quatromoni, and Andrew Duchon, for their insights and support; and the Greenleaf Book Group team, especially Dee Kerr, for their invaluable guidance. A special thanks to Tim O'Brien for sharing his experience in writing and his words of encouragement all along the way. Finally, my gratitude to the staff at Mount Holyoke College for providing access to their archives in researching my mother's college years.